DEATH OR GLORY

RYAN WILLIAMSON

JASON ANSPACH

WARGATE

An imprint of Galaxy's Edge Press

ISBN: 979-8-88922-060-2

Library of Congress Control Number: 2024934838

Edited by David Gatewood

Published by WarGate Books, an imprint of of Galaxy's Edge, LLC.

Cover Design: Mike Corley

Cover by: Marc Lee.

CHAPTER 1

The taloned hand raked my chest as I leapt away, and my back slammed against the wall of the pit. Above, the chitter and squeaks of the cheering crowd urged us on. My opponent was small, about four foot seven, but the scaly lizardman was fast as he danced toward me. He hissed, and the dewlap under his chin unfurled bright red. The spines running down his head and back quivered.

Blocking another swipe, then kicking straight out to give myself some room, I struck with a low round kick, hitting his thigh with my shin, and heard the satisfying *crack* of his femur breaking. He stumbled to the left with a squeak of pain, and whipped his long tail in my eyes. I managed to catch the barbed tip on my forearm and strike out with a snap kick to his clavicle that sent him sprawling in the bloody sand of the pit's floor.

The cheering of the reptilian crowd rose to a crescendo.

I surged in, leaning low as he attempted to get to his feet, batted away a feeble strike, and then jabbed a feint with my left before delivering a right cross that caved in the frontal bone of his skull.

Dancing back, I wiped the blood and sweat out of my eyes and surveyed the carnage before taking stock of my own injuries. Three of the pygmy saurians lay motionless in the sand. I had a cut on my forehead that was bleeding profusely but probably wasn't serious, lacerations and bites on my arms, legs, and chest, and some tender spots that were going to turn into pretty spectacular bruises. The barbs embedded in my forearm made the swollen skin numb and red, but better my forearm than my eyes.

I looked up at the crowd of lizard people rimming the pit, wondering if they were going to throw in any more opponents. I was shaking from the adrenaline dump, and my mouth felt like dry parchment. Someone tossed down a waterskin and my claw knife.

Sir Angus McKenzie, the only other human I'd seen in this village and a slave fighter like me, had warned me the pit matches could go all day. I'd been here one week now, ever since the scaly freaks had captured me when they ambushed my platoon, but most of that week I'd spent curled up next to the chamber pot in my cage vomiting out of both ends as my body tried to accustom itself to my new diet of pulped corn and larva and whatever was in the murky water they gave us.

One hellish week I honestly didn't think I'd live through, and now I was in the pit for the first time.

Sir McKenzie was an interesting man. He claimed to be a World War I flying ace and renowned explorer, but I don't recall hearing about him in any history lessons. He was a big Scottish-Canadian man, with long matted red hair and a bushy beard, and had been a prisoner of the little saurians for over a year. He was convinced he was lost somewhere in the British Honduras and the year was still 1919, even though I'd tried to explain we weren't even on *Earth* anymore. When I told him how my platoon of Cavalry Scouts had been sucked into this realm of the Aztec god Smoking Mirror from Panama in 1989, he declared me insane and said the lizardfolk had bashed me on the head too hard when they captured me.

During some of the worst days of that first week, I wondered if he was right.

Picking the waterskin and knife off the sand, I pulled the cork out with my teeth and drank the tepid water. It tasted slightly fresher than whatever my keepers delivered to my cage each morning.

Another prisoner, a female, was frogmarched to the edge of the pit and thrown down. She was a dun green color and lacked the dewlap and bright blue cheeks of the males, but like most females of her species she was bigger than the males, probably five-two and a good hundred and thirty pounds. A bone-tipped spear was cast down after her, and she picked it up, watching me warily and keeping her distance as I drank.

She was a slave like me, a captive from some other lizardfolk tribe. One of us would live to fight again another day; the other would have their head shrunk and be eaten. We had no way to communicate. They spoke in a language of squeaks, hisses, and chittering chirps that was impossible to mimic—or understand.

When we'd first arrived in the Land of the Black Sun, the god—or *extra-dimensional entity*, as Captain Brown insisted—Smoking Mirror had granted us Outworlders the ability to understand the other beings of his realm, what the Kuauchanejkej called the "Gift of Tongues." But he'd apparently withdrawn that Gift not long after we'd descended into the underworld realm of Mictlan and destroyed his soul-powered forge. One moment we were conversing fluently with our native allies, and the next we were a mass of confusion with them speaking dialects of Nahuatl and us English and neither able to understand the other any more than I could now understand my lizard captors.

It was fortunate that I already possessed a working knowledge of Nahuatl from the time I spent in Southern Mexico on my proselytizing mission, and so could serve as a translator with the Kuauchanejkej, and they knew some Spanish from their friar who had lived among them for decades, so we got by with a sort of pidgin of English, Nahuatl, and Spanish. In fact we did remarkably well, considering. Captain Brown speculated that months of using the Gift had also unconsciously accelerated our understanding of each other, because once loss of the Gift forced us all to learn the other's language, the learning came rapidly. Within a few weeks of dedicated effort we'd smoothed things out to a point where our pidgin allowed communication that was almost as good as it had been before Smoking Mirror's take-back. The only person in our group whose speech still had a flavor of "Me Tarzan, you Jane" was Epasotl, and that was because she insisted on using English only. "So I learn."

Still, the withdrawal of the Gift meant we could no longer speak with anyone else. Like the lizard people. Sir McKenzie had no issue communicating with them—as an Outworlder who *hadn't* pissed off Smoking Mirror by destroying his precious soul forge, he possessed the Gift of Tongues—but I was reduced to communicating in pantomime.

My hissing, chittering opponent leveled her spear at me and circled slowly. I tossed the drained waterskin away, testing the weight of the knife in my hand. It was a good weapon, well balanced, with a five-inch claw-like blade and a ring in the hilt. Our platoon medic, Doc, was a savant with the things and had been teaching me the finer points of their use. I held it in a reverse grip in my right hand, with my index finger in the ring, and settled myself into a steady crouch, awaiting her inevitable lunge.

When it came, I was ready, slapping the spear point away as I sidestepped and let her momentum carry her past me, then whipping out my right fist and slashing deeply into her flank.

She pirouetted and swung the butt of the spear in a low feint before reversing her strike, thrusting the bone tip at my throat. I blocked with my left and struck out with my right, but she was too fast and ducked, slamming the butt of her spear into my inner thigh, just inches away from some very exposed and tender bits.

Did I mention I was naked? Yeah, so I had that going for me.

She jabbed again with the butt, going for my solar plexus, and I hopped back, knocked the spear away, and followed through with a reverse roundhouse to her head that managed to connect with a whole lot of air as she rolled past me and did her best to impale me through the gut. I spun, blocking the spear with a high left knee, and simultaneously whipped out with my right hand in a low diagonal arc that slashed across her chest. Then I dropped and swept her feet, but she was already airborne and flipping over me. I let my momentum carry me around on my knees to face her, blocking a series of strikes before I found an opening and struck at her thigh. I must have hit her femoral artery, because the spray of blood blinded me and I had to execute a backwards somersault to get some distance.

Back on my feet, I wiped blood from my eyes with my forearm as she staggered around the pit drunkenly, trying to level her spear tip at me. She didn't stagger far before collapsing and falling over backwards, her chest rising and falling in great heaves that soon gave way to a shudder and then stillness as she bled out.

Thumps on the sand alerted me to fresh opponents behind me, and I leaped forward in a roll that ended with me on my feet and facing two spear-wielding males who were already advancing in a rush. I dodged to my right, placing one opponent behind the other, and hammered the nearest in the eye with my claw knife's ring. He reeled back, and his companion surged forward, aiming his spearhead at my groin. I twisted aside and managed to get several inches of sharpened, serrated bone in the meat of my left thigh as a reward for being too slow. He ripped it out and went again for my gut while his one-eyed friend moved to circle behind me.

I let them come and flowed into the attack, grasping the spear coming for my belly and using my attacker's momentum to draw him into the path of my right hook, catching his throat with my blade and nearly severing his head clean off as the second spear whipped past my shoulder. One-Eye overextended, and I swung in low with a disemboweling blow that sent him stumbling backward as lizard guts poured out onto the sand.

My thigh was bleeding heavily, and I limped to the center of the pit, trying to apply some pressure. The spear hadn't hit an artery, but I wasn't feeling so hot. The crowd above jeered in chittering taunts, and I screamed up at them hoarsely and, I'll admit, somewhat incoherently.

Their medicine man, or whatever he was, came to the edge of the pit and began chirping at me.

"You want some too?" I shouted back. "Come on. Get some!"

He replied in a series of squeaks and clicks, and made a throwing-down gesture with his right hand.

I held up my knife threateningly. "What? This? You want me to drop it? *Screw you!*"

Several of the warrior lizards, male and female alike, raised their spears over the edge of the pit, readying to throw and turn me into a pincushion.

I got the message.

"Fine!" I tossed the knife onto the sand. "*Fine.* There. I dropped it. What now?"

Someone lowered a rope ladder into the pit. Apparently showtime was over. I sighed. False bravado aside, I was totally beat, and bleeding from more cuts and bites than I could count, plus there was the ragged hole in my thigh.

I climbed the ladder and heaved myself over the lip of the pit to be greeted by a forest of spears. I just stood there, naked and sweating and bleeding, my chest heaving.

"What now?"

More clicking and chirping from the medicine man as he snorted a fine white powder out of half a clamshell. Then two males with gourds scuttled up and dipped their long fingers into some kind of green goop and moved in to—I didn't know what. I backed up, and one of them squeaked. He sounded angry. The medicine man was angry too, and the warriors jabbed their spears at me.

I held up my hands in surrender.

The green goop was some kind of medicine that they painted my wounds with. It had a numbing effect, and it hardened after just a few moments, closing up the worst of the punctures and lacerations like wintergreen Krazy Glue. My thigh wound got a plug of something nasty-looking inserted in, then sealed inside with more green goop. Finally they escorted me back to my cage.

Once they had me secured, the medicine man gave me a long lecture accompanied by wild gestures I couldn't begin to parse.

I turned to Sir McKenzie in the cage next to me. "What's he going on about?"

"The fights were too fast," McKenzie replied. "Gotta give 'em a show, eh? Take your time."

"Seriously?"

The medicine man chittered something more.

"Or they'll wound you *before* the fight to make it fair," McKenzie added.

"Fair? *Fair?* I barely made it out alive!"

"We're here to entertain the king." The big man shrugged. "From what Ezekiel is saying, it sounds like the king wasn't so entertained this morning."

McKenzie had given all the lizards names, usually Biblical ones. I wasn't even sure how he managed to tell them apart.

"Ezekiel, huh?" I turned to the medicine man. "Okay, *Ezekiel*, next time I'll give you a show. Sound good?"

He chirped something that could have been approval and wandered away with his retinue of guards.

I leaned back against the stoutly woven branches of my cage and inspected my injuries. Whatever that green glue was that they'd used to treat me, it worked; I didn't feel a thing. I absently traced a black vein running down my leg.

"You sure that isn't catching?" McKenzie asked.

"What? This?" I gestured to the spiderweb of blackened veins across my chest, face, and limbs. "No. Like I said before, it's a cancer of the soul… and body, I suppose. I'm death-touched. I'm dying. But it's not contagious. I was infected when one of the ravenous undead blew some kind of powder in my face."

"Ravenous undead, eh?"

"Servants of the death god Mictlāntēcutli. Zombie cannibals. Most death-touched turn into them. Some don't. I didn't."

And most who don't turn become psychopathic murderers anyway, I didn't add. Beyond killing me slowly and giving me a bad temper, I wasn't sure what the effects of being death-touched were. The changes had been gradual, but I felt stronger and faster than before. Better reflexes. Harder strikes. I'm hardly an expert at combatives, but I'd fared well enough in the pit. I felt my arms and chest. I didn't seem noticeably bigger—not all swole and pumped like my friend Sergeant Wilson, but I had more definition where maybe there hadn't been before. Although that could also just be from hard living over the last several months in the Land of the Black Sun. I wasn't sure. Either way, in my mind I was just a kid from Utah; I was no killing machine.

But maybe I was becoming one.

"Mictlāntēcutli," McKenzie repeated in a low voice. "The Lord of Mictlan. I explored a crypt dedicated to him once. Evil place, that was. You could feel it in your very bones."

"I've *been* to Mictlan," I murmured.

"So you say." He gave a low chuckle. "I still say you were hit on the head too hard, Future-Man."

I gave a shrug.

Some guards approached his cage, and he got up.

"Looks like it's my turn," he said with a sigh. The guards led him away to the pit, and a few minutes later, I heard his deep voice rumbling through the persistent mist.

"*Moritūrī tē salūtāmus!*"

"*Avete vos,*" I muttered.

CHAPTER 2

The king of the lizardmen, whom McKenzie had dubbed "Zedekiah," sat under the lone surviving wing of a crashed plane, being fanned by two servants. Slaves, probably. He was tall for a male, and grossly obese. The plane was of the smaller twin-prop cargo variety, and hung a couple meters off the ground, caught in low branches and vines. It looked like it'd been hanging there for a long, long time.

"They practically worship the thing," McKenzie said. "Say it was a gift from the sky gods. Or its cargo, rather. You ever seen an aeroplane like it? I say it's no wonder it crashed. Damn thing's made all of metal, eh? Wonder it could fly at all."

"The cargo?" I asked.

"Powdered cocaine," the large man replied. "Crates and crates of it."

"You've been up there? Inside?"

"Once. There's weapons and ammunition too. Whole load of 'em. Didn't get much of a peek, but the markings on the crates were U.S. government."

"I don't see any of the lizards toting modern weapons."

"They don't know what they're for, eh? They just care about the blow. Now *that* they worship." He turned to one of the guards standing next to us. "Ain't that right, Peter? You love your powder of the gods."

The diminutive lizardman chittered in reply and snorted from a shell.

McKenzie smiled at me. "Peter and I are old mates."

"He's your *jailor*."

"They're not all bad sorts, once you get to know them."

"And they're all addicted to cocaine. Explains a lot."

He gave me an amused sidelong glance. "Them an' us, lad."

"Speak for yourself. They offer it before fights, but I always refuse."

He laughed, a rough sound from deep in his belly. "Laddie, it's in your slop."

"Fantastic." I'd thought my increased energy and sharpened senses were somehow due to my... unusual condition... but apparently I was simply a junkie now. "Just great."

He shrugged. "Why're your knickers in a twist? I always took a tab or two of Forced March before a flight. Gave me an edge. An' when you're up in the sky trading bullets with Jerry, anything that gives you an edge is a good thing." He motioned to the wide pit before us. "Same as down there, eh?"

"I don't smoke. I don't drink. And I certainly don't do drugs. Not intentionally."

"Ah, one of those. You Mormon or something, lad?"

I nodded sourly.

"Crivvens! Got yourself a bundle of wives then, eh?"

"Just the one."

He spit off to the side. "That be one too many if you ask me. Bairns?"

"What?"

"Kiddos. You got little Bennetts?"

"Uh, no."

"That you know of, eh?" He elbowed me in the ribs. "I 'spect there be a couple or three wee McKenzies running about. Maybe you left her with a bun in the oven, eh?"

My wife, Xochi, was back at the refugee camp we'd relocated her people to after the attack on their villages. I hadn't seen her in over a month. The thought of her possibly being *pregnant* was something I hadn't considered. It didn't seem possible. We hadn't been married very long, only a few weeks really, and I told McKenzie as much.

"All it takes is once, lad," he replied with a deep chuckle.

We hadn't been married long, but we'd certainly made… good use of the time we had together before my platoon shipped off to this strange land of perpetual mist. The prospect of potentially being a father was sobering, and my thoughts turned once again to escape. It'd been two weeks now, with no sign of rescue. I'd tried making a run for it twice, and I'd keep trying, no matter how severely they whipped me before throwing me back in my cage.

My platoon had arrived here, wherever *here* was exactly, several weeks ago through a portal our Chaneque guide and resident sorceress Epasotl had conjured. It transported us from the Kuauchanejkej refugee settlement of Tepeuakan to this land of mists, which was possibly another continent in the Land of the Black Sun, or possibly another world altogether—we simply didn't know. All we did know was this was the place where we'd find a critical piece of the puzzle that would get my platoon-mates back to Earth in 1989. We didn't even know exactly what we were looking for, other than it was some sort of navigational aid, an artifact, or codex, or something, which would provide us, or Epasotl rather, the intel she needed to create a portal back home to what the guys called the "real world."

And somehow in all of this I was the key to finding what we were searching for.

The entire op was based on what Captain Brown was referring to as Metaphysical Intelligence, METINT. More specifically, we were relying on a vision that my wife, Xochi, had long before we'd even arrived in her world. It didn't seem much to go on, although both Xochi and Captain Brown knew a lot more about this vision than they were willing to share with me. But some intel was better than no intel, and if the captain felt it was actionable enough for us to come here, I'd follow where he led. He'd never let us down yet.

I sighed as limp and bloody lizard bodies were dragged out of the pit to make room for the next round of contestants. McKenzie slapped a hand on my shoulder.

"Showtime, laddie."

I rolled my shoulders and cracked my neck. Today the big man and I would be teamed up against whatever they threw down after us;

tomorrow I might have to fight *him*. I wasn't looking forward to that. We'd become friends, but I had no doubt he'd kill me if we were matched against each other.

Nothing personal, of course.

***

Since my second escape attempt, my keepers had taken to trussing me up like a hog when I wasn't under guard, even in my cage. The ropes were strong and the knots were clever, and my bindings had a way of cinching tighter the more I struggled against them. Eventually I stopped trying.

But I didn't stop plotting.

I'd run some of my schemes past McKenzie, but he'd already tried them all, plus some things I'd never even considered. For Stone Age saurians, these little lizard people knew how to keep prisoners. They'd give a supermax prison a run for its money, and I was no Houdini. It was depressing.

Pierce squatted down on the opposite side of my cage and studied his fingernails.

"Can't sleep?" he asked.

The appearance of my dead teammate didn't startle me. He'd been coming and going for weeks. I hadn't told anyone yet—I wasn't exactly sure why. Being haunted by your best friend certainly wasn't the craziest thing we'd encountered in the Land of the Black Sun.

"I need to get out of here," I said.

"You really do."

"It's been two weeks… I think… the days are starting to run together."

"About that long, yeah. The guys are looking for you. Don't lose hope."

"You've seen them?"

"No, I still can't wander far from your sorry white ass, but I know Captain Brown. He won't give up until you're found."

"How're you holding up?"

He gave a fractional shrug. "Being dead is boring as hell."

"Haven't met any hot dead chicks?"

He looked around melodramatically and waved a hand. "I don't see dead people, man. Only the living. And only you can see or hear me."

"Bummer."

"For real. Can't recommend it." He shot me a Lando Calrissian smile. "You think that Sir McKenzie bro is right? Think you knocked up the princess? God knows you tried. You two were at it like rabbits."

"We weren't *that* bad."

"Oh, I don't know about that."

"Please tell me you didn't—"

"Watch?" He mock-gagged. "Gross, bro. I got as far away from you two nymphos as I could."

"Crazy to think she could be pregnant. I need to get out of here. I should be with her."

"Roger that. So how're we gonna bust you out?"

As the night wore on and McKenzie snored, Pierce and I brainstormed and rejected new ways to free myself. Hours passed, and gradually the persistent mist grew into a thick fog. There was something unnatural about it, and it seemed to worry the sentries too. They chittered and squeaked in agitation as tendrils of silver-blue haze snaked along the ground and up over the village. A feeling of intense weariness came over me, and I sat up straighter, blinking hard to try and stay awake.

And then one by one the guards fell over where they stood—asleep, comatose, or dead.

The next thing I remembered was waking abruptly from a dreamless sleep with the smell of something horrendous in my nostrils.

***

Large green eyes flecked with gold glowed in the torchlight inches from my face. A bluish feline nose below them wrinkled.

"Wake up, Ben-Ette," a soft voice hissed.

"What is that awful smell?" I asked in a daze. "Eps?"

She pulled her head away from mine and gave a Cheshire grin full of needle teeth. She was… not a pretty sight, but Chaneque never are. Pretty, that is. Even the women. Imagine a child-sized bluish-gray-skinned gremlin with the features of a Sphinx cat—you know, the hairless naked ones—adorned with a mop of lanky blue hair and no less than four large, bat-like ears full of bone piercings.

"You naked," she observed.

"So are you," I replied, averting my eyes from the glowing blue paint she'd daubed over her belly, breasts, and… other parts. Apparently it wasn't just her ears that were pierced. Ouch. "Wait… why are *you* naked? Is this a dream?"

Nightmare, to be honest. Dreaming of Epasotl naked was a nightmare.

"Not dream," she said. "Rescue."

"But you're naked."

"No duh. Sleep magic work better this way." She stoppered the small vial she'd been waving under my nose and swapped it in her haversack for a knife, which she used to quickly cut through my bindings. I rubbed my wrists and tried to look at her without, you know, *looking* at her.

"I wish you weren't naked," I said.

"Do not get excited."

"Believe me, that's the furthest thing from my mind."

"Lucky for Xochi." Epasotl gave a staccato hissing laugh and held her finger and thumb apart maybe half an inch. "Not much there if you were."

"Thanks, Eps."

"Come, we get the di di mao out of Dodge now. Your captors will wake soon."

I scurried out of the cage after her and then paused. "Wait, we need to get McKenzie."

"Who?"

"My friend. He's in that cage. We can't leave him."

She loped over to where I'd indicated and called back to me in a hiss over her shoulder. "Are you sure he not sisimito?"

"Very funny." In truth there was some resemblance between the big, hairy man and the gigantic, shaggy, red-haired beasts the Chaneque used as shock troops. "Here, give me the vial. I'll wake him up. If the first thing he sees is a wrinkly naked blue cat-woman with glowing lady parts, he'll freak out."

She put her fists on her hips. "I look *nothing* like *cat.* And am not *wrinkly.*"

"You do and you are, a little. Come on."

She handed over the vial. "Hurry. Little Kahuna wonder what take so long."

"Moving with a purpose," I muttered as I unfastened the cage and got the foul-smelling vial under McKenzie's nose. He woke with a start and nearly throttled me before he came to his senses.

"Ach, Bennett! Scared the bejeezus outta me. What's that smell, eh? What's going on?"

"Jailbreak," I said hurriedly. "My friends are getting us out."

He was about to exit his cage when his eyes fixed on Epasotl. "What the bloody hell is *that*?"

"That's Epasotl," I said.

"What in the blazes is an Epasotl?"

"Me," she said proudly with a toss of her lanky blue hair. "We must break like wind and blow bicycle stand. Sleep fog wear off."

"Quite right," McKenzie said, slapping me on the shoulder. "Lead the way, lassie."

***

"Might be easier to ask if there's any part of you that *isn't* cut, bruised, or lacerated," Doc said as he gave me a twice-over under the light of his red penlight. "You were pit fighting?"

We were off to one side of the platoon's assembly area deep in the jungles of… wherever we were exactly. We didn't know for certain.

"Every day," I said. "Before that I had a bad stomach bug."

"Explains the weight loss. Damn, you're a mess. I'd hate to ask what the other guys look like."

"Dead. They look dead, Doc."

He pursed his lips. Johnny "Doc" Yazzie was our platoon medic, a former Ranger E-7 busted down to buck sergeant and thrown out of the Bats for unknown but energetically speculated-upon reasons. I wasn't sure myself—the man was one of the most squared-away dudes in the platoon—but bets ran high it involved a colonel's daughter. Maybe a general's even.

He touched one of my numerous scabbed-over cuts. "Looks good for less than a week old. You said they *glued* you back together?"

"Something like that, yeah. It was this green goop. Like menthol Krazy Glue."

He grunted and felt my ribs.

"There's, uh, more, Doc…"

"What's that?"

"They fed us… well, they put *cocaine* in our food."

"You mean like coca leaves? I wouldn't worry. I give the guys shit for chewing them just because Captain isn't totally down with it, but there really isn't a risk to be honest. No worse than coffee or tobacco, which were two of my three major food groups before we ran out, same as most of the guys here. And it doesn't seem to hurt the Sugar Skull Gals any. They chew it by the bushel."

"No, I mean like *cocaine*. Real cocaine. The little freaks are total junkies. Some plane running drugs and guns went down, and they built their village around it. They snort it, drink it, put it in the food. They worship the stuff."

"Ah. Well, I still wouldn't worry. Withdrawal doesn't have any serious physical side effects. You'll be tired, grumpy, anxious, irritable, that sort of thing, but it'll wear off. Let me know if you start getting seriously paranoid about shit or whatever. Mostly you'll just be jonesing bad. Listen, get some leaves from Flaming Feather or Wilson to chew, or make a tea or something. That'll help."

"But Captain—"

"He'll come around."

"It's against my—"

"Religion? Suit yourself, man. But if you start getting freaky, I'll force-feed you the damn leaves."

"Roger, Doc." I stood and got dressed. "So, what's your other major food group?"

He grinned. "Hate, of course. Caffeine, nicotine, and hate."

"Once a Ranger…"

Doc laughed and then turned as McKenzie strode over, wearing nothing but a poncho liner around his waist. He'd been talking with Captain Brown and the senior NCOs and now it was his turn to get poked and prodded.

"Sir Angus McKenzie," the big man said, offering a shovel hand.

Doc shook and motioned to a log. "Kindly step into my office, Sir McKenzie."

I left them to it and headed over to where Captain Brown was sitting with Sanchez, our platoon sergeant.

"Take a seat, Nephi," the captain said as I approached. "Doc clear you for duty?"

"Yessir. I look worse than I feel. Glad to be back."

"Took a lot more trouble to track you down than I care to admit," Brown said. "Shouldn't have taken two weeks."

"Roger that, sir," Sanchez said. "These indigs are a pain in my ass."

"The lizardfolk, Sergeant?" I asked.

"Scaly bastards been on us like white on rice. They hit, we fade. Repeat. But we found you, and we got you out. That's what matters."

"Hooah," I replied.

"What can you tell us about them?" the captain asked me.

"Smarter than they look, sir. Tough, skilled fighters, but you know that. We can't communicate, although McKenzie understands a bit of their odd language. I think there are several tribes, all at war with the others. They made me fight their captives in death matches. The ones who nabbed me, I think they're the biggest group. They've built their village around a downed cargo plane. McKenzie said it's got a load of arms and ammo inside. American, he thinks. The lizards don't know what they are and haven't touched them. I don't know planes, sir, but it looks like it's from our time. It's full of drugs too."

"Cartel?" Sanchez asked Brown.

"Or CIA," the captain replied. "Sounds like you found us a resupply option. That's welcome news. We're going to need to stock up."

"Sir?" I asked. "I thought we had plenty stored back at the Kuauchanejkej settlement. Especially after we raided the armory in Amoloyan—I mean, if we're running low, Eps can just open a portal for resupply."

"That was the plan, but it's off the table now," Brown said with a grunt.

"Off the table—I don't understand."

"The PFC can't make a portal back to the settlement," Sanchez said with a look of indigestion.

"I don't under—"

"The dagger has been lost," Brown clarified.

"Lost—!" I blurted. "But that was our exfil!" My wife's bronze dagger, an artifact from an ancient people, the original inhabitants of the Land of the Black Sun, was a key component in the creation of temporal portals that could link vast distances. Without it we were stranded in this land of mists, and that meant I had no way of getting back to my wife. That was my first thought—Xochi—even though the larger concern for the platoon was that the dagger was necessary if we were ever going to get anyone back to the real world. The artifact we were here for, whatever it was, was just a navigational aid; it couldn't create portals on its own. Or so we believed. Like I've said, we had very little intel. "I can't believe she lost it!"

"Destroyed more than lost," Sanchez said.

I looked at my platoon sergeant blankly.

"We were being overrun and attempted a hasty exfil," the captain explained. "Too hasty, apparently. The portal was unstable and the dagger shattered. Epasotl blames herself, but I take responsibility for making her rush the procedure. Without a lodestone like the arches we used to access Mictlan..."—he spread his hands—"portal creation is riskier than we believed."

"I thought..." I shook my head. "Isn't Atzi supposed to help with that?"

"She was unavailable at the time," Brown said. "I made a bad call and I own it."

I could respect that. I *did* respect it. It takes a big man to own up to a mistake, and I didn't envy the calls he had to make each and every day. The fact that he was right most of the time and admitted when he was wrong instead of shifting the blame when he easily could've, just made him a better leader. But losing the only means we had of getting back to my wife… that was a hard blow.

"You said you were being overrun, sir," I said. "If the exfil failed, how'd you escape?"

Sanchez barked a laugh. "It was pretty spectacular when the portal failed. Scared the daylights out of those scaly little shits. Hell, I nearly pissed my own pants, truth be told. They haven't bothered us since."

"As for getting back…" The captain shrugged his massive shoulders. "We'll figure it out. The dagger was an artifact of the very people we've come here to find. We'll just have to beg, borrow, or steal a replacement."

CHAPTER 3

The good news, for me at least, was that my kit and weapons had been recovered. The lizardfolk didn't know what to do with most of it and the guys had salvaged what they could from the trash heap outside the village, including a few dozen rounds of hand-loaded .338 Lapua Magnum. Those were precious, especially since we couldn't pop back to the settlement to fetch more from our stockpile. My NODs were busted, but Sybil, Pierce's M24 sniper rifle I'd inherited, seemed no worse for wear. She was filthy though, and I spent most of the next morning giving her a thorough cleaning along with the rest of my gear.

Sergeant Wilson ambled over and slapped me some skin.

"How's it hanging, Bennett?" the former surfer and bodybuilder asked as he took a seat on the log beside me.

"Righteous now that I'm back with Crazy Horse Platoon, Sarge."

"So, pit fighting, huh? Pretty hardcore. You look like shit. I mean, you looked like shit before," he motioned to the spiderweb of black veins on my face and forearms, "but now you *really* look like shit."

"Thanks, man. How're the gals holding up?"

"Gals are good. Super squared away, like always. You know Flaming Feather wasn't hip to breaking up the Blackhearts and dividing them among the platoon like we did when we set out on this op, but it works better this way. She's adjusting."

The "gals" were our female Kuauchanejkej allies, known affectionately as the Sugar Skull Gals due to the striking warpaint they wore. Flaming Feather was the older sister of Wilson's girlfriend, Dressed-in-Stars, and one of the more seasoned warriors of the bunch we'd integrated into the platoon. Most notably, Flaming Feather was… intense.

"And Stars?" I asked.

"Driving me crazy, bro." He puffed out his cheeks. "This no fraternization in the field rule's got me seriously bent. Captain says look but don't touch. Bogus."

"As if, man. I don't believe you're not sneaking off."

"No bueno. Feather would have my balls and Captain would bust me down to private. Same as any guy who touches her girls. Don't matter. Stars and I, we have a history, you know? We got a *thing*."

"Probably for the best."

"Still blows chunks."

I nodded and scrubbed more nasty gunk off my assault pack.

Wilson slapped his thighs. "Anyway, bro. Tell me about the fights."

"Not much to tell."

"Don't want to talk about it?"

"Not really."

"Now that Sir McKenzie dude, he's got some stories. Seems like a good dude. He on the level?"

I gazed across the assembly area to where McKenzie was chatting up Takahashi and García, two of our senior NCOs. Someone had given him a spare pair of ACUs that actually fit him. Probably Captain Brown's.

"I think so," I said. "I've only known him a couple weeks, and half that time I was vomiting out of both ends, but yeah, I think he's cool."

"He said he's fought some of those jaguar-men characters we're looking to make contact with."

"The Tlacaōcēlōtl. Yeah, he told me about that."

"What a trip. I thought they were, you know, like men who dressed in jaguar skins or something. Not actual *jaguar*-men."

"Last one he fought almost killed him. He was out of action for a month."

Wilson gave a low whistle.

"You guys find any trace of them?" I asked.

"Not yet. Just those lizard dudes always on us like flies on shit until the portal went kablooey and scared them off. That was some seriously bad mojo. Eps almost died, you know? Portal just about sucked her in when it collapsed. Would've, too, if Sanchez hadn't snatched her back just in time."

"I didn't know. I should go see her."

"Think she's still sleeping off the spell she used to put the village to sleep. Working magic like that knocks the kid out cold when it's over. Still pretty dope she can do that shit. She's gotten better, too. Spending time with that kitty Jedi Master while we were gearing up for this op taught her a bunch of new tricks."

"Ueueokichtli's not a *Jedi*."

"Whatever. Dude was like a blue Yoda."

I couldn't help from laughing, because it was true. The Chaneque *Teōicpauhqui*—literally "one who makes with threads of god" in their dialect—was totally a blue Yoda. The master god-weaver even had funny backwards speech patterns. He was also a foulmouthed drunk, but that only added to his charm… if you want to call it that. Epasotl had sought him out via handy portal magic shortly after our little raid into the Underworld to destroy the soul forge, which, now that I thought about it, was a lot like Luke going to find his teacher on Dagobah—except in her case, she brought him back with her. Ueueokichtli had spent weeks training her while the rest of us relocated the gals' people, the Kuauchanejkej refugees, to the secret settlement of Tepeuakan in the vast wilderness of the southern subcontinent and then prepared for this operation.

I stood and slung Sybil over my shoulder.

"I'm going to see if she's awake," I said.

"Roger that, bro." He gave me a fist bump. "Glad to have you back. Almost missed you."

"Same feels."

Epasotl was up when I made my way over to where she and Sanchez had parked their rucks in for the night. She was chattering away with her spirit guide, Atzi, who inhabited a floating infant's skull wreathed in blue flame.

"How goes it, sister from another mister?" I called out.

"I am tired, but doped up," she replied.

"It's just 'dope.' You're dope."

"Whatever. Is same."

I didn't bother correcting her again as I sat down cross-legged by her sleeping bag.

"Atzi," I said in greeting to the flaming skull. It, or she rather, turned her glowing eye sockets at me and giggled, a sound like spring rain. "Thanks for saving my bacon, Eps."

"Is what bros do, no?" Epasotl replied with a shrug.

"True that, sis. Still, thanks."

I didn't mention that I'd caught she'd said "bros" and not "slaves." Technically, according to Chaneque custom at least, she was my slave and I was her master, since I'd captured her. The fact that she now thought of us as bros was major progress. Maybe she'd even stop asking me to torture her to death so she could regain her honor.

She fingered one of her ears absently—the one with all the notches cut out of it; every time she healed one of us she had to sacrifice her own flesh. There wasn't much of that ear left now. But, as she would often quip, she had three others, so "no biggie, bro."

"Was I interrupting?" I asked, motioning to Atzi.

"No," Epasotl said. "We talk about you and Pierce."

"You know about Pierce? Can you see him too?"

"I cannot, but Atzi can."

"Pierce, Pierce, Pierce," Atzi chittered in a singsong toddler's voice. "He is not gone!"

"How long have you known?" I asked.

Atzi gave the floating, flaming skull equivalent of a shrug.

"Do you know why he can't… you know… *move on*?"

Atzi just giggled in reply.

"Load of help she is," I said to Epasotl.

"Spirits are flighty," Epasotl replied. "Rain Spirit most of all. She believe he bound by duty to you and others, to help see them home. Then he go home too. That you see him and we cannot suggest strong connection between you. Why you not told anyone?"

"I don't know… it just seems too crazy for anyone to believe."

"Should tell Little Kahuna at least."

"Sergeant Sanchez?" I pursed my lips. "Maybe. Captain Brown might be more open-minded to… this sort of thing."

"Tell me what?" a quiet voice said behind me, and I nearly jumped out of my skin. Our platoon sergeant was the softest-spoken man I'd ever met, and he could move like a ghost. It was hella creepy.

He squatted beside us and gave me *The Look*. For a short wiry guy, he had all the presence of a rock giant.

"Uh, hey Sarge," I croaked.

"What sort of thing would the good captain be more open to, Bennett?"

"Well… ghosts… and ah… well, it's… you know… Pierce. He's…" I waved a hand aimlessly. "… Always around. Somewhere nearby. We, uh, talk… about… stuff."

"Is true," Epasotl confirmed. "Atzi see him. He not gone."

"Not gone! Not gone!" the skull twittered.

"You talk about 'stuff' with Pierce's ghost?" Sanchez asked very softly.

"Yes."

He nodded slowly and squinted at me.

"I'm not crazy, Sarge."

"Maybe." He quirked an eyebrow. "A ghost would make a good scout. We could use that edge. I'll inform the captain we potentially have a new asset. And you tell Pierce just because he's dead don't mean he can slack off, you read me?"

"Lima Charlie, Sarge."

"Good. As you were."

He stood and walked away. When he was out of earshot, I exhaled, and Epasotl gave a staccato, hissing laugh.

"See, Ben-Ette?" she said. "Told you so."

"I hate the way he sneaks up on me all the time. You knew he was there, didn't you?"

"Of course," she said. "But the look on you face—!"

***

Captain Brown had made some major changes to Crazy Horse Platoon in preparation for Operation MacGuffin with an eye to integrating the guys and gals. We were reorganized into two fully manned combat squads for this operation. Sergeant Takahashi led Gold Squad, which was composed of two full rifle teams led by Sergeant Wilson and Corporal Stanley. Wilson was in charge of three of the gals: Falling Leaves, Jade Talon, and Obsidian Tears. Stanley kept PFC Lawrence and got Specialist Cohen, plus he was given a young but accomplished warrior named First-to-Dance to fill out his team. Stanley was a pig when it came to women, and I wondered about the wisdom of adding one of the gals to his team, but I needn't have worried—Dance made it clear on Day One she wasn't someone to be trifled with.

García, who was the leader of Blue Squad, kept Specialist Cameron as an AG and got Private Anderson as his M240B gunner, plus Flaming Feather and Dressed-in-Stars as a second crew with a woman named Heart-of-Darkness to fill out his squad as a rifleman. Riflewoman, rather.

And apparently Sir McKenzie was coming with us as another rifleman in Blue Squad. Made sense, I guess. I mean, it's not like he had anywhere else to go—and after having a long chat with the captain, he'd seemed to come to terms with the fact he wasn't in the British Honduras anymore.

I guess the captain explained it better than I did.

As for me, seeing as I didn't have a team to lead with Pierce KIA and all, even though he's still around, sorta, I got rolled into HQ with the captain, Sanchez, Doc, and Epasotl. Lieutenant Whitlock had stayed behind at the settlement as an advisor.

But I kept my sweet X-Men call sign, so I wasn't complaining.

All told, we were a couple squads short of a full infantry platoon, even though we were *technically* Cavalry Scouts, but 19Ds are basically infantry anyway, right? I mean, we carried everything on our backs now, so might as well give us a blue cord and call it good.

Just kidding. I'm a trooper 'til the day I ride off to Fiddler's Green. We were still cavalry. We were just… permanently dismounted.

Captain Brown had decided to hit the lizardman village immediately and secure the weapons and ammo from the plane, so we had a day and a night to kill before we raided the village at dawn. At some point in the evening, Captain Brown found me. It looked like he wanted to chat about something serious.

"Is he here?" he asked.

"Pierce?"

He nodded.

I thumbed behind me. "Yessir, right there."

The captain squinted in the direction I'd indicated and furrowed his brow. He'd debriefed me earlier in the day, and I'd given him the four-one-one on my invisible friend. Later Sanchez told me Brown was "displeased" I'd withheld the intel for so long.

Translation: he was pissed.

And he's not a man to piss off.

"I wasn't so sure I wasn't crazy myself, Sarge," I'd told Sanchez.

"Doesn't matter. You know something, you say something. That's true back in the real world, and it's double true here. You have intel, you share it. Crazy or no. Read me, son?"

I read him. Lima Charlie, Sergeant.

Now Captain Brown glanced at me, back to where Pierce was standing, then back at me.

"Not going to lie, Nephi," he said. "I'm still skeptical."

"Understood, sir."

"Turn around."

I nodded and pivoted to face away, somewhat confused by the order.

"Ask Stanford how many fingers I'm holding up."

"Three," Pierce told me. "Now five, now a fist, now the sign for nine. Now he's repeating it all over again except it's eight at the end, not nine."

I relayed what Pierce said, and Brown grunted.

"I'm still skeptical, but Atzi corroborates it, not that I consider her the most reliable of sources. Either you're right, or you're hallucinating *and* suddenly telepathic. You can turn back now."

"Yessir. I don't know what to say. Like I told you before, I didn't even tell Xochi. *I'm* still skeptical, sir."

"A third option occurred to me," Brown mused.

"What's that, sir?"

"A malignant entity has attached itself to you and taken on Stanford's appearance to gain your trust."

Pierce swore. Rather creatively.

"That… something from *X-Men*, sir?"

One of Captain Brown's quirks was quoting from the Gospel of Chris Claremont. It might sound a bit silly, especially coming from an officer, and a former *Ranger* at that, but trust me, it wasn't. The wisdom he pulled out of those comics had saved our skins more than once.

"Bible, actually," Brown corrected.

It took me a few seconds to make the connection, but I automatically blurted out, "2 Corinthians 11:14."

Not for nothing, I *was* a missionary for two years. I might not know *X-Men*, but I know my Bible verses.

"What the hell is a Second Corinthians?" Pierce asked.

"Means you could be a devil disguised as an angel," I said over my shoulder. "Basically."

"Oh for Chrissakes," Pierce said. "This is bullshit. I'm not the damned Devil. Not an angel either, bro. I'm just dead and stuck haunting your sorry ass."

"He says he's not the devil, sir," I told Brown. "Or an angel. He's just stuck haunting me."

"I don't think he's a devil or angel either," Brown said. "But I question if this *entity* you see and hear is truly the spirit of the late Specialist Pierce."

"I can't believe this," Pierce sighed.

"We've talked a lot, sir. If it's not Pierce, then whatever it is, well, it does a dang good impression of him."

"Good enough to trust your life to it?" the captain asked.

I pivoted and considered my friend standing behind me. He stared daggers back at me.

"You have to admit Cap'n has a point," I told Pierce.

"Seriously, bro?"

I shrugged and spread my hands helplessly.

"Okay," Pierce finally admitted. "He has a point. *Maybe*. But if I'm not me, *whoever* I am is doing a damn good job of pretending to be me, because they're fooling even *me*." He frowned. "Wait! Ask me something only I would know."

I thought for a few moments. "Ireland or Crawford?"

"Neither. My vote's for Adaora."

"Who the heck is that?"

"Remember the *SI* from the future? The one with that Upton chick on the cover? Polar *Bare*?"

"I never saw it. You only told me about it."

"Yeah, well there was this Nigerian chick in it. Adaora Akubilo. She gets my vote."

"Better than Upton? Better than *Ireland*?"

Pierce shrugged. "She's a sister, so yeah. Duh."

"Why are you talking about swimsuit models?" Brown interjected.

"Sorry, sir. Forgot the conversation's one-sided. Just a sec… Hey Pierce, what did you ride on your dad's ranch?"

"Beat-to-hell-up KDX."

"And where'd you finally *really* pop your surfer's cherry?"

"No one actually says that, bro, but Jalama."

"Dunno, sir," I said to the captain. "He's three for three. Sergeant Wilson could probably interrogate him on surfer stuff. I doubt a malignant entity would know all that. When it comes to surfing, I'm just a Scoobie."

"*Shubie*," Pierce corrected, rolling his eyes.

"Four for four," I said. I would've given Pierce a high five, but… ghost.

"That'll do, Nephi," Brown said. "It doesn't necessarily prove anything, but I suppose it's encouraging, assuming you're not simply imagining him. We'll proceed with optimistic caution."

"Imagining? But, sir. Counting the fingers—?"

"Delusional and telepathic is also an option."

I sighed. "Roger, sir."

Brown moved off to attend to officer things, and I pulled my assault pack around to rummage for a bite of Epasotl's famous pemmican; I was saving my last MRE for a special occasion. Pierce plopped down beside me and blew out his cheeks.

"I'm not some kind of 'malignant entity,' bro. You know that, right? It's just me."

"I want to believe that, man. I really do. But Cap'n's got me a little freaked out now. Being haunted by my best friend is one thing… but being haunted by some… *thing* pretending to be my friend… that's seriously bad mojo."

"Well, shit." Pierce plucked at a small shoot and flicked it away.

"Don't sweat it. I'm sure you're *you* and—holy crap!"

"What?" Pierce said in alarm.

"You just—you picked something up and *threw* it!"

"Damn! I did, didn't I?" He tried and failed to pluck up another shoot. "Dammit! How'd I do that?"

"I have no frigging clue, but that was totally rad. It's progress!"

Pierce grinned from ear to ear.

CHAPTER 4

Later that evening Sanchez called the NCOs together for a briefing. Captain Brown was in attendance, naturally, as was Epasotl. She might be a PFC, but she operated more like a warrant. I still wasn't sure why they hadn't just made her one. Is there a military designation for "Platoon Witch"? Maybe Sanchez just couldn't stomach the idea of having to salute her and call her "ma'am." That seemed the most likely reason. Sanchez had also invited McKenzie to attend as an advisor.

"Take a knee, gentlemen," Sanchez said, gathering us around a sand table of the lizardfolk village he'd constructed in the dirt with the help of me and McKenzie. It even had a little plane woven from twigs. "As you all know, we're about to head out on a long recon, and we've lost our resupply and evac option. Fortunately, Sir McKenzie has identified a promising store of weapons and ammunition. Now, we don't need 'em yet, but we're gonna, and it doesn't make sense to backtrack here later, so we'll be hitting the target at first light, *before* we head out into the unknown."

"If we pick up extras now, we'll be pretty loaded down," Takahashi observed.

"Can't be helped," Brown said. "I'd rather we hump more now than need it and not have it later. It might slow us down, but consider the alternative."

"Roger that, sir," Takahashi said.

Stanley raised a hand, and Brown nodded. "Just how much stuff are we talking about?" the corporal asked.

Brown looked over to McKenzie, who cleared his throat and spread his hands. "Several crates. Nothing I'm familiar with, but it looked like someone was set to outfit a small army. Cap'n here helped me interpret some of what I saw. Looked to be a load of rifles and a mess of ammunition."

"Mixed bag of M16s and a lot of five-five-six," Sanchez said. "Grenades too. But at least one M60, and more importantly, boxes of seven-six-two, which we need as much of as possible since the whole platoon is chambered for that."

"Linked?" García asked hopefully.

"Affirmative," Sanchez said. "Sounds like several M19A1 cans at least."

"That's what the markings said," McKenzie affirmed. "M19A1."

"We'd better start saving M13 links, all the same," García said.

"Wise policy," Brown agreed.

"So what's the plan then?" Takahashi asked. "PFC Epasotl puts the village to sleep again and we slip in, load up, and slip out?"

Epasotl waggled her hand in a "more or less" motion, but her face said "not exactly."

"The spell might not work as well a second night in a row," Brown explained. "They'll be on alert since they just lost two valued prisoners."

"And magic is unpredictable," Sanchez said with a sour face. "So we expect some resistance."

"That might be putting it lightly, Sarge," I said. "That plane is sacred to them. It's their holy of holies."

"I have other tricks down my pants," Epasotl said.

"Up your sleeves," I corrected.

"Is same."

"No, it's really not."

"Whatever."

"Point is," Sanchez said irritably, "we can't expect things to go as smoothly as last night. Expect direct action and plan accordingly. We want to avoid it if we can, but the probability of violence is high."

"Just need to be more violent than they are," Doc chimed in.

"Hooah," said Wilson.

"So where do you need our teams, Sarge?" Takahashi asked, moving closer to the sand table.

"It'll be a two-pronged assault..." our platoon sergeant began, moving a rock that represented Wilson's team.

***

"Execute!" Sanchez's voice was soft over the radio, and I shifted my butt in the forked bough of the tree I was positioned in. It gave me a great view of the sprawling village and the plane that hung a couple meters above the forest floor suspended in vines and branches. I could even see the skeletal faces of the pilot and copilot in the cockpit. I wondered how long that rusted-out hulk had dangled there. Decades, maybe, or perhaps only a few years. Doc said a body could be reduced to a skeleton in a matter of weeks, if not days, so that was no clue.

Epasotl, naked and painted in glowing blue stripes, held out her hands as she cast a silvery fog over the buildings near the plane. Tendrils of mist snaked out and climbed over walls, and one by one, the guards began to fall to the ground just as they had the night before. Wilson's team moved in from my right, and Stanley's took a position on the left, the two rifle teams leading the machine gun crews who set up in positions that would allow them to talk their guns.

Wilson leveled a knife hand, and Jade Talon scurried silently under the belly of the plane to set up her lightweight machine gun on its bipod. Falling Leaves got into position to cover her with the grenade launcher, and then Wilson and Obsidian Tears ran over to the plane's open cargo hatch. Dropping her SCAR-H on its sling, Tears drew her knife and scaled the rope ladder leading up into the belly of the plane, a coil of rope slung over her shoulder. She paused to listen just under the lip of the fuselage, then heaved herself up and into the cargo hold in a single fluid motion.

Wilson waved to Stanley and Cohen and First-to-Dance, who detached themselves from their team's formation and ran on light feet to where Wilson was waiting under the plane.

I admonished myself for paying too much attention to what my teammates were doing and resumed my survey of the village. So far all was quiet. I'd attached my thermal monocular to my scope and scanned the buildings and pathways. I couldn't see through the walls *into* the huts—thermal doesn't work that way—but it was helpful to catch where various guards were patrolling—or more often had fallen asleep at their posts due to Epasotl's spell.

I scanned past the plane, noting the crates and cans descending on the rope to where Wilson was overseeing Cohen and First-to-Dance, who were hustling the cargo back to our rear security element. As I repositioned myself slightly to get a better view around the body of the downed aircraft, I spotted a patrol of four guards advancing toward the plane. They must have been out of range when Eps cast her spell. They nearly stumbled over a sleeping sentry and were slapping him awake when one of them caught sight of the activity at the plane and gave a sharp, trilling cry.

"Havok, Longshot," I transmitted. "You've been spotted."

"Just need a few more minutes," Wilson replied.

"Don't think you're going to get them."

Other guards throughout the village picked up the cry of alarm, and soon the misty dawn air was filled with a chorus of squeaks and sharp barks. Lizardmen poured out of huts clutching spears, clubs, and flint daggers.

Sanchez gave the order to go weapons hot, and I started pink-misting targets of opportunity from my perch as the two-forties lit up and drummed out steady bursts. I spied a large cluster of maybe twenty warriors assembling across the village and got on my radio.

"Gold Eight, Longshot."

"Go for Gold Eight," Falling Leaves replied.

"Give me some AB at your two o'clock, one-eight-zero meters."

"Roger," she replied.

I heard the thunk of her FL40GL and watched for the air burst. The grenade detonated several meters to the right and past the rushing warriors, and I did a rough guesstimate to correct for leading them.

"Gold Eight, Longshot. Left ten. Drop twenty."

"Roger. Left ten, dropping twenty."

This time the air burst caught them full on and blew the group apart in a red-hazed bloom.

"Target neutralized. Thanks, Gold Eight."

"Any time, Longshot."

I had just shifted to take out another target of opportunity when a veritable horde of lizard warriors came rushing the plane from seemingly out of nowhere, and I called out a warning on the radio. Epasotl popped up and charged straight at them, holding out her hands, fingers splayed, sending a sheet of searing blue flame leaping from her fingertips. It immolated the nearest warriors, but the group was too large and quickly engulfed her. I saw visions of my friend being hacked to pieces when there was a terrific thunderclap and the ground around the mob literally heaved, throwing bodies like bowling pins. I could feel the tremor from where I sat in the tree.

Glowing blue, Epasotl backed away quickly, leaping over the cracked and uneven ground, MP5 to her shoulder as she fired bursts into the stunned warriors.

García's machine gun crews quickly shifted and belched fire into the lizardmen, cutting down the few that remained like wheat as Epasotl turned and loped drunkenly back to the plane. She made it about halfway before she collapsed.

Takahashi was on the radio as he sprinted forward toward her. "Xavier, Sunfire, prize is secured." He scooped Epasotl up with one arm and fired from the hip into a charging trio of lizardmen. "Gold Squad, execute Bravo Delta Three."

García held his machine gunners' positions as Gold faded, then ordered Blue Squad to fall back. Half a minute later, two distant thunks sounded and the plane exploded, showering the village with scraps of metal and a fine cloud of white dust that instantly ignited in a secondary explosion that nearly knocked me from my perch.

Witnessing a cocaine-fueled air bomb hadn't been on my bucket list, but I'm not going to lie: it was pretty spectacular.

"Xavier, Longshot," I transmitted. "Moving to Point Charlie." I slung Sybil, shinnied down the tree, and then faded into the forest, heading to our rendezvous.

CHAPTER 5

We rolled up the assembly area around midmorning—just a rough guess, because the sky in this land was permanently gray. If the sun was permanently eclipsed here, there was no way to know it; we'd never actually seen it. We headed west, at least according to Epasotl, during a moment of lucidity from her post-spell-coma-induced haze. Compasses didn't work any better in the Land of Mists than they did in the Land of the Black Sun. Maybe the two were one and the same; I really didn't know. Even Epasotl didn't know for sure. But without being able to see the sun and with no magnetic north, not to mention no maps, navigation was mostly a matter of faith on this op. Thankfully Epasotl has an uncanny sense of direction, so it wasn't quite *blind* faith.

Still, to be honest, I'm surprised they found me at all.

Anyway, no maps, no navigational aids save one diminutive Chaneque witch, and no real intel on our objective made for suboptimal operating conditions. But we were undaunted. At least Captain Brown was. I'm sure some of the guys were less optimistic. As for me, I was just happy not to be fighting pigmy lizardmen in a pit, and thrilled that I hadn't started to jones for that corn and larva mash, because it was disgusting. I wasn't even starting to feel tired or irritable, so that was a good sign. Maybe it took a couple of days for the withdrawal symptoms to kick in.

Or maybe I'd get lucky and there wouldn't be any side effects at all.

I was very much hoping for the latter.

***

Two days later we found the village. It'd been a difficult hump through thick jungle as we left the coastal lowlands and made our way into the foothills of… wherever we were. This land of mists. There hadn't been any sign of the lizardmen, or much of anything else for that matter. Just quadruple-layer canopy dripping condensation, stifling humidity, and swarms of biting insects. Epasotl had made a disgusting paste that helped with the bugs, but there wasn't much we could do about the constant damp and heat. It was like living in a sweat lodge.

"I don't see anything alive down there," Pierce reported back to me. I was lying prone on a tall rocky outcropping that offered a decent view of the village. It was more of a hamlet than a village, with a cluster of stone and adobe buildings arrayed around a small central pyramid. Woven grass-and-leaf huts radiated farther out beyond the core, but most were burnt to the ground. There had been perhaps eighty families, I guessed. Had been, because what I saw through my spotting scope looked like a massacre.

"Xavier, this is Longshot," I transmitted. "I have eyes on a Tlacaōcēlōtl settlement one point seven klicks to your two o'clock. No signs of life. Something bad happened here. There are a lot of adult and juvenile bodies."

"Roger," Sanchez replied over the radio. "Any sign of hostiles?"

"Negative."

"How recent?"

"Hard to say. A while. The bodies are in an advanced state of decomposition."

"Hold your position and continue observing. We're coming. ETA thirty mikes."

"Roger, out." I turned to Pierce. "Cavalry's on its way."

Captain Brown was exercising what he continued to call "cautious optimism" and had begun sending Pierce and me out on recon probes ahead of the platoon. So far it had gone well. Having a teammate who was silent and invisible was a definite edge. X Team was back in business.

Assuming it *was* Pierce and not… something else pretending to be him. I didn't really believe that theory, but still…

"This place gives me the creeps," Pierce muttered.

"Roger that. Mind going back down there? Make sure there aren't any surprises."

"Will do, bro. But I'm telling you, there's something off here. My Spidey sense is tingling."

"Say again?"

"Can't explain it. Just feels off. Like something real bad went down."

"Well, sure. It was obviously a slaughter."

"More than that. This village… it's *dark*, bro."

"Okay… I read you. You don't have to go down there again if something seems off."

"Nah, I'll go. Just sayin' is all."

I pursed my lips. "You should stay here and wait for backup. If there are hostile… entities… Atzi can probably help with that."

He considered that for a minute and nodded.

I got out my notebook and began sketching a rough map of the village and surrounding terrain, noting the best places for weapons emplacements, routes, and potential ambush sites.

***

"Based on the state of these corpses, I'd estimate the attack happened two, maybe three weeks ago," Doc said, prodding a skull with his forceps.

"That recently?" Sanchez asked.

"In a climate like this, with all the insect life, not to mention scavengers? Sure. I've heard of carcasses being stripped to bone in as little as ten or fifteen days."

"Looks like they gave a fair account of themselves," Captain Brown observed. "It must have been a ferocious battle. Neither side gave nor asked for quarter. Even the juveniles fought. It's clear the Tlacaōcēlōtl aren't a united people." He bent down and picked up a bronze short sword, testing the balance in his hand. "This wasn't a raid. It was an extermination. We've wandered into a civil war."

"And they wield powerful magic," Epasotl chimed in. Atzi twittered in agreement.

"Why do you say that?" Brown inquired.

"Magic leave shadow. Shadow everywhere here. Gnarly dark magics."

"But light too," Atzi giggled as she bobbed in the air.

"Yes," Epasotl said, considering. "Light and dark magic in conflict. Both used in battle. But dark magic leave grody stain. A stench. It stink here. Bad mojo."

"Pierce felt something was off, sir," I added. "Maybe that's what he was sensing."

"What kind of dark magic?" Brown asked Epasotl. "Can you be specific?"

"Summoning and binding of evil spirit to do you will."

"Sorcery," Brown stated. "And the light magic?"

"It is…" Epasotl moved her hands around as if she were weaving something. "It is the working of pure *teōtl* to create something from nothing."

"Teōtl?" Brown asked.

"It's sometimes translated as *god*," I offered. "But that's not exactly accurate, sir. In this context it's more like… a supernatural force? Maybe something like the East Asian concept of qi, I guess? Sort of. It's very nuanced."

"Or *mana* in Oceanian cultures?" Brown suggested. "Or maybe the Force in *Star Wars*, if you want a watered-down version. Interesting. If I'm understanding this right, Epasotl, you evoke a form of elemental energy to manipulate reality. Is that correct?"

She waggled her hand and shrugged. "Sure, I guess."

"So she *is* a Jedi," Doc said.

"Yes!" Epasotl beamed. "Like Luke Walking Sky. That more rad than 'witch.'" She drew herself up to her full three feet, six inches. "I am Jedi."

"More like Doctor Strange than a Jedi," Brown said. "You'd like him, Epasotl. I'll have to tell you about him sometime."

Takahashi's voice came over the radio. "Xavier, Sunfire," he said. "We got something."

"Go for Xavier," Sanchez replied.

"Gold Niner reports possible contact at her ten o'clock, twenty meters. Likely a single individual."

"Roger," Sanchez replied. "Capture if possible."

"Roger, capture if possible. Sunfire out."

"Where are they right now?" Brown asked.

"Clearing the south end of the village, sir," Sanchez replied. "But it's just Wilson's team. Stanley is clearing the pyramid and adjacent structures."

"I want a weapons team in support then."

"Roger that, sir." Our platoon sergeant relayed the order to García, and I saw Flaming Feather and Dressed-in-Stars rushing past a break in the buildings with McKenzie covering their six.

"You too, Nephi," Brown ordered.

"Hooah, sir," I said. "On it."

"Sunfire, this is Longshot," I transmitted as I ran to the south end of the village. "Coming in from your seven o'clock. Where do you want me?"

"See that two-story adobe structure? Get on the roof."

I clicked twice in reply and posted up at the door.

"Pierce, you mind clearing it for me?"

"Will do, bro."

He walked through a wall and less than a minute later poked his head back out—of the wall.

"All clear."

"Both floors and the roof?"

"Duh."

I nodded, ducked through the doorway, and scaled a ladder to the second floor and then onto the flat roof. Shimmying on my belly, I set Sybil up on the low wall and got my bearings. I could see the weapons team posted up to my nine and Wilson's team spread out and advancing on a cluster of huts.

"Gold Niner, this is Longshot. I'm in position. What am I looking at?"

"Movement in door of second hut on left," Jade Talon replied. "Only see shadow, but look maybe man."

"Roger, out. Havok, Longshot."

"Go for Havok," Wilson replied.

"Be advised hostiles may employ magic."

Wilson swore over the net and I saw him halt his team's advance. "Can you be more specific?"

"Something nasty, probably," Epasotl cut in. "Be careful, broski."

I fixed my thermal monocular to the front of my scope and zeroed in on the doorway. With the ambient temperature it was hard to make out much of anything, but I caught what certainly looked to be a large man, or at least man-shaped figure, crouching in the shadows of the hut past the doorway.

"Havok, Longshot. I've got thermal on at least one unidentified individual in the second hut on the left in that cluster."

Wilson gave a hand signal, and Falling Leaves and Obsidian Tears cleared the adjoining huts while Jade Talon provided cover with her Mk 48 lightweight machine gun. A minute later Falling Leaves signaled the all-clear, and Wilson got back on the radio.

"Xavier, Havok. Area is secure. We got at least one individual holed up here. You still want him warm? Because cold would be a whole lot easier."

"Bishop wants him breathing," Sanchez replied. "Call him out. If that doesn't work, smoke him out if you have to."

"Roger, Havok out."

Wilson shouted something a couple times that I couldn't make out, paused for maybe half a minute, and then gave Falling Leaves a signal and threw a knife hand at the doorway. She nodded and loaded the FN40GL mounted under her SCAR-H and popped an egg into the shadows. A few moments later red smoke billowed out of the doorway, and one side of the hut caught fire. Something from within the hut gave a terrific roar that rattled my ribs from fifty yards away, and a huge shaggy figure stumbled out into the open.

He was… a big dude. And he was pissed.

***

From where I watched, I estimated the jaguar-man was at least seven feet tall and probably a good three hundred pounds of solid muscle that rippled under his sleek fur. He wasn't wearing anything besides a belt with bronze links around his waist and a small haversack slung over his shoulder. He carried a long staff capped in bronze on either end and shook it threateningly as he hissed and spat and roared at Wilson's team, but he seemed to understand the objects they held were weapons that could reach out and touch him, so he stuck to intimidation instead of attacking them outright.

Wilson was shouting ineffectively at the jaguar-man to drop his weapon and put his hands up when Captain Brown quickly made his way over and took control of the situation, letting his rifle hang on its sling while making the universal gesture for "Let's all chill out. It's cool, man. Put the weapon down and let's talk."

After a couple of minutes of pantomime diplomacy on the captain's part, the jaguar dude stopped roaring at least, but I could tell there wasn't much in the way of actual communication happening. The Tlacaōcēlōtl used a lot of gestures when he talked, sort of like an irate Italian, and Pierce clucked his tongue beside me.

"What's up?" I asked.

"I think it's sign language."

"What?"

"My mom's deaf, so I know ASL, right? What he's doing with his hands looks a lot like that."

"These jaguar guys know ASL? Where'd they learn that?"

"Don't be a 'tard. Of course they don't know ASL. I said it was *like* it."

"Gotcha. That's going to make communication interesting if he's deaf."

"I don't think he's deaf, bro. But cats probably can't speak all that well, right? Sorta makes sense they'd use sign to talk."

"Point."

Meanwhile, Brown had somehow convinced the big cat dude to put down his weapon, and now they were both sitting in the dust of the street looking frustrated and waving their hands.

"Think you could help?" I asked Pierce.

"How? He can't see me."

"But you could show me what to sign."

"He wouldn't understand it anyway. There's like three hundred sign languages back in the real world, all totally different, with different accents even. It's not like Sign's universal. I don't recognize anything he's signing. I can just tell it's a language."

"Longshot, Bishop," Brown transmitted. "Get down here."

"Roger. Longshot moving." I packed up my thermal monocular and slung Sybil before scurrying down the ladders and beating feet over to where the captain was sitting with the Tlacaōcēlōtl man.

"Take a seat, Nephi," Brown ordered. "His vocalizations are limited, but some of them sound a lot like Nahuatl. Maybe you can make out something. He seems to use an auxiliary sign language to communicate complex ideas."

"Pierce guessed the same thing, sir."

Brown grunted. "I haven't made much headway, but I think his name is Kiktú. Something like that."

"McKenzie could help with interpretation, sir. He had no problem communicating with the lizardmen."

Brown shook his head. "Epasotl said she has a solution. She's preparing something for us. See how much progress you can make while we're waiting."

I nodded to Brown before bowing to the jaguar-man. "Is your name Kiktú?" I asked in Nahuatl.

"My name is Kiktú," he replied in what sounded very much to be a strange dialect of Mayan, while making a sweeping motion with his left hand and touching his heart. He made the same sweeping motion in reverse and pointed to me. "What is your name?"

"My name is Corporal Nephi Bennett."

He shook his head and pointed at me, echoing a decent approximation of my name, then said something else I couldn't understand.

I held up my hands in what I hoped was the universal sign for *I have no idea what you just said*.

"Troubles?" Brown asked.

"He might speak and understand some Nahuatl, sir, but most of the words he's using… they sound Mayan."

"You speak Mayan as well?"

"No, sir. Not hardly. I learned a few phrases." I turned back to Kiktú and spoke again in Nahuatl. "How are you?"

"I am hungry," he replied in his Mayan dialect, motioning to his mouth and belly.

"I asked him how he was, sir, and he said—"

"He's hungry," Brown finished. "That much I get. Give him something to eat."

"Pemmican, sir?"

"Sure."

"You are hungry?" I asked Kiktú, pulling a chuck of pemmican out of my assault pack.

He shook his head vigorously and then took the pemmican from me and sniffed at it suspiciously.

"Weird," I said to Captain Brown. "I asked if he was hungry and he shook his head, but then he took it."

"A head shake means yes in some cultures. Indians, for example."

"You mean Native Americans?"

Brown quirked an irritated eyebrow at me. "Dot, not feather, Nephi. Don't assume to get politically correct on me."

"Right. Sorry, sir."

Kiktú took a bite and grimaced, but proceeded to eat all of it. He made a sign and said something I didn't understand.

"No clue, sir," I told Captain Brown.

"I think he was thanking you," Pierce interjected.

"Ah." I bowed to Kiktú. "You are welcome."

"Is ready," Epasotl said, joining us. Kiktú eyed her suspiciously, and his tail started twitching again, but at least he didn't reach for his staff. If anything he looked more curious than alarmed.

She unstopped a small gourd and handed it to Brown. "Is how we speak with our sisimitos."

He took a sniff and frowned at her. "Smells like chocolate and cadavers. What's in it?"

"Is made with plants, herbs, tongue of bird, eyes of frogs, and... other things." She smiled proudly. "Make with chocolate so taste good for human, see?"

"What other things?" I asked.

"You no ask, I no tell. You make sour face. Whine like cub."

Brown shrugged and took a tiny sip, then held the gourd away from his mouth and spat. "What other things?"

"Special ingredient make magic work. Need brain of who you want speak to. His kind."

"*Brain*?" I said. "Where did you find jaguar-man—? Oh, that's gross, Eps."

"Where else to find?" She shrugged. "Most brain gone to rot. Look hard find brain."

"You did good, Epasotl," Brown said. He handed me the gourd, and I took it from him with a raised eyebrow.

"Sir?"

"Bottoms up, Corporal."

I must have made a face, because Epasotl said, "See? Already whine like cub. Just one full mouth. Is no big deal."

I sighed, then held my nose as I gagged down a mouthful of the slimy goop. Not vomiting it back up was... extremely difficult, and it left a disgusting film on my tongue.

"So how does this work?" I asked Epasotl.

"You know his tongue now. Speech. Sign. Try and see."

I turned to Kiktú, who'd been watching all this with interest, and I realized I somehow *knew* what words to say and signs to make. It was like how I just knew English or Spanish without having to think about it. Their language was mostly sign, but it still had a component of speech to it.

<Can you understand me?> I signed while interpreting aloud in English for the captain's benefit.

<This is a good Making,> Kiktú replied, and again I interpreted aloud in English. <The small blue one must be very skilled.>

Brown clapped his hands together. "Excellent. Now that we can understand each other, Kiktú, I have some questions..."

CHAPTER 6

Once the language barrier had been breached, Kiktú became downright chatty. He was fascinated by us, asking what manner of creatures we were, where we came from, what Epasotl was, and if we had more food. But he answered Captain Brown's questions guardedly, and I got the impression he viewed us with caution. Brown was guarded too, supplying only vague answers as to our origins and purpose. He soon worked the conversation around to the matter of the village.

"Tell me how you survived the massacre," he said.

I continued to act as interpreter, signing to Kiktú as Brown spoke and telling the captain what Kiktú was signing in reply.

<When I returned on the day before the last, it was as you see it. I do not know when my village was attacked, but it must have happened after the great rain, so not long ago.>

"No more than two weeks," Brown stated.

<I do not understand that word, but no more than ten-day and three.>

"And you stayed here? Among the dead?"

<I stayed here among the dead. Where was I to go?>

"Are there no friendly settlements?"

<My people are scattered like leaves in the wind. To travel far is dangerous.>

"You said you *returned*. Why were you traveling alone if it's so dangerous? Where did you come from?"

<I was walking alone,> Kiktú replied, as if it were the obvious answer.

"I know you were alone. I'm asking why."

<I was walking alone.>

"Maybe he means like a *walkabout,* sir," I cut in. "You know, like the Aboriginals in Australia. Some kind of rite of passage."

Brown pursed his lips. "Kiktú, perhaps we don't understand the meaning of..." He attempted the sign for "walking alone."

The jaguar-man looked surprised. <To become a man. Why else would one go walking alone? It is very dangerous. Have not all of you also walked alone? You are all each of you here men, are you not?>

I cast a glance over my shoulder at my platoon-mates assembled around us, male and female both now that the Sugar Skull Gals had joined our unit. Maybe he couldn't tell the difference between the human sexes.

"We have all 'walked alone,' in our way," Brown affirmed. "The rite of passage is somewhat different for us. So you are a man now?"

Kiktú gave a deep sigh and hesitated a minute before growling the negative.

"But you walked alone," Brown stated.

<All the men are dead! There were none to receive me and dock my tail. I am neither a child nor a man.> He hung his head. <I am merely a woman.>

I turned to the captain. "That's... odd."

"Certain human societies have a similar distinction for sexually mature males who either fail or voluntarily choose not to participate in rites of manhood," Brown explained. He addressed Kiktú. "If you find other men of your people, can you still become a man yourself?"

Kiktú shook his—*her*? I'll stick with *his*. He shook his head in that peculiar way that meant yes.

"I need to know more about who attacked your village."

<The Kábi, or perhaps the Míchli.>

"And they are...?"

<Tribes sworn to worship...> He looked around cautiously before whispering, "*Tohil.*"

"And this... god, is it? That they worship. Can you tell me about him... or her?"

<He is the great Obsidian Jaguar who drinks the blood of men, women, and children like an infant suckling its mother. It is said the ancestors of the Kábi and Míchli people summoned him when our world was young and we covered all the land, before the sun swallowed the moon and we were driven to the Land of Mists. They gave our world to him as tribute in exchange for dark powers.>

"But *your* people don't worship Tohil," Brown said.

<No! We worship the Feathered Serpent. He is the true god of this world, and he will come again to end the sacrifices and bring peace.>

"Quetzalcoatl," I breathed excitedly. "It has to be, sir."

"Could be," Brown considered. He dropped his voice. "And I'll bet dollars to donuts this Tohil and Smoking Mirror are one and the same."

"Tezcatlipoca," I murmured.

Brown slapped his thighs and spoke to Kiktú. "We are also friends of the Feathered Serpent, and sworn enemies of the Obsidian Jaguar. We defeated the Lord of Mictlan in a great battle."

"We didn't exactly *defeat* him, sir," I said out of the side of my mouth in a low voice. "I mean, he's still around, and probably more than a little teed-off."

Brown waved me away irritably, and Kiktú cocked his head to the side.

<I do not know this Lord of...> he signed before attempting to pronounce "Mictlan" and giving up.

I racked my brain for a few moments before snapping my fingers. <Xibalba. The Lord of Xibalba. We were there. We hurt him good.>

<You descended to the Place of Fright and did battle with One Death?> Kiktú's eyes widened and he shook himself before bowing low and stretching out his arms.

"Please, Kiktú, that's not necessary," Brown said.

Kiktú raised himself high enough to sign, yet kept his gaze downcast. <But I have treated you as men, and you are gods.>

"We're certainly not gods," Brown drawled. "Not quite. We're cavalrymen."

I wasn't sure if that last would translate via Epasotl's magical goop, but Kiktú straightened and raised his eyes, nodding somberly before casting his gaze around us.

<I see you are like the fearless men of the Ónik clan. I believe such, as they would brave even the Place of Fright. But then… where are your thunder-stags?>

"We had to leave them behind before we came to your land," Brown told Kiktú with a trace of feigned sorrow in his voice. "It was a great but necessary sacrifice."

l wanted to ask what exactly a "thunder-stag" was, but Brown was already skipping past the interesting bits to more pressing matters. He reached into his assault pack and pulled out a small cloth, which he unwrapped to reveal the shards of my wife's bronze dagger—the one Epasotl had used to create her teleportation portals.

"Have you seen something like this before?" he asked Kiktú.

The huge jaguar-man leaned in to peer at the shattered weapon closely, hesitating to touch it. <It is a dagger, but I have never seen one shattered thus… and the writing is strange.>

<You can't read it?> I asked.

<No.> He cocked his head and narrowed his eyes. <Where did you find it?>

"It was an ancient relic thought to be of your people that came into our possession," Brown said. "What do you know of teleportation portals?"

<Doors?> Kiktú looked confused. <To enter and leave a building?>

"No… Magical doors in space that allow one to cross vast distances with a single step."

Kiktú's eyes grew wide. <That is how the Obsidian Jaguar was invited into our world—through a doorway connecting his realm and ours. It is said we once traveled the stars through such doorways, when our ancestors were gods.>

"Might some of your people still know how to work such magic?"

<Those are only stories.>

<We came to your land through a portal,> I signed. <But we used this dagger. Without it we're stuck here.>

<Are you sure you are not gods?>

Captain Brown ignored him. "Kiktú, I think we could be of use to one another. You need to find men of your tribe to complete your rite of passage, and we need a guide to find more of your people. Someone who knows more about portal magic. We walk the same path."

<There is a place where you may find answers.>

"Where?"

"Chlŭmpu," Kiktú chirped. The jaguar-man flattened his ears. <It would be a great honor to be your guide there, but I am only fit to cook and keep camp, not to guide a war party.>

"But you know the way?" Brown asked.

<I know the way.>

"Then we will travel together," the captain concluded. He stood and motioned for Kiktú to rise before turning to me. "I want you to act as a liaison, Nephi. You've proved capable in that role before."

"Hooah. Thank you, sir."

The captain gave a curt nod before striding away and getting on the radio to give the five-minute warning to mount up.

Mount up on what, you ask? Our LPCs. Leather Personnel Carriers. Aka boots.

<Looks like you're with me, Kiktú,> I signed. <You have anything you need to collect before we go?>

He picked his staff up off the ground and then went back into the hut to recover a large bow and a quiver of arrows. Other than that, the small haversack hung over his shoulder, and a flint dagger he'd thrust into his belt, he didn't carry any possessions.

<Travel light?>

<I require little; the jungle provides much.>

<Lots of good weapons lying around here,> I signed. <You might want to upgrade.>

<It is not permitted for a woman or child to touch weapons of war.>

<What're those?> I gestured to his staff and the bow he'd slung over his back.

<A bow for hunting and stick for walking.>

<And the dagger?>

<A tool for preparing food.>

<So only men are warriors?>

<Only men are men.>

<I mean, women cannot be warriors?>

He gave me a puzzled look. <That is contrary. A woman cannot be a man.>

This was getting confusing. Maybe "warrior" and "man" meant the same thing. <But a boy can become a woman?>

<I do not understand that word.>

<What? Boy? You know… like a man child.>

<A child is not a man or a woman. It is a child. A child is a child until they walk alone and their tails are docked, then they become a man.>

<And if they don't complete their walk alone, they become a woman?>

He shook his head in the manner I was learning meant the affirmative. It was really more of a bobble than a shake from side to side, but it was still confusing. <Many children also choose the woman's path and never walk alone. I do not understand. Is it not the same with you?>

<No. I mean, not really. I mean you cannot choose if you're a man or a woman. You're just born that way.>

"It's, like, a social thing for them," Pierce said after I explained to him what we were talking about. "I remember reading this *Nat Geo* article about some tribe in the Amazon… or maybe it was Indonesia… anyway, they don't really have a concept of biological sex, just gender roles. But they had like five genders or something."

"Five? How many do you need?"

Pierce shrugged. "Ask Curly when we get back. The Navajo have at least three."

<Who are you talking to?> Kiktú asked me. <Do you have a spirit guide?>

<Not a guide. A… friend.>

<So you are a Maker also, like the small blue one.>

<Not quite. I do not know Making.>

<But you have a spirit guide.>

<It's complicated.>

Kiktú breathed out a puff of air that sounded like a "Hmph."

<Why are you marked?> he asked, motioning to my face.

<The black veins? It's a long story.>

<Are you a great man in your war party?>

<Not remotely.>

<But you are marked, and I assume older than the others, for your head fur is going to gray.>

<That's complicated too. I'm much younger than I look. We came across one of your people's abandoned cities and ran into… undead warriors they left behind. Guardians, I guess. Mummies. I was cursed.>

<Ah, I have heard legends of such crypt guardians. The curse makes one turn to grave dust. How did you escape?>

<Epasotl saved me.>

<The small blue one?>

<The same.>

<That one must have great skill in Making.>

I shrugged, then nodded. <She does.> The truth was, Epasotl had more skill in "Making" than she gave herself credit for.

We reached the assembled platoon and Sanchez motioned us over.

"Yes, Sarge?" I asked.

"Time to motor. Lead the way."

I glanced around the village square. "We're not going to do anything about the bodies?"

"No time, Bennett."

"Hooah." I turned to Kiktú. <Which way?>

He pointed roughly northwest, assuming I had my bearings straight. <We go into the mountains.>

CHAPTER 7

Kiktú paused and moved some ferns aside, revealing a large footprint. Huge, really. Terrifyingly huge. It looked somewhat like the prints the gals' warbirds made, only much larger; the three splayed toes must have been a couple of feet wide. He loped ahead a few meters and found another.

<I don't want to know what made these,> I signed.

<You do not?> Kiktú signed.

<Not really, but tell me anyway.>

<They are made by the great and terrible earthquake-birds, but none come this far down the mountains this time of year.>

<Earthquake-birds? Just how big are these things?>

Kiktú considered the question. <Over the height of two tall people.>

<You have seen one?>

<I have seen them from afar.>

<Are you tall?>

<No.>

And he was a good seven feet at least. That made whatever this was… a really big bird.

Pierce squatted by one of the footprints and pursed his lips. "Bro, this isn't a bird. I've seen these prints before, on a field trip to the natural history museum."

I took off my boonie and ran my fingers through my sweat-and-salt-caked hair. "Let me guess. Frigging T-Rex."

"Yup."

<Is your spirit guide speaking with you?>

<He's seen these prints before too.> I hit the transmit button on my radio. "Xavier, Longshot. Be advised we've found T-Rex prints."

"Say again," Sanchez replied.

"I say again: we've found Tyrannosaurus Rex footprints."

There was a long pause. "Are you certain?"

I looked at Pierce, and he nodded.

"Pretty certain," I transmitted.

"How old?"

I asked Kiktú, then relayed that they were fresh. A week old at most.

"Roger. Hold fast. We'll come to you. Xavier out."

"Right about now I'm not so bummed to be a ghost," Pierce said.

<You think there's just the one?> I asked Kiktú.

He gave his head a bobble-shake. <They hunt alone and are extremely territorial.>

<That's good news, I guess.> I caught sight of Obsidian Tears and gave her the signal that I'd seen her and it was clear to approach. Wilson came into view a few moments later and hoofed it over to me.

"Did I hear that right, bro?" he asked in a low voice. "T-Rex?"

I motioned to the footprint. "Sure looks like it."

"Holy shit, that's huge." He turned to Falling Leaves. "What do you make of it?"

She crouched low and measured the print with her hands and arms. "It is like a wolf-vulture, but many times bigger. Many, many times. The print is heavy and the claws on each toe go deep into the earth, see? The claws may be over fifteen fingers long." She motioned to a tree that had large gashes in its bark well above my head. "It marks its territory like so. Whatever left this print could weigh as much as… six of our warbirds? Perhaps more."

That would be… eight tons or so, I figured. Eight tons of enraged, hungry, territorial dinosaur.

"Kiktú said they're over sixteen feet tall," I told Wilson. "His people call them 'earthquake-birds.'"

"Awesome," Wilson said. "Not."

"What do we got here?" Captain Brown asked, joining us. Sanchez accompanied him.

"The king, sir," Wilson said. "And I don't mean Elvis."

Brown puffed out his cheeks and gazed off into the forest. "We'll have to modify our patrol formation."

"I don't recall dinosaurs in FM 17-98 or FM 7-70," Wilson said. "Maybe you got something special in the Ranger Handbook, sir?"

"Don't be a smartass," Sanchez said.

Brown chuckled. "No, Dave, nothing in Ranger doctrine for rampaging dinosaurs. But I don't suspect it's much different from operating against high-mobility mechanized units."

"Except *this* high-mobility unit can swallow you whole," Wilson pointed out.

"Then it's a good thing we reconned Carl from the armory," Brown said. "Who's got it now?"

"Heart-of-Darkness, sir," Sanchez supplied.

"How are we on four-oh-one?"

"Sergeant García has three remaining," Sanchez answered. "We used one when things were getting dicey in the lizardmen raid before the portal blew."

"Good. Make sure she's got at least a couple rounds of it ready at all times. I suspect we won't have enough warning in this terrain to hit it before it gets too close and personal for a warhead to arm."

ADM 401 was a nasty round for the venerable Carl Gustaf recoilless rifle. It fired over a thousand flechettes across a wide area, essentially turning the weapon into a giant shotgun. Anything caught in the cone of fire was effectively hamburger.

Hopefully it would do the trick against a T-Rex.

***

We continued to proceed up from the lower foothills at a cautious pace in a somewhat unorthodox formation, with Wilson's team in front and Stanley's on trail; García split his two weapons crews on either flank. Heart-of-Darkness was on the left with Cameron's M240B, but could quickly maneuver the Carl to wherever it might be needed in the event of a face-to-face meeting with an enraged eight-ton dinosaur.

T-Rex wasn't our only concern though; there was always the chance we'd come across a roving patrol of hostile jaguar-men, packs of feral and possibly rabid jungle dogs, solitary giant cats who preferred to snatch their victims and make a run for it, or wild thunder-stags, which I'd worked out to be reptilian quadrupeds at least the size of a moose who traveled in small herds and were about as friendly when they feared for their young as bears were, which is to say: not very.

Oh, and then there were the death-vines, so that was cool. Carnivorous plants that could whip out tendrils and pull you up into the trees to be digested. Those are always a bonus, right? Especially when they keep you alive but paralyzed while they slowly feed on you for weeks. Or months.

But at least there weren't any clever weapon-wielding zombies, so I was counting my blessings.

I was taking a break from being on point when Doc caught up to me.

"How're you doing, Bennett?" he asked conversationally in a low voice.

"Sweating like a pig, but otherwise peachy, Doc."

"Fun fact: pigs don't sweat."

"Huh. Good to know."

"It's been a few days. Withdrawal treating you okay?"

"Actually I feel fine, no more irritable than anyone else in this heat and humidity. A bit tired, but we've been humping it uphill for forever without much sleep. A little paranoid, but we might have a T-Rex stalking us, so maybe that's a good thing."

"The leaves helping?"

"Haven't touched 'em."

"Huh."

"Honestly, I think I'm doing *better* than most of the others. I don't feel any different from when I was fighting in the pit, or before I was captured for that matter. If anything, I feel like I'm getting stronger every day. Sharper focus, too. Need less sleep."

Doc spit out a stream of coca leaf juice and nodded. By now virtually everyone except me was chewing the stuff; even Captain Brown kept his canteens full of coca tea. I couldn't blame them. I probably would've given in too, religious convictions notwithstanding, but I didn't need a boost.

"You know, Doc, I think it's my… condition. I don't think it was the coke at all. It's like I was immune to it or something."

"Could be," he said, considering. "How's your digestion?"

"Digestion?"

"Your poop, son. I'm dealing with more than a few cases of the runs, even though we're doing our best to collect rainwater and treat it before drinking. Not full-blown dysentery yet, knock on wood, but still, the pathogens here must be vile. You have any symptoms?"

"Negative, Doc. My poop is just fine and I'm staying plenty hydrated."

"That's music to my ears."

"Know what else is weird?"

"What's that, Bennett?"

"The bugs don't touch me anymore. I haven't used Eps's ointment for days."

"Lucky you. To be honest I'm more worried about the bugs than I am the water. Last thing we need is for the platoon to come down with some exotic variant of malaria or whatever. Pathogens are our number one enemy out here. Kill you deader than T-Rex or whatever it is that has everyone all jumpy for no reason."

"I don't know, Doc. T-Rex or malaria, you end up just as dead either way. Unless you're Pierce, I guess. You're not worried about a dinosaur the size of a school bus?"

"Nah. We got plenty of belt-fed seven-six-two and Carl G." He slapped my shoulder. "Gotta do the rounds. Let me know if anything changes."

"Hooah, Doc."

He had just turned to leave when a vine shot down from the canopy, wrapped itself around his neck like a noose, and instantly snatched him up into the air. It all happened so fast I'd have missed it if I blinked. There were shouts of alarm from others in the formation, and I watched in horror as bodies were hauled off the ground by more of the snaking vines. They seemed to be everywhere at once. Stanley was hanging upside down by one leg, hollering, and Flaming Feather was wrestling with no less than three vines looped around her torso like pythons. I spotted Anderson and García struggling uselessly as they were hauled upward, but McKenzie was faring better, swearing and slashing at the vines as they struck at him.

I wasn't spared, either. A vine latched on to my right arm, and I felt stinging barbs pierce my sleeve as it constricted and began hauling me up. I managed to draw my machete awkwardly with my left hand and set to hacking at the thick vine. It took three hard strokes to sever the tendril, and I dropped to the ground, landing in an awkward roll. I got back on my feet and slashed at another vine as it whipped past my face, its spiny, sucker-like blossoms puckering.

I didn't see what happened, but I heard the *whump* as Doc plummeted down from above. He must have drawn his claw knife and cut himself free, and now he was lying in an unconscious heap on the jungle floor. As I hacked at another vine, I saw First-to-Dance leap up and grab Stanley's outstretched hand, then begin scaling his flailing body even while holding her obsidian-edged war club. Then the vine that had caught Stanley's leg pulled them both up into the canopy out of my sight.

Kiktú roared my name, and I spared a glance over to where he was pulping vines with his staff as they lashed out at him. <We must kill the body!> he signed urgently before casting his staff aside. He leaped a good eight feet up onto a trunk and began to scurry up the tree.

I dodged another vine and peered up into the thick branches overhead. The vines were attached to bulbous red sacs suspended high in the canopy. Was this "the body"?

After one more solid hack at the nearest vine, I dropped my machete, unslung Sybil, aimed at one of the sacs, and fired. The sac exploded, showering us with burning, foul-smelling digestive acid.

Anderson plummeted to the ground cocooned in slime.

I shifted my aim and shot at another sac before getting on the radio. "Target the red sacs up in the canopy."

"Roger," Heart-of-Darkness replied, and Cameron hefted the two-forty, shoulder-firing into the trees overhead. I was already targeting another bulbous, throbbing mass when Jade Talon went cyclic with her Mk 48, screaming her bird-of-prey war cry.

A small blue shape darted past me. There was a blinding flash, and forked blue-white lighting arced overhead, rupturing three of the sacs at once in a terrific spray of corpse-rot acid.

Sanchez got on the radio, ordering a ceasefire once we'd tagged all the sacs and the vines hung limp. Epasotl stood wavering in the middle of our formation, her hair standing on end and smoking. She plopped down on her butt, blinked twice, and fell over.

I scurried over to her and checked her pulse as Sanchez barked out a request for ACE reports from the other NCOs. She was stable, but out cold. I started to sigh a breath of relief that caught in my throat as I felt the ground tremble.

"Contact, nine o'clock!" Dressed-in-Stars announced over the radio. "Fifty meters and closing fast!"

"Holy shit, it's huge!" García announced a moment later. "Light it up!"

Flaming Feather got on her sister's machine gun and started firing long, rapid bursts as McKenzie fed the two-forty.

And then we were hit by a roar so loud and deep, it felt like it was shaking the fillings out of my teeth and turning my guts to liquid.

I was about to end up with the runs after all.

CHAPTER 8

The first bad thing that happened, other than an eight-ton monster barreling down on us, was Lawrence panicking and firing a grenade at the charging beast well within a range you'd call "danger close."

Rex was probably only thirty meters away when the kid cried out in fear and I heard the telltale *thunk* of the forty-millimeter launcher.

I threw myself over Epasotl and got as low as possible.

Meat-spray and shrapnel exploded out of the side of the dinosaur, taking off one of its stubby little arms, and it veered into a tree, uprooting it. The beast roared again and leapt most of the remaining distance toward us in a bound that shook the earth, nearly landing on Dressed-in-Stars's gun emplacement.

Jade Talon was already moving and firing, working her lightweight machine gun over Rex as Cameron and Heart-of-Darkness repositioned their two-forty.

I rolled onto my knees and fired a round squarely into the beast's head, hoping the .338 Lapua Magnum would be enough to penetrate its skull, but either it wasn't or I missed the thing's little brain.

Or it was too stupid and angry to know it was already dead.

We were all falling back as Takahashi and Wilson were busy directing what was left of the rifle squad to provide flanking fire. I had Epasotl over my shoulder and was dragging Doc by his plate carrier.

"Blue One-Eight, fire when clear," Sanchez barked over the radio.

"No shot. Friendlies in the blast area!" Heart-of-Darkness replied.

I whipped my head around, trying to make sense of the chaos as Rex bellowed and stomped, smashing trees and snatching at my platoon-mates with its massive jaws. García was limping bad and shooting one-handed, and McKenzie had Flaming Feather in a fireman's carry as Dressed-in-Stars covered their retreat, shoulder-firing the two-forty.

Obsidian Tears raced up beside me and grabbed Doc's arm, and together we heaved him back to where Takahashi was positioned with Sanchez and First-to-Dance. Lawrence was lucky Taks hadn't clocked him with the butt of his rifle after the kid had gone stupid with forty mike-mike and nearly got us all fragged. I had a feeling someone would be on latrine-digging duty for a long, long time. Not that we stayed in any one place long enough to need latrines, but just 'cause we wouldn't use them didn't mean he wouldn't be ordered to dig them.

Wilson and Falling Leaves had formed up with Cameron, who was talking his gun with Jade Talon, providing enfilade fire as García circled around to get into a position that would clear Heart-of-Darkness to let loose with the Carl G without any friendlies in the cone of certain death. But Captain Brown raced up beside her, grabbed the recoilless rifle out of her hands, and charged directly at Rex with a bloodcurdling scream that got its attention on the double.

As the tyrannosaurus bore down on him, Brown threw the weapon up on his shoulder and fired directly into the dinosaur's face.

It's hard to describe the sound it made. The ADM 401 is a pressurized gas canister and there's no explosive back blast, so it's something like a tire blowout, sorta, followed by the scream of eleven hundred fin-stabilized steel projectiles ripping apart the fabric of reality.

T-Rex might be king of the dinosaurs, but Carl G don't care.

The headless monstrosity reeled back a few steps and then fell over with a crash that nearly knocked me off my feet.

Brown, covered head to foot in blood, walked back to Heart-of-Darkness and handed back her Carl before wiping his face with a handkerchief.

"Bring it in," he ordered. "Get me a head count, Diego. Dave, you're in charge of security. Form a detail."

Wilson shouted a "Hooah" and got to work securing the area while the rest of us searched for platoon-mates and dragged bodies over to the casualty collection point Sanchez had established.

Turns out Doc wasn't unconscious after all. He, Stanley, Anderson, and Flaming Feather were all wide awake, just completely paralyzed. They weren't alone—García was paralyzed on practically his entire left side, and several other people had barely functioning, or at the very least numb, limbs or faces. Epasotl was on her feet again though, recovered from her lightning spell—the only sign of her ordeal was the fact that her hair was still standing on end—and amazingly no one had been stepped on or eaten, although Dressed-in-Stars and McKenzie had caught some shrapnel from Lawrence's grenade.

I looked at my arm, peppered with spiny barbs. Apparently I was immune to the paralyzing toxin. I had some bad welts on my face and hands from the burning digestive acids we'd been showered with though, just like everyone else in the platoon. No one had been spared that; we all looked like hell and smelled like death.

Some of us smelled worse.

Okay, I'll be completely honest here: I'd crapped my pants.

At least I wasn't alone in that.

"It happens to the best of us, boys and girls," Sanchez told us casually. "More than you think. Don't sweat it. When I was back in the Corps in Quang Tri, I remember Gunny—"

On second thought, maybe that's not my story to tell. You'll have to ask Sanchez—just make sure he's in a good mood first.

Kiktú was unharmed, although death-vine juice was caked to most of his fur. He'd scaled forty feet up a tree and attacked one of the sacs directly with his flint knife, fighting off paralyzing vines the whole way. Pretty ballsy if you ask me.

<There is a plant that can neutralize the toxin,> he signed to me. <I will collect some and make a poultice, but we cannot stay here. The carcass of the earthquake-bird will attract scavengers.>

Meaning feral and potentially rabid dogs, or possibly even another T-Rex.

So we set out at a limping pace, carrying our immobile platoon-mates on improvised stretchers made from ponchos and tree limbs, and resumed the arduous climb uphill until the growing darkness and fog forced us to stop for the night.

***

Even with Kiktú's poultice, it was late morning before everyone was on their feet and ready to go. My eyes were bleary from pulling tiny barbs out of people's skin for hours, but I wasn't complaining; those who'd been poisoned with the death-vines' toxin had been puking up their guts most of the night and looked like they had a bad case of the flu. Kiktú didn't have anything to help with that.

<The sickness should not last long,> Kiktú had signed to me. <It is unfortunate your thunder-rod and lightning magic attracted the earthquake-bird, but without it I fear we all may have been devoured by the death-vines. I have never encountered so many in one place.>

<It's a shame you didn't spot them before we were attacked. You're a good guide.>

Harsh, maybe, but I was tired and cranky after nearly being devoured by carnivorous plants and then a dinosaur, followed by a long and tedious night of playing medic—not to mention literally crapping myself along the way. Plus, Epasotl's wonderful potion that allowed me to communicate with the jaguar-man only lasted for a few hours before I needed to quaff another dose. I'm pretty sure it affected my breath because people were keeping their distance.

Anyway, sarcasm must not have translated because Kiktú simply agreed with me and then moved on to asking what kind of magic could vaporize an earthquake-bird's head.

"Swedish magic," I replied.

By midafternoon we were out of the foothills and making our way into a pass that cut through the mountain range. Once again Kiktú and I were scouting ahead of the platoon. The thick jungle had begrudgingly given way to scattered copses of wind-bent trees and rocky expanses of lush grassland and giant ferns.

<It is here we are most likely to encounter wild thunder-stags,> Kiktú signed. <If we keep our distance and do not startle them, all will be well, but it is also the hunting ground of the earthquake-birds, so we must be cautious.>

<I would really *not* love to run into one of those again. This is my last clean set of clothes.>

He gave me a perplexed look. <You often speak in riddles. Is that common among hairless walking monkeys?>

<Probably not. This place you are taking us to, it's over this pass>

<It is over this pass and across the river. The journey will take one ten-day.>

<What river? You never mentioned a river.>

<Did I not? There is a river.>

<How do we cross it?>

He cocked his head. <Swim, of course.>

Heck, he was a huge cat-man. Swimming was probably second nature to his kind. Big cats like jaguars love to swim, right? I figured most of the guys could swim, or at least dog paddle, but I knew the gals couldn't. Xochi had explained to me that, what with the killer tentacle-tailed hyena-opossums infesting their lakes and rivers, the Kuauchanejkej never entered deep water.

Which meant we'd have to find a ford.

<Is there any place we can walk across?> I asked.

<Such as a bridge? I do not believe so.>

<Is there a shallow place where you can cross on foot?>

<I do not know.>

<How wide is the river? How fast?>

<I do not know.>

I stopped dead in my tracks and faced him. <What do you mean? You've crossed it before, haven't you?>

He gave a head-bobble.

<What's that supposed to mean?>

His head bobbled again.

<Be honest with me, Kiktú. Have you or have you not been across the river?>

<I know many men who have.>

"Oh my heck!" I ran my hands through my hair. <That's not remotely the same thing. You said you knew the way.>

<I do know the way. It is over this pass and across the river. Are you unwell? Your face is turning red.>

I took a deep breath and held up my hands. <We'll figure it out. Come on, we need to find a secure place where everyone can spend the night.>

***

"All quiet on the western front?" I asked McKenzie and Flaming Feather as I climbed onto the elevated rock shelf we were using as an observation post to watch the pass. It was dark, but the big man looked slightly embarrassed and Feather had a brief coughing fit. If I didn't know better, I'd have suspected some fraternization was going on in the cozy OP.

"Go down and get some real food," I told them. "I'll take watch."

Kiktú had caught a small deer, which was currently cooking on a fire in the back of a cave he and I had scouted out earlier in the day. Fires were never a good idea in hostile territory—they might keep wild animals away, but they were signal beacons for any bad guys in the area—so we rarely lit them. But the cave was deep and screened by a copse, so the captain figured it would be safe enough. Besides, Doc would've had an aneurism if anyone ate raw meat.

I was just happy to be eating something other than Epasotl's pemmican.

After they left, I got comfortable and let my eyes get accustomed to the darkness. And it was quite dark. We had yet to see stars here due to the perpetual cloud cover, and we didn't even know if there was a moon in this place. But I could hear just fine.

I sensed someone beside me and caught Pierce's profile out of the corner of my eye.

"Where you been, stranger?" I asked.

He shrugged. "Around."

"You mean hanging with Falling Leaves."

He shrugged again.

"I still can't believe you two had a thing going right under our noses," I said. "Sneaky."

"She talks to me."

"She can hear you?"

"No, but I think she can sense when I'm near. She talks to me sometimes."

"What about?"

He gave me a sidelong glance. "None of your business, bro."

"Fair enough."

"Hey, check it out." He picked up a tiny pebble and flicked it off the ledge.

"Holy crap! That's awesome."

"I've been practicing."

"No doubt. That's really cool."

"I can go further away from you too now. Little more each day."

"How far?"

"Around two hundred meters. And I figured out how to... I dunno... jump, I guess."

"Jump?"

"Like, I don't need to walk everywhere. I think of where I want to be and I'm there, so long as it's not too far from your sorry ass."

"That's rad!" Without thinking, I held out my hand, and he slapped it. Or tried to. But I could've sworn I felt *something* when his hand passed through mine.

The distant roar of a tyrannosaurus echoed through the pass like thunder on the wind, and I shivered.

"Really hope we don't run into one of those again," I said after a minute.

"No doubt. That was bad mojo. We were lucky no one got crushed or eaten."

"Really lucky. And those vines. What the heck, man?"

He shook his head, and we sat in silence for several minutes.

"I think someone's following us," Pierce said eventually.

"Really? You're telling me this just now?"

"Wasn't sure."

"Someone or some*thing*?"

"Someone. A few someones, actually. They're hella sneaky whoever they are. Don't leave a trail, and I haven't had eyes-on."

"Think you can scout 'em out? Get more intel? Cap'n will want to know."

"Already on it."

"Hooah."

He tossed another pebble off the ledge. "Cap'n still doesn't trust me, does he?"

"Me or you, man. He's being 'cautiously optimistic,' remember?"

"S'pose that's his job."

"I guess."

"*You* trust me though, right?"

"Of course," I lied.

Truth was, the captain had planted a seed of doubt in my mind, and it was taking root.

CHAPTER 9

"Kiktú says we'll be out of the pass and at the river soon," I told Captain Brown. "But his estimation of distances is messed up because his people run everywhere and he's never been here before himself. Could take all day, maybe two. And we need to find a ford for crossing," I said. "No telling how long that might take."

"We don't need a ford," Brown said. "Just a place where the current isn't too strong."

"The gals can't swim, sir."

"I know."

His tone signaled me to drop the subject. Whatever his plan was for getting non-swimmers across a river would be announced when the time came. I switched topics.

"Sir, Pierce says we're being followed, but he doesn't know by whom, or how many there are. He wants to try and get more intel, but he still can't range too far from me. Might be a good idea if I pulled rear security."

The captain shook his head. "They must be more curious than hostile, or they would've already made contact. I need you on point with Kiktú. I'll have Epasotl look into it."

"Roger that, sir."

Pierce grumbled as we walked away to collect the jaguar-man.

"Orders are orders," I said with a shrug.

I called out to Kiktú, and he loped over.

<We're moving out,> I signed to him. <Captain wants eyes on the river before nightfall. Can we make it?>

He gave a head-bobble in reply. <Perhaps. Please do not be offended, but hairless walking monkeys do not travel as swiftly as The People.>

<I understand. But I need to see the river as soon as possible. I'll move as swiftly as I can.>

<You could move more swiftly if I carried your belongings. You are burdened by a great load. To carry the camp supplies is a woman's duty; a man should be unencumbered.>

It wasn't the first time he'd offered to carry my ruck, but until now I'd stubbornly refused. Part of it was personal pride, and part of it was distrust. If he decided to abandon us and ran off with my kit and extra ammo, I'd be screwed. On the other hand…

<All right. You carry my pack, and we'll try to cover as much distance as we can.>

I informed Sanchez that Kiktú and I were heading out on an extended recon, and we took off. The jaguar-man was fast, even carrying my ruck, and I had to hoof it to keep up with his long, bounding strides. He was stealthy, too, darting silently through the tall grass and ferns. I was… not so stealthy, but I found my pace and was surprised to find that second wind that runners talk about. I've never been a good runner. Sprinting, sure, but I wasn't made for distance. Or I hadn't been before. Maybe this was another side effect of being death-touched. If it was, I wasn't complaining.

A couple hours later he called a halt and crouched low in the tall grass. He wasn't even breathing hard. It was obvious he'd been pacing himself so I could keep up.

<Thunder-stags,> he signed.

I took off my boonie and wiped the sweat from my eyes, trying to peer above the grass. There were large moving shapes in the distance, but I couldn't make them out very well.

<How many?> I asked.

<It is a small herd, perhaps ten and two adults and half that number of juveniles.>

<Can we get a better look?>

He sniffed at the air and gave a head-bobble. <We must stay downwind.>

I called it in, informing Sanchez that the herd was approximately thirty klicks from where we'd spent the night. The platoon must have been at the extreme range of our team radios, because it was hard to get a clear signal.

I tapped Kiktú on the shoulder and we moved out, stalking the herd and angling to keep the wind blowing toward us.

We stopped again about five hundred meters away from them, and I pulled out my spotting scope to get a better look. From Kiktú's earlier description I'd expected some kind of weird moose-lizard, but instead they were a variety of duck-billed dinosaur with a large bony crest on top of their relatively small heads. They moved on all fours, grazing on the grass, the adults forming a protective circle around the young. Every so often one would stand up on its hind legs, searching for dangers and communicating with the others through a series of low-pitched trumpeting calls that reminded me of elephants.

They were about as big as elephants too, and the thought of riding one of them into battle was equally thrilling and terrifying.

Kiktú traced a wide arc with his hand and signed that we would draw back and skirt around the herd. I nodded and followed him at a cautious pace. One of them must have caught our scent, because it got on its hind legs and raced a few hundred meters in our direction, trumpeting angrily before pausing to paw at the ground and toss its head, uprooting a couple of giant ferns. It gave another trumpet blast of warning and then turned and loped back to the herd at a casual trot.

"Impressive," I breathed. <I would *not* want to be on the receiving end of a charge. Some of your people actually *ride* those?>

<Did you not say you also ride thunder-stags into battle?>

<Our mounts are a little… different. Come on, we need to reach the river before dark.>

We set off again at a brisk pace that ate up the miles, and by late afternoon the pass began gradually descending into a vast jungle valley thick with trees.

We passed through a gap in the trees, and I got my first good look at the river.

We're not talking Mississippi big, but it was a good few hundred meters across at the narrowest point I could see, far broader than I'd care to try and swim while kitted up. Or without any gear at all, for that matter; I'm not the world's best swimmer. From our vantage point, it looked like a wide brown slash snaking through the multi-canopied forest, and as I tracked its course I saw it fed a distant lake, where I could just make out a walled city built on an archipelago in its center. The islands of the archipelago were connected to each other, and to the shores of the lake, by narrow causeways and floating bridges, but most of these were now coughing smoke. Smoke also roiled from the high walls of the city, and I could make out fires here and there.

Kiktú's expression was grim. "Chlŭmpu has fallen," he trilled softly in his strange Mayan tongue.

I tried to get on the radio, but the platoon must have been out of range.

<Do you think there will be survivors?> I asked.

<All will be captured for sacrifice to the insatiable thirst of the Obsidian Jaguar.>

It was a sizable city. I guessed maybe a hundred thousand inhabitants. Maybe even twice that.

<All?> I repeated.

<All who breathe.>

***

Captain Brown lowered his binoculars and pursed his lips. "The walls are manned. I don't think the city has fallen."

It had rained overnight, extinguishing most of the fires, but a haze of fog and smoke still hung low over Chlŭmpu, capital of the Yínchani, largest of the tribes who worshiped Q'uq'umatz, the Feathered Serpent. Through my spotting scope, I could make out banners featuring the tribal god on the city walls. And yes, there were jaguar-men manning the battlements.

Jags, as Wilson called them.

"Could be occupiers, maybe, sir."

"Could be, but I don't think so." He turned to Kiktú in our OP set high up on a bluff. "Would the attackers sacrifice the captives here or transport them?"

<They would move them to their own temples.>

"I figured as much," Brown said. "And I don't see any massed movements of prisoners in or out of the city, or any troop movement at all for that matter, so I suspect the assault was repulsed. In fact..." He paused to gaze through his binoculars again. "It looks like refugees are *returning* to the city. That's the good news."

"And the bad news, sir?" I asked.

"A defeated army always leaves behind marauders. It'll make the river crossing that much more dangerous."

"We're still going to try to swim across?"

"Never said we were, Nephi. We're going to *float* across. You've never made a ruck-and-poncho raft?"

"Can't say they covered that in Scout School, sir."

He grunted something dismissive in reply and got on the radio. "Xavier, Bishop. I need Havok to take a patrol down to the river and secure a suitable crossing point."

"Roger, Xavier out," Sanchez answered.

Aside from Sanchez and Doc, Sergeant Wilson was probably the best choice for this duty, given he'd been to Pathfinder School. I doubt I would've known what to look for.

<You sure there's nothing dangerous in that river?> I asked Kiktú.

He gave an unconvincing head-bobble in reply, and I arched an eyebrow at the captain.

Brown shrugged. "Can't be worse than Florida Phase in Ranger School."

"Are you forgetting the hyena-possums, sir?"

"Tackle a hungry full-grown daddy 'gator and we'll compare notes, son."

"Point, sir."

***

"Then just roll it up, like you're making a burrito with your poncho and the ruck's the filling," Doc said, standing over me in nothing but the clothes he was born in, arms akimbo. "Keep it tighter than Sister María back in boarding school, so there's a good air bubble trapped in there, and tie it off with five-fifty. Bennett, you should've packed your skivvies, instead of wearing them. Nothing worse than wet skivvies. You'll get chafed later."

"I got a dry spare," I replied.

"Suit yourself." He turned to the other guys and gals in our circle, most of them stripped down to nothing like him. "I'll take lead. Wilson, I know you're a strong swimmer, so I need you on trail. Stanley and Bennett, you guys are behind me."

Sanchez had divided the platoon into three groups to each be led across the river by him, Captain Brown, and Doc, respectively. Two groups would hold security while the third crossed.

"Can you two swim okay?" Doc asked me and Stanley.

"Swim" was a relative term when talking to a former Ranger.

"Sorta," I said.

"Dog paddle," Stanley admitted.

Doc gave a grunt and turned to Falling Leaves, Jade Talon, and First-to-Dance. "I know you all can't swim, but this'll be easy. You just hold on to your raft and kick your feet. We'll all be connected with five-fifty, so don't worry about drifting off. And Sergeant Wilson's got your six."

"Hooah," Jade and Dance replied in unison. Leaves seemed less enthusiastic and raised a hand.

"Yes?" Doc said.

"What if we let go of raft?"

"Then sink to the bottom as fast as possible and run like hell," he replied with a straight face.

She gave him a dubious look and nodded slowly.

"Bro's joking," Wilson said. "You'll be tethered to your raft, but if anything happens, I'm right behind you. That goes for nasty critters too. Anything attacks us, don't panic. Just keep moving forward. Doc and I can both handle whatever might come looking for a taste. I've killed sharks with my bare hands."

Knowing Wilson, he probably wasn't kidding. He seemed like a goof-off most of the time, but he was as hardcore as anyone in the platoon when it came down to it.

Except for Sanchez. Our platoon sergeant took the title when it came to being a badass.

"All right then," Doc said. "We're second to cross, so there'll be time for questions if anything comes to mind. This is a simple river crossing in daylight with an easy current, so it'll be a piece of cake. Just don't get *somehow* once you're in the water."

"Easy like a Sunday morning," Wilson added. "That's the ticket. Ain't nothing but a thing."

I looked at the slow-moving brown river and hoped he was right.

CHAPTER 10

Sanchez's group was first to cross and made the trip without incident, posting up on the opposite bank with Flaming Feather and Dressed-in-Stars on the two-forty. He signaled for us to cross after he was satisfied with security on his side, and Doc stood, unlimbering his arms and legs.

"All right, boys and girls, ready to get wet?" he asked.

We gave a hushed chorus of "hooahs" and grabbed our weapons and rafts. Doc paused by the river's edge and looked back at Wilson, who threw a shaka sign.

Stanley and I eased our rafts into the water and walked them out into the river until it was deep enough for us to kick off after Doc. Once in the murky water, the current didn't feel nearly as sluggish as it looked, but Doc led us at an angle upstream and we made reasonably fast progress. The river was a good four hundred meters across, and by the time we'd passed the halfway point, I was starting to feel optimistic about the whole venture. Stanley wasn't doing quite as well and had his eyes screwed shut and was mumbling something.

His eyes shot open and he turned to me in alarm. "Something just brushed past my leg!"

It wasn't like the conceited show-off to admit fear, so whatever it was must have spooked him good.

"Could've been anything," I said with bravado I didn't really feel. "Don't stop kicking. Probably a log or something like that. Lotsa crap probably gets washed down this river."

"Didn't feel like a frigging *log*, Preacher."

Falling Leaves cut off a yelp behind us and I heard Jade Talon laugh at her, only to stop short and give a muted cry of her own.

When Wilson swore, I knew we were in the crapper for sure.

There was a huge splash behind me, and Falling Leaves screamed. I looked back and saw her go under in a whirlpool of foaming brown river water and blood. Stanley froze and started unexpectedly reciting Psalms 23 in a panicked voice, and I remembered he'd attended a Catholic private school as a kid. Apparently at least one thing the nuns had tried to beat into him had stuck.

"Keep kicking, dammit!" someone shouted. Me, I think. Maybe Doc. I looked back again and couldn't see Wilson either. Jade Talon had one arm across her raft and a knife in the other hand, searching frantically around the area where Falling Leaves had been, and First-to-Dance had both arms wrapped around her own raft, looking like she was kicking for all she was worth.

Doc was suddenly at my side. "Keep your heads front, guys. Kick harder! Bennett, you have the lead. Keep us angled upriver. Don't swim to Sanchez. You need to lead him in order to fight the current. You got this?"

"Yeah, okay, yeah," I sputtered.

"You got this?" he repeated. "Because Stanley sure don't."

"Yes, Sergeant! I got this."

"Good." He slapped my shoulder and then vanished under the water.

"Come on, Stanley," I shouted. "Kick!"

"—shadow of death," he said mechanically, holding on to his raft with clawed hands. "I will fear no evil—"

"Jade, Dance, you two with me?" I called over my shoulder.

"Yes, Corporal!"

"—thy rod and thy staff, they comfort me—"

"Just focus on getting us across, gals. Doc and Wilson got this."

"Yes, Corporal!" they repeated in unison.

"—thou anointest my head with oil; my cup runneth—"

Stanley's stranglehold on the raft slipped, and he almost went under. I got an arm around him and tried to heave him up. He's not the smallest of guys.

"—I will dwell in the house of the Lord—"

My foot kicked against something slimy and I almost panicked before I realized I was touching the river bottom. We were still a good hundred meters to the shore.

"Stanley, snap out of it! I can't drag you."

"—is my shepherd; I shall not want—"

"Jade, Dance, can you touch the bottom?" I asked.

"I can," Jade replied.

"Good. Jade, take Stanley. Try to slap some sense into him. Dance, help me reel all the rafts in."

"—leadeth me beside the still waters—"

"Slap him?"

"Whatever."

"—though I walk through the valley—"

Half holding him out of the river, she backhanded him so hard it sounded like a gunshot, and he flailed to his feet, sputtering.

"What the f—?" Stanley yelled.

"Stop praying and help with these rafts, Joe," I barked.

"Bitch!" He took a blind swing at Jade. She ducked, then hit him with an uppercut that sent him sprawling back into the river.

"Oh my heck! Jade, help Dance with the rafts." I handed her the loops of five-fifty cord and pulled Stanley's limp body out of the water. "You knocked him out!"

"I am sorry," she panted. "He has a weak jaw for such a big man."

I got my hands under his armpits and started hauling him toward the bank. I could hear people from Sanchez's group splashing out to help us.

It was about then that the water erupted in front of me and something horrific took hold of Stanley's leg and wrenched him violently from my arms. The monster was huge, a good fifteen feet long at least, with a wide mouth like a crocodilian frog and two stout forelimbs. Its fishlike tail slapped the water as it corkscrewed my platoon-mate away from me in a spray of blood.

I staggered back, fumbling to unsling Sybil from behind my back, when Sanchez shot past me in a blur with his Ka-Bar and tackled the beast, driving his knife into it with massive piston-strokes of his arm. It flipped over, carrying Sanchez with it under the water, Stanley's leg still in its mouth.

But only the leg.

Casting about numbly, I found the rest of Stanley floating nearby and hauled him out of the bloody water, not even realizing at the time that McKenzie and García were there beside me, helping carry him back to shore.

"Tourniquet!" I shouted, trying to stop the blood pouring out of his stump with my hands. "Dammit! Somebody get me a tourniquet!"

García hauled me up and spun me around, snapping his fingers in my face. "He's gone, man. You can't do anything."

"He needs a tourniquet, Sergeant!" I shouted back.

"He's gone, Bennett. *¿Comprende?* Gone. *Muerto.* He's lost too much blood."

Doc had Falling Leaves laid out beside Stanley and was giving her CPR. She had a nasty bite mark covering most of her torso; it was bleeding badly and she looked far too pale. Wilson was hunched over her, trying to dress the wounds while Doc pumped her chest and gave her mouth-to-mouth.

"Sure as shit didn't have Toadzilla on my bingo card," Wilson panted.

García snapped his fingers in front of my face again. "You with me, Bennett?"

"Where's Eps?" I asked in somewhat of a daze. She might not be able to help Stanley, but she could save Falling Leaves at least.

"Captain's group," García replied. "Still on the other side."

"Contact!" Dressed-in-Stars shouted.

García yelled back, asking for a direction and distance, but he was drowned out by the sound of the two-forty.

"Bloody everywhere!" McKenzie cried.

Jags were pouring out of the jungle on our side of the river, seemingly from all directions. García grabbed Jade Talon, who was loading a new belt into her oversized SAW, and started shouting out sectors and moving people into defensive positions.

"Motherf—!" Sanchez roared, storming out from the water behind us, caked in mud and blood. "What is it with this hellhole? Swear to God, it's one damn thing after another!"

Something whistled by my head and a second later I felt a sharp burning pain in my leg. I looked down to see an arrow sunk deep into my thigh. I dropped to a knee and unslung Sybil in one motion, casting about for the jerkwad who'd stuck me.

I got a bead on the archer and blew out his heart before he was able to draw another arrow. Working the bolt, I pivoted and found my next target, another jag with a wicked-looking spiked club closing in on Doc and Falling Leaves, and dropped him in a cloud of pink mist minus his calvaria. Wilson had tackled a third assailant, but I didn't have a clean shot, so I moved on to the next target of opportunity.

García had somehow managed to form an impromptu fireteam with Jade Talon, Heart-of-Darkness, McKenzie, and Lawrence; Sanchez and First-to-Dance were both lobbing grenades off into the jungle in a coordinated duet of destruction. I figured the best place for me to be was to cover Doc while he fought to save Leaves.

I dropped another would-be attacker charging Doc and pink-misted another archer hidden in the trees. I knew there was a third archer sniping us when I caught an arrow in my chest plate; I spotted him and took him out with my last round.

By then Wilson had somehow managed to crush his opponent's skull with the jag's own club, and was standing with his hands on his knees breathing heavily and bleeding from multiple lacerations. The two-forty gave a last bark, and just like that the assault was over. Sanchez started calling out for ACE reports.

Wilson panted and pointed at me. "You, uh… you okay, bro?"

"Fine," I said. I fingered the arrow in my leg. "Quads are gonna be sore, but I don't think it's serious."

"Not the one in your leg. The one in your chest, bro."

"Oh yeah. Can you believe that? Stuck right in my plate carrier!"

"You ain't wearing a plate carrier, man. You got nothing on but your boxers."

"And *you're* naked as a jaybird!" I started laughing. Heck, half of us on this side of the river were fighting naked. It struck me as insanely funny.

Then I passed out.

CHAPTER 11

When I awoke, Doc and Epasotl were leaning over me with concerned looks on their faces.

"Hey, Doc," I said. "Eps."

"Hey," Epasotl said.

"What's wrong? Is my leg going to be okay?"

"Leg's fine," Doc said. "But you... you should be dead."

"Was it poisoned?" I asked. "Did you save me again, Eps?"

"Bennett... I don't know how to say this..." Doc began.

"You totally shot in heart," Epasotl finished.

"Hit my plate carrier," I said.

"You weren't wearing a plate, man," Doc said.

I raised my head and noticed I was still dressed in only my soggy boxers.

"You sure?" I asked.

"Oh, I'm sure."

"Well, thanks for taking it out."

"Thing is... I didn't. It kinda... extracted itself. Like your body pushed it out."

I felt my chest. Aside from a lot of dried blood, I couldn't find a bandage... or a wound... and I said as much.

"Yeah, that's the thing," Doc said. "It just... healed right up."

"Very funny, Doc. You almost had me for a minute there."

Epasotl gave Doc a look. He nodded, and she unsheathed her claws and raked my forearm. Hard.

"Son of a—what the heck, Eps!" I held up my arm and watched the blood flowing freely from the four deep slashes. After a few seconds, the bleeding slowed to a trickle and the cuts closed up completely. There weren't even any scars.

"Whoa," I breathed.

"Same as last time," Doc said. "Consider my mind blown."

"Wait, last time? You've been letting her claw me while I was unconscious?"

"Just a little," Epasotl said. "For science."

"So, what?" I asked. "I'm like Wolverine now? How'd that happen?"

"Beats me," Doc said. "Maybe it's part of your… you know. *Condition.*"

"Cool… I guess."

They both stared at me for a long minute.

"Can I get dressed now?" I asked.

"Sure," Doc said. "You feel… any different?"

"No," I said, sitting up. I checked my leg. Aside from a lot of dried blood, it didn't look like I'd been stuck with a few inches of arrow. I glanced around to get my bearings. We were still on the riverbank, but it looked like the whole platoon had made it across. "Falling Leaves?" I asked.

Epasotl fingered a new scabby notch in her ear. "She is okay."

"Stanley?"

She shook her head, and I sighed. Stanley had been a total pig—especially toward Xochi—and a jerk in general, but he was still a brother. And I had to admit he'd been a good team leader. A good soldier. I don't know if I'd ever seen him freeze up—until today in the river.

"We buried him, and Cap'n said a few words," Doc said. "Better get dressed. We're moving out. We were just waiting on you."

"Don't want to be the holdup," I said, getting to my feet.

I found Kiktú squatting near my ruck.

<Nothing dangerous in the water?> I signed.

"*Imix*," he said quietly.

<What is that?>

<A sea monster. I have never heard of one this far from the ocean. They live only in brackish waters.>

<And yet here we are.> I rummaged through my ruck and dressed quickly in my ACUs.

<What manner of man are you?> Kiktú asked.

<A man who's angry one of my brothers was ripped apart by a sea creature because you are a bad guide.>

<I saw you die.>

<It was just a flesh wound.>

<It pierced your heart. Are you a ghost?>

<No. I'm not a ghost.> I slapped my plate carrier. <See? Just me. Alive and in the flesh.>

<Perhaps you are a demon. Perhaps that is why you are marked.>

I reloaded Sybil's five-round magazine and double-checked I had extra mags in my pouches. <Perhaps,> I admitted. <I may very well be a demon. I don't know anything about this sickness, or curse, or whatever it is, other than I'm dying slowly yet somehow getting stronger and… other stuff. Come on.>

Tossing my ruck onto my back, I set off to find our platoon sergeant without bothering to check if Kiktú was following me.

***

"Straight ahead, about a hundred and fifty meters," Pierce said. "About a dozen of them. Headed this way."

I held up a fist to halt the platoon and then got down on one knee and pivoted slightly so I could see Wilson. I relayed Pierce's report with a few quick hand signals, which he then passed on to Captain Brown.

A couple minutes later Sanchez got on the radio, ordering us into an ambush formation that put me, Cohen's team, and Cameron's two-forty crew in a wide vee. Wilson's team hung back with Flaming Feather's gun and would circle around to provide flanking fire once contact was made. Kiktú fingered his staff nervously.

<I cannot join the battle,> he reminded me. <It is forbidden.>

<We just need you to identify them. If they're friends, it is good. If they're not, you fade back to the captain's position while we light them up.>

<It is unmanly for me to deceive them into entering this trap.>

<Good thing you're a woman then.> I shot him a shark-tooth grin.

He grimaced, showing his teeth, but gave a resigned head-bobble in response.

Pierce appeared next to me again. "Still heading this way. Closing on fifty meters."

Kiktú sniffed at the air. <It is fortunate they are upwind.>

I keyed my radio. "Fifty meters and closing."

Scanning the trees through Sybil's high-powered scope, I caught my first sight of one of the jags at forty meters. He was a big dude, much bigger than Kiktú, slinking through the underbrush like a ghost. If I hadn't been actively looking for him, I don't think I would've seen him.

"I have eyes on one," I transmitted. "One o'clock. Forty meters." Without looking up, I tapped Kiktú on the shoulder.

He stood slowly, and my target stopped cold.

"How is your path?" Kiktú chirped in the traditional greeting.

My target's friends must have been moving into positions to rush and flank Kiktú, because García's teammates started quietly calling out targets and positions over the radio. I kept my scope fixed on my target. The wind shifted, and I swore silently. If they smelled us, things could get messy.

My target moved slightly out of the shadow of a tree and sniffed at the air cautiously.

"I am well," he growled. "And you, woman?"

Apparently that was enough for Kiktú to identify the stranger as an enemy, because he started back-stepping and hissed a warning to me in a low voice.

I keyed the prearranged short and long clicks on my radio that signaled to the platoon we were dealing with bad guys, and Sanchez responded with a simple, "Execute!"

I'd already taken the slack off my trigger and felt it break like glass as I gave it a final few ounces of pressure. The stock slammed back against my shoulder and my sight picture jumped momentarily.

When I had my target back in the scope, he was falling, surrounded by a pink cloud.

Cohen's team instantly began firing and communicating, and I could hear Cameron shouting targets and elevations as Anderson woke up the M240B and started belching 7.62 downrange in ragged bursts.

Wilson was quick to maneuver his team, swinging them around our right to enfilade the enemy, but by the time Flaming Feather got her gun in position, it was all but over.

Anderson spit out a couple more bursts before Cameron shut the kid down, and I inhaled deeply, savoring the smell of cordite in the afternoon. Smoking barrels mixed with the mist as we moved forward to clear the kill zone.

"Got a live one here," McKenzie called out. "Medic!"

"Here too!" Lawrence cried.

Doc rushed over to McKenzie and I heard a guttural rasp as Takahashi secured the one Lawrence had found.

Wilson was already directing his team into security positions and García was busy repositioning his crews to defend our perimeter when I made my way over to Takahashi and Lawrence. The jag Lawrence had found struggled against his zip ties and hissed at me as I approached with my med bag. I could see his leg was chewed up pretty bad and bleeding heavily, but I asked Takahashi if he had any other wounds.

"Just the leg, far as I can see," the sergeant replied.

The jag roared at me, baring his impressive teeth, before his eyes rolled back and he slumped to the ground. I had a tourniquet out and was about to try and get it around his massive leg when the blood stopped pumping out of his thigh.

I took his pulse and then looked up at Takahashi, shaking my head. "He's gone, Sergeant."

"Oh well," Takahashi said in a bored voice. "Sounds like the other one's still kicking at least. Short Round, report to Cohen and get on security."

Lawrence scowled at what had become his permanent nickname —his reward for shooting off that grenade danger close at the T-Rex —and rushed off.

From McKenzie's position, I could hear a jag hissing and growling obscenities and questioning someone's parentage. Doc's, probably. McKenzie was swearing too.

"Just hold him down," I overheard Doc say in a frustrated voice.

"I'm trying, Sarge," McKenzie replied. "He's a big lad. Little help here, Miss Stars?"

I beat feet over to where they were struggling to restrain three hundred pounds of wounded man-cat and grabbed Kiktú on the way.

The prisoner saw Kiktú and roared more obscenities, nearly tossing McKenzie, Doc, and Dressed-in-Stars off him. He was quite inventive with his curses too. It was impressive, even if half of them didn't cross the cultural barrier so well.

Captain Brown apparently was out of patience. He walked right up to the jag and punched him in the snout. Brown was a big man, as I've said, and an amateur heavyweight boxer, so it was a solid punch to say the least.

That got the guy's attention.

"McKenzie, kindly tell this gentleman we're trying to treat his wounds," Brown said.

"I've been tryin', sir! He donna want to listen," McKenzie replied.

"What's his name?"

"Béktül, sir," McKenzie said after a short exchange with the prisoner.

"Tell Béktül to at least shut up and stay still so we can treat his wounds," Brown grumbled.

Doc pulled me aside after he was finished treating Béktül, and we left Brown to resume attempting to interrogate him with McKenzie as interpreter.

"Hey, Bennett, check this out."

"Eh? What's up, Doc?"

"Har har. Shut up and look at this."

He led me over to one of the jag bodies and lifted the warrior's kilt. I'd noticed they all wore these same cloth-wrap skirts, unlike Kiktú who wore nothing but a belt to hold pouches and tools. I wasn't sure why Doc wanted me to look up a cat-man's kilt though.

"What do you see?" Doc asked.

"Uh… is this a trick question?"

"Obviously a male, right?"

"Yeah, pretty obvious."

He led me to another corpse and tossed the kilt back. "What about this one?"

"Also male."

We examined a few more.

"All apparently male," Doc pronounced. "So how can Kiktú, a woman, become a man?"

"I've talked to him about this a little. I think it's a social thing. 'Man' means 'warrior'; it's not a reference to sex. I don't think they even differentiate between biological sexes. Not the way we do anyway. He's a 'woman' because he failed to complete his rite of manhood."

"But he's *actually* a woman."

"Just because he calls himself a woman doesn't make him one."

"No. I mean he *is* female, Bennett. Now that you've seen a male of this species, it's pretty obvious they have something Kiktú lacks. The jags might not exhibit other signs of sexual dimorphism, but these guys have *balls*, don't they? And Kiktú doesn't."

I pinched the bridge of my nose. I hadn't really been paying attention to Kiktú's nether regions, but Doc was right.

"Is there a point to this biology lesson, Doc?"

"How would completing a rite make Kiktú, who's female, a male?"

"It would make him a *man*—it wouldn't make him biologically *male*. The ritual makes him a warrior, and the jags think of warriors as men and non-warriors as women. Like I said, it's a social thing. Just because this group of warriors is all male doesn't mean there aren't female warriors."

Doc shook his head. "I think it's more than that. I think the tail-docking causes a physiological change. Most likely the juveniles are neuter—possibly female, but my money's on neuter—and if they don't get their tails docked by a certain age, they *become* female."

"And if they get docked, they become male?"

"Exactly."

"That's… an interesting theory," I admitted.

"Easy enough to confirm," Doc said. He whistled to get Kiktú's attention and called him… or *her* I guess… over.

"Interpret for me, Bennett," Doc said. He lifted the kilt on the corpse at our feet. "What's this?" he asked Kiktú, pointing to the anatomical objects in question.

Kiktú turned half away with an angry hiss, shielding her eyes and signing rapidly that they were sacred and not to be exposed.

"I think you've offended her," I told Doc.

"Tough breaks. This is science," Doc said, but he lowered the kilt. "Kiktú, why don't you have those?"

<He is very rude,> she signed to me after I interpreted his question in sign.

I sighed.

<I refuse to speak of sacred things.>

"She says they're sacred and she won't answer you and also says you're extremely rude," I told Doc. "I agree."

"How about this then," Doc said. "Are you a woman yet, Kiktú? A full woman?"

She gave a vague head-bobble.

"What happens if your tail isn't docked soon?" Doc asked.

<I will be a woman forever.>

Doc nodded sagely. "But if your tail *is* docked before you reach a certain age, you'll grow sacred parts and be a man?"

She hesitated and growled low in her throat.

<It's okay, Kiktú,> I added in sign. <He doesn't mean to be profane.>

<It is as he said,> she signed to me begrudgingly.

"She says yes," I told Doc.

He reached up and slapped Kiktú on the shoulder. "Thanks, ma'am."

As he strode away, Kiktú gave me a quizzical-slash-horrified look, and I did my best to explain why he was so interested in sacred dangly bits. She seemed somewhat mollified after I was done but repeated that he was a *very* rude man.

CHAPTER 12

With Cohen's team on prisoner detail, the platoon was stretched pretty thin from an operational standpoint. Béktül hadn't been terribly forthcoming with details, only that he was from the Míchli tribe, which controlled a narrow neck of land northward and had come down with a vast army to sack the Yínchani capital city of Chlůmpu, conducting a scorched-earth campaign on hamlets and farmsteads along the way. They had been repulsed at the city, barely, and the invading army had shattered into bands of marauders as Captain Brown had suspected.

The next day we came across a ransacked hamlet, its houses and buildings burnt to the ground. Not a living thing had been spared.

I was inspecting a pen of slaughtered turkeys when Kiktú came up beside me.

<It is always so when the worshippers of the Obsidian Jaguar attack,> she signed. <They take what they can carry and destroy the rest.> She glanced over her shoulder to where Cohen, Lawrence, and First-to-Dance were guarding Béktül. <I would kill him, and slowly, if it were not forbidden for a woman to shed a man's blood.>

"I wouldn't blame you." I looked around at the bodies scattered about the razed settlement. There were many children among the dead, and the adults had been obviously tortured. "I might even help."

Doc came over, his mouth set in a grim line. "Kiktú," he said. "Is it usual for an enemy to remove"—he glanced at me—"the sacred parts of a man?"

I interpreted for her, and she answered, <It is done to make them a woman in the hereafter.>

"And the eyes?" Doc asked.

<So he will wander in blindness forever.>

Doc nodded. "Figured. Ritual mutilation isn't an uncommon practice. Neither are rape and infanticide. All too common in war."

"Found something," Heart-of-Darkness called out. "It's a man!"

We hurried over to where she was squatting. She turned over the partially fire-blackened human corpse. He was dressed in armor decorated with eagle feathers and wore a beaked helm. Most striking, though, was the spiderweb of black veins on his skin.

Heart-of-Darkness jumped back when she saw the sign of the curse. "It is a Child of Mictlāntēcutli!" she hissed, and quickly drew her knife and jammed it hilt-deep into the corpse's eye.

"I don't think so," Doc said. "I don't see any signs of decomposition or rictus around the mouth. He wasn't undead. He was... like Bennett."

"Death-touched," I whispered, stepping back involuntarily. My boot scraped against something metallic on the ground, and I bent down to pick it up. I showed it to Doc.

"Fifty cal," he said, taking the expended cartridge from me and turning it over in his hand. He called Sanchez to come look, and the platoon sergeant in turn called Takahashi over and instructed him to get everyone searching the area for brass.

<Have you ever seen something like that?> I asked Kiktú, motioning to the casing now in Sanchez's hand.

<It contains the magic that powers your thunder-rods, does it not?>

<But before you met us,> I asked. <Ever seen one? Or heard stories of men with thunder-rods?>

<I have not. I recognized them as weapons when you came, but have heard no such stories.>

<And you thought our kind were only stories to frighten children, right?>

She gave a vigorous head-bobble.

Brown arrived, took the brass from Sanchez, and marched over to Béktül, waving McKenzie over to join him as an interpreter. He showed the cartridge to the captive and then pointed back at the human corpse. I couldn't make out what they were saying, but I caught the distinctive head shake the jag gave to the captain.

Brown talked with Béktül via McKenzie for another minute, then came back to us.

"We've got a problem. Seems these human 'eagle warriors' are working with his tribe. They're led by four pale gods with magic weapons that spit fire and cough out golden metal."

"Four… pale gods?" I asked. "You think he's referring to—"

"Alpha Section," Sanchez said.

"I'd say it's just a coincidence," Brown grumbled, "but he says they've been sent here by Tohil and are hunting for a war party of their own kind."

"You think Smoking Mirror sent Alpha here to kill us, sir?" I asked.

"I do."

Sanchez cracked his knuckles. "Well, if you wanted to get that bastard's attention by destroying his soul forge, sir, I'd say you succeeded. Let them come. I've got a score to settle with that sonofabitch St. James."

"That's not all they're hunting for," Brown added.

Sanchez quirked an eyebrow.

"Appears ol' Smoking Mirror has his eyes on a Tlacaōcēlōtl artifact and is looking to grab it before we do."

"Our ticket home," Sanchez said.

"The very same," Brown said with a grunt. "Béktül called it the Compass of the Gods."

<Have you ever heard of something called the Compass of the Gods?> I asked Kiktú.

She shook her head. <Only in stories, from a time before time when we were gods and walked the stars.>

"What was it exactly?" Brown asked her after I'd interpreted for him.

<I do not know. It is a myth.>

I translated for the others.

"Béktül doesn't know or won't say either," Brown said with a frown. "But we now have a name for it, which is more intel than we had starting this op. Hopefully we can find someone in Chlůmpu who knows something concrete."

***

"Still don't know who they are?" I subvocalized.

"Not a damn clue," Pierce said. "I just know they've been riding our asses ever since we left the lowlands. They're sneaky bastards for sure."

"Got to be, to hide from a literal ghost."

Kiktú sniffed at the light breeze.

"Anything?" I asked her.

She lifted her upper lip, exposing her teeth, and hissed the negative. It sounded like someone exhaling in disgust.

Somehow it was easy to forget she was three hundred pounds of natural-born killer until she bared her fangs. Béktül was even bigger, and when I thought about it, the three-man guard we had on him seemed laughable. He could probably break through his zip-ties, then claw his guard to shreds without breaking a sweat. I wondered why he hadn't already.

Now that we were running into more signs of marauding bands and things were getting dicey, Captain Brown had decided that the time had come to find out who had been tracking us all the way from the lowlands. I personally wondered why we hadn't forced contact sooner, but the man obviously had his reasons. We'd set up our ambush two hours earlier, and the light was beginning to fade as the mists thickened. Much longer and we'd have to switch to NODs or give it up and try again later.

I'd attached my thermal monocular to my scope and was continuing to scan the forest when I caught a smudge of light on dark against a tree trunk about thirty yards away. I got off the scope to check with my naked eye, but saw nothing there. Returning to my scope, I confirmed the target and called it in on my radio.

Pierce was hunched down beside me. "I don't see anything, bro. You sure?"

"Got something on thermals," I subbed. "Definitely."

"Big tree at two-thirty, twenty-six meters?" he reconfirmed.

I nodded, and he vanished.

A minute later he was back beside me. The smudge hadn't moved an inch the entire time, but it was shifting subtly, like something breathing.

"Negative," he said. "There's nothing there. Maybe your scope's malfunctioning."

"Scope's fine. There's something there. I can see it breathing. It's about Eps-sized. Maybe a little bigger."

"I swear to God I was all right up around that tree and nothing's there."

I gave a fractional shrug.

"Ben-Ette," a soft voice hissed beside me.

"Cripes, Eps," I muttered. "I didn't know you were there."

"I am scouting out. Do not shoot me in ass-kisser."

She low-crawled past me silently and vanished into the undergrowth.

"All elements, this is Longshot," I transmitted. "Be advised friendly entering the kill zone."

A long minute or two later I caught her on thermal crouched low about a dozen meters away. She gave a low yowl, and the smudge against the tree was immediately outlined in a glowing blue light, as were several other figures hiding in the gloom. My target gave a surprised chirp and detached itself from the tree, its skin shifting from the mottled brown of the bark to a light green.

I swore.

Lizardmen.

People started calling out targets over the radio, and Epasotl scurried back to my side, her MP5 up against her shoulder.

"Wait!" McKenzie called out. "Hold your fire!"

He stood from his hidden position beside Flaming Feather and Dressed-in-Stars's machine gun. "It's all right. It's the lads! Bartholomew, that you, laddie?"

My target was trying to pat out the ghostly blue light surrounding his body and quirked his head up at McKenzie's voice. He gave a sharp, trilling cry.

"Safe?" McKenzie laughed. "Yes, you dafty. Of course it's safe! Come on out, all you lads."

The blue-glowing lizardmen, twelve in total, assembled cautiously before us. McKenzie stepped out of formation and strode over to them, greeting them all, and then turned to us.

"These are my lads," he told us. "This one here's Peter, that's Bartholomew, and this one's James. That over there's John, and this is Andrew, and that… well, you get the idea."

What McKenzie's "lads" were doing following us, I didn't know, but if they'd come to take us back to the fighting pit, they were wasting their time. And their lives.

Peter, or maybe James, chirped and clicked at McKenzie, and the big man threw back his head and laughed.

"Mind explaining this, Sir McKenzie?" Brown asked, approaching the gathering.

McKenzie nodded to the captain, then turned Andrew—or maybe *that* one was Peter. "Why have you been following us?"

The lizardman took a small shell out of a pouch in his belt and snorted from it. His tongue flicked out, licking the white power caked to his nostrils, and he gave a long trilling explanation as he gazed at Brown expectantly from one eye.

"Seems it's somewhat complicated," McKenzie interpreted. "See, they were sent to fetch me and Nephi back, originally, but they've been watching us for some time now and they've decided they like what they see. They want to join us, but they've been wary about making contact. Weren't sure if you all might see fit to eat them, you know."

<The Spirits of the Forest,> Kiktú signed to me. <I have never seen one before. It is said they deceive travelers and lead them on false paths where they steal their souls.>

"No," I said bitterly. I was beginning to think I'd encountered this Peter after all; he'd overseen my flogging after one of my escape attempts. I couldn't be sure, though. They all looked pretty much the same. <They don't steal souls,> I signed. <They make you fight in a pit and shrink your head and eat you if you lose.>

"You want the big man to be your new boss?" McKenzie asked Peter.

The diminutive lizardman chirruped in reply and squared his shoulders. I wasn't sure, but it looked like he was flexing too. His dewlap unfurled bright red and he gave a series of croaking barks. One by one the other lizardmen followed his lead and banged their spear butts on the ground.

McKenzie laughed. "They say they took a liking to you and yours after you walloped them and blew up their holy site. Not sure how true that is, but they do take a fancy to the strong man in the room— like to follow the winners. And after watching us all for a goodly long time, they've decided we're the winners."

Brown took off his boonie and rubbed his great bald head. "I'm not so sure about this."

"Ach, sir," McKenzie said. "It'll be braw. Dafty, the lot of 'em, but these are basically good lads, each and every one. I've known them all for over a year now; we're all mates, you know. And they're excellent scouts, as you can see. They tracked us all this way undetected. Well, mostly undetected."

Peter trilled something and McKenzie nodded. "And brave warriors too. Can't forget that."

Peter took an object from his belt and held it aloft. Kiktú hissed. It was unmistakably a shrunken jaguar-man head. The lizardman chirped and barked proudly as he shook the head and did a little dance on one leg.

"His conquered foe," McKenzie explained. "Taken in single combat."

<They are savages,> Kiktú signed to me.

<Can't disagree,> I signed back. "How can we trust them?" I called out to McKenzie. "Pretty sure the one shaking that head flogged me. And don't forget it could easily be *your* head he's waving around."

Peter stopped dancing and leveled his spear at me, chirping irritably.

McKenzie held up a hand to the pigmy saurian. "Nah, Peter, Nephi's a good lad, he is. You saw him fight. Right gallus one, he is."

Peter cocked his head and considered me with one eye, then strode boldly toward me, flipping his spear around. He tapped me on the shoulder once with the butt and chirped proudly.

"What the heck was that?" I asked.

"Counting coup," McKenzie answered.

"Cheeky little bastard," Takahashi commented from off to the side.

"Try that again and see what happens," I warned Peter.

He flared his dewlap at me and then marched back to his brothers.

Brown replaced his boonie. "All right. We'll give it a shot. You're responsible for them, Sir McKenzie." He thumbed back toward Béktül. "Have 'em guard the prisoner."

"Yessir," McKenzie said crisply. "You heard the boss, lads. We're to guard the big cat-man."

Peter trilled an order and the "lads" formed up smartly and marched over to Béktül. The jag roared at their approach, and Peter tapped him on the shoulder with his spear butt. The other lads chirped in amusement.

"Don't antagonize the prisoner," McKenzie ordered. "Look sharp now. Ten-hut!"

"This is ridiculous," I muttered under my breath.

Brown stepped in close to me and leaned down. "Problem, son?"

I straightened up. "No, sir."

He gave a low, gravelly chuckle. "They certainly seem enthusiastic. If Angus trusts them, I figure we can too. Plus they've been watching our six for days with no trouble. Stopped some, in fact."

"How so?"

"I've had Epasotl keeping an eye on whomever it was we had trailing us. She never caught sight of any of them, but they left a trail of bodies. Based on her reports I figured they were watching our backs, quietly dispatching any marauders who'd picked up our trail."

"I suppose that's… something, sir."

"Certainly is." He rested a shovel hand on my shoulder. "I'm sure you have a bone to pick with them, Nephi, after what you experienced, but try to let it slide and keep an open mind if you can."

"Hooah, sir. But… prisoner detail?"

He shrugged a massive shoulder. "I want to keep 'em where I can see 'em for a bit. And I doubt Béktül is going to try anything anyway. It seems to be a matter of honor with their kind."

"Like the Chaneque?"

"Not quite. Didn't say I trust him. Just not particularly worried."

"Four-hundred-plus pounds of apex predator with huge teeth and razor claws would have me worried."

"Well, he isn't a pussycat, that's for certain. Not letting my guard down, just not losing sleep over it. Neither should you."

"Hooah, sir."

"How's Pierce doing?"

"Eager to help."

Brown nodded. "He's been useful on recons. You two and Kiktú make a good team. Helps me rest easy knowing I don't have to worry about my point men. I know it's a taxing job, especially the long-range patrols, but I appreciate your diligence."

"Thank you, sir. Just doing my part."

"And you're giving it a hundred percent and then some. I notice these things." He paused for a moment. "You should know Sergeant Sanchez wants you to fill Stanley's slot. He wants to see you get more leadership experience, and I agree with him. But I need you where you are for a while longer. You'll get your chance to lead a rifle team soon enough."

To be honest, I hadn't considered being assigned as a TL in Takahashi's squad, and I wasn't sure I even *wanted* the position. It'd been just me and Pierce for so long, and then just me. But I appreciated the captain trying to smooth any ruffled feathers I might have had over Cohen getting the spot.

"Understood, sir."

He gave my shoulder a slap and strode off to talk one-on-one with some of the other guys and gals.

It was getting dark, so I was surprised when Sanchez announced over the team channel ten or fifteen minutes later that we were moving out. We didn't usually travel at night, mostly to save the batteries on our NODs. We had solar rechargers from our raid on the armory in Amoloyan, but with the perpetual overcast, batteries took forever to charge. In fact this was the first time we'd needed the NODs since my escape from the lizardmen—and so it was only now that I was reminded that my night vision had been busted by my captors.

I hurried over to Sanchez.

"Sergeant, my NODs are busted."

"And?"

"I'm on point."

"You kids and your damn tech. Swear to God. A real recon man don't need fancy gadgets to see in the dark. I really need to start making y'all run night patrols without 'em, otherwise the whole lot of you gonna curl up and wet yourselves when the batteries run out."

"Yes, Sergeant."

He moved away, muttering something about not needing no damned NODs in no damned Cambodia or no double-damned Laos.

I turned to leave and felt a viselike grip on my arm. Sanchez shoved his NODs in my hands.

"Bust 'em and you'll be on intimate terms with your e-tool."

"Thank you, Sergeant."

I hopped across the unused and unneeded latrine pit Lawrence was filling back up and found Kiktú.

"Ready to rock and roll?" I said in English. Kiktú had surprised me by picking up a few phrases, and I knew that particular idiom wouldn't translate.

She gave an awkward shaka sign, and it suddenly occurred to me who Kiktú was learning our language from.

<Epasotl teach you that?> I asked.

<The small blue one has been helpful in understanding your odd gestures. Did I do it right?>

<You did it right. Come on, we're burning darkness.>

CHAPTER 13

Pierce held up a fist and I took a knee with Kiktú. His form ahead of us blurred for a moment and then he was beside me.

<One Uniform, eleven o'clock, fifty meters,> he signed with patrol hand signals. He could've shouted—no one would hear him but me—but old habits die hard.

I pivoted to catch Takahashi's eye and relayed to him with a few gestures that we'd spotted an unidentified individual ahead of us, then signaled to Pierce to get a closer look. He nodded and blurred out of sight.

<Did your spirit guide see something up ahead?> Kiktú asked.

<He saw something ahead, but we don't know if they're friends or enemies,> I replied in sign.

<They are upwind,> she signed with a snarl. <It is likely they know we are here and are stalking us. I doubt they are friends.>

I double-checked that Sybil had a round in the chamber and flicked the safety off. I would've preferred my SCAR-H PR, but I'd loaned it to McKenzie back when he joined us.

Pierce tapped me on the shoulder. Literally. I was so intent on listening to, watching, and yes, even smelling my surroundings that I didn't register the physical contact was from a ghost. I swiveled my head toward him and he signaled that he'd seen ten more, including archers, closing in an arc around us from our one o'clock to our eight.

I pivoted back to Takahashi's position and relayed the intel. He signaled me to hold and watch. I updated Kiktú in sign language and she gave a low, throaty growl.

<How will they attack?> I asked her.

<A feint from there>—she motioned to our ten o'clock—<followed by simultaneous attacks from there and there.> She pointed to our two and seven, and I nodded. Classic pack tactics: distract from the front and hit on the flanks.

"Xavier, Longshot," I transmitted in a low voice. "Expect a feint from our ten with coordinated assaults on our two and seven."

"Roger. Wait one," Sanchez replied. Several seconds later he transmitted, "All Crazy Horse elements, execute Foxtrot-Bravo-Niner on my mark. Three… two… one… mark!"

We had a whole list of coded maneuvers, like football plays. FB-9 was the signal to form the platoon in a left echelon and move to contact as rapidly as possible. It was designed to break through ambushes. We'd been drilling in these maneuvers for weeks and I automatically fell back into my position on the right flank of Cohen's team in the rear rank of Takahashi's squad. Wilson's team led the charge.

Our stalkers obviously hadn't accounted for their prey counter-ambushing them, and the ferocity of our assault caught them flatfooted. My platoon-mates called out targets, and my NODs lit up with muzzle flashes as things went from deathly silent to deadly kinetic in seconds, and was over just as fast. It was so fast in fact I didn't get a shot off and my ears rang from the thunderous chatter of Lawrence's lightweight machine gun on my left.

My adrenaline was still going strong when somebody, Heart-of-Darkness I think, called out contact on our left flank and then García was shouting we had contact to the rear and Falling Leaves started lobbing grenades to our front.

I was on the right, saw multiple jags charging in from that flank as well, and dropped to a knee to draw a bead on the closest tango while shouting out a warning to Cohen. I took my shot, dropping the cat-man, and when Cohen didn't respond, I risked a glance back. He looked panicked, and instead of organizing his team's fire on our flank, he was shooting his rifle to the rear.

"Short Round!" I shouted, getting Lawrence's attention. "We need suppressive fire"—I had to turn him bodily in the right direction—"*there*! Now!"

He gave a quick nod and started laying down bursts at the mass of jags threatening to roll up our flank. An arrow hit Last-to-Dance in the shoulder, and she fell down on her ass.

"Cohen!" I screamed. "Tim! Wake up, man. Cover Short Round!" Cohen looked at me wide-eyed and shifted his aim. I snap-fired Sybil at another tango, blowing out his spine.

Last-to-Dance was trying to get back into the fight. I called out to Doc that we had wounded and tried to force her back down.

"It is not bad," she protested.

"Give me your rifle and bandoleer," I said, slinging Sybil behind my back. "Use your sidearm. Cover us."

She nodded and I took her rifle, loaded a round of AB in the tube, and then lobbed it with a *thunk* into the rear of the massed attackers.

Lawrence called out a belt change and Cohen, regaining his senses somewhat, was finally picking off targets with some degree of efficiency. The jags were learning quickly that closing to melee range was suicidal and instead were now hanging back and sniping us with arrows and javelins.

And worse.

Sickly green rays of energy lanced through our position sporadically, splashing against tree trunks. One hit Jade Talon and she began retching violently.

Epasotl swore and produced a staff capped with a rattle of snake skulls from… I wasn't sure where actually… and shouted at Cameron, pointing her staff off into the forest. "Do you see the tall thin one? Wreathed in black flame? Light him up!"

Anderson laid into his two-forty and was walking his bursts as Cameron corrected his elevation when the private suddenly screamed and held his hands up to his face, his flesh erupting in sores. Cameron and Heart-of-Darkness were instantly covered in them too, and it seemed like every living thing within several feet of them was withering and dying. Somehow Cameron managed to take hold of the weapon and resume firing despite whatever the heck was happening to them.

Holding her staff like a rifle, Epasotl caterwauled something I couldn't understand and a bolt of pure energy shot out of it, momentarily lighting the jungle in a blaze of brilliance that washed out my NODs.

"Tango down!" she cried.

Takahashi gripped my shoulder and yelled in my ear. "We're moving. You're taking over Bravo team from Cohen. Squad column, fire teams abreast."

"Hooah, Sarge," I replied. "Cohen, Short Round, we're moving. Squad's forming a column, teams abreast. Dance, stick by me. Let's move!"

Gold Squad shifted into a roughly circular formation with Takahashi and Kiktú in the center, and we advanced under the fire of arrows. I ignored the searing pain as one found its mark in my upper arm and focused on sending HE grenades downrange. Lawrence screamed that he was hit, but he kept moving and firing his machine gun anyway.

"Hit your plate carrier, PFC," I heard Takahashi yell. "You're not dead yet, Isaiah! Give 'em hell!"

"Mag out!" Cohen cried, and I shifted fire to cover him. First-to-Dance's slide locked back and she dumped the mag, then managed to smoothly reload and chamber a round one-handed on the move.

"You hanging in there?" I asked her over the whistling of arrows and bark of automatic weapons fire.

"Hooah, Corporal," she answered. She was smiling, so that was a good sign.

Sanchez barked something I didn't quite catch and then Takahashi ordered us into a line facing the rear. "Fall back by teams. Alpha on me."

By this point I'd lost all sense of direction, but I trusted that Brown knew where he was leading us to. How the man could orient himself while controlling the movement and fire of eighteen men and women was beyond me; I was totally consumed with my little world of Cohen, Lawrence, and Dance.

For the next half hour Takahashi bounded our teams backward at a steady, measured pace and our fire slackened as we shifted from a desperate attempt to avoid being overrun to an ordered withdrawal under irregular arrow fire.

Sanchez finally ordered another formation change and I glanced over my shoulder and saw that we were nearing the lake. I felt a momentary panic that instead of Captain Brown leading us, the jags had been herding us straight into the water, when I caught sight of an undamaged causeway leading to the city.

Clever one, our captain.

Our enemy must've seen it too, because they began roaring in rage and suddenly burst through the trees in a full-on kamikaze charge. I tried to swallow the lump that formed in my throat, but my mouth was too dry. There were just too many of them. We were going to be overrun and hacked to pieces.

Then Epasotl stepped calmly to the front of our formation and held Atzi aloft, the infant's skull blazing in a wreath of blue-white flame.

I felt a wind pick up off the lake to our backs, which rapidly grew in intensity. Sand and stones were kicked up by the gusts, and in moments the wind reached hurricane force not ten feet in front of us. Shrubs and small trees were uprooted, and the massed charge of jags was thrown back in disarray as they fought blindly to press through the gale.

The supernatural wind held back most of the horde, but not all.

Overheated weapons went hot again, and Lawrence swore as his machine gun jammed. My bolt locked back just as Cohen announced another mag swap, and I dropped the rifle to draw my sidearm as a truly huge warrior broke through the defensive wall of wind and charged me, bringing his war club up in an overhead sweep. My pistol cleared the Kydex holster cleanly, but everything seemed to be moving in slow motion, and I knew I wouldn't have the weapon up before that massive club with its football-sized obsidian head came down on my skull.

First-to-Dance was firing, although I couldn't hear anything except for a distant popping sound. Her shots bloomed red on his fur, but nine-millimeter doesn't really have any stopping power against nearly five hundred pounds of battle-crazed man-cat.

Then a blurred form knocked Dance and me aside and barreled into the warrior like a tornado of claws, fur, and fangs.

Kiktú hissed and spat as she wrestled with him, blood and fur flying in all directions. He threw her off with a terrible roar and raised his arm to bring his club down on her when Lawrence's machine gun resumed coughing lead and quite literally ripped him to shreds.

Epasotl was on her knees now, holding the flaming skull over her head as the hurricane wall continued to beat back our attackers. It had begun raining, and I could hear Atzi giggling over the wind.

Lightning flashed, splitting an old tree, and the jags unexpectedly began to withdraw, fading back into the jungle.

I was about to breathe a sigh of relief when someone shouted a warning that we had contact to our rear. Risking a glance back, I felt my heart drop as scores of jags rose out of the waters of the lake, brandishing spears, clubs, and bronze axes.

Kiktú gave a joyful chirrup, and I turned to her.

She flashed me a smile full of sharp teeth. <They are friends,> she signed.

"Oh," I wheezed. "Thank God."

CHAPTER 14

The city elders had placed us in a high-walled, windowless courtyard to rest and recover—whether we were prisoners or guests seemed to be an open question. And they had taken both Kiktú and Béktül somewhere else for questioning.

Jade Talon was still retching violently, and Doc had her hooked up to an IV while healers from the city tended to Cameron, Anderson, and Heart-of-Darkness, all of whom had open, rotting lesions covering their bodies. It reminded me of the necrotic decay that had infected Wilson when one of the witches scratched him back in the forests of Kuauchanko, except this time we didn't have any antibiotics.

Other than those casualties, and several punctured CamelBaks, we'd gotten off relatively unscathed. A few arrows had found flesh, but nothing serious; my own wound had healed completely before we were even out of the jungle.

And of course Epasotl was unconscious again—and this time she was running a fever. Whatever toll the magic had taken on her body, it wasn't good.

I sat beside my small blue friend and tried to cool her with wet compresses as she shivered and muttered incoherently.

Without a prisoner to guard, McKenzie's lads were crouched in a corner leaning on their spears and playing a game with carved knucklebones that involved a fair amount of chirping and a lot of drinking from wineskins. Eventually one of them got up and sauntered over to me. He peered at Epasotl with one eye and trilled something that sounded like a question.

"Peter wants to know how she made the great wind," McKenzie explained, joining us.

"I don't know how she does it," I answered.

Peter chirruped another question.

"He asked if it was the skull of fire," McKenzie interpreted.

I shrugged. "Really, I don't know."

The lizardman took the shrunken jaguar head off his belt and held it out to me, uttering a series of clicks and chirps.

"Peter says the head is from a great warrior and will make you mighty in battle. He wants to trade."

"Trade for what?" I asked. "Atzi? Absolutely not."

Peter gave an agitated series of short barks and thrust the head at me.

"For these wee folk, to refuse a trade made in good faith is considered offensive," McKenzie said.

"Let him be offended then," I said. "I couldn't care less. And the skull's not mine to trade anyway. He'd have to ask Eps." I pointed to Peter and then to Epasotl. "You ask her trade. Later. See how far that gets you. Now go away. She's sick."

Peter's dewlap flared and he considered me with one eye for a minute, then hissed and produced a shell from his pouch, offering it to me. I quirked an eyebrow at McKenzie.

"Peace offering," he explained. "Some cocaine to smooth any ruffled feathers."

I held up my hands. "I appreciate the offer, Peter, but no thanks. I'm good."

His dewlap flared again and he motioned with the shell to Epasotl and gave a long trilling explanation that I could've sworn ended with a sound like "Eps."

"My mistake," McKenzie said. "It seems it's for her. To cure her magic sickness. Apparently their medicine men use it for that purpose."

"Might work," Doc said, joining us. "Theoretically. Sorry, couldn't help overhearing."

"You're not serious, Doc," I protested.

"I said theoretically. If it's pure. We could dissolve some and administer by IV. But who knows what the hell that might be cut with, so no."

I breathed a sigh of relief.

"Oh, stop clutching your pearls, Bennett," Doc chided. "Just because it's abused doesn't mean it can't have medicinal uses if administered properly. I don't recall you having problems sticking people with morphine."

"Point," I admitted.

Doc squatted beside the lizardman. "Anyway, thanks… Peter, is it? Thanks, Peter, but no."

Peter bobbed his head, chittering something as he gestured to Doc and then to me. He gave a final chirrup and left us to return to his brothers.

"What was that about?" I asked McKenzie.

"Ah, oh, he was just commentin' on how nice and polite Doc here is and, ah, well you're a mite rude, Nephi, says he."

Doc laughed and then motioned to Epasotl. "How's our little Jedi?"

"Hasn't woken yet. Still running hot, and delirious," I said. "What about Jade?"

Doc blew out his cheeks. "Not vomiting or dry heaving finally, but not good. It's like she was poisoned."

"Is she going to pull through?"

"Without knowing what the toxin is…" He spread his hands. "Hard to say. I was hoping Eps could figure it out. Maybe one of the healers here has some idea. They seem to have arrested the spread of the necrosis in Cameron and the others. Hopefully they can repair the tissue damage, because it's… extensive."

Nightmare fuel would be a better term. They looked like something from a horror movie. Doc had given them morphine for the pain, and whatever the healers were doing helped with that too, but… it wasn't pretty.

"Doc, whatever got them… it was like some kind of area-effect weapon. Like something chemical or biological. Everything around them just… died. Scary as heck. And we don't have any NBC gear."

"That's assuming getting kitted up in MOPP 4 would do any good. Remember, this ain't chemical or biological. It's *magical.*"

"Ugh."

"Yeah, double ugh. My guess is some form of magically weaponized necrotizing fasciitis or some other bacteria like syphilis on some serious effing steroids, but I'm not an expert. Listen, I gotta get back to Jade. I know Eps has been through the wringer after saving our collective asses and all, but when she wakes up, I need to talk to her."

"Hooah, Doc."

He moved off, and I turned my attention back to Epasotl. Her eyes were dancing rapidly under her eyelids, and she'd broken out in a cold sweat. I wrung out another cloth in the bowl of cold water, folded it, and laid it across her forehead.

The door to the courtyard opened, and one of the city elders entered. He was an old warrior with gray on his muzzle and scarred fur and wore a purple kilt and sash embroidered with gold. Captain Brown moved to greet him, extending his right hand, palm up, and motioned for me to join him.

"Sir?" I said, jumping to my feet.

"Interpret for me."

"My dose of the potion, uh, expired. I don't have more on me, and Eps isn't awake yet, sir."

"Just fetch it out of her bag."

Rummaging around in Epasotl's haversack of disgusting things was about the last thing I wanted to do. Plus I wasn't sure I'd get the *right* ointment.

"What if I fetch the wrong thing?" I asked Brown. "She's got a lot of crazy stuff in that bag. No telling what could happen. Could be... awkward, sir."

He rubbed the bridge of his nose, nodded, and then called McKenzie over to interpret.

"Angus, thank this gentleman for sheltering us and helping with our wounded, and ask him how long we must remain here, in this courtyard. Politely, of course."

"Aye, sir." McKenzie turned to the jaguar-man and politely repeated Brown's words. He nodded as the jaguar-man replied, then told Brown, "He says in time they may greet you as friends."

It's hard to describe how weird it was *not* understanding the jaguar sign language. Hours earlier I was fluent, and I could remember my conversations with Kiktú in detail. But now as I looked on, McKenzie and the elder looked to me like they were just waving their arms about. It kind of blew my mind.

"Okay, so not guests," Brown said. "Prisoners, for now. We can work with that."

The elder held up a hand and then signed rapidly. McKenzie quirked an eyebrow and turned to Brown. "He says Kiktú claims you're friends of the Feathered Serpent and have done battle in the Place of Fright against One Death. That you are sworn enemies of the Obsidian Jaguar."

"Tell him that's true."

The elder considered that. From what I knew of their culture, a man didn't lie, and to infer he did was a grave offense demanding a duel of honor.

"He says he doesn't know our kind, and we aren't 'The People.' He asks if you're a man or a beast."

"I am a man," Brown replied.

"He says a beast may speak with two faces, but a man may not."

"I am a man," Brown repeated.

The elder growled low in his throat. I couldn't tell if it was a threat or a sign of satisfaction with the captain's answer.

"He says he'll treat you as a man in that case," McKenzie interpreted.

"Angus, tactfully ask him what became of my prisoner. He was under my protection, and I expect him to be unharmed."

"Says he chose to be tried by the gods for his crimes against the tribe, and his guilt has been proven in blood."

"Trial by combat..." Brown grumbled.

"So soon?" I asked him.

"Apparently justice is swift here."

Brown frowned at the elder. "He was my captive. He was under my protection."

The elder signed to McKenzie.

"Says the jag was a criminal, and so your honor is unblemished," McKenzie said.

"And what of the woman?" Brown asked.

More signing, then McKenzie frowned. "Says she drew a man's blood and has been chastised."

Captain Brown laid a warning hand on my shoulder.

"Also says if you wish, she'll be returned to us, in her shame," McKenzie added. "She no longer has a place with The People."

"So she's dead to them," I said bitterly.

McKenzie repeated the question and shook his head after the elder replied. "No, not dead. Not living. She is… anathema."

"Tell him we'll have her, shame or no," I told McKenzie. "Right, Captain?"

Brown nodded and squared his broad shoulders. "Angus, tell him she has a place with my people."

The elder considered McKenzie's statement and gave a dismissive wave of his hand.

"So be it," McKenzie interpreted.

***

Two hours later the door opened again and Kiktú was pushed through by the guards. She stumbled several paces and collapsed in the center of the courtyard on her hands and knees. Her fur was still matted with blood from her fight with the man who'd almost killed me, but she also had new marks, fresh and bloody. Her left eye was swollen shut, and her right hip bore a hideous brand.

I rushed over and knelt beside her.

"What the hell happened to her?" Doc asked.

"They beat her and branded her because she saved my life. She's been exiled."

"Damned barbarians," Doc hissed. "I'll get my med bag." He raised his voice. "You see what those assholes did to her, Captain?"

"I can see," Brown grumbled from where he stood off to the side with Sanchez.

"Kiktú, it'll be okay," I said. "You're safe now. With us. You're one of us. We'll protect you."

She stared at me in fright, not comprehending what I was saying.

Doc rushed back with his med bag and surveyed the damage. "Holy hell, they beat her good. I'll take care of the burn first. And she's going to need stitches. A *lot* of stitches. Kiktú, this is gonna hurt me more than it hurts you."

I tried to pantomime what Doc had said as best I could, and she gave a head-bobble before hissing as Doc poked and prodded. Then I motioned for her to stay put before running over to Epasotl. She was still unresponsive, so I reluctantly found her haversack and flipped back the flap. I'd just have to risk imbibing the wrong thing, awkward results or not. I desperately wanted to be able to communicate with Kiktú—and communicate directly. I didn't want to speak through McKenzie.

But the haversack seemed oddly... empty.

I felt around inside, and my hand wrapped around a small gourd. I pulled it out, unstopped it, and then took a good whiff that nearly bowled me over. Yeah, that was the right potion. Chocolate and cadavers. Unless there was another... nah, couldn't be. The scent was unmistakable. I forced down a swallow before plugging the gourd and tossing it back in the haversack, then ran back to Doc and Kiktú.

<You must be in great pain,> I signed when I returned to her.

<I have been chastised. It is no less than I deserve.>

<You have been beaten,> I signed angrily. <And branded. This is barbaric.>

<It is the law.>

<I am so sorry. You are safe now. With us. You are one of us. We'll protect you.>

<I have no tribe. I will be a woman forever.>

<You have us now,> I replied. <We are your tribe now. Tribe... Crazy Stag.>

Fixing me with her good eye, she signed, <Tribe Crazy Stag?>

<We are. Us, and you. Brothers and sisters.>

<Sisters? But you are all men.>

<We are not.> I pointed out some of the gals. <They are *women*, Kiktú. Not men.>

<But they fight.>

<Man, woman, it does not matter. We all fight for each other.>

<I understand now. At the river crossing, I noticed the differences between you. I thought they were a different race of hairless walking monkey. But they are women of your kind. Who fight. I did not think such a thing was possible. It is unnatural.>

I shrugged. <Perhaps, but these gals are some of the fiercest fighters I've seen. They're my battle sisters.>

<Battle sister.> She bared her fangs. <I would be a battle sister also?>

I called Falling Leaves over.

"Yes, Corporal?"

"You gals have room for one more?"

Leaves gave me a savage grin. "Hooah, Corporal!"

CHAPTER 15

Epasotl's fever broke in the night, and the next morning she cracked open her big, green, gold-flecked eyes and blinked at me.

"I feel like the shits," she hissed. "How long this time?"

"Couple days, more or less. You had a bad fever this time. I'm worried about you."

"Is price of being gremmie."

"So it won't always be this bad?"

"Depends."

"Depends? On what?"

"How fast learn."

"I suppose that's encouraging."

She tried to sit up and look around but gave up. "I tired to the boner."

"Bone. Tired to the bone."

"Where are we?"

"In the jag city. We're… sort of prisoners. For now at least."

"That sucks big one. We all make it?"

"Yeah, mostly. Cameron's team is recovering from the… whatever was eating their flesh. I think the jag healers are using magic. Jade is in bad shape. Poisoned, Doc thinks. He wants to get your opinion. What the heck happened back in the jungle?"

"Bad mojo. Powerful life magic."

"More like death magic."

"Is same."

"How do we defend against magic like that?"

"Maybe Atzi know. I ask her. For now have my staff. Is big guns."

"Ah, about that… it kinda… it got lost, I think. We couldn't find it."

She eyed me quizzically. "Lost?" She peered into her small haversack. "No, it is here, safe."

"What? In there? It can't fit in there."

"Is bigger on inside." She lifted the bag onto her lap and opened the flap. "See?"

I looked inside, but again all I saw was darkness. "It's empty."

"Not empty." She reached into the haversack and pulled out the infant's skull. "See?"

Just like I had done with the speech potion.

"How did you do that?" I asked.

She looked at me like I was an idiot. "I reach in, take out."

"So… whatever you want, when you reach in…"

"I take out." Again she gave me that *idiot* look.

"And you're saying the staff is in there too?" I again checked the size of the bag. Not even close to big enough to hold a staff.

"Has everything I need."

"When you say *everything*…"

"Can not hold *everything*. But hold much."

"Doesn't it get heavy?"

"No."

"Then why the heck are we humping all this extra ammo? We could just put it in your little magic bag!"

She shook her head. "Too much. Too heavy. Put too much and will rip."

"Then what? Everything falls out?"

"No. Space inside tear apart. Then things come in, maybe get out of bag. Bad mojo."

That didn't sound good. "What kind of things?" I asked.

"Better not worry pretty head."

I eyed the bag suspiciously. No way on Earth I was reaching into that thing again.

"Where did you get that anyway?" I asked her.

"Ueueokichtli give. Dope graduation present, no? Is rad." Epasotl got to her feet unsteadily and wrapped her poncho liner around her head and shoulders. "Come. We see Doc. See what is up."

Jade Talon was in a fetal position, wrapped in a couple of poncho liners of her own, shivering. Doc looked up from where he was organizing his med bag.

"Ah, you're up. How's my favorite Jedi?" he asked.

"Baller," Epasotl replied. "Jade Talon not look well."

"Yeah." Doc rubbed his face. "I've done all I can. It's some sort of toxin."

Epasotl squatted down next to Jade and held out her hand. "Spit."

"What?" Jade asked deliriously.

"Spit in my hand."

After Jade had done as requested, Epasotl sniffed her palm and then licked it. I tried not to gag. She looked thoughtful, then reached into her bag and pulled out a mortar and pestle, a variety of herbs, and some tiny stoppered gourds. Working swiftly, she ground her various, and in same cases dubious, ingredients into a fine paste. Then she drew her knife, sliced her thumb, and squeezed some blood into the mixture. She rummaged around in her haversack some more, pulled out an MRE spoon, and scooped up the paste.

"Eat this," she told Jade, who nodded weakly and let Epasotl feed her. Her eyes bulged and she made a gagging sound.

"You must swallow," Epasotl said.

"I cannot," Jade said around a mouthful of the nasty paste.

Epasotl pinched Jade's nose and held her mouth shut. "Swallow!"

Jade squeezed her eyes shut and gave a shudder.

"Good. Now lie on you back."

Epasotl lifted Jade's ACU blouse, exposing her stomach, and placed her palm over Jade's navel. A pale blue radiance spread across Jade's skin, and she broke out in a heavy sweat. Epasotl closed her eyes and massaged Jade's stomach in a circular motion while muttering something I didn't understand. After a few minutes Jade abruptly gagged, rolled over onto her hands and knees, and vomited with a sudden heave that wracked her whole body. Then she fell back to the ground, shaking and sweating.

Epasotl examined the mucus and bile critically before reaching into it and pulling out a long, thin worm. Doc swore softly. Meanwhile my stomach was threatening to disgorge its own contents.

"Gnarly," Epasotl said. She dropped the worm into a small gourd, corked the top, wiped her hands on her pants, and then began putting everything back in her haversack.

"That's it?" Doc asked.

"That it," Epasotl said.

"What the heck *was* that?" I asked.

Epasotl gave me a sidelong glance. "Bad mojo, Ben-Ette. Very bad mojo."

***

By late afternoon, Cameron, Anderson, and Heart-of-Darkness were awake and eating. They looked much better, relatively speaking. Not *good*, but at least they no longer looked like something out of a horror movie. García was with them, chatting and cracking jokes.

"Must be powerful magic healers use," Epasotl commented as we stood off to the side. "You say they no sacrifice they flesh?"

"Not that I've noticed."

Epasotl fingered the stub of her much-sacrificed ear thoughtfully. "Must learn. What they call they magic?"

"'Making.' I think it means the same as 'god-weaving' in your language."

"But weaver must weave part of self. Flesh or life force."

"Is that why magic always knocks you out? You're sacrificing part of your soul?"

"My life force. Yes."

One of the healers had come by to check on Cameron and the others and caught sight of Epasotl. The woman flowed—that's the only way I can describe how she moved—over to us, squatted down beside my friend, and signed to her.

"She's asking if you're a Maker, a god-weaver," I told Epasotl.

Epasotl nodded.

The cat-woman was short for her kind and had large, soft brown eyes and petite ears, with a slim, graceful build. She gazed at Epasotl with deep compassion.

<You are so weary,> she signed. <So tired. The Making demands a high price from you.>

Epasotl sighed deeply after I'd interpreted, and I looked at her, I mean, really *looked* at her, and realized with a shock that she'd been aging before my very eyes and I hadn't noticed. Her hair hung limp and dull, her skin was ashen and sagging, and she had large black circles under her eyes. When I met her she'd been a young woman, and now she was old.

The healer cocked her head to the side and signed to me.

"She wants to touch you, Eps."

Epasotl shrugged.

The jaguar-woman smiled and traced her hands over Epasotl's head, stroking her ears, her eyes, her face, and as her hands moved a glowing white radiance followed her touch. Epasotl's hair began to gleam like cobalt, her skin firmed and glowed with a healthy blue-gray sheen, and—I caught my breath—her ears became whole. She looked young again and… I had to admit… actually sort of pretty.

For a Chaneque anyway.

Epasotl reached up and touched her ears. "What magic is this?" she asked.

"She says it is a pure Making that requires no sacrifice," I interpreted.

"Ask her if I can learn this!"

"Perhaps, she says."

The jaguar-woman smiled and stood. <I fear I cannot heal the curse that lives in you,> she signed to me. <That you must heal yourself. But>—she touched my cheek with a velvet palm—<I restore the youth that was robbed from you.>

Epasotl laughed when she saw my transformation. "Xochi be disappointed. You young again. She say you no look distinguished now. At least still have you scars."

<Thank you,> I signed to the healer.

<It is my gift to give, and I give it freely. Go in peace.>

<Go in peace,> I replied.

She smiled and flowed away from us.

Epasotl fingered her ears again and followed the healer with her eyes as the woman exited the courtyard. "*Must* learn this weaving."

Wilson was crossing the courtyard and did a double take. "Whoa, bro, that you? You look like you again instead of like your old man."

"The healer…" I began.

Then Wilson caught sight of Epasotl and stopped short. "Eps? Wow. You look all… spunky."

"Admit it, broski," Epasotl said. "You have hots for me."

"Not in a million years, sister." He gave her a fist bump, then turned back to me. "I guess they couldn't do anything about…?" He gestured to my black-veined face.

"Apparently not. Still death-touched."

"Eh, don't sweat it. At this point you'd look weird without it. Like shaving off a mustache." He dropped the subject, much to my relief. I was already wondering whether I'd now have to have this exact same conversation with everyone in the platoon. "You have any inside intel on when we're getting out of here?" he said. "I'm going stir-crazy."

I shrugged. "No clue."

"Damn." He chewed his lip. "Double damn."

"Look sharp," I muttered.

"Heya, Cap'n," Wilson said as Brown approached. "When we gettin' out of here?"

"Same as I said when you asked half an hour ago, Dave. Soon." He regarded Epasotl and me for a moment, and I prepared myself to receive his congratulations and then condolences. But he just grunted then said, "Walk with me, Nephi."

There wasn't really anywhere to walk to, but I detached myself from my friends to join him, and we moved off a short distance.

"Sir?"

"Need to talk to you, son."

I waited.

"I've never known you for holding grudges, Nephi, but you're beginning to acquire the habit. First with the lizardmen, and now with our hosts over Kiktú." I opened my mouth but snapped it shut as he raised a hand. "I get it. I'm angry about how they treated her, too. But that doesn't make them the bad guys. We're dealing with a foreign culture here—hell, a *nonhuman, non-Earth* foreign culture— and we can't judge them by our standards. I'm not saying there's no absolute right and wrong, but when you're dealing with allies, you sometimes gotta let cultural things slide, even if it sticks in your throat. I'm saying this because I need you to interpret for me, and you can't be having a chip on your shoulder while you're doing that. Understand?"

"Yessir."

"But?"

"But nothing, sir. I can be diplomatic."

"How's Kiktú?"

I looked over to where she was sitting with Falling Leaves and some of the other gals, teaching them how to sign.

"Better. The healers won't touch her, but Doc says she'll be okay. The gals have taken her in as one of their own."

"That was well done, encouraging them to do that. Giving Kiktú hope for a new life. What'd you call 'em?"

"Uh, battle sisters, sir?"

"I like that."

"Kiktú's a good person, sir. Haven't known her all that long, but we have a connection. I think she's a kindred spirit. Guess that sounds sorta sappy."

"Maybe. But that's what I like about you, Nephi. You got a big heart. And you see people's souls. It's a rare quality. Don't lose it."

"Yessir."

"And no grudges. Forgive and move on."

"Forgive? I thought Rangers were fueled by hate, sir," I said with a smile.

"Only for the enemy. Gotta know the difference."

CHAPTER 16

It was another several days before Captain Brown was invited to speak with the chief elder of the tribe. By then the healers had restored Cameron and the other magical flesh-eating bacteria victims to something very close to their old selves. The change was really quite miraculous. Epasotl had stuck to the healers like a puppy, asking questions and learning all she could about this form of god-weaving that required no sacrifice on the part of the weaver.

I found her in a corner of the courtyard sitting in a lotus position with her hands palms-up on her knees, her body illuminated by a faint silvery-blue aura. I paused, not wanting to interfere with whatever was going on.

She cracked an eye open. "Wassup, Ben-Ette?"

"Sorry, didn't want to interrupt…" I waved a hand. "Whatever you're doing."

"I practice draw teōtl, to store for weaving later. It how jaguar Makers work they magic."

I sat down beside her. "Is it difficult?"

"Require epic concentration." Her aura flared and vanished, and she frowned. "If I stop thinking hard, it all go away."

"You'll get there. I'm sure the healers have been training for years."

"We no have years."

"How does it work? This… teōtl?"

"Is energy. I store, use later."

"Like charging a battery?"

"Battery?"

"Like on our NODs."

"Yes. Is like how NODs store sun. But if I lose focus, it escape."

I considered. "Could you store the teōtl in something else?" I asked. "Like a gemstone or something? I've read stories where the wizard had, like, a big ruby or whatever full of magic."

"I no have big ruby. Or even small one." She reached into her bag and produced a small withered and blackened hand. "I have mummified hand of virgin, but I no think that work for storing teōtl."

"How do you know it's a virgin's hand?" I regretted the question as soon as I asked it.

"You really want know?"

"Probably not. What about this?" I took out my dog tags and removed my grandpa's old West Point class ring. My dad had inherited it, and he'd given it to me when I completed OSUT. "It has an amethyst. Could that work?"

She took it from me and peered at it from various angles. "Is valuable?"

"I don't know. I mean, it's an antique by now, and it's real gold, so maybe. But it was my grandpa's, so it means a lot to me and my family. Amethyst was my grandma's birthstone. They were married the year he graduated."

"Epic sacrifice," she said. "You would sacrifice it for me? That is sick."

"Uh…" I had meant to let her maybe *borrow* it. The idea of actually losing it hit me harder than I'd thought it would. "I was planning on giving it to my son, if I ever have one."

"No worries. It cool. I find something else," she said, handing it back to me.

"No." I held up my hands. "If it can help you, that helps the mission, so it's worth the sacrifice. Take it."

"You are rad," she said, fishing a thin leather thong out of her haversack and stringing the ring onto it. She tied it around her neck and tucked it under her ACU blouse. "I try. If it no work, I give it back."

The door to the courtyard opened and a guard leaned in, calling for Captain Brown. "That's my cue," I told Epasotl before gagging down a fresh dose of the putrid potion. "Good luck."

She shook her hair and closed her eyes. "You too, bro."

I hurried over to Captain Brown, and we followed the guard out of the courtyard and across a plaza to a large pyramidal stone building crafted out of giant blocks with no mortar. The architecture was distinctly Olmec, with a subtle Mayan flavor. Large stone jaguar heads sat around the grounds, and reliefs of feathered serpents had been carved into the walls. This part of the city didn't appear to have seen much fighting, but there were still walls covered in soot from where fires had burned.

The guard led us through the pyramid, passing sentries posted at intervals along the halls and staircases. Eventually we passed through a great arch flanked by more guards and entered a spacious chamber. It was lit by braziers, and at its center sat an old jaguar-man, cross-legged on a cushion. I had only a vague idea of how their species aged, but his dull fur had gone to silver, and most of his rosettes had faded.

<How is your path?> he asked after we seated ourselves.

<It is smooth and untroubled, thanks to the generosity of your tribe, High Elder,> I replied. As always, I interpreted everything into English for the captain's benefit.

He gave a head-bobble. <I have waited many, many long seasons for this meeting.>

<You expected us?> I asked in surprise.

<I have expected you.>

<Was our visit foretold?>

<It is ancient history. We have met before, as we meet now, as we will meet again.>

I glanced at Brown, and he quirked an eyebrow and asked me to clarify.

<We do not understand, High Elder,> I signed. <We do not remember meeting you before.>

<Nor do I, but we *have* met, and will again, forever. Time is one eternal round. Always repeating, unbroken, with no beginning nor

end. This land is in time and yet outside it, like the gods.> He smiled, and I noticed one of his yellowed fangs was broken. <But you have come not to meditate on eternity with an old man, but to seek answers.>

<We have come to seek answers,> I replied in their fashion. They had no word for "yes."

Captain Brown produced the cloth holding the bronze dagger shards and spread it out on the floor.

<Have you seen anything like this before?> I asked.

The high elder squinted at the remains of the dagger. <My eyes… > he signed in apology. <They grow dim.>

He picked up a small bronze bow with two gemstones affixed to it, placed it over his muzzle like spectacles, and peered at the shard again.

"It is a key," he hissed, in the same Mayan dialect that Kiktú had used. His voice was like a dry wind.

He put the shard back down to sign. <A key from ages past to open doors to other lands and realms, when we roamed across all the land, before this place. Thirteen were created, but the Obsidian Jaguar hunted them down one by one. How did you come by this?>

<We do not know its history,> I explained. <It was my wife's, and before that it was in the possession of a giant. How he acquired it, I cannot say. We used it to come to this land. Can it be repaired?>

<Physically, yes, but its power is gone. It will never function as a key again.>

I began to sign, but Brown motioned me to stop. "Ask him how we can get back to the Land of the Black Sun without a portal."

<Without the key to open doors to other places, how might we find our way back to the land we came here from? The Land of the Black Sun?>

<You stepped not through space alone, but out of time and into time and through to a space inside space, a reality coexisting independently from what you perceive as real.>

"A pocket dimension," Brown muttered to himself.

<Are we stuck here then?> I asked. First stuck in whatever world Smoking Mirror brought us to from Earth, and now double stuck in a

"pocket world" inside that world… or something. It was confusing. At least to me. The captain seemed to be following along well enough.

<Not after you find what you seek,> the high elder replied. <It is the key to all doors.>

<The Compass of the Gods?> I asked. <What is it? An artifact? A map? How do we find it?>

<It is hidden away, far from here, protected and safe. The Obsidian Jaguar seeks it, for it is how he reaches across space and time to fetch his playthings to his realm.>

<But if he used it to bring us to the Land of the Black Sun from our world… why doesn't he have it anymore?>

<He has it and yet does not have it. You will find it and lose it to him and he will steal you from your reality to fetch it for him again, as you have done from the beginning and will do forever. All is one eternal round. Unbroken and unbreakable.>

"I'm totally confused, sir," I said to Brown.

He grunted. "It's a bootstrap paradox. Practically a cliché, really. I'll explain later. What matters is the artifact is here and we can use it to get back home. If Smoking Mirror gets ahold of it later and uses it to bring us here in the first place, there's nothing we can do about that. The future has already happened and the past can't be changed. He's an extra-dimensional entity, remember. He exists *outside* space and time."

"I… *really* don't understand."

"You need to read more. It's an overused trope, if you ask me. We need to know where this 'Compass' is. Ask him again."

I turned to the high elder. <High Elder, where will we find the Compass of the Gods, and how do we know what to look for?>

<You will receive it northward of the narrow neck of land, far to the edge of the world, where the last battle of The People takes place and we war one with another to our very extinction. You will find it in that future place of desolation where you have always found it.>

"Now I'm even more confused, sir," I told Brown. "It's hidden in the *future*?"

"I suspect time works in this realm asynchronously," Brown explained. "This battlefield he mentioned is probably an ancient place, and yet also the site of a battle that will happen far in the future. Don't try to think too hard about it. It is what it is. We just gotta roll with it. I'm curious though. Ask him if he has the Compass."

"But he said it's hidden—"

"Just ask him."

I sighed. <Do you have the Compass of the Gods, High Elder?>

<Of course,> he signed. <I will give it to my son who will give it to his, down through the generations, until my descendant will give it to you.>

"What?" I exclaimed, forgetting to sign and that he didn't understand English. "Why the heck can't you just give it to us now?"

"Because, Nephi," Brown said patiently. "If he gave it to us *now*, then he couldn't give it to his son and on down the line until Junior hands it to us. The timeline has already happened. We're just actors on a stage following an eternal script."

"That's like destiny. What about free will?"

"Ask a philosopher."

I gave another deep sigh.

"Can we see it?" Brown asked the high elder, leaving it to me to interpret.

The old jag bobbled his head and reached for a wooden box bound by bronze bands, which he moved in front of him and opened. He lifted a spherical golden object engraved with curious glyphs out of the box and handed it to me. I took it with both hands. It was heavy, about the size of a softball, and appeared to be made of multiple sections like a puzzle box. It glowed faintly with a buttery yellow radiance that seemed to come from within.

"Think we could get out of here with it?" I asked Brown in a low voice. "Maybe Sanchez could infiltrate tonight and steal it."

Brown laughed.

I shrugged. "Just saying."

"Wouldn't work anyway," he said. "Remember, the timeline is fixed. We can't steal it *now* because we get it *later*. Even if we tried, it wouldn't work."

"Well, that sucks. I mean I'm holding it in my hands *right now*."

I gave it back to the high elder with another sigh and signed to ask how it worked. He placed it back in the box.

<That is for you to discover, with the help of the Feathered Serpent, after you receive it.>

<I'm sorry, but I still don't understand how we obtain it exactly.>

<*You*, young man. Only you. *You* will receive it into *your* safekeeping. You will find it, and it will find you.>

<Me?>

"Xochi's vision, son," Brown reminded me.

I groaned. My wife's cryptic vision of me—which she'd had before she even met me—was the reason we were here looking for the artifact in the first place. And she'd said the mission success relied on me. So no pressure.

"Well, at least we know we win," I said.

"No one has said that," Brown corrected me. "Not the high elder, and not Xochi's vision."

"Fine—at least I live long enough to get the Compass. That's encouraging."

"Or you don't, and someone else will take your place in the timeline."

"But you said—"

"Son, you *really* need to read more."

CHAPTER 17

We never got to explore the city, but our hosts let us rest and recuperate for another several days before escorting us to the northern gate and across a wooden walkway that stretched across the lake to the far shore. The farewell wasn't hostile, but it wasn't exactly friendly either. *Perfunctory* might be the right word. They had loaded us up with provisions, though, mostly dried meat cakes similar to Epasotl's pemmican. I tried a bite of one, and while it took some water to get it down, it wasn't all that bad. The small bite felt surprisingly filling, too. They had also given Captain Brown a map painted on a hide that had been scraped until it was paper thin and nearly translucent.

"Copy this map down into your notebooks and memorize it," the captain ordered me and the other NCOs clustered around him on the shore. "Make sure your teams make copies as well. We'll be traveling through this pass to the north"—he looked around to get his bearings, then pointed—"and from there out of the mountains and into this narrow stretch of lowlands skirting between the western ocean and this mountain range here. From there we make for this peninsula here to the northeast. Our objective is a plateau near the eastern coast. There are still scattered bands of marauders, so we need to move cautiously, but once we're out of this valley, the territory all the way to the objective is controlled by the Míchli tribe, so we won't be able to let our guard down for a minute. Except perhaps here." He stabbed his finger down on an isolated valley on the map.

"And what's there?" Takahashi asked.

"Clan Ónik," Brown replied. "They're related to Kiktú's people. I'm hoping they'll be amenable to helping us out a little."

"Helping how, exactly, sir?" García asked.

"We'll need more provisions," Brown answered. "But I'm thinking of mounts, specifically."

"Thunder-stags, sir?" I asked.

"Exactly."

"Wait." García held up his hands. "You mean those weird dinosaurs we saw in the pass? We're going to use those as *mounts*?"

"That's the plan," Brown said.

García made a sour face. He hadn't even been particularly fond of riding *horses*. Wilson, on the other hand, was stoked.

"Bitchin'," he said with a broad grin. "That's *totally* bitchin'."

"Bit of a detour to get to their valley," Brown said, "but worth it if we can procure a faster means of transportation."

"And how far to our final objective?" Takahashi asked. "I'm guessing this map isn't to scale."

"Too many variables to say," Brown answered. "Outside estimate is three months. The jags measure distance in how far they can run in a day. Converting that to miles and how fast we can travel in enemy territory is guesswork at best."

Takahashi pursed his lips. "Is this even doable, sir?"

"Not like we have a choice," Sanchez put in. "This is a no-fail mission. There aren't any alternatives aside from giving up and going native with the jaguar-folk. And that's not happening. The gals need to get back to their people, and I want to go home."

"Point," Takahashi conceded. "Wish we had the motorcycles and dune buggies."

"So do I, Hachirō," Brown said. "But even if we did, I don't see any fuel depots on this map."

"Point again." Takahashi barked a laugh and then frowned. "Still... months deep in enemy territory with no resupply..."

Sanchez shrugged. "Been there, done that. The T-shirt wasn't worth it. It ain't nothing but a thing. Embrace it, son."

Brown grew serious. "Any doubts about the mission end here and now. We can't have griping and second-guessing among the cadre.

You're all leaders, and our men and women need you to project confidence."

"I know that, sir," Takahashi said. "But here and now is when we poke holes in the plan."

"So poke away," the captain said.

"Sir, speaking plainly, you haven't given us anything specific to poke *at* other than the whole plan in general. I know you're acting on limited intel and I'm not criticizing that, but we're not an LRRP unit. Sure, we have you and Doc, and Wilson's a pathfinder, McKenzie's apparently a world-famous explorer we've never heard of, and Sergeant Sanchez's a total recon stud, but the rest of us? The men and women in the platoon? We don't have the training."

"Sure you do," Doc interjected. "What do you think we've been doing since Panama? This has all been one *long* LRRP. Just 'cause you don't have a Ranger tab or been to some special school or whatever doesn't mean you don't have the experience by now to do this job."

"Yeah, why the sudden negative vibes, bro?" Wilson asked.

Takahashi blew out his cheeks and looked at me and García. "Is it just me?"

"Not just you," García admitted.

I won't lie—I was having my own doubts, especially now that I'd been officially given what had been Stanley's team. Cohen wasn't the least bit bent about the demotion; he wasn't leader material yet, and he knew it. I wasn't sure *I* was leader material either, but after I'd stepped up during the ambush, Sanchez had insisted I take the slot.

"I want to see my wife again," I said. "So it doesn't matter if this mission feels impossible. Like Sergeant Sanchez said, it's no-fail. We *have* to succeed, whatever the odds."

"We're almost home," Brown said firmly. He held up his hand, thumb and forefinger slightly apart. "We're *this* close. I'm not giving up. I swore an oath I'd get all you men home. I intend to see that through."

"Not all of us, sir," García said quietly. "We've lost a *lot* of people. We'll lose more." He turned to me. "You want to see your wife? I don't want to see any more of our brothers die. Even if that means I never see my family again."

"Is that what this is about?" Sanchez asked.

García shrugged.

"He's right," Takahashi said. "There aren't many of the original platoon left. We've lost twenty of our brothers already."

"And we almost lost Ross and Cory to some flesh-eating death magic not a few days ago," García added. "And come to find out, four of our lost brothers who turned into psychopathic murderers are now *hunting* us."

We also had one *haunting* us, but I didn't say anything about that. People looked at me weird whenever I mentioned Pierce.

"Let them decide," Brown said.

"Sir?" Sanchez asked.

"Let the boys decide. Ladies too. Anyone wants out, I'm sure we can find a place for them in the city." He thumbed over his shoulder. "It's right there."

"We're gonna break up the band?" Wilson asked, dumbfounded.

"This was an all-volunteer mission," Brown said. "I was clear about that from the start. No pressure, remember? Every one of you had the option to stay back with the Kuauchanejkej refugees and make a life for yourselves there. You *all* elected to come here. And you can choose to stay in this land of mists too. *I'm* getting home to my family. Or die trying. Either way. Those are *my* only options. But you all have a third option, and it's just across that bridge."

Wilson shook his head. "I can't believe we're even discussing this," he said with disgust, and threw an accusing knife hand at Takahashi and García. "You're seriously thinking of giving up and cutting out? Not cool, bros. Not cool at all. No bueno. We came because we thought you were in it to win it. I had a life back there, with Stars."

"We're not giving up or cutting out, Dave," Takahashi said. "All Jesus and I are saying is that we don't want to lose any more people."

"Then turn in your stripes if you can't stomach it," Wilson spat. "I've lost good men too. And women. You think that doesn't keep me up at night?"

Sanchez cleared his throat. "Let's take a walk, Dave."

Takahashi rubbed his face with a palm, and García looked like he wanted to be anywhere but right here, right now. Brown waited until Sanchez and Wilson had left before continuing.

"Speak to your people," he said in a calm voice. "Lay out the options and the risks. Let them decide. But"—he held up a knife hand—"Sergeant Wilson is correct. If the burden of leadership has become too heavy for any of you, you need to be bluntly honest about it with yourselves. And more importantly, with *me*. That is all."

Garcia and Takahashi both nodded and returned to their squads, and Captain Brown strode off with his map and gazed at the mountains, leaving McKenzie and me alone.

"Well, that was a mite awkward, eh?" the big man said, rubbing the back of his neck.

"Could've been worse," I said.

"Cap'n seems like a good sort. Better than a lot of officers. Listens to his NCOs, lets them speak their mind."

"Yeah. I don't think he sleeps much though."

"Good ones never do. Suppose I should talk to the laddies too. Lay it on the line for them."

He gave a mock salute and strode away.

I sighed and trudged up the beach in search of Epasotl. I found her off under a huge dead tree, meditating. There was an array of ingredients spread around her, and the mummified virgin's hand was busy with the mortar and pestle grinding herbs and seeds. I hadn't realized the creepy relic was animated, and did a double-take.

"Am too busy mediating now to make potions, so put Maitl to work," Epasotl said.

"Maitl? You named the hand?"

"She useful. I teach her things. Say hello to Ben-Ette, Maitl."

The blackened hand paused working and gave me the finger.

I rolled my eyes. "Real cute, Eps."

She laughed in her staccato hissing way and stood to stretch.

"How's the meditation going?" I asked.

"So-so. Is hard work, but I have some success with you grandfather ring."

"It works?"

"It works."

I was surprised. I hadn't really expected… but maybe there was some source of truth in those old stories. This was good news. Great news, really.

Although it also meant I wouldn't be getting my grandfather's ring back.

"Can store a little teōtl now with it, not much, more later I hope," Epasotl said. "But I have to weave first. That is the trick."

"I don't understand."

"Cannot store raw teōtl. Must give it shape first, *then* save in ring. Pros and cons."

"How so?"

"When need it, weaving is nearly done, so make magic very fast. That is rad. Bad is I must guess what shape to weave before I need it. So must plan forms of magic in advance. *¿Comprende?*"

"Yeah, I think so. It's like packing for a trip. You gotta figure out what you'll need and hope you're right and don't need something you didn't pack."

"He is smarter than he look, Maitl."

The hand gave a thumbs-up and returned to grinding.

"That hand's hella creepy, by the way."

"You said same thing about Atzi, and now you friends."

"True. Where is she anyway?"

"With Pierce. They talk often."

"Oh yeah, I've been wondering where he's been, too. What do they talk about?"

"I no know. He dead and she rain spirit. Who can say?"

"Captain was thinking he might not be, you know, *him*. Like he might be an entity pretending to be him."

Epasotl shrugged. "Could be. Spirits like play games."

"But Atzi thinks it's really him?"

"So she say. Maybe he fool her too. Spirits not so smart."

"Hmph. I dunno. I mean, he knows everything Pierce would know. It sure seems like it's really him."

"Cannot say." She shrugged. "Him, not him, I am not much worried."

"What if it's an evil spirit?"

"Only few spirits really evil. Most spirits just spirits. Play games. Sometimes play tricks. But spirit-Pierce made friends with you. That is good. No nasty tricks. He is helpful. That is good mojo. Is cool. Besides, maybe he is dead bro after all. That would be dope. Ah, here they come now."

I turned and caught sight of Pierce and Atzi coming out of the forest. The floating infant's skull bobbed along, wreathed in blue flame and giggling.

"Hey, man," I said to Pierce. "Whatcha up to?"

"Atzi's been teaching me how to manifest," he replied. "You know, become visible to other people. Not just you."

"Is it working?"

"I think so. Let's try it on Eps."

"Sure." I turned to Epasotl and thumbed over to Pierce. "He thinks he's figured out a way for you to see him."

She nodded and looked in the direction I'd indicated. Pierce crouched down in front of her, squinted, and held his breath. Several long seconds passed, and then Epasotl jumped back a pace, her ears flat against her head.

"Warn first," she hissed.

"What?" I said. "I did warn you."

"You not say he ugly son of a bitch. Sorry, I startled." She smoothed back her hair and motioned in Pierce's general direction. "Try again."

Pierce shrugged and held his breath.

Epasotl cocked her head. "Pierce, you ghost is… super grody. So sorry."

"What does he look like?" I asked. "He looks like Pierce to me."

"Me too! Me too!" Atzi twittered.

"Look dead," Epasotl said. "Like very, very dead."

Pierce exhaled. "I was hoping to surprise Falling Leaves."

"Whatever you do, do *not* do that," Epasotl said emphatically. "She scream and shoot you."

"Aw, man. Being dead sucks big, sweaty, hairy, diseased donkey balls. I'll never get laid again!"

"Wait," I said. "You can *hear* him, Eps?"

She scrunched up her nose. "Still see him too. Is super gnarly in bad way. Gag with spoons. Happy can not smell him."

I laughed. "I didn't think anything could gross you out."

"When is bloated rotting corpse of friend with maggot in mouth and eye, yes. Big-time grody."

"Sorry, man," I said to Pierce. "Maybe you need to work on manifesting more. You still look like you to me and Atzi, for what it's worth."

"Yeah, but I don't want to put the sweet moves on you or Atzi."

"Maybe Leaves will love you anyway."

"Doubt it," Epasotl said.

"Maybe we need to ease into this," I said. "You could try manifesting to the captain."

"Worth a shot," Pierce agreed.

***

Captain Brown didn't even raise an eyebrow. He simply nodded.

"I see him."

"Does he look, like, you know, *Pierce*?" I asked.

"Not really."

"What then, sir?"

"Like a body in an advanced stage of decomposition."

Pierce swore.

"Can you still see him?" I asked Brown.

"Yup. Heard him, too. Well, at least we know you weren't hallucinating him. He looks normal to you though?"

"Yeah." I gestured at Pierce. "I mean, he looks like he always looked. Totally not rotting. Very alive. About five-eleven, dark brown complexion, lady-killer mustache—"

"Solid six feet, bro," Pierce corrected me.

"Five-eleven, tops."

"Interesting," Brown said.

"Six," Pierce hissed at me.

I held my hand flat, palm down. "Maybe five-ten."

"*You're* five-ten, bro! I'm a good two inches taller than your short ass. Maybe three."

"You two done?" Brown asked.

"Sorry, sir," we said in unison.

"I don't recommend manifesting to anyone else, okay, son?" Brown said. "Especially not your girlfriend."

"You told Cap'n about Leaves and me?" Pierce asked me, looking betrayed.

Brown laughed. "I knew about you two before either of *you* did. It's sort of my job."

"Oh," Pierce muttered.

"Can you do anything else?" Brown asked. "Manipulate the material realm?"

"A little, sir. I've been practicing. I can throw pebbles and stuff a few feet."

"Keep practicing." Brown folded his arms and cocked his head to the side. "Keep me in the loop with your progress."

"Will do, sir."

Brown looked Pierce up and down, then grimaced. "And *definitely* don't go manifesting to your girlfriend."

CHAPTER 18

To a woman, the gals protested even the suggestion of anyone staying back in the jag city. They'd all volunteered for this mission because they felt honor-bound to help us after we'd destroyed the soul forge and saved their people from being sacrificed to it, and their conviction hadn't wavered in the slightest.

"Death comes for all," Flaming Feather had said, speaking passionately. "Let us meet it with weapon in hand, and if we fall, then we fall in honor. I would rather die for my sisters and brothers today than grow old knowing I had abandoned them. Who could live with such shame?"

"My elder sister speaks true," said Dressed-in-Stars. "But we are bound by more than duty and honor only. We are no longer Outworlder and Kuauchanejkej, but one people, one family, our bond forged in blood when we fought back to back in the Underworld. Our destinies and our lives are entwined. It is a bond of love."

"*Maiorem hac dilectionem nemo habet ut animam suam quis ponat pro amicis suis,*" First-to-Dance quoted softly.

The gals echoed a reverent "Amen." Brown was nodding, and several of us guys looked to him questioningly.

He simply answered, "John 15:13."

"Hooah to that," Sanchez muttered.

Wilson and a few others turned to me to supply the verse in English.

"Greater love hath no man than this," I recited, "that a man lay down his life for his friends."

García put his head in his hands and sighed.

Silence hung over the assembled platoon for several minutes as we listened to bird calls from the forest, and the lake water lapping the shore. I half expected Brown to say something like we wouldn't fault anyone for staying behind or think them a coward, but he didn't, because that wasn't true. We would, and everyone knew it. We'd been through hell together, literally and figuratively. To abandon the mission now... to give up... I could hardly comprehend it. And I didn't even need to be here. I wasn't trying to get back to Earth. My home was with Xochi. I had come for *them*. Because they were my brothers.

"If anyone stays behind," Cohen finally said, "you'll come back for them, right, sir?"

The anger hit me so fast I had to literally bite my tongue. I tasted blood and clenched my fists. Come back? For men who wouldn't see it through? Come back for someone who'd sit back while others took the risks? I looked around and could tell Sanchez and a few others were feeling the same as me.

But the captain was completely calm when he answered Cohen. "That's not a promise I can make, son. Anyone stays here, it's likely for good. I can promise I'll try, but I can't promise anything more."

I ground my teeth. That was a hell of a lot more than I'd promise a deserter. Harsh? Maybe. But that's all I could feel in the moment. I had a wife—who might even be pregnant—and I didn't *need* to be here in the first place, dammit.

Brown slapped his thighs and stood. "Think it over. You have an hour. Daylight's burning, and we need to Charlie Mike. Come see me if you want to talk through it. My door's always open. You know that."

Wilson clapped me on the back after the captain had left the circle. "You good, bro?"

"I'll be fine."

He dropped his voice. "Because you look like you're about to murder Cohen."

"I'll be fine."

"Don't bullshit me, bro. You mad? Good. So am I. But if you go kinetic on Cohen or anyone else, I'm gonna have to knock you on your ass and keep you there."

"Not so sure you could anymore," I said with a thin smile.

"Point," he said after considering it for a long moment. "But Sanchez still could. That wiry old hobbit could put down a damned Balrog."

I laughed. "Thanks."

"For what?"

"Being you. I'll be fine, really. Just need to walk off some steam."

"Want company?"

"Nah, Sarge. It's cool."

"Don't 'Sarge' me, man. We're bros. Screw rank."

"You don't say that when Sanchez is handing out work details."

"Can you blame me?"

"Nope."

"Don't wander far."

"I won't."

***

I kept close to the assembly area, but I didn't want to see who might need to have a chat with the captain. Instead Pierce and I skipped rocks in the lake and chatted about everything and nothing. Mostly nothing. Books. Music. Old girlfriends. Movies. Stuff I'd almost forgotten about. It made me a little homesick to be back in what the guys called *the real world*. But then I thought about Xochi. She was *my* world. My reality. She and the family we were going to have. Might already have.

"You got quiet fast," Pierce said. "Thinking about your girl?"

"Yeah."

"Why didn't you stay back with her?"

"You know why."

"I know what you say, but is that the *real* reason? Did you *really* want to come on this mission?"

I thought about it for a minute. "Honestly?"

"Duh."

"No."

He skipped a rock. "So if it wasn't for duty and honor and brotherhood and all that jazz, why'd you sign up for this?"

"It sounds stupid."

"Try me."

I shrugged. "It's my destiny. I didn't have a choice."

"Xochi's vision," Pierce stated.

"Yeah."

"But you *did* have a choice."

"I don't think I did." I gazed toward the city. "The high elder said time is a circle; the future's already happened. I've been here before, and I'll be here again. Forever."

"'All the world's a stage, and all the men and women merely players.' You believe that shit's literal?"

"I didn't before. I don't know now. Maybe free will is a lie we tell ourselves so everything doesn't seem pointless."

"Bullshit. Listen, man. You know what my dad said about fate and free will? He said life's like a game of cards. The hand you're dealt is fate; the way you play it is free will. You made a choice, and I think you're bullshitting yourself if you say it *wasn't* because of duty and honor and brotherhood. All that jazz. I know you. You're that kind of guy. Xochi's vision foretold what *you* chose to do. You follow me?"

"Sorta." I picked up a rock, tossed it away, and picked another, running my thumb along the edge. "I'm no hero, Stanford."

"That's the biggest load of bullshit I've heard yet come out of your mouth."

"Really, I'm not. Even if I made a choice and it was for all the 'right' reasons, I didn't want to do it. I don't want to be here. Everything I've done in my life has been for duty or whatever you want to call it. Because I thought it was what I was supposed to do. Because it was the 'right' thing. I hated Boy Scouts. I didn't want to leave my girlfriend and spend two years in Mexico having doors slammed in my face while she ran off and married my best friend. I didn't want to take care of my mom when she was sick and my friends were going out. I didn't even want to enlist. But my dad and grandpa served, and it was my turn, so I did." I skipped the rock hard, watching it bound across the glassy water. The ripples spread out, intersecting until I couldn't tell where one ended and another began. "I'm a *fraud*, Stanford. I'm pissed at the idea of any of the guys abandoning us, but I'm no better than them. Not really."

"You don't get it, do you? *That's* what makes you a hero, Nephi. Because you do the right thing even if you don't want to. Not wanting to means you're human. Doing it *anyway* makes you a man. That's why my dad was always riding my ass. Because I did what I wanted instead of what I should. I see that now. Now that I'm dead, of course. Don't sell yourself short, Nephi. Living a life of doing what needs to be done is a whole lot more fulfilling than chasing what you think you want. My dad said that too. I wish I'd listened."

"Why'd *you* enlist?"

"Honestly? G.I. Bill, plus my recruiter said chicks dig the uniform."

I laughed. "How'd that work out for you?"

"Actually pretty good, until I got killed saving your ass in Hell. I'll never go to college. My mom will be pissed."

"Yeah, about that. Thanks."

"No sweat. I'd do it again."

"Really?"

"Probably not."

"Jerk."

"Asshole."

I caught movement on the walkway stretching across the lake from the shore to the city. "Cap'n's walking someone to the gates. I think... dang. It's Cameron."

"Holy shit, it is."

"Wow. I figured on Cohen, after that remark. Anderson, maybe. Lawrence wouldn't have *totally* shocked me. But Cameron..."

Pierce shrugged. "You just never can tell."

***

Cameron choosing to stay in Chlǔmpu with the jaguar-men, perhaps permanently, wasn't the biggest shock of the day, however.

García had turned in his stripes.

"He did what?" I asked Wilson.

"Had a long chat with Brown and Sanchez. Handed his rank over."

"So… what's he now?"

"Spec Five, apparently."

"Is that even a thing?"

"Used to be. Sanchez is bringing it back."

"What's happening to Blue Squad now?"

"Flaming Feather will be acting SL, with García in an advisory role. Stars and Touchdown are making up one of the crews, with García and Kiktú on the other. Heart-of-Darkness keeps the Carl G and will be wherever she's needed."

"Touchdown? Who's that?"

"What rock have you been living under? Anderson. We've been calling him that for ages."

"Why Touchdown?"

"Well, you know. Kid's got a touch of the Downs if you ask me. Not all there."

I didn't much care for that—one of my cousins had Down syndrome, and he was just about the nicest person I've ever known—but I let it pass. Being offensive in the platoon was like water to a fish—the stuff you breathed. "Is Kiktú good with this?"

Wilson pointed over to where the jaguar-woman was squatting with García next to a M240B. "Oh yeah. She's stoked to be a gunner."

I watched García running her through the manual of arms for the weapon. García was using a lot of pantomime to communicate, but he was going to have to bite the bullet and drink the brain potion if he really wanted to be able to speak with her.

"He looks… happy," I said.

"Weight off his shoulders. Being an NCO isn't for everyone. Speaking of, you'd better get to your team, bro. We're settin' to move out."

My team.

Cohen, Lawrence, and First-to-Dance. I joined them and made sure everyone was squared away. Not that I really had to, but it seemed like a good idea to go through the motions. Give speeches about hydration. Slap shoulders and mag pouches. Project confidence. That sort of thing.

I'd sort of helped lead a rifle team before and… well, hopefully this time would go better.

Sanchez gave the order to move out, and we entered the forest, McKenzie and his lads forming a screen on our front and flanks. My team was the trail element, and I gave Chlŭmpu a last look before the trees closed around us and blocked the view.

And I wondered if we'd ever see Specialist Cameron again.

CHAPTER 19

It took three days of hard marching through the thick jungle surrounding Chlůmpu to reach the foothills and the northward pass; going forward we'd be entering enemy-held territory. We came across a few burned-out villages and farmsteads along the way, but encountered only one band of marauders. The skirmish was brief and one-sided, hardly worth mentioning, and the jags broke contact quickly. Whatever bands might still be in the valley, it was apparent word had spread about the war party of hairless walking monkeys and their thunder-rods, and hostile forces seemed to be actively avoiding us. That was the good news. The bad news was that if rumor of us was spreading, it would attract the attention of our former platoon-mates, who apparently were trying to track us down and kill us... aided by whatever death-touched friends they'd brought with them to this realm of perpetual mist.

Captain Brown kept us busy in our spare time crafting and training on "new" weapons. And by new, I mean old. "Our ammo won't last forever," he'd told us. "So best start familiarizing yourselves with Stone Age weapons now, because that's what it's gonna come down to before the op is over: sticks and stones and real harsh language."

Me and a bunch of the gals were tasked with fletching arrows and carving spear throwers—also known as atlatls. An atlatl is a simple tool about as long as your forearm with a cup or spur at one end that holds the butt of the spear. You hold it at the farthest end from the cup and cast overhand, and the leverage from the thrower launches the spear at a far higher velocity than you'd get without it. It's a primitive tool found in various forms across many cultures—and worlds, apparently; the Chaneques had used them against us, as did the giants we'd encountered on the plains—but it's highly effective. I was put on atlatl-carving duty after I made the mistake of mentioning that I'd learned how to make and use them way back in Boy Scouts. Me and my brothers had spent more than a few summers running around in the woods casting spears at each other until my dad got sick of trips to the ER. But I did bag a rabbit once with an atlatl from fifty yards, so that was cool.

I was also "volunteered" to assist with archery training. I was decent with a bow, thanks again to General Baden-Powell, but the only bow we had on hand was Kiktú's huge monstrosity, and it turned out only McKenzie, Wilson, and Brown were strong enough to draw it. She ended up making smaller versions for others to practice with.

The gals were familiar with spear throwers already, and highly skilled in their use. Bows were a new concept, but they took to it right away. In turn they introduced us to the bola, a weapon consisting of several balls connected by strong cord, used for entangling opponents.

The lizardmen had no interest in archery, but they had Stone Age weapons of their own, including one of the most primitive, simple, and yet effective ranged weapons in human history: the sling.

The lads were scary accurate with slings.

They also had blowguns fashioned out of reeds, and thin darts they coated with some kind of paralyzing neurotoxin. It had been one of those darts that had taken me down and led to my capture by the lizardmen originally.

But of all the primitive ranged weapons, the bow was probably the most effective, and we also judged it the easiest to learn, relatively, so the guys and gals who showed aptitude would be focusing primarily on archery.

When I asked Takahashi if he could help with the training, he just laughed. "Sure, because all Japanese people know how to shoot a bow, right? I don't have a clue. Never studied Kyūdō."

But to everyone's surprise, Anderson had. And Cohen had grown up recurve bow hunting with his uncle, so between them, Kiktú, and myself, we had a cadre of capable instructors already.

What we needed more of was time. Most people spend a lifetime acquiring the skill; we had only until our ammo ran out. And then the greatest advantage we had in this world—our firearms—would be worthless.

Bows, slings, and spears. Things were about to get savage.

***

The evening of our fourth day since departing the city found us high in the northward pass. It had rained earlier in the day, and a heavy mist hung in the treetops, giving everything a gloomy, spectral feel. Kinda creepy, to be honest. It was cooler at the higher altitude, and the humidity was less oppressive, as were the biting insects, which was a welcome relief to everyone.

We'd formed our assembly area under an overhanging wall of rock that jutted out from the side of a cliff, and Cohen and I had just wrapped up running Gold Squad through an hour of archery practice.

I massaged my shoulder as we strolled back to our rucks.

"Sergeant Wilson's not doing too bad," Cohen said. "But I think Taks is focusing too hard on aiming."

"Maybe you need to tell him to be more zen," I joked.

"Right. He'd twist me up in a pretzel. Dance and Jade are naturals though."

"Yeah, they're picking it up surprisingly fast. Short Round shows some potential. Leaves, not so much."

"Or Tears," Cohen said. "She's struggling."

"It's only been a couple days though. Too soon to tell."

"Oh yeah, totally."

"How long you been doing this?" I asked.

"My whole life, basically. Got my first bow when I was eight. Bagged my first deer at thirteen. Biggest thing I've scored was a bear. That was the season before I shipped off to OSUT."

"A bear? Seriously?"

"Just a black bear, but yeah."

"That's impressive."

"Spent three days on that stalk." He took off his boonie and ran a hand through his shock of pure white hair, courtesy of the ghosts who'd attacked him back in the ancient abandoned jag city we'd found. He'd been blinded then too, temporarily. And then had his ear cut off by a Chaneque commando. Doc had sewn it back on, but it looked rough even now, months later. The kid had been through a lot, come to think of it. "That was a good trip. I love Montana. Ross and I are planning a hunting trip when we get back to the real world. He—" Cohen cut himself off. "Well, guess that won't be happening."

"You and Cameron were pretty tight, huh?"

"We were the last Spec Fours in the platoon. E4 Mafia gotta stick together, you know?"

"Why'd he... do you know why he chose to stay behind?"

"That whole flesh-eating magic thing was the last straw, I think. He was just... done. I mean, he didn't say that, but... I could see it. I know you guys think he's a coward and a deserter or something, but it's not like that at all. He just couldn't go on."

"He's definitely not a coward. Doesn't he have anyone to go home to?"

"Not really. He's an only child, and his parents are divorced. Mom's batshit crazy and dad's a drunk. I don't think he has any other family."

"No girl?"

"Guy in his case, but no. And I didn't say that. Don't ask, don't tell, right?"

"Doesn't matter to me. Ross is a stud. He was the last person I expected to stay behind."

"Figured *I* would, huh?"

"Honestly? You or Anderson."

"Captain squared me away. Besides, I have family to go home to. And a girl."

"You got a girl?"

"Don't have to sound so surprised, man. Yeah, I got a girl. Fiancée, actually, kinda." He fingered his scarred ear. "If she still wants me."

"'Course she will," I said. "Chicks dig battle damage."

"You think Captain would leave Ross behind if this works and we figure out a way home?"

"No. Absolutely not. He'll come back for him if he can find a way. Trouble is"—I spread my hands—"we just don't know how this'll all work in the end."

Cohen shook his head. "The thing that sucks is, I *know* Ross will come around and regret it sooner or later, probably sooner, but now he's stuck here. Maybe forever. I tried to talk him out of it... but it was like he was already dead on the inside, you know? He just... shut down."

"Captain won't go home without him, Tim. Not unless something prevents it. And then he'd probably blow his way through that to get him out anyway."

Cohen sighed and flopped down on his ruck. "I'm beat. What's the watch schedule?"

"Dance and I have first watch. Grab something to eat and then get some sleep. We'll wake you and Lawrence when it's your turn." I looked around. "Where are they anyway?"

"They joined up with Blue Squad to practice some more."

"They've been spending a lot of time together."

"Well, sure. We're a team. We're supposed to be tight."

"Think that's all it is?"

Cohen laughed around a mouthful of dried meat cake. He swallowed and grinned. "Like you're one to talk."

"Is that a yes?"

"Dude, they're *friends*."

"You'd tell me if there was anything going on though, right? You're my ATL."

"Sure thing, Corporal." He snapped a mock salute. "I'll keep an eye on them. Like a hawk."

"Mmhmm." I was going to have to ask one of the other NCOs about managing a coed team. And how not to come off as a colossal hypocrite doing it. That was going to be tricky. Xochi might be the crown princess of her tribe and no longer a member of the platoon, *and* my wife, but it hadn't always been that way. I gave a mental shrug and strolled off to find Epasotl before my watch began.

***

I found Epasotl's stuff, but no Epasotl. The mummified virgin's hand was energetically grinding ingredients into a foul-smelling paste and paused to give me the finger as I approached. I was going to have to talk to Epasotl about that before the hand flipped off Sanchez or the captain.

"Uh, hi, Maitl." Talking to a desiccated hand was weird, to say the least. "You, uh, know where Eps is?"

The hand gave a thumbs-up and then pointed off into the forest.

"Uh, thanks."

Maitl flashed a shaka sign and then went back to work.

I followed the direction indicated and found Epasotl in a small, mist-draped clearing. She was standing motionless, staring at a log a few yards away from her.

I cleared my throat.

"Wait one," she said without looking back at me. She stretched out her hand and flexed her fingers.

"*Xia!*" she yowled.

A lash of lightning energy struck out from her fingertips, entangling the log and wrenching it violently toward her at a high velocity. When it neared her, there was a blinding flash and thunderclap and the log exploded in a spray of rotten fragments across the clearing.

She danced around in a circle. Her hair was standing on end and smoking a little.

"You see that, Ben-Ette?"

"Yeah," I said, brushing rotten wood pulp off my ACUs. "New trick?"

"Is totally rad," she said.

"You're like Wonder Woman."

"Who?"

"Superhero. She's got this magical lasso. Well, except it doesn't blow stuff up; it makes people tell the truth."

"Lame. I not like Wonder Woman at all."

"Yeah. Bad comparison."

"Blowing stuff up is tubular."

"Got me there."

"You not seem stoked."

"What?"

"New trick is rad but you not stoked."

"I'm totally stoked about your new trick."

She wrinkled her nose and squinted. "You are sick? I make potion. You feel better. Come."

"No, I'm not sick. Just wanted to say hi before I go on watch."

She shook her head and put her hands on her hips. "What is up?"

"I dunno."

"All men same. Human. Chaneque. 'I dunno.' Bah! Come. Sit. Talk to bro." She sat on the ground and patted next to her. "Doctor is in. Five cents."

I sat down beside her and sighed.

After a few minutes, she tapped my knee. "Talk to me."

"Why… why are you here, Eps?"

"Why here in clearing? To practice weaving."

"No, *here*, in this place, with us. Why'd you come on this mission?"

"You go, I go."

"Because you still think you're my slave? Because I captured you."

She gave a hissing laugh. "That dumb Chaneque custom. Is stupid. They say I dead because captured. Now they say I live because survived Underworld and make magic. Honor restored. Stupid. Does not even make sense." She tapped my chest and then hers. "You go, I go."

"But you don't owe me anything. You could've gone back to your people. Your family."

"Platoon my people now. All bros. Better than family. And you, you more than family. More than bro. You, me, we are bound." She wrapped two fingers around each other. "You go, I go. You stay, I stay. See? Question I think you ask not why I go, but why *you* go? Why leave mate? Xochi."

"Yeah."

"So? Why?"

"Because it's my duty. They're my brothers. Because they can't go home without my help."

"Duty?"

"Yeah, duty. Because it's the right thing. It's the honorable thing. I always do the right thing, even if I don't want to. Even if I resent it. I've made a lot of sacrifices for people because it's my duty."

"Like who?"

"Like... like my mom when she was sick. I missed out on a lot taking care of her."

"You angry at mother?"

"Not *angry*, but... sometimes I guess I resent her for it? That sounds pretty horrible, doesn't it."

"Hmm. Maybe."

"Ugh."

She tapped my knee again. "Ben-Ette, I have news flash for you."

"What?"

"You not perfect! Problem is you think you should be. Nothing perfect. Not people, not gods, not anything."

"Pretty sure God is perfect."

"Are you God?"

"Not even close."

"Then cut you some slacks. Listen." She got up on her knees and looked me straight in the eye. "You think you a bad person?"

I nodded.

"Bad persons not care. You care. You not bad person. But I not think you do what is right for duty or honor. I not think you leave mate and come here for brothers for that. You not take care of mother for that. You not do anything for that—no, do not shake head, Ben-Ette! Listen!" She held a slender finger in front of my face.

"You not driven by honor. Not by duty. Not by what people think of you." She stabbed my chest hard. "You driven by *love*."

"Love?"

"Yes. Love. You taught me love. You love everyone. Yes. Do not shake head! Yes, everyone. You have much love. Too much sometimes. But that is why where you go, I go. Because you love even dead Chaneque girl with no honor. And *I* love *you*. Oh, do not make sour face. No mean *mating* love. No mean *hots*. Gag with spoons! You have nasty mind sometimes. Bag you face, Ben-Ette."

I held up my hands. "I wasn't thinking that, I swear."

She punched my chest. "Do not make jokes when I serious about heart-things."

"I'm sorry. I love you too. Like a sister. The best sister I never had."

"I know." She wiped her eyes. I'd never seen her cry before, not even when her village was burned and her people slaughtered. "Now give you sister hug."

She wrapped her thin little arms around me, and I embraced her, awkwardly at first, surprised by how tiny and frail she felt. She always seemed larger than life, but she was really a very small creature, no bigger than a young child. She squeezed me fiercely for a minute and then pushed me away, drying her eyes again.

"If you tell Broski about heart-things and cry, I cut off you skin with dull knife and make woobie," she sniffed.

"I won't tell Wilson, or anyone else. I swear." I gave her bony little shoulders another squeeze. "Thanks for the talk, sis."

"It help?"

"Yeah, it helped."

"Good. You still owe me five cents." She wiped a tear from my cheek. "Chaneque no cry. Only cubs. Is dishonor. Human cry drop of pants."

"Hat. Drop of a hat."

"Whatever. You have to watch, no? Go now. Leave sister in shame for cry and speak of heart-things."

"Nothing shameful about that," I said. "That's a stupid custom too."

"Anyway now you know." She patted her heart and then mine. "I love you. You love me. You heart, my heart. You go, I go. But now you go, I stay. Hurry, or Little Kahuna grab you ass."

"*Kick* my… never mind." I looked around the darkening clearing. "Be safe."

"Is cool, I have many traps. Oh! No worry, Ben-Ette! They know you friend."

"You sure? What kind of traps?"

"Mean and nasty, like me." She bared her needle teeth. "Now get lost."

CHAPTER 20

The huge jag rushed us, cough-barking a deep roar that shook my rib cage. I was swinging Sybil around, wondering if I'd be able to stop him with the one shot I'd manage to get off if I was lucky, when I heard Epasotl yowl and a whip of pure energy lashed out, entangling him and pulling him right off his feet. He flew through the air past me, the tether of blue lightning crackling, and dropped in a heap before her. She laughed maniacally and pounced on him, driving her knife deep into the back of his head.

"Never mind the light show, Short Round!" Cohen yelled to Lawrence. "Get me some supportive fire on that bunch of archers!"

"Hooah!" Lawrence shouted back, hunching behind his Mark 48 machine gun. He squeezed off a long burst as I sprinted behind him, the hiss of arrows slicing past my head.

I dove for cover and rolled up beside First-to-Dance. She ducked below the log she was behind as a sickly green bolt struck it, splashing over our heads.

"You good?" I asked.

She nodded and set her mouth in a firm line.

"Get me a round of AB to your twelve-thirty." I paused to do a quick calculation in my head. Sixty-five meters would be about... "Twenty-six land rods."

"Hooah, Corporal!" She pulled an M397 grenade from her bandoleer and loaded it in the launcher mounted under her rifle, set the leaf sight for the range I'd called, and then popped up over the log and fired before taking cover again.

I poked my head up and watched the grenade hit the ground in front of a vaguely man-shaped writhing void in space. An instant later the air burst detonated and the nothingness imploded into itself.

"Sunfire, Longshot," I transmitted. "Deadhead Charlie down." I clapped Dance on the shoulder. "Good shooting."

"Roger," Takahashi replied. "Havok is dealing with Deadhead Alpha. Swing your team right and see if you can't take down Tree-Hugger Bravo. Should be on your two, forty meters."

We'd so far identified and tagged two distinct types of Unmakers, as Kiktú called the spellcasters among the worshippers of the Obsidian Jaguar: Deadheads, who Captain Brown said were necromancers, and Tree-Huggers, who were some kind of twisted druid-slash-shaman dudes. Both were bad news.

"Roger, Sunfire. Mystique, Longshot. Moving my team to known point Golf-Echo."

"Roger, Longshot," Flaming Father responded. "Will cover your move."

Dance was firing over the log, and I reached up to tap her shoulder. "Moving," I said. "On me."

We sprinted over to Cohen and Lawrence, and I squeezed Cohen's shoulder. He gave me a thumbs-up and then I took off with Dance, moving into position, and covered Cohen and Lawrence as they bounded past while García and Kiktú's two-forty chattered away, clearing our new front.

The jag druid was about forty meters away, advancing through the jungle with a guard of three spearmen, casting a screen of fog before him from a bushel of branches. He seemed to be wearing some sort of skin-tight bark armor—or maybe his skin *was* bark— and 7.62 didn't seem to do anything but annoy him.

Lawrence lit them up, taking out two of the spearmen, and the druid stretched out his hand toward us. The ground began to shake under me and then Cohen and Lawrence's position erupted in a fountain of earth and rock like it'd been hit with an artillery strike. Dance and I hugged the ground as clods of earth and stones rained down.

"Longshot, Mystique. We lost Tree-Hugger Bravo in the fog. Do you have eyes on the target?"

"Wait one," I replied, lifting my head and peering into the thick haze rolling over our position. "Negative, Mystique. Switching to thermal."

I dug into my assault pack and fished out my thermal monocular, affixing it in front of my scope as Dance snapped off shots into the fog. Getting to one knee, I shouldered Sybil and got a bead on the druid, only to have my sight picture blocked by something.

I was cursing and trying to reacquire my target when a shadow resolved in the fog, materializing in front of us as a large feral dog with glowing red eyes. It leapt it me, barking and slavering, but Dance was faster and tackled it, crashing off to the side and rolling through the underbrush, her shrieking war cry piercing the cacophony of battle. Wherever that dog had come from, it didn't look natural, and I remembered Epasotl's warning that casters could summon *things*, and the best way to defeat them was to kill the summoner.

Spellcasters were Priority One targets, no matter what else was going on.

Snapping Sybil back to my shoulder, I danced my scope back and forth until I caught the big light-on-dark image of the druid closing on us in my thermal scope. Steadying myself, I took a breath and then squeezed smoothly, feeling the trigger break and Sybil slam against the pocket of my shoulder. Racking the bolt, I loaded another round and followed the blurry shape of the great jag as he fell headless to the ground.

"This is Longshot. Tree-Hugger Bravo down. I've lost—my whole team."

First-to-Dance emerged from the undergrowth with her rifle dangling from its sling and holding a bloody bronze tomahawk.

"Correction, Gold One-Two and One-Three MIA."

She shoved her hatchet in her belt and snatched up her rifle, getting down beside me and breathing heavily.

"You good?" I asked her. "Injured?"

She shot me a thumbs-up and scanned the dissipating fog through her sights.

"Cover me," I told her. "I'm going to look for Cohen and Lawrence."

An arrow hissed past, and Dance snapped off a shot that dropped an archer edging toward us. "Hooah, Corporal."

"How's your ammo?"

"Yellow all around."

"They get too curious about us, don't wait for me. Just lob AB at 'em until they lose interest."

She grinned, her golden eyes sparkling. "Hooah!"

I sprinted over the rocky, uneven ground and jumped into the crater that had formed at my other teammates' position. Lawrence was sitting against one wall, caked in dirt and looking dazed. I dashed over to him and started patting him down for blood.

"How's it going, Isaiah? You with me?"

"Where the hell are we?"

"Nowhere good. You hurt?"

"Ribs are critical, dog. Got a wack hangover."

"Where's your weapon?"

"Dunno."

"You seen Tim?"

"Dunno."

I called for Doc on the radio as I finished checking Lawrence over. "You're not bleeding, so that's the good news. Probably have a concussion. Doc's on the way. Just lie back and take it easy." I considered giving him his sidearm but didn't want him shooting Doc. "Just hang tight for a minute, okay?"

"Yeah, I'm just gonna chill."

I scrambled up the other side of the crater, lifted my head to check for hostiles, and then rolled over the rim. Huge dirt clods and rocks the size of basketballs littered the forest floor, crushing the undergrowth. As I scuttled through the churned-up earth, I heard a *thunk* followed by a distant explosion and then screaming jags. I smiled. At least Dance was holding down the fort all right.

It took a few minutes before I found Cohen's hand. It was sticking out of a pile of dirt and stone, and I began digging, scooping earth and rock like a dog, terrified his hand would be *all* I found. But slowly his arm emerged, and then a shoulder, and then I was pulling him free and checking his vitals: a faint pulse, but not breathing. I had to scoop dirt out of his mouth before I could start on getting him breathing again, but after a long tense minute, he coughed violently and rolled over onto his side, moaning.

I told him to hang in there and radioed that I'd found him as I patted him down for blood and checked his limbs for any obvious breaks. I'd been calm throughout, but now that the worst was over, my heart was thudding in my chest and I felt a strange sense of vertigo.

"Short Round?" Cohen croaked.

"Dazed, but alive and in one piece."

"Dance?"

There was another *thunk* followed by a boom and more cat-man screaming over the sound of small arms fire.

"She's good," I said.

"We get hit by arty or something?"

"Something. Can you move? We're too exposed here."

"Yeah, sure. God. Feels like something chewed me up and spit me out. Where's my weapon?"

"Still attached to your sling."

"Ah, cool."

I helped him into a crouch, and we duck-walked to the crater and slid down to the bottom. Doc was there, shining a penlight into Lawrence's eyes.

"How is he?" I asked.

"Major concussed, but he has all his fingers and toes and I don't think there's any internal bleeding. Cohen?"

"Okay, far as I can tell. You'll want to check. He wasn't breathing. Got buried alive under a ton of dirt. You good here, Doc? I gotta get back to Dance."

"Right as rain."

"Hooah." I crawled out of the crater, checked for bad guys, and then sprinted back to First-to-Dance.

"Miss anything?" I asked, clapping her on the shoulder.

Her head lolled back and she slumped against me. An arrow protruded from her chest, just above her plate carrier, which was drenched in blood.

Cursing, I laid her out and ripped open a field dressing, wrapping it around the arrow shaft and applying pressure as I called for Doc. She had a pulse, but it was extremely weak, and there wasn't much more I could do but keep more blood from pumping out of the wound.

Something hit me hard just under my right armpit, and I felt an intense burning sensation radiating from the inside of my chest. The arrow was still quivering when I looked down to see what had hit me. Then I looked up and saw the archer not twenty meters away, drawing another arrow back.

It was all slow motion: him drawing, releasing, the arrow floating toward me. I could see every detail of the barbed bronze arrowhead and the colorful fletching. I wondered what kind of bird the feathers came from. The archer was already drawing yet another arrow before the previous one hit my right arm, punched through, and embedded itself in my side, pinning my arm in place.

A haggard, gasping roar erupted from somewhere deep inside me, and I awkwardly drew my sidearm with my off hand, pivoted, and lined up the sights.

The third arrow hit my left shoulder, tearing straight through the muscle and sinew, and my shot went wide. Somehow I managed to correct my aim despite my shattered shoulder and rapidly tunneling vision, and started squeezing off rounds. The slide locked back, but I kept pulling that trigger until the jag finally fell.

I wheezed again, finding it hard to breathe, dropped my pistol, and resumed applying pressure to Dance's wound. I think I was calling for Doc, but it felt like my lung had collapsed and all I could manage was a harsh rasping sound.

"I got you," Pierce said, kneeling beside me. "I think you have an arrow in your lung, bro. This is... well, it's not gonna feel good."

The searing pain flared as he grabbed hold of the arrow… and then… it felt like he was literally ripping my insides out.

"There, got it. Now the other one…"

"No!" I gasped as my lung inflated. "Thanks."

I snapped off the other arrow and pulled my right arm free from the shaft. My body would work the arrowhead out; I wasn't about to go through a barbed arrow being drawn from my flesh again anytime soon.

"Where the hell is Doc?" I said.

"Other wounded."

"Get Eps."

"Will do," Pierce said, vanishing.

By then I could feel my left shoulder already knitting itself together—not a pleasant sensation—and I was seeing clearly. Dance's face was ashen, and I checked her pulse again. Still there, but so faint I wondered if I was imagining it.

A few eternities later, Epasotl bounded up beside me and tsked, shaking her head.

"Roll her on side," she ordered.

The sound of small arms fire and the chatter of the two-forties was still echoing through the jungle, and my radio was filled with platoon chatter. I wondered just how many jags had attacked us this time. The entire army? We weren't even out of the northward pass yet.

"It went through!" Epasotl snapped in admonishment. "She bleeding from back whole time. Why not check back?"

I shook my head. That was dumb. More than dumb. I should've checked for an exit wound. I knew better. *Dance…*

"Hold her still," Epasotl said. "I pull arrow through."

"That could kill her!"

"She dead soon anyway. Hold!"

"Uh, guys?" Pierce said urgently.

"What now?" I cried.

"Is it just me, or do you see that too?"

Epasotl and I both looked where he was pointing. Off in the trees and closing fast, a nightmare was approaching.

It stood at least nine feet tall, cloaked in swirling shadow. Its head was the skull of a stag, the broad antlers festooned with black ribbon, and its body was that of a skeletal, emaciated jaguar-man. But the limbs were wrong, with too many joints, and it didn't so much move as *ooze* through space. It threw its head back and wailed, a sound so filled with anguish that I felt a despair I'd never before known.

"What is—?" I choked, unable to move, unable to form more words. I was overcome with grief and hopelessness. I wanted to give up. To crawl into the deepest hole I could find. To curl into a ball and just… die.

Epasotl cursed in Chaneque and pulled the infant's skull from her haversack. Without hesitation she smashed it on the ground, where it shattered into a million fragments of light that swirled around us like luminescent dragonflies, forming a protective dome.

"We must work fast, Ben-Ette," she said. When I didn't answer, she slapped me hard. "Ben-Ette!"

"It's no use," I moaned. "She's dead. We're all dead. We should've never come here."

She slapped me again. "Hold her!"

"No use…" I sobbed, but I held Dance firmly anyway, even though there was no point. No point in anything. No point in…

I shook my head, fighting to force the hopelessness away.

"What the heck is going on?" I asked Epasotl, wiping my eyes with a hand.

"Is evil spirit. Spawn of shadow. Is spirit of misery. Now hold." She took a firm grasp on the arrow's shaft and pushed it deeper into Dance, then grabbed the other end and pulled it out with a grunt. "Is summoned thing. Is wuss. Make you feel sad. Boo-hoo. No power if you be strong. So be strong, Ben-Ette. Lay her down."

I moved Dance onto her back. She looked… very dead. Above us the dragonfly sprites swarmed, a million points of radiance. I could sense the overwhelming despair just outside our cocoon of light, pushing in, fighting, and the swarm pushing and fighting back just as fiercely.

Puffing out her cheeks, Epasotl placed her hands over Dance's wound. There wasn't any more blood pumping out of the hole. That was bad. Her skin was gray and her lips had gone blue. Her eyes were dull and vacant.

Epasotl looked at me. "You too," she said. "I not have enough teōtl alone. Help sister."

"Me?"

"You hands, my hands."

Confused, I placed my hands over Epasotl's. "What am I doing?"

"You heal others with touch, no?"

I hesitated. Missionaries are often asked to give blessings of healing… but had I actually healed anyone, or was it just coincidence when they got better? I wasn't sure. My faith was… not the strongest anymore. Hadn't been for a while. And besides, even if it wasn't coincidence, it wasn't *me* who had done anything. I didn't have any special power. I just had faith. Once. Back then.

"How do you know about that?" I asked.

"You had hands of healer once. You make god-weaving too, in faraway place."

"I didn't make magic, Eps. I just prayed over people. Sometimes they got better. It's not the same."

"Is same," she said confidently. "Weave with sister." She closed her eyes, and I felt a surge of warmth emanate from her hands beneath mine. I closed my eyes too, unsure what to do. I didn't know if I should pray, or just hope, or…

"*Yoli,*" Epasotl whispered softly.

First-to-Dance gasped, and light filled her eyes.

CHAPTER 21

There wasn't time for rest or recovery. Captain Brown figured we had stumbled into the vanguard of an army marching southward to attempt another assault on Chlůmpu, and he wanted us out of its path as quickly as possible. Sanchez redistributed the dwindling ammo and we were off again, climbing the steep eastern slopes of the pass and making for an alternate path out of the mountain range.

We'd lost two of McKenzie's lads, Philip and James, but amazingly that was all. We had a lot of wounded, but everyone was ambulatory and morale was generally high; we'd hit a vastly numerically superior force, including several spellcasters, and had routed them. We found several human eagle warriors among their dead too, all death-touched, and I wondered if St. James and the others from Alpha Section had joined this army, perhaps even participated in the battle.

"Is Atzi gone now?" I asked Epasotl when we stopped for a brief rest the next day atop a high bluff that overlooked the pass. We'd been humping straight through the day and night. Sleep wasn't an option yet.

"Is gone," she said.

"Dead?"

"Spirit not dead, not alive. Spirit just spirit. She go back to spirit place. Not come again."

"That's sad. I was getting used to her. What are you going to do now?"

"Call for new spirit. Am preparing home." She pulled Peter's shrunken jaguar-man head out of her bag and rolled it between her hands.

"How'd you get that?"

"Make trade. Lizard bros like make trade. He happy, I happy."

"What did you trade?"

"Weapon. I no need anymore."

"You gave him your MP5? Does Sanchez know?"

Epasotl rolled her eyes. "I not dumb. Ask Little Kahuna first."

I was genuinely surprised our platoon sergeant had agreed to it. "Does Peter even know how to use it?" The idea of one of the psychotic cokehead lizardmen running around with a submachine gun didn't exactly give me the warm fuzzies.

"What to know? Point and shoot."

"I suppose."

"No worry pretty head."

"So… what kind of spirit are you going to get now?"

"Do not know. I call, spirit come. If like home, spirit stay."

"Hope it's a good spirit."

"Duh. Why call evil spirit? Evil spirit strong but dangerous. Maybe turn on you. Make bad tricks. No bueno."

I chewed on some dried meat cake for a minute.

"How Dance?" Epasotl asked.

"Really good. You'd never guess she'd almost died. Thanks again for saving her."

"You help too."

"I don't think I did anything."

"You summon teōtl to help make weaving. Not do without you, not without make flesh sacrifice again." She touched her restored ear.

"I did?"

"You draw teōtl like I not see before. Like tree draw water from ground. You god-weave too if you practice, like before in faraway place."

"I told you, Eps, I didn't make magic. Magic doesn't exist in my world. I wasn't weaving some kind of mystical energy. I just prayed."

"Heal people, no?"

"Maybe? I don't know. But if they were healed, it was God working through me. It's not magic. It's faith."

"Is same."

"No, it's not. Trust me. Faith isn't magic. It's... hard to explain, even for me, and I used to teach people about it every day. It's... hope? Trust? It's a belief in God. Well, it's more than just believing. It's... confidence, assurance that comes *from* God that He's real and will answer prayers."

"Big Kahuna say man with faith like tiny seed move mountain. Is true?"

"I've never seen that happen, but I suppose so. I mean, I believe it's true."

She pursed her lips. "I think you god and teōtl is same, but way you weave in faraway place different."

"I don't know about that."

"We see." She shrugged. "You weave in faraway place with what you call 'faith.' I weave with potion and spirit. Used to weave with sacrifice. No more. Like ears pretty. Not look like old woman. We both weave. Is same, is different. Different-same. I give potion for you see teōtl, see god. You make weaving to heal bros. Be rad, no? Not rad as sister. But rad. Much stoked."

She held out her fist, and I bumped it with a sigh.

"Not stoked?" she said.

"Just tired."

"Need seed of stag? Much energy. I have some still."

"Hard pass, sis. I'm not that desperate yet. Listen, I gotta get back to my team. We'll be moving out soon."

"Suit youself." She dropped the shrunken jaguar-man head back in her haversack and stood, stretching. "Hang loose, bro."

I nodded and stood as well, rolling my left shoulder and taking a deep breath. I'd fully healed, but the memory of the pain remained. I wasn't sure what to make of Epasotl's claims about magic... and faith. It was undeniable that magic existed here, and it was clear that some forms of it came from a good source and others from evil. But I didn't know how to reconcile that with my concept of divine power.

My experience battling the curse when it threatened to consume me had led me to believe that the God I believed in operated here on some level—that had been a battle of faith more than will. And yet the curse that was the cause of that battle… was magic.

Faith.

Magic.

I just couldn't wrap my head around the two things together.

But what was magic, anyway, but a word to explain the unexplainable?

Maybe Captain Brown had a theory. I'd have to ask him. Later.

***

The high, narrow path we'd taken as a detour made for slow going, and our walking wounded slowed us down further. No one was critically injured, and Epasotl did what she could for them without depleting her store of magical energy too much in case of an emergency. She seemed to have a limit to how much she could draw without having to resort to self-sacrifice, and my grandfather's ring, while able to store "juice," as she had taken to calling teōtl—undoubtedly Wilson's influence—apparently had a short magical half-life.

"It's leaking?" I'd asked her.

"No, ring good, not leak. But juice go bad. Not stay fresh. Not last more than day before too weak to weave. And we move. Always move. No rest. No time for meditate."

"We'll be stopping soon. We have to. Some of the guys and gals won't be able to push much farther. We've been humping it through these mountains for three days and nights. Short Round is starting to hallucinate."

"So sorry. Cannot help. Seed of stag all gone. Gave last to Broski. He make team drink."

"That explains why they're so chipper."

"I make more. Find stag. Is trick to milk seed from stag, you know. First you—"

"Don't want to know, Eps."

She shrugged, and I tightened my ruck's straps as we climbed, sometimes hand over foot, up the winding path.

At dusk Captain Brown called a halt and Sanchez set up a watch roster. They knew the platoon was hurting, and to push any further was to invite accident and injury. After over seventy-two hours without sleep, most of the guys and gals looked like the living dead.

"We move again at first light," Sanchez told me and the other NCOs.

"And make sure everyone's changing their socks," Doc added. "I'm already dealing with one of you people's feet rotting off because the dumbass has been wearing the same funky pair of socks for a week."

We all knew he was talking about Anderson. Flaming Feather apologized profusely for her failure in leadership and offered to cut her hair and resign in shame.

"Denied," Sanchez said curtly. "Sometimes I wonder if you gotta hold that kid's dick to help him piss."

"I do not, Sergeant," Flaming Feather said in all seriousness. "Is that one of my duties as squad leader?"

"If it comes to that, I'll give Touchdown a catheter," Doc said deadpan, but I could tell he was struggling not to laugh.

Feather looked confused and nodded, folding her arms across her chest. "He tries hard to be a good warrior, but he is…"

"Ate the hell up," Sanchez said. "It boggles the mind, I know. I'll have another chat with him."

Translation: Anderson would be pounding sand and digging a new latrine pit with Lawrence whether we needed one or not.

Speaking of, I found my teammate half-asleep kneeling and hacking at the hard soil with his e-tool after the NCO meeting broke up.

"Latrine looks good for now," I told him. "Hydrate, change your socks, and then rack out. You have watch with Cohen in four hours."

He nodded wearily and dragged himself over to his ruck. Cohen had his boots and socks off and was massaging his feet. He looked up at me and grimaced.

"Blisters?" I asked.

"Yeah."

"Gotta change your socks more often."

"I *have* been! But we've been walking nonstop forever. Damn, Corporal. My Hush Puppies are killing me."

"I don't even know what that means."

"I don't either!" He started laughing.

"Get some sleep, man. You're delirious."

"Yeah, get some sleep, Hush Puppy," Wilson called over.

Cohen stopped laughing and groaned.

I shook my head. "Sorry, man."

First-to-Dance was snoring, and I shook her shoulder.

"Watch," I told her. She rubbed the sleep out of her eyes and grabbed her weapon, following me with a yawn over to where Heart-of-Darkness and García had set up an observation post. After exchanging some small talk they went to rack out, and Dance and I got comfortable.

"How about you make us a range card," I said to Dance.

"They left us one," she pointed out, holding up the page García had torn out of his notebook.

"Yeah, but it's good practice. Make another. You still need to work on converting land rods to meters."

"Roger, Corporal," she said, pulling out her notebook and the stub of a pencil. She got busy sketching, and I set up Sybil and made my own. We had a good view back southward about a klick along the path we'd followed, which looked like a far gentler climb than it had actually been. A low ridgeline obscured the lower pass to the west, and to our east the mountains rose into the low mist and clouds. At this altitude the trees had turned to scattered stands of pines and moss-covered scrub oak. The temperature had been dropping the higher we climbed, but it wasn't what I'd call cold, even with the strong wind that swept up the side of the mountain and rustled the lush ferns and grasses.

"You ever seen snow?" I asked Dance.

"Snow? I do not know that word."

"White stuff that falls from the sky. Very cold. Covers the trees and the ground like a blanket."

She made a sour face. "That sounds horrible."

"It's really pretty. I miss snow. Maybe we'll see some if we climb high enough."

"It is already too cold," she said.

"This? This is nothing. Where I grew up, it got so cold the lakes and rivers would turn solid—freeze—and you could skate on them."

"Skate?"

"Like running, but with blades on your feet. Feels like flying."

"You are making a joke."

"No joke."

"Water cannot become hard."

"It's called ice. When it's cold enough, the water turns hard. Like rock."

"I do not believe you."

I shrugged.

She handed me her notebook. The sketch was really good. She'd made marks of dots and lines and what looked like arrow feathers at various ranges. I asked her to explain.

"Dots for one, two, three, four. Lines for five. Arrow with five feathers on right is one hundred. Five feathers each on left and right is two hundred. Ten feathers on right, five feathers on left is three hundred. And so on."

I scribbled down the equivalent Arabic numerals on her range card. "Is this meters or land rods?"

"Land rods," she said. I double-checked her ranges against my own, converting the units of measurement. She was really close, but I already knew that. She always dropped her grenades right where I asked. She was a savant with a grenade launcher.

"Convert the ranges to meters," I told her. "One land rod is about two and a half meters, so that's easy. And use my numbers."

She set back to work, the tip of her tongue sticking out between her teeth, and then handed me back the notebook when she was finished. I nodded in approval.

"See?" I said. "Not so hard. But you need to be able to think in meters, not convert in your head."

"I will practice more." She turned to a fresh page and started redrawing the terrain features and marking ranges. "But writing your numbers is difficult. They make no sense."

"Only up to nine. Ten and above is much simpler than yours. You just have to memorize one through nine. Then it's easy."

"I memorized your letters. I can read your tongue, a little," she said proudly.

"Really? Where'd you learn that?"

"Lawrence is teaching me. We read from a codex about a short burglar and a magic ring."

"That's awesome." I paused. Was it time for the fraternization talk? I hadn't had a chance to ask any of the other cadre about dealing with that. "So... you and Lawrence..."

"Umhmm?" she asked, busy with trying to write Arabic numerals.

"Are you... close?" I asked.

"Close?"

"You know... *close.*"

I don't think I could've said it more awkwardly.

She laughed quietly. "You mean like you and Princess Flower Eagle or Sergeant Wilson and Dressed-in-Stars. Or Flaming Feather and—"

I held up a hand. "I don't want to know. But, yeah. Like that."

"Lawrence is a good man, but still a boy really. He is not my... how do you say? Type?"

"Oh," I said in relief.

"Now, Sergeant Takahashi, *he* is my type."

I frowned. That would be fraternization with a capital 'F.' Definitely. Absolutely verboten. Go straight to jail. Do not pass go. Do *not* collect $200.

"He's our squad leader," I reminded her.

"I know the rules, Corporal." She sighed. "Still, it is too bad. He is a stud, no? Mmm, yummy."

I wrinkled my nose, and she covered her mouth to keep from laughing out loud.

"Do not worry. I will not seduce him. I am a good girl." She gave me a sly grin and leaned in toward me. "Most of the time." She handed me her notebook. "How is this?"

"Very good." It was. Her range estimates nearly matched my own.

"I was not sure about the range here," she said, pointing to her sketch. Some of her hair had come out of her topknot and brushed my cheek as she leaned in to study the range card with me. "Is it close?"

"You're… very close."

"It is a cold night, no?"

Was she flirting with me? I wasn't sure. I'm about as dense as osmium when it comes to women. Whatever she was doing, it was making me feel uncomfortable. She breathed a throaty sigh and then leaned back, giggling.

"Princess Flower Eagle is right! You blush very easily. You look like you swallowed a chili pepper. She will laugh so hard when I tell her."

"Brat," I said, tossing her notebook back.

"But my estimates are good?"

"You're a natural."

"Maybe I can become a sniper too." She motioned to Sybil.

"Well, it's more than just estimating range. You need to know how to read the wind across the whole distance of the shot, how the bullet rises and falls. Lots of factors. Humidity, altitude, tons of stuff. I'm still learning."

"But you could teach me?"

"Sure, why not? You're already a crack shot." I pursed my lips. "Come to think of it, so is Jade. You and her would make a good team. I'll talk to Sergeant Takahashi about it."

"Baller," she said, tucking the errant strand of hair behind her ear and grinning broadly.

We sat in silence for a long time, watching the mountainside and listening to the wind and insects; the birds had long since settled in for the night.

"Sure is taking a really long time to get dark," I commented.

"What do you mean? It has been dark for a while now."

"A little. Not much." I waved my hand in front of me. "Not at all, really. I mean, the colors are muted, but I can see just fine."

She gave me a puzzled look. "It is quite dark now, Corporal. I can see maybe twenty land rods—I mean fifty meters. Maybe."

"Really?"

She nodded.

"Weird." I could see *much* farther than that. Detail was blurry, and the colors were almost monochrome, but otherwise I could see well… fine. In fact it was like I was using really good night vision. "Can you see that outcropping at three hundred twenty-five meters?" I asked. "You marked it on your range card. Number four."

She squinted. "Maybe the shadow of its shape. Maybe. Nothing more."

I chewed on my lip. I could see it clearly. Not like during the day, maybe, but no worse than dusk. I got behind my scope. "So weird…"

Something moved around the edge of the rock I was examining.

"I've got movement," I said.

"What is it?"

"Dunno." The shape moved slowly, almost imperceptibly. It was either a medium-sized animal, or… I dialed up my magnification to maximum. "Get down!"

Without looking away from my scope, I flailed with my arm to catch Dance's sleeve and pulled hard. My scope lit up with a blinding flash and less than half a second later something split the air where she'd been only a moment before, followed almost immediately by a thunderous boom. I was already reflexively sinking into my shooting position and exhaling. Bright dots danced in my right eye from the afterimage of the muzzle flash, but my aim hadn't shifted, and I fired. I couldn't be sure if I'd hit him.

I rolled to the right a couple of meters and low-crawled to a better position. If there was a second shot, it'd be where he'd seen *my* muzzle flash. I tried to reacquire the target while I keyed my radio. "Contact, contact. OP Echo. Sniper at eleven o'clock, three-two-five meters."

"Known point four," Dance said to me calmly. "AB, Corporal?"

"I thought you couldn't see it."

"I can still *hit* it."

She wasn't bragging; I knew she could.

"Let 'er rip."

She loaded the air-burst grenade, rolled up onto her knees, paused for the briefest of moments, and then fired before hitting the deck again. There was another blinding flash in my scope followed by the scream of a round ripping the air between us and then the slightly delayed report of what could only be a Barrett fifty-cal.

Three hundred meters and change was practically point-blank range for a rifle like that. Dance was lucky she still had her head on her shoulders.

Her egg hit the ground and popped the air-burst charge, detonating in a red flash.

I was still trying to blink away the spots dancing in my shooting eye. "Dance," I said. "Catch."

I tossed her the thermal monocular. She crawled a couple of meters and crouched up cautiously, holding it to her eye.

"See anything?" I asked.

"Yeah. Something. It is not moving."

"That doesn't mean anything," I grunted. "Get back down. Shift somewhere unobstructed you can observe prone. Stay low."

I blinked again, shook my head, and got back on the scope. He was still there, prone and hugged up tight to the outcropping, motionless.

Sanchez called me for a sitrep.

"One tango," I replied. "We have eyes-on. Thermal and visual. Hit him with AB but can't confirm neutralized. He might be playing possum."

"Put another round in him," Sanchez replied.

"Roger, Longshot out."

Sybil barked, but the sniper didn't flinch. I moved to a new position. "Xavier, Longshot. Tango didn't so much as twitch when I hit him."

"Hold position, Longshot. Havok's coming to investigate. Xavier out."

Wilson crawled up to me a couple minutes later. "What do we got, bro?"

"Sniper. Fifty-cal. Possibly neutralized. Three-two-five meters. Eleven o'clock. Under that outcropping."

He peered through his NODs in the direction I'd indicated and chewed on his mustache. "You can see that without night vision?"

"Yeah. Believe it or not. I think it might a new side effect of… you know. My…"

Wilson made air quotes and mouthed, *Condition*. He slapped my shoulder. "Gnarly. Okay. We'll swing left. You got my ass covered, bro?"

"Hooah, Sarge."

"No sign of anyone else?"

"Negative. You want more forty mike-mike on his ass just to be sure?"

"Nah, save it. I got this."

Wilson got on the radio to announce he was advancing, and then moved out. Leaves, Jade, and Tears flowed past me a few seconds later, silent but for a faint rustling that could've been the wind.

"Dance," I called out softly. "Keep scanning with the thermal. Watch for any more hostiles."

"Hooah, Corporal."

I dialed back the magnification on my scope to get a wider sight picture and focused on breathing calmly. The sniper still hadn't moved.

Several minutes later Wilson's team came into view and took up positions around the body. Wilson turned the corpse over and paused for a long time before keying his radio.

"Xavier, Havok."

"Go for Xavier."

"Tango down." Wilson broke off for a few seconds. "It's Sergeant Wright."

CHAPTER 22

"What's left of him, anyway," Wilson said to me. I was squatting next to Wright's mangled corpse. A forty-millimeter air-burst grenade does nasty things to a body, even if Dance's aim had been slightly off, but it was Wright, without question.

"Great shot, Dance, by the way," I called to her in a low voice.

She raised a hand in acknowledgment from where she was pulling security.

"She made it blind, from memory of the terrain feature on her range card," I said to Wilson.

He gave a low whistle. "I couldn't have done that. She's some kind of thumper wizard." He laughed softly. "That's your new name, Dance. *Thumper*."

She gave a thumbs-up.

I pivoted, scanning the area. "So where's the rest of Alpha?"

"That's the million-dollar question," Wilson said. "Either they cut and ran, or he was working solo."

"If he was solo, giving himself away by taking a shot at us wasn't the smartest thing he could've done."

"Yeah, well, it *is* Wright we're talking about. Probably figured he could bag one or two of us and pull a fade."

"All Crazy Horse elements, this is Xavier. Moving out in five mikes."

"So much for my beauty sleep," Wilson muttered.

"Xavier, Longshot," I transmitted. "What about the body? Shouldn't we... bury it or something?"

"Food for buzzards and worms. Get back up here. Xavier out."

I looked at Wilson, who shrugged.

"I call dibs on his rifle," he said.

"You're welcome to it, Sarge. I'm not humping that."

"Wuss. I thought you were all Mr. Macho Death-Touched Man now."

"I am, but I'm still not carrying that cannon. Sybil suits me just fine."

"Losers weepers." Wilson collected all the ammo he could find and slung the Barrett over his shoulder. "Lead the way, bro."

We were moving again as soon as Wilson and my teams formed up with the rest of the platoon. Brown pushed us as fast as possible to get distance from the skirmish, but the platoon was hurting. Within two hours Kiktú was carrying Anderson, and before dawn we had to halt again. Sanchez ordered all the junior enlisted to rack out while the NCOs buddied up to cover the first watch. The whole platoon was reeking of ammonia from our muscles breaking down. If there were any jags in the area, they'd find us by smell alone.

We were situated on the broad shoulder of a mountain near a cliff to the north overlooking a canyon far below. East and west of us the mountains climbed into the low clouds. My watch-buddy was Sergeant Takahashi, and we set up our OP with a view southward back down the wide draw we'd climbed during the night. He was looking pretty rough around the edges.

"Get some sleep, Sarge," I told him. "We can switch in two hours."

"Thanks, but I'm too amped at the moment. Was that really Wright back there?"

"It was. Did you know him well?"

"As well as any of the squad leaders back in the real world, I guess. Not like we were drinking buddies or anything. He was always off with St. James, picking fights with jarheads or whatever. Not really my scene. Sergeant Douglas was a hardass about that sort of thing anyway. Kept his people in line."

"I miss him."

"Miss a lot of people," Takahashi said. "Losing Stanley hit me hard. He was my gunner, remember? When we first got ripped out of Panama."

I nodded, trying to be sympathetic.

"I know you two hated each other," Takahashi continued. "But Joe wasn't all bad. Man was squared away and always stepped up."

I gave a vague grunt of acknowledgment, and Takahashi laughed softly.

"Just because he had his eye on your girl doesn't make him a bad man," he said.

"Frankly, Sergeant, he was foul about it. And he made threats. Veiled threats maybe, but still. I was worried about her safety around him."

"I seriously doubt he would've done anything. He was yanking your chain. Getting you riled. You're not exactly hard to rile, Preacher."

I bristled.

"See?" Takahashi said. "That's what I'm talking about."

"Point."

I watched our sector as the overcast sky grew from black to gray, lost in my thoughts.

"So random," Takahashi said, startling me. I'd thought he'd fallen asleep.

"Say again, Sergeant?"

"Death. It's so random." Takahashi rubbed his face. "Living one minute, gone the next. Guy next to you buys it and you don't. Random. No reason for it. It just is. Why am I still here when so many others aren't? I think you and Wilson had the right idea. Forget the real world. Go native. Find a girl and make the best of it in this nightmare."

"So why'd you volunteer for this mission?"

He shrugged. "Because I'm the senior NCO next to Sanchez. If he buys it, I'm responsible for you all. Because Captain is a good man and I want to see him home with his family. You know why he left the regiment?"

"No clue." We all wondered of course. There had even been a pool once betting on the reasons a high-speed, low-drag Ranger officer would *choose* to lead a ragtag platoon of green Cavalry Scouts.

"Family," Takahashi said. I gave him a glance, and he nodded. "The regiment took him away from his family too much. He wanted a gig that would let him be home more."

"That's…"

"Ironic? Yeah, I know. He's held us together. He's the only reason *any* of us are still alive. The man deserves to go home. Seeing this through is good for the ol' karma, as my father would say. Or maybe… this *is* my karma. *Sode fure-au mo tasho no en*, my grandmother always said."

"I didn't think you believed in anything like that."

"I don't. Didn't. Don't know anymore." He held up a hand. "Don't get excited, Preacher. I'm not converting. I don't believe in God or destiny. Didn't. I don't know. Maybe my grandma was right all along; maybe even our sleeves brushing together is fate."

"The future's already happened," I said to myself. "I don't know, Sarge. I think we still have a choice. I think fate is just the sum total of our and everyone else's choices. Maybe the tapestry is already complete, but *we* wove the threads."

"Poetic. Very zen."

I shrugged, and he gazed at a bird flitting in the branches overhead, dancing through the mist.

"Karma cannot change," he said,

"The tapestry is complete,

"But we wove the threads."

Then he chuckled. "I suck at haiku. Get some sleep, Bennett."

***

"Wake up, Bennett, we're pulling out."

Takahashi was shaking my shoulder. For a moment I forgot where we were, and I rubbed the sleep out of my eyes with the heels of my hands.

"Already?" I croaked.

"We got company."

That woke me up. "Where?"

"Coming up the draw. Tripped a couple surprises Captain left on our trail. Don't know how many, and they're a few klicks away, but they'll be on top of us soon enough. Gotta move."

"What time is it?"

"Beats me. Early afternoon." He moved off, calling over his shoulder for me to get my team together and report for a leaders' meeting ASAP.

Cohen was snoring beside me, and I nudged him awake.

"What?" he asked irritably.

"We're moving out."

"I just got off watch."

"Bad guys on our trail. They'll be here any minute."

"Oh, shit." He sat up. "This sucks. Where are Short Round and Dance?"

"Pulling security. I have a briefing. Can you get the team's kit ready to go?"

"Yeah. Yes. Right on it."

"Thanks." I grabbed Sybil and hurried over to where the other NCOs had already assembled in a huddle with Captain Brown.

"—leaving us one direction," Brown was saying. "We go *down*."

"The cliff?" Takahashi asked. "It's gotta be, what? A hundred meters down to the river valley?"

"Hundred and thirty, give or take," Doc said, tying the eight feet of rope we all carried into a harness. "Won't be fun, but it's doable."

"Do we have that much rope?" Takahashi asked.

"We have enough," Brown said. "We're not rappelling everyone straight down four hundred feet. There are ledges and scrub we can traverse and anchor to. Doc will go first and set up the route while Dave supervises everyone tying their Swiss seats, then the two of them will belay the platoon down one by one from point to point. There are a couple places along the route we can stage groups of people from, so we can get everyone over the side fairly quickly, but it's going to be slow going to the bottom, and we don't have much time. Hachirō, you'll take Dave's people and a weapons team down first with me and we'll set up security at the bottom. Sir Angus, your team is next."

McKenzie cut in. "That won't be necessary, sir. The lads can make their own way down."

"Free climb?" Doc raised an eyebrow.

"If you mean without ropes, aye," McKenzie confirmed.

"That'll speed things up," Brown said. "In that case, I want the rest of Blue Squad next—is Kiktú going to have any problems getting down?"

I had a brief exchange with her before turning back to the captain. "She'll manage, sir."

He nodded. "Good. Next is your team, Nephi. Sergeant Sanchez and PFC Epasotl will be last, and are responsible for retrieving all the rope; I'd rather not leave an easy way down for our friends. In fact, maybe some of the lads can be on rope retrieval duty, Angus."

"Bloody good plan, sir," McKenzie replied.

Questions?" Brown asked us.

Takahashi and I exchanged a brief glance with Flaming Feather, but the rest of the leaders were experienced mountaineers. If they were confident, I was confident. I just wouldn't look down. Four hundred feet is a long way to fall.

"No questions, sir," Takahashi said for the both of us.

"No, sir," Feather echoed.

"Then let's move with a purpose," Captain Brown said.

***

Getting everyone and all the gear down was taking longer than anyone had hoped, and the bad guys made their appearance all too soon.

The death-touched human warriors with the eagle-beaked headdresses came out of the mist-shrouded trees, blowing whistles that sounded like inhuman screams of terror and beating their weapons on hide-bound shields. They ran fearlessly against the heavy fire coming from Dressed-in-Stars and Anderson's two-forty until they were within bow and javelin range, and then they took cover, bounding toward us methodically to get within accurate killing distance.

And some of them were armed with more than that.

I heard the crack of incoming rounds and swore. Sounded like 7.62.

We were doing our level best to hold the eagle warriors back, but the warriors must have had a similar healing ability to my own, because no matter how many times we put them down, they just got back up a minute later. Except for headshots. Those seemed to put them down and *keep* them down.

Note to self: don't get shot in the head.

Sanchez yelled at Flaming Feather to get her people to the rope, and the two-forty went quiet. A couple of squads of eagle warriors took this as a cue to charge, but Sanchez had taken the Carl G from Heart-of-Darkness and calmly raised it to his shoulder. There was that tire-bursting explosion of air and the screaming hiss of hundreds of tiny flechettes spreading out all at once, and then twenty or so eagle warriors erupted into a red cloud not thirty yards from our position.

They didn't get back up.

The antipersonnel round must have found more targets downrange, because there was suddenly a *lot* of screaming.

Epasotl threw a handful of small round objects in the air above her, and they instantly caught fire and began orbiting her head. She threw a knife hand, and one of them sped off, connecting with a tree forty meters away that was being used as cover. The tree exploded in a shower of razor splinters. She threw a second knife hand, sending another tiny meteor downrange where it practically flattened an advancing squad.

Lawrence called a belt change as First-to-Dance lobbed forty-millimeter HE at ranges that were about to become danger close far too quickly.

"Now your people," Sanchez said, clapping me on the shoulder after I'd pink-misted an eagle warrior and was swapping magazines.

"Cohen!" I yelled over the report of small arms fire. "Get Short Round to the rope and get yourselves down."

Epasotl sent two meteors simultaneously off into the forest and grinned at the resulting screams.

We'd been pulling back, closer to the edge of the cliff, tightening our defensive perimeter, and the eagle warriors were now drawing around us from the southern draw and the slopes to our east and west like a noose. Then Lawrence's lightweight machine gun went quiet, and they shouted as one body and rushed.

I was backing up to the edge of the cliff, rifle shouldered, snapping off headshots rhythmically, when a familiar face appeared in my crosshairs.

Specialist Bond.

I froze when our eyes met through the scope. His expression was twisted in hate and his eyes looked dead. Whatever I'd hoped might remain of my friend was gone.

But I still couldn't take the shot. My finger took the slack out of the trigger, but it wouldn't break.

He brought his carbine up in what felt like slow motion. And I knew in that moment that whatever hesitation I might have, he had none.

Then with a sudden rush of wind and heat, a searing wall of blue-hot flame leaped into the air between us, twenty feet tall. My skin prickled and I broke out into an instant sweat. Lawrence was already over the edge and Cohen was getting ready to follow; Sanchez was yelling at them to haul ass; and Epasotl's face was contorted in concentration as she shaped the wall of fire around us.

One of the eagle warriors burst through the barrier, wreathed in flame, and fell only feet from me, where he writhed on the ground.

I drew my sidearm and shot him.

Brain and skull fragments splattered over my boots.

Cohen's head disappeared over the lip of the ledge, and I called to Dance to hook onto the rope.

I looked to Sanchez.

"It was Bond," I said.

"Not anymore he ain't."

"I couldn't take the shot."

"He's gone, son. *That* wasn't your friend." He glanced at Epasotl. "How long can she keep this up?"

"Don't know, Sarge."

He pulled a grenade from his punch and pulled the pin, then nodded to the rope. "Your turn."

Epasotl fell to her knees, and the roaring flames wavered.

"What about you and Eps?"

"Get your ass down that rope or I'll kick you off the edge."

I nodded and clipped onto the rope, easing myself down, trying not to look.

"Nice and steady now," I heard Wilson calling up to me. "I got you. It ain't nothing, bro. Just like the rappelling tower."

Except the fall would be almost ten times farther. And I'd only done the tower a couple of times. In Basic. And I'd been terrified. I have an intense fear of heights.

"Don't kick off," Wilson called. "Just walk yourself down. You're just taking a stroll."

I heard small arms fire erupt from below and then the chatter of a two-forty. People on the radio were calling out targets. From *below*. At the base of the cliff. We were surrounded.

And I was dangling four hundred feet in the air.

Screwing my eyes shut to ward off the vertigo, I began moving down, step by step, the rope feeling far too thin in my hands to be holding my weight.

"That's it!" Wilson said encouragingly. "Just another forty feet. You got this."

I moved faster, working into a rhythm as I descended.

"Not *that* fast, bro," Wilson warned.

Sanchez peered over the edge. "Clear the rope, Bennett, I'm coming down."

Wilson swore. "Okay, change of plans. You're gonna have to fast-rope it, bro. Unclip and just slide down the rope like a fire hose. I'll catch you."

"You'll do *what*?" I cried.

"It's fine. I'm on a ledge. Plenty of room. Unclip and let 'er rip, man."

Trembling, I squeezed the rope between my boots while gripping it for dear life in one hand as I fumbled to unclip myself with the other. Sanchez yelled something from above and Wilson was shouting from below and the whole time my heart was about to beat itself out of my chest. As soon as the rope was clear of my carabiner, I took a deep breath, gripped the rope with both gloved hands, and dropped, leaving my stomach somewhere above me.

As I fell—well, slid, but it felt like falling—I watched Sanchez step off the edge with Epasotl in one arm, using the other hand to break himself while *running* down the cliff, *facing* me, rock and shrapnel erupting above him.

Wilson caught me and had to peel my fingers off the rope to get me out of the way. Sanchez braked at the last moment and touched down coolly on the ledge. My hands were clenched in fists and my forearms were cramped, swollen, and rock-hard. My palms burned even under my assault gloves.

"Haven't done that in a while," Sanchez said, putting Epasotl down on the ledge. She wavered a little and sat down.

"That was *rad*, Little Kahuna," she slurred before passing out.

"Wilson, get Bennett the rest of the way down. I've got you covered. How's the progress?"

Wilson peered over the ledge and pursed his lips. "Slow, Sarge. Taks and Captain are engaged at the base. McKenzie's lizard dudes must be down there somewhere too. Can't see them anyway."

Sanchez followed Wilson's gaze. "Looks like Blue Squad is halfway. Where's Bennett's team?"

"Under that outcropping," Wilson replied. "It covers a ledge. They're staged to descend once Doc gets Blue all the way down."

Sanchez glanced back up. "Well, we can't stay here. They'll pick us right off the side of the cliff. Gotta get behind that cover."

As if in answer, a warrior poked his head over the edge above us. Sanchez snapped up his rifle and brained the guy before he could release his arrow.

"Give me your ammo and get going," he said to Wilson.

"Hooah, Sarge." Wilson handed over his magazines, then clipped himself to the next rope and dropped out of view.

"I can't open my hands, Sergeant," I told Sanchez.

"Try harder, kid. I'm sure as hell not carrying you and Little Miss Kitty both." He was staring upward and fired off a couple more shots.

A flailing body fell past us, screaming.

"On belay?" Wilson shouted up after us.

An arrow skipped past us and snapped off the narrow ledge we were standing on. Sanchez returned fired and then glanced at me. "That's your cue, Bennett. Haul ass." He fired off another few rounds. "And you'd better move with a purpose because I'll be right behind you."

Rappelling with cramped forearm muscles was difficult to say the least, and incredibly painful, but I didn't have a choice. After what seemed like forever with arrows hissing past my head and javelins skipping off rocks—plus the occasional bullet whizzing by—I got to the ledge and under the overhang. Sanchez wasn't far behind, with Epasotl under one arm. With us and Wilson plus the rest of my team, the little scree-covered lip of stone was getting downright cozy.

"Fast-roping sucks," I told Wilson. "I can't believe I put in for Air Assault School."

"Well, you're supposed to use a big-ass rope," Wilson explained. "Real thick, like your wrist. Well, *your* wrist, not mine. Fast-roping on a thin rope like this is retarded. Not to mention suicidal."

"Right. Thanks, Sarge."

He clapped me on the shoulder.

"We can't stay here all day, people," Sanchez grumbled. I noticed he had a snapped-off arrow sticking out of his leg.

"I'll go first," I said. "I can cover the rest of you from the bottom."

"You'll have to go fast," Wilson warned. "But again, not *too* fast. If you lose control, Doc might not be able to break your fall."

"I got this, Sarge."

"I know you do." Wilson stroked his beard. "I'll still go first to belay you at the next anchor point. Then you can pass me and traverse ten meters to the one after that. Doc is at the bottom of that one. From there someone on the ground will belay you the rest of the way."

"Hooah," I said, with more confidence than I felt.

Sanchez had put Epasotl down, and she seemed to be getting her strength again. She groaned and pulled herself to her feet. "We make it?"

"More than halfway there," Wilson said, clipping himself to the rope. "I'll call for you when I'm set, Bennett. Remember, fast, but not too fast. Steady and smooth."

He kicked off the ledge and disappeared from view.

"I can't do it again," Lawrence told me, eyes wide. "I just can't."

"Well you can't stay here, son," Sanchez said. "Man up. You're first after Bennett." He peered around the overhang and swore. "They're coming."

"Without ropes?" I asked.

He climbed out around the outcropping and fired his pistol. Someone screamed, hit the shelf above us, and bounced out into the open air, flailing all the way down. We might be more than halfway, but it was still a long way to fall.

Sanchez ducked back under cover as an arrow flew past and another snapped off the rock above us.

"On belay!" I heard Wilson shout from below.

I flexed my stiff fingers and tried to ignore my burning palms, clipped myself to the rope, and took a deep breath before I lowered myself down, feet braced against the wall. I gave myself a mental count of three and then kicked off, letting the rope play through my hand as I plummeted.

"Break!" Wilson cried out. "Holy shit, bro. Shorter intervals. You're going to rappel straight off the end of the rope!"

I took another deep breath. My throat was so dry, it felt like it was closing up. I tried to ignore the arrows whistling past and kicked off again, breaking when I figured I'd gone maybe fifteen feet, then again, and again until I was hanging beside Wilson.

"Where's the ledge?" I asked.

"No ledge, bro. This is the hardest part of the route. You need to traverse ten meters to the next anchor. Don't worry, there's lots of handholds." He let go of his rope and dangled, clipping me and tying a new rope off on my carabiner. "This is in case you fall. But you'll have to untie yourself and clip onto the new rope on the other side yourself. Got it?"

"Uh…"

"Bro, if Touchdown can do it, you can do it."

"Right."

"With a purpose!" Sanchez called down after us.

I reached for the first handhold and climbed out into open space. If I slipped, all I had keeping me from falling to my death was a short length of rope attached to the anchor Doc had hammered into the rock. I moved sideways, first one foot, then a hand, another foot, another hand, inching my way along the face of the cliff. Those ten meters climbing under fire were probably the longest I've crossed in my life. My whole body was shaking when I reached the next length of rope.

"On belay," Doc called from below. He sounded a long way down, but I didn't dare look.

Somehow I managed to clip onto the rope and untie my tether. I braced my feet and tried to work some spit into my mouth, but I couldn't speak.

Taking a breath and screwing my eyes shut I kicked off, slid, and braked at intervals, mentally chanting to myself that slow was smooth and smooth was fast.

I felt the rope tighten and I stopped abruptly, dangling in the air.

"Shit, man, you gotta look where you're going," Doc said from somewhere nearby. "Open your damn eyes and walk down the rest of the way. It's only ten feet."

I lowered myself to the scrub-covered ledge and unclipped, risking a glance down and then back up. Lawrence was already making the descent to Wilson, and archers were taking potshots at him.

Unslinging Sybil, I flattened myself against the wall. It wasn't a sheer vertical rise to the top, but it was close enough that I could rest her bipod on the rock above me.

Kinda like shooting prone, but standing up. Strange feeling.

I got behind the scope and started picking off archers leaning over the top of the cliff. Five shots, five kills—more or less—mag swap, repeat.

At some point, high above, something detonated, flinging bodies that had been crawling down the cliff out into open space. Then I sighted Sanchez clinging to the rock like Spider-Man with his grenade launcher extended in one hand. I realized Lawrence was already beside me and Dance was coming down Doc's rope while Cohen traversed those terrifying ten meters. Epasotl had nearly reached Wilson.

I got back on my scope and continued taking out archers until Dance cried out that Sanchez had been hit.

Swinging my rifle, I caught sight of him rappelling far too fast down Wilson's rope, an arrow in his chest. Wilson was trying to break his rapid descent, but they collided, and Sanchez pinwheeled off into open air. Wilson somehow managed to catch a handhold and clung to the cliff like a limpet, crying out after Sanchez as he fell.

CHAPTER 23

The next thing I knew, Epasotl, whom I'd last seen traversing between anchors, propelled herself like a rocket off the side of the cliff, directly into Sanchez's downward path.

She'd always had a death wish, but I thought she'd outgrown that. I'd hoped so, anyway.

She struck Sanchez dead-on and wrapped her arms and legs around his body as they both plummeted down, down, the trees rising up to meet them.

And then…

They just… floated through the branches to the forest floor. Like a feather.

"What the hell…?" Doc said.

"Magic," I replied. Wilson was already traversing to Doc's rope, and I turned to Lawrence. "You, go."

He nodded dumbly and clipped off, lowering himself down the final rope. I turned back to the rest of my team. "Dance, you're next. Then you, Cohen. I'll be right behind you."

Whoever the platoon had been fighting below must have been taken care of by this point, because the two-forties turned their attention to the eagle warriors scaling down the cliff above us, picking them off like roaches. Bodies fell past, and they didn't float to the ground like feathers.

I don't really remember the last hundred and fifty feet or whatever it was down to the canyon floor. I hit the ground, unclipped, and ran to where I'd last seen Epasotl and our platoon sergeant. She was kneeling beside Sanchez, holding the shaft of the arrow with one hand and stroking his brow, mumbling something. Pink froth bubbled out of Sanchez's mouth, and his eyes were screwed shut.

I skidded to a stop and dropped to my knees by his side, opposite Epasotl.

"Weave," she said. She looked exhausted. "Weave with sister for Little Kahuna."

"Okay. Weave. What do I do?"

"No time explain."

"Like with Dance? My hands on your hands?"

"Teōtl too weak. Must sacrifice." She looked like she was going to pass out again.

"Flesh sacrifice?"

Her eyes rolled back in her head, and she fell over, unconscious.

I cried out in frustration.

I didn't know what to do aside from falling back on my combat lifesaver training. Sanchez had a punctured lung; I had to seal it off. I turned him gently onto his side and felt for an exit wound. Nothing.

"Okay, Sergeant," I said. "We gotta get you sitting up. Nice and easy. Okay?"

He hissed something. I took that as an affirmative and got him into a sitting position. I helped him remove his plate carrier and strip down to the waist, then I examined the shaft. It had entered just to the left of his chest plate at an awkward angle, and I needed to cut it. I was about to warn him that it was going to hurt, but from his expression I decided I'd best get on with it. Using my knife, I pared the shaft as deep as I could all around, gave him a three-count warning, and then snapped it off about an inch from the wound. I always keep a few MRE wrappers in my kit, and now I placed one over the wound, covered it with a field dressing, and applied a cravat to tighten it up. Then I worked my fingers under the plastic until I could get a couple underneath.

I exhaled in relief and supported him as we waited for Doc. The rest of my team had assembled and were watching him anxiously.

"Stop gawking," I told them. "Link up with Sergeant Takahashi and find something useful to do."

Sanchez grunted a laugh. "Make an NCO of you yet."

"Doc's on his way, Sarge. Meanwhile I need to take care of the *other* arrow. In your leg."

"Right. Forgot about that one."

"What do we got?" Doc asked as he approached.

"Arrows in his leg and chest," I replied. "Think it hit his lung. Cut off the shaft and got it covered with plastic. He's stable, but the head's still in there."

"Good," Doc said, double-checking my work. "Good. Okay, Sarge, good news is I can remove it. Bad news is we need to move, so it'll have to wait. Really bad news is when we get to it… it's gonna hurt like hell. But it'll hurt me more, so it'll be all right."

Sanchez suggested Doc go and do something I was certain was anatomically impossible. "Just get me on my feet."

***

"We gotta move, people," Takahashi shouted.

Doc and I wrapped Sanchez in a woobie and helped him stand, and I got one of his arms over my shoulder. He grunted in pain but allowed me to help him limp to the fast-flowing river cutting through the narrow canyon. Several dugout canoes our attackers had used to reach this position in the river valley rested on the bank, and Blue Squad was already moving two of them into the water.

"McKenzie, you and your team take those two," Captain Brown barked, knife-handing.

"But, sir, the lads say they dunno how to paddle!" McKenzie replied.

"Feather!" Brown called out. "You'll have to take some of the lads. Mix and match."

"Yes, sir," she replied, hurrying over to coordinate with McKenzie.

There were jaguar-men bodies everywhere, but no sign of the death-touched humans who'd attacked us atop the cliff. It'd been a sizable party though, and I saw the bodies of a few Unmakers among the dead.

Takahashi ordered several of the gals to demolish all the remaining canoes while Wilson and Cohen maneuvered the two that Gold Squad would be using off the shore. I splashed out with Sanchez to one of them and helped him climb aboard. I could tell he was hurting bad, even though he was making an effort not to show it. After we were aboard, Doc handed me Epasotl. She was still unconscious, and I laid her out in the bottom of the canoe.

"Thought I'd bought it," Sanchez muttered, staring at her.

"Sarge?" I asked. I hadn't quite heard him.

"Nothing," he grunted. "Move to the stern. You're on overwatch for our six."

"Hooah." I got up gingerly and edged past him to the back of the narrow, wobbly boat, where I set up Sybil on the deck.

"Gold Squad set," Takahashi transmitted as he settled into our canoe.

"Blue Squad set," Flaming Feather echoed.

Captain Brown ordered the platoon to paddle out into the current and follow the river as it flowed eastward. Brown had made sure each boat had a "captain" with some degree of experience to guide it, but we were going with the current, so there wasn't much to do but steer. As long as we didn't hit any serious whitewater, we'd be fine.

Assuming there weren't any monsters in the river looking to overturn a canoe for a late-afternoon snack.

I didn't know how far we traveled—the current moved at a rather lazy pace—but when dusk settled, Brown ordered us to shore. We disembarked and dragged the dugouts up onto a rocky beach. The cannon was narrower here, and the walls seemed much higher. Scrub oak hung precariously from the cliffs, and the ghostly shapes of bats flitted through the gathering mist. Everyone was exhausted, and more than a few people were just staring off into the distance. Epasotl had been awake for a couple of hours by now, but she was looking haggard. If I had to rate our combat efficiency, I'd put it at *Not Very*.

Brown got the platoon to work on clearing brush around our assembly area and building a simple perimeter of branches. It was obviously more of a make-work project to get people moving than any sort of effective defense, but it did the trick well enough.

Doc found me perched on a shelf of rock providing overwatch. "Need you, Bennett," he said.

I called to Dance to take my spot and followed him over to where Wilson, McKenzie, and Kiktú had taken a knee by Sanchez. Epasotl was squatting nearby, rolling the shrunken jaguar-man head from hand to hand.

"Gotta get that arrowhead out, Sergeant," Doc told Sanchez.

He nodded. "Where do you want me?"

Doc had laid out a double layer of poncho liners and motioned to it. Sanchez nodded again, and Wilson helped him lie down.

Captain Brown strode over and chewed on his lip. "How can I help, Doc?"

"More hands the better, sir." He glanced at each of us. "You're all going to have to hold him still. And I do mean *still*. If I had a table, I'd tie him down." He turned to Epasotl. "And I need light."

"Can do," she said, shoving the shrunken head back into her haversack. She fished around for a few moments and pulled out a small polished white stone. She blew on it and whispered, *"Tlauilli."*

The stone glowed faintly in her palm at first before increasing in brightness until our small group was bathed in a pure, cool light. Oddly, the luminance only lit a dome of space about ten feet around us. Beyond that it simply… ended.

"No one outside circle see light," Epasotl explained.

"Handy," Brown remarked.

"Okay," Doc said. "Everyone, get a good hold of him. He can't move while I'm working. Not even a little." His eyes met Sanchez's. "I've already given you morphine, so you're probably feeling pretty good right now, but it's not going to stay that way."

"Just get it over with," Sanchez replied.

Doc looked at me. "Bennett, you're on knife duty. I've sterilized these two blades. Work them down along the shaft and pry the wound open so I can get at the arrowhead with my pliers. You need to be rock steady. Understood? We might have to spread his ribs, so don't be dainty about it. Be firm. Careful as hell, but firm."

I swallowed the lump forming in my throat and nodded, taking a thin-bladed knife in each hand.

Doc motioned to Epasotl to hold the light over Sanchez's wound and pulled out an old leather wallet. "So you don't scream or bite your tongue off, Sarge," he explained to Sanchez, who simply grunted and bit down.

"Can't you do something for the pain, or put him to sleep or something?" I asked Epasotl.

"So sorry," she answered. "Use all juice in fight. Ring empty. No time meditate."

Doc removed the dressing and inspected the wound, probing a little with his forceps. Sanchez twitched, and Doc frowned in thought.

"Okay, Bennett. One blade here, the other here. Right alongside the shaft. Work them down a little and spread it open. We need to figure out how deep this goes."

I did as instructed, working the knives down about an inch, and pried the wound apart slowly. Sanchez grunted and bit down harder on the old wallet. Sweat was breaking out on his brow.

"Little more, Nephi," Doc said. "Little more. Pry it open. Good. Okay, a little more—" He shot a look up at Kiktú. "Hold him *steady*."

She hissed an apology.

"Need to open it up more, Bennett," Doc repeated.

I was trying. It wasn't easy, and I knew my every movement was putting Sanchez in agony. Tears were streaming down his face now, and his groans were louder, more raw.

"That's good," Doc said. "Little deeper… perfect. Hold there."

He slipped his medical pliers between my blades and gently twisted and tugged. He instructed me to open the wound still more, and then with a final gentle pull he extracted a nasty-looking barbed bone arrowhead, which he handed to Epasotl.

"Got it out cleanly. Doesn't look like any fragments are still in you, Sarge. Bennett, work your knives out slowly, real gentle. I'll dress the wound. Barring infection, we should be good to go. That's the good news. Bad news is we have to repeat this all over again for your leg."

Sanchez spit out the wallet and took a deep breath. "Thanks, boys," he grunted. He was surprisingly calm after what we'd just put him through.

Epasotl pulled a small stoppered gourd out of her haversack and handed it to Doc. "For Little Kahuna. Help heal faster. Stop wound rot. No need bandage."

Doc pulled the stopper and wrinkled his nose. "Smells like peppermint and death."

"Is from lizard lads."

"Oh, is it that green superglue they use?" I asked.

"Is green, yes."

"Works like a charm," McKenzie added. "Better than anything I've ever seen."

Doc smeared the green goop over the wound. It dried quickly, sealing the hole as it crystallized. He was about to wrap a bandage over it, but McKenzie held out a hand.

"Needs to breathe, Doc," he said. "Donna need no bandage."

"Interesting," Doc said. "Find out if they have more of this stuff, or if they can make it. Meanwhile..." He patted Sanchez's shoulder. "We need to get that other arrow out of your leg."

CHAPTER 24

"How's our ammo?" Takahashi asked Wilson and me the next morning as the platoon was getting ready to move out again.

"I had everyone turn their packs and pockets inside out looking for loose rounds," Wilson said. "My team's just shy of a combat load per person, and the surplus is all gone."

"Pretty much the same," I said.

Takahashi pinched the bridge of his nose. "Don't shoot the messenger, but I need two magazines from everyone in the squad. Blue is low on belts. They're down to linking spare ammo by hand."

"That'll get them, what? Three belts?" I said. "Not even that."

"Oh, and a pouch of linked rounds from each of your gunners," he added.

"You're killin' me, Taks," Wilson said.

"Yeah, well, it's that bad." Takahashi spread his hands. "How about you personally, Bennett?"

"Two and a partial magazine for Sybil. That's it. Once those are gone, she's a really expensive paperweight."

"I got three full magazines for the Barrett off of Wright," Wilson offered. "Ten-rounders, bro. That should keep you in business a while longer. *And*—" He grinned. "A handful of Raufoss for special occasions. But we're yellow on forty mike-mike. Leaves only has three AB and five HE left."

"Dance has about the same," I said. "Minus one of each."

"You mean Thumper," Wilson said with a smile.

"She's a better shot with the FL40GL," Takahashi said to Wilson. "Have Leaves give her another two of each."

Wilson looked wounded, but nodded.

"Green on nine-millimeter though," I said.

"Same," said Wilson. "Once the SCARs run dry, I'll take these Glock-whatevers over a sharp stick and harsh language. They're good pistols."

"Not much stopping power against a jag though," I said. "Takes half a mag to put one down."

"That's why you gotta aim for the kill switch." Wilson aimed a finger gun at my nose.

"Doesn't matter," Takahashi said. "All the extra mags are going to Captain and us NCOs anyway. Everyone else keeps what's loaded in their sidearm, no more. And even then, sidearms are a last resort. We need to keep our people focusing on bows and sharp sticks. Harsh language too."

"We need a loot drop," Wilson said.

"Say again?"

"Loot drops. Dude back in Amoloyan I was drinking with told me about them. You see, in the future, there's these video games where you get dumps of ammo and healing packs and shit along the way. They call it a loot drop."

"Unless a C-130 loaded with pallets of ammo and Snickers bars crashes in our path, I think we can scratch off that possibility," I said.

"Stranger things have happened here," Wilson pointed out. "We did find that plane full of cocaine."

"*Anyway*," Takahashi said. "Two mags of seven-six-two from each of your people and a pouch to Blue Squad, and their extra mags of nine-millimeter go to Sanchez for now."

"Roger that," Wilson said. "And two rounds each of AB and HE to Miss Thumper. Want a pint of blood while you're at it, Taks? Maybe my left nut too?"

"Just the ammo, smartass."

"Right." Wilson snapped his fingers and then clapped his hands together. "I'll go assemble the Avengers."

"Don't let Captain hear you say that," I warned.

Wilson shrugged. "Avengers could kick the X-Men's asses any day, you ask me. Wish my call sign was Thor."

"Sergeant Thor, eh?" I said. "Kinda has a nice ring to it."

"Instead I'm Havok, whoever the hell that is."

"Captain didn't give you the lowdown?"

"Of course he did. Something something mutant plasma bolts. Dunno. Sounded lame." He pointed a finger at both of us. "That's all off the record, bros. Captain asks, I think X-Men are totally rad."

"Come to think of it, you're really more Thing than Thor," I told Wilson.

"Yeah, I could work with that," he said. "It's clobberin' time!" He laughed and gave me a fist bump. "That's totally my new battle cry."

Takahashi just shook his head. "You can geek out over comic books later. Redistribute the ammo, and let's form the squad up in fifteen."

As Wilson turned to go collect his team, I gave Takahashi a nod and left to find my own people. Dance was sitting by our rucks cleaning her rifle, and I gave her a wave as I wandered over to Cohen and Lawrence's OP.

"How goes the war?" I asked them after I'd announced my approach and we'd exchanged the sign and countersign.

"Quiet for once," Cohen said.

"We're forming up by the boats in fifteen," I said. "So start packing up. I need two magazines of seven-six-two, Cohen, and a pouch of linked from you, Short Round, and whatever extra nine you two guys got for your sidearms."

"For what?" Lawrence asked.

"Orders, that's what."

"That's some squiggly shit there, man," Lawrence said.

Cohen just rolled his eyes and handed me his mags.

I looked at Lawrence. "I know you have spare mags for your pistol, Short Round. Hand 'em over."

"Can you stop calling me that?" He pulled out a stick of nine-millimeter.

"No can do, Shorty. Where's the other one? You were issued three. One for your weapon and two spares."

"Lost it," he said.

"Bullshit," said Cohen.

"No, really. I lost it," Lawrence protested, but he looked shifty.

"I'm calling bullcrap too," I said. "Sanchez is going to count the mags, and I guarantee you don't want me telling him you *lost* it. We can't afford to lose ammo. Not a single round. You finally just got off latrine duty, man."

"Fess up," Cohen urged. "God help you if you lie to Sergeant Sanchez."

Lawrence suddenly looked very uncomfortable. "I… traded it," he mumbled.

"Traded it?" I said. "With whom? For what?"

"Peter. He wanted it for the MP5."

Most of the lads were relying on slings, but McKenzie had put Peter through special training on the submachine gun. I wasn't sure how I felt about that, but… the lads were McKenzie's responsibility, and if Brown wasn't complaining, I wasn't going to.

"He was issued ammo. He doesn't need more. What did you trade it for?"

Lawrence mumbled.

"Say again, PFC?" I had a pretty good idea what the answer was, but I wanted him to say it.

"It's just I'm so damn *tired*, and it *helps*."

Cohen groaned. "You're an idiot, Isaiah, you know that, right?"

"Hand it over," I said.

Lawrence looked up at me in alarm.

"Your stash," I said. "Hand it over."

He hesitated.

"Man, you're in such deep shit you don't even know," Cohen said. "Don't dig yourself any deeper."

"But I *need* it," Lawrence whined.

"No, you don't," I said. "Just man up and hand it over. I'll do what I can to convince Captain and Sanchez to take it easy on you. You really only have two options here. That's option one."

"What's option two?" Lawrence asked.

Cohen and I just gave him a look.

"Oh." Lawrence sighed. "Fine."

He reached behind his plate carrier and pulled out a small leather pouch. Giving it a wistful look, he handed it to me. I shoved it into a cargo pocket along with the magazines they'd given me.

"Pack it up, grab your stuff, and meet Gold Squad by the boats," I said. "Ten minutes."

***

I found Sanchez sitting on his ruck eating some dried meat cake. He seemed tired, more tired than usual, and a little gray around the edges, but after what he'd been through, I couldn't blame him.

"Got the nine-millimeter from my team for you, Sergeant. As requested."

"Dump 'em here." He motioned off to his side.

I unloaded the magazines.

"Missing one?" he said.

I *knew* he'd notice.

"Yes. Lawrence was one short."

"He have an explanation for that?"

"Well…" I rubbed the back of my neck. "Well, see, Peter's been scrounging ammo for the submachine gun, and he, uh… well, Lawrence traded him the stick of nine for, uh… you know."

Sanchez gave me a hard look. "I don't know, Bennett. That's what you're here to tell me."

"Cocaine, Sarge."

Sanchez sighed. He really was tired if that's all the reaction I was gonna get. I'd expecting an ass-chewing at the very least.

I pulled out the little leather pouch and handed it to him. "He gave it up without too much fuss, Sarge," I said. "Was hoping you'd go easy on him."

"You were, huh?"

"He's trying," I offered. "We've been pushing so hard, and he was using it to keep up with everyone else and… I guess that sounds pretty lame, Sarge."

"You think? Don't make excuses for the kid," Sanchez said. "That's not your job." He stood and stretched gingerly, testing out

199

his injured leg and holding a hand to his side. He looked like he'd aged ten years overnight. He scowled, then gave an evil little smile. "As it turns out, Doc doesn't want me carrying my ruck. I'll need a porter. Send Lawrence over. I'm assigning him to HQ for now."

"Right away, sir."

I trotted back to where Gold was forming up. "Sergeant Sanchez has a job for you, Isaiah. You're reassigned to HQ."

He moaned and muttered something under his breath.

"Move with a purpose, PFC," Cohen quipped.

"Swap weapons," I told them. "You won't be needing the Mark 48, Short Round."

Cohen gave Lawrence his magazines while the other grumbled and unslung his remaining pouch of a hundred linked rounds.

"She's got about half a belt loaded, plus this full pouch," Lawrence said. "Take care of my homegirl."

"Will do, man," Cohen said. "Congrats on going back home."

"That's right," I said. "You were Sanchez's driver when this all kicked off." I laughed. "Be like old times."

"Screw you," Lawrence said.

"That's 'Screw you, *Corporal*,'" Cohen said.

Lawrence flipped him off and beat feet over to Sanchez.

"I should probably work on discipline more," I said.

"Nah. You're doing fine, Corporal."

****

"We board in five mikes," Takahashi told Gold Squad. "Wilson's boat will be the lead element in the convoy and Bennett's will be trail. I'll be in Wilson's boat. Our job is to watch for rapids. If we encounter any whitewater or falls, we'll have to..." He paused, looking for the word.

"Portage," I supplied.

"*Portage* the boats past them."

Jade Talon raised a hand. "What is 'portage'?"

"We'll carry the canoes past the dangerous water," I explained.

"Carry them?" she looked at the large dugouts skeptically. Each was nearly forty feet long.

"They're lighter than they look," I assured her.

"Obsidian Tears, you'll be with Bennett's team to even the loads," Takahashi said.

She gave a "Hooah" and moved beside First-to-Dance. They slapped palms and bumped fists. Not a Kuauchanejkej custom, by the way. All the gals by this point had been infected by Wilson's surfer slang and mannerisms.

Takahashi glanced back to where the rest of the platoon was staging and then turned to us. "Okay, get on board. Gold is responsible for security while the rest of the platoon gets off shore."

Dance and Tears were already maneuvering our dugout into the water. I splashed out to help them, and Cohen climbed aboard, moving to the stern.

"Dance, you're on the bow. Tears, you're in the middle. I'll be steering from the stern."

They chorused hooahs and climbed aboard. I followed, and we pushed off the riverbed with our paddles and entered the current.

"Now this is the tricky part," I said to Dance and Tears. "We need to hold our position in the river. So we're paddling *backwards*, against the current. Smooth, strong strokes. I'll call out a cadence. We row as one."

We managed to stay more or less stationary relative to the shore as I called the strokes and corrected mistakes. Captain Brown's dugout was already in the river, followed by Sanchez's, while Blue Squad held security on the rocky beach. García's canoe followed, and then finally Flaming Feather boarded and her team pushed off into the flowing water. Finally Wilson's boat struck out for the center of the river, and soon the whole column was moving downstream, the mist-draped canyon walls narrowing and the river flowing ever faster.

CHAPTER 25

First-to-Dance gasped for air. "I thought you said these are not as heavy as they look."

"They aren't," I grunted.

"Still… plenty heavy… man," Cohen panted.

"Well…" I said. "Usually there'd be… six men… carrying it."

Our little team struggled with the forty-foot canoe down a steep, narrow trail covered with shale and scrub, working our way along the canyon wall while trying not to fall over into the raging whitewater below. It was early afternoon, and we'd already portaged one waterfall, but that'd been a cakewalk compared to now. This stretch of rapids was going on a lot farther than we'd anticipated.

"Havok, Longshot," I transmitted.

"Go for Havok."

I frowned. Wilson didn't sound even mildly winded.

"You hit… the end of this… yet?"

"Negative. We're working past an obstacle right now."

"What… kind of… obstacle?"

"Gnarly rock wall. About, oh, fifteen feet high. You'll need rope. You sound tired, bro. Thought you were all Mr. Macho now."

"Golf Foxtrot Yankee," I replied. "Longshot out."

"Did he say… fifteen feet?" Cohen gasped.

"Something… like that… yeah."

"How're we gonna… get this ark up a… fifteen-foot wall?"

"Rope… apparently."

"No bueno," Tears wheezed.

"Come on." I shook the sweat out of my eyes. "Move… with a… purpose."

Dance gave a weak "Hooah," and I laughed. Coughed, really. My mouth was dry, and the whitewater rushing below us was making me thirsty.

"Longshot, Xavier."

"Go for… Longshot," I replied.

"Trail widens a hundred meters from you. Take ten. Rest and recover then Charlie Mike. Xavier out."

"Oh thank God," Cohen practically sobbed.

We made the hundred meters without dropping the canoe or ourselves into the rapids, and collapsed on a bed of shale. I sipped from my water tube and stared blankly at the high cliffs rising above us. It was dark and chilly at the bottom of the canyon, the sky above only a thin ribbon of gray.

"How high you think those cliffs are?" Cohen asked.

"Sixteen hundred meters, give or take," I said automatically. I'd been estimating ranges so long now I didn't have to think about it. Even vertically.

He gave a low whistle. "Wouldn't want to climb down that."

"Heck no," I said. "If you fell from the top, you'd hit terminal velocity just over a third of the way down."

"How fast is that?"

"Fast enough you'd be a smear when you landed."

"Sergeant Wilson jumps off cliffs," Obsidian Tears offered.

"Sergeant Wilson is crazy," I said.

"How does he not die?" Dance asked.

"Parachute," I said. "It's like a big blanket that catches the air and makes you float down slowly."

"Like Epasotl and Sergeant Sanchez," Dance observed.

"*That* was magic," I said. "Parachuting isn't magic, just crazy."

"When a girl is to become a warrior, she must prove her bravery by climbing the tallest tree and jumping with vines tied to her ankles," Dance said. "Sergeant Wilson did it when he lived with us."

"Of course he did."

I'd heard of a tribe that did that in the South Pacific, but never among Mesoamerican people. Maybe some insane bungee jumper at some point had been sucked into the Land of the Black Sun and had taught them how.

"He was the first man to do so in the memory of the tribe," Dance continued. "That is why he did not have to live with the other men and could stay with Dressed-in-Stars in the royal village. He proved himself to be a warrior."

I grunted.

"You will have to do the same, if you are to live with Princess Flower Eagle in the royal village," Tears said casually.

That got my attention.

"What?"

"You must prove yourself to be a warrior," Dance said.

"Figured I'd already done that."

"Unless you demonstrate your bravery, you will have to live with the other men," she explained.

"Or become a eunuch," Tears added.

"Yes, that is an option," Dance said seriously. "But I think the princess wants children."

"She could have children by another man," Tears proposed.

"Oh yes, that would work also," Dance agreed.

"Wait." I held up my hands. "You're saying if I want to live with my wife, I need to do some crazy bungee jump with vines tied to my feet or get castrated? Those are my only options? Just how tall is this tree I'm supposed to jump out of?"

"Twelve land—" Tears began.

Dance cut Tears off proudly. "Thirty meters!"

Cohen started laughing.

"But Corporal Bennett is the princess's royal consort," Tears said.

"True." Dance pursed her lips. "How tall was Princess Flower Eagle's tree?"

"Oh, fifteen land rods at least."

"Xochi jumped almost forty meters?" I said. "With nothing but vines tied around her ankles?"

"Yes!" Dance exclaimed. "She is very brave. You will have to match her bravery to be a suitable consort."

"You're making this all up," I said. "You can't have a custom for this if Wilson was the *first*."

"Queen Skull-Dancer gave Sergeant Wilson the option of that or being made a eunuch if he wanted to stay in the royal village with Dressed-in-Stars," Dance said. "I do not see why her daughter, the new queen, would not insist on the same from you."

"They've established a precedent, man," Cohen said, trying and failing to keep a straight face. "Can't argue that. Gotta take the jump or"—he made scissor fingers—"snip, snip. Say goodbye to your boys."

"Forty *meters*?" I repeated. My cousin had once talked me into bungee jumping off a tower less than half that tall, and that had been plenty, thank you very much. *And* I'd had a harness *and* there was a net at the bottom.

"There is no shame in becoming a eunuch," Dance said seriously. "The queen had many consorts, and the princesses called them father."

"Although you cannot sire children, you will raise them as your own," Tears added. "And a eunuch can still nest with a woman."

"*Obsidian Tears!*" Dance admonished.

"What? It is true!"

"It *is* true," Dance admitted.

"And it is safest to nest with a eunuch because then a warrior cannot become with child," Tears said. "That is what eunuchs are for, after all."

"But Friar Bastía teaches us the practice is ungodly," Dance pointed out.

"*That* is what confession is for," Tears said with a laugh.

"Oh!" Dance threw up her hands. "You are *wicked*, sister."

Cohen was crying now and trying not to howl with laughter.

I stood, brushing myself off. "I think that's enough rest," I said. "We need to catch up with the rest of the platoon."

***

The fifteen-foot wall Wilson had encountered was a sheer cut like a giant step in the side of the canyon. With some rope and a lot of sweat and a lot more profanity, we managed to get our dugout up to the next part of the trail. Cohen would've put any sailor to shame, and the gals taught me some colorful new Kuauchanejkej metaphors; even I dropped more than a few F-bombs (sorry, Mom). But we managed it, barely, and motored on through the growing dusk.

"It is so cold," Dance panted as we maneuvered the canoe through a particularly dense clump of thorny bushes. "Will the river become like rock, Corporal?"

"It can't be less than fifty degrees," I grunted. "That's nothing. How can you be cold? I'm sweating buckets."

"We're going to have to stop," Cohen wheezed. "I can't see anything."

"Stop where?" I asked. "You heard Sanchez. They found a place to stop for the night. Think how good your sleeping bag will feel."

My foot slipped and I grabbed at a small tree growing out of the canyon wall to steady myself as part of the trail gave way and crumbled down into the frothing water ten feet below. The canoe teetered, and for a moment my heart caught in my throat as I had visions of it falling. But we managed to right it and keep moving forward.

"Watch that part of the trail," I warned everyone behind me. "It's eroding fast."

"What trail?" Cohen moaned. "I'm telling you, man, I can't see a damn thing."

"It *is* becoming dark," Tears agreed.

"Just stick close to the canyon wall; feel the way with your feet," I said. "I'll guide you. It gets wider up ahead."

"How can you see anything?" Cohen asked.

"He has been blessed with the eyes of an owl," said Dance.

"Not blessed," I grunted. "I think it's part of the curse."

"Some curse," Cohen gasped. "You're stronger, faster, heal like some kinda freak, and now you can see in the dark. Wish *I* was cursed."

"Yeah, except I'm *dying*," I said bitterly. "I can feel it, like a cancer."

"Are you truly?" Dance asked.

"Yes. Less talking, more moving. Trail widens up here just enough that we can put the canoe down for a minute. Just another few meters."

Gasping and panting, we inched forward until it was safe to lower the dugout to the ground.

"Xavier, Longshot," I transmitted. "Taking five mikes to rest."

"How far away are you?" Sanchez asked.

"Unknown. Few hundred meters maybe?"

"Turn on your strobe."

I fished in my pack for the IR strobe, turned it on, and held it above my head.

"Solid visual. Estimate three hundred fifty meters out. Nightcrawler is ETA ten mikes to the AA. Take five, no more, then Charlie Mike."

"Roger. Longshot out." My team was looking beat. "Get out your NODs."

Cohen gave a vague nod and blew out his cheeks. "Three fifty to go?"

"That's what the man said."

"How far do you think we've been carrying this damn boat?"

"Too far," Tears said.

"Roger that," Dance agreed. "Ugh. It's *so* cold."

Cohen laughed. "Not nearly. I was on a stalk once with my uncle. Got caught in a freak snowstorm in the mountains. Hit minus twenty. Thirty maybe with the wind chill."

"How cold is that?" Dance asked.

"Cold enough to kill you quick if you don't have the right gear."

"Cold enough to turn water like rock?"

"Cold enough to turn your fingers and toes to rock. It's called frostbite. Your flesh freezes and dies. My uncle lost two fingers and a toe."

"That is horrible." Dance shuddered. "I cannot imagine such cold."

"Yeah, fortunately there was a shelter nearby, or we'd have been toast. But we scored a bull elk the next day. An imperial."

"What is that?" Tears asked.

"Like a deer, but bigger. An imperial has seven points on each antler."

"Seven!" Dance exclaimed. "Most stags have only two."

"I speared one with three," Tears said proudly.

"Enough chitchat," I said. "Time's up. Charlie Mike."

Cohen groaned and put on his NODs.

"Come on, man," I said. "Just think of it as three and a half football fields. Then you get to sleep."

"Just," he muttered, moving to the stern of the dugout. Dance and Tears each took a position in the middle. I positioned myself at the bow and keyed my radio. "Xavier, Longshot. Moving."

"Roger. Be advised Nightcrawler reports the trail is eroding. Stay frosty. Xavier out."

"On three." I counted down, and we heaved the canoe up and advanced forward. "Trail gets narrow again up ahead. Slow and steady. Watch your step."

The trail not only narrowed, it was unstable, the edge crumbling away as we moved along. It had probably been eroding bit by bit as the rest of the platoon passed. We had to slow to a shuffle, and soon the dugout was scraping along the side of the canyon wall.

"Longshot, Xavier. You're still over two hundred meters out. Need assist?"

"Now he asks?" Cohen griped. "Could've used an assist an hour ago."

"Platoon was still on the trail," I said irritably. "García just got into the assembly area not ten minutes ago. You know that." I keyed my radio. "Affirmative on assist. Be advised there's not much of a trail left anymore."

"Hold your position. Sunfire and Havok en route. Xavier out."

"You heard the man," I said. "Cavalry's coming."

We held the dugout propped against the cliff and waited. After several minutes I saw Wilson working his way carefully toward us, followed by Takahashi.

"No good," Wilson called out. "Trail's too dangerous to continue."

"Well what the heck are we supposed to do, Sarge?"

"Wait one." He keyed his radio. "Xavier, Havok. Trail's eroded too much. It's too dangerous to move this tub any farther. Recommend we lose it."

"Roger. Confirmed. Drop it in the drink. Xavier out."

"We're ditching it after carrying it all this way?" Cohen cried. "This is bullshit!"

"Embrace the suck, Hush Puppy," said Wilson. "It is what it is. Huge chunk of the path fell into the river over here. No way you'll be able to get it past that point. Hella too dangerous."

"So, just toss it over?" I asked Wilson.

"Yeah, but carefully. Taks and I will help. Hold one."

I watched as he and Takahashi moved closer. Only when they shuffled slowly around one spot did I see the chunk taken out of the path there. He was right. There was no way.

"All right, Bennett, I got the bow," Wilson said. "Get yourself and your team farther down the length of the hull. Slowly. Shit! There goes more of the path. Taks, you got ahold of it?"

"Hooah."

"Okay, nice and easy, people," Wilson coached. "We're gonna need to—"

Obsidian Tears screamed and dropped from view as the trail collapsed under her, but I didn't hear a splash. I craned my neck and saw her dangling one-handed from the branch of a tiny but hardy tree sticking out of the canyon wall just below us. The river crashed and foamed under her, snatching at her boots.

"I'll get her," I said as calmly as I could manage. "I'm letting go of the boat on three, okay?"

"Roger, bro, we got it," Wilson confirmed.

I counted down and then squatted by the crumbling edge as everyone else held the dugout above me. Tears had gotten her other hand on the thin branch, but the current was slapping and tugging at her feet, trying to drag her away. I looked back at the wall and found a crack big enough to wedge my fist into as an anchor, then leaned out over the edge, but she was just out of reach.

"Get your feet out of the water," I called down to her. "Brace them against the rock. I'm going to have to get some rope. Hang in there. You're going to be fine."

She stared at me with terrified eyes and nodded.

Then the branch snapped and she was gone.

CHAPTER 26

I didn't even think about it. I ditched my ruck and weapon on the trail and jumped in after her.

The torrent caught my feet and swept me under, pummeling my body against the rocks. Fighting against the undertow, I surfaced and caught sight of Obsidian Tears's arm flailing above the whitecaps. I angled my feet like some sort of insane aquatic luger toward her, and the current rocketed me forward; I almost swept past her, only just catching her drag handle by some miracle. Pulling her close, I wrapped myself around her, protecting her with my body as best I could. Her ruck was gone, but her weapon was catching against rocks and slapping us like a jackhammer. I fumbled for the quick release on the sling and let it go before it brained one of us.

Getting to shore didn't seem like an option. The best I could do was try to ride the current like a human kayak with her on my chest and hope a rock didn't crack my skull open. I'm sure there's a proper way to rescue someone from rapids, but they didn't exactly include that in 19D training, so I was making it up as I crashed along.

Rule one was probably *Don't Jump In After Them.*

The river curved, and I tried to angle us toward the inside bend—some part of my panicked brain was telling me the current would be slower there. Whitecaps rose and slapped at my face, nearly drowning me, while rocks beat against my backside. I kept trying to lower my feet to break against the riverbed, but the undertow would always snatch my boots back up again and propel us forward. At least I was making progress toward the inside curve, and the current *was* slower here, relatively.

Then something abruptly snatched at Tears and I nearly lost her. Somehow we'd come to a dead stop in the river.

I floated, confused for a minute, and then discovered the water was shallow enough to stand in. In fact it wasn't much above my thighs. Floating her inert body in front of me, I searched for what had stopped us and discovered her sling, though released, had gotten itself wrapped around one of her arms, and her rifle had anchored between two rocks. I untangled her and then made for a small ledge of rock, where I laid her down.

She had a steady pulse, if weak, but she wasn't breathing. I gave her mouth-to-mouth until she started coughing up half the river. Then I rolled her on her side and got her in the rest position. When I was sure she was breathing fine on her own, I waded out to retrieve her weapon.

Wearily, and feeling every bruise and blow I'd sustained in the rapids, I climbed up onto the small ledge beside Obsidian Tears.

I said a prayer. A good one. But brief.

She was mumbling something in her native tongue, but it was slurred and I couldn't make it out. She was shivering. Come to think of it, so was I. And I felt drowsy. I mean, it'd been a long, hard day, and I was exhausted, but I felt… foggy.

That meant something, but I couldn't remember what.

I should probably check in on the radio.

I just wanted to lie down beside her and sleep.

I dug a soggy piece of meat cake out of a cargo pocket and chewed for a minute. Tears's teeth were chattering. Then I remembered my med kit and the thermal blanket inside. It was still strapped around my waist. Another small miracle.

"Okay, Tears," I said, my voice slightly slurred. "Sorry about this, but you can't stay in these wet clothes."

But I should really check in with the platoon.

Except my radio was shattered.

I checked Tears's radio and held the headset to my ear. "Any Crazy Horse element, this is Longshot. Radio check, over."

I tried a couple of times before Sanchez responded asking for a sitrep.

"Uh, we're both alive," I said. "Though I had to resuscitate her. No idea where we are. Except it's on the other side of the river. I, uh, got her rifle and we're good on ammo. She's stable. But we're cold. I got my med kit. Going to wrap her in a thermal blanket."

"Is your position secure?"

"Secure enough. Got a cozy little shelf of rock here. Only way to us is through the river."

"Roger. Can you hold there until morning?"

"Sure," I replied. "Don't have anything better to do."

"Longshot, this is Beast," Doc cut in. "Have you checked Gold One-Zero for hypothermia?"

Hypothermia! That's what I was trying to remember.

"Yeah, she's shivering and mumbling. Shallow breathing. All that."

"You're slurring really bad. Sounds like you got it yourself," Doc replied. "Is your position sheltered?"

It wasn't, really. But farther back along the rock, there was an overhang we could scoot beneath. "Sheltered enough, Doc. Cozy cave here." It looked anything but cozy.

"Okay, listen, you already know this, but you're probably not thinking straight, so I'm going to spell it out for you. You need to get both of you out of those wet clothes. Everything. Underwear too. This is no time to be shy. Get yourselves wrapped up in that emergency blanket together and get her as far into your shelter as possible. I want her against the back wall and you behind her, like a sandwich. Are you following?"

"You want me to… spoon her… *naked*?"

"Affirmative."

I paused.

"Longshot, do you read me?"

"Lima Charlie." I rubbed my face. "Roger and all that. Take off everything?"

"Everything. Or she could die. Maybe you too. Understand? It's not *that* cold out, but cold enough, and I'm not taking chances if you're both showing signs of hypothermia and you just had to resuscitate her."

"Roger."

"Good. Beast out."

I laid out the thermal blanket against the back of the little shelf, as far under the overhang as I could reach, then undressed Obsidian Tears and moved her into position against the wall before pausing to quickly function-check the rifle. Good to go. Solid weapon, that SCAR. But I was stalling.

Placing the rifle where it'd be in reach, I stripped off my gear and clothes and slid in behind her, wrapping us both in the thin metallic blanket as tight as I could manage. She'd stopped mumbling, and her breathing became less shallow as I held her. Eventually we both stopped shivering.

Sleep came quickly.

***

I awoke to the sound of soft laughter, and it took me a minute to remember where I was… and who I was with.

"Good morning, Corporal."

"Uh, morning." I shifted awkwardly. "Sorry about… *that*… I, uh… it has a mind of its own."

"Why are we naked?"

"Er… hypothermia. Staying in wet clothes could've killed… It was cold… Doc said…"

"It is not so cold now."

"No."

She snuggled her back against my chest. "Is this Outworlder medicine for cold sickness?"

"Something like that."

"Hmm. Good medicine."

Soft light was pouring through the opening I'd left in the blanket for air, and I could hear the river rushing by.

"We should probably get up," I said.

"You already are."

"Please don't make this any more awkward than it already is."

She laughed. "Do not worry. I do not want to nest with you. You belong to the princess, and besides, I do not want children. Not for many years. But lying here with you is more pleasant than drowning in the river, no? Thank you for saving me."

"Of course."

"It was very foolish of you."

"Yeah."

"And brave."

"I suppose."

She twisted around until she was facing me. "You are an unusual man."

"I get that a lot."

"Not in a bad way, but still, you are somehow different from your brother warriors. I can see why the princess was drawn to you. You two are a good match, I think."

"I like to think so too."

"Mmm." She put her head under my chin. "I do not want to get up. Keep me warm a while longer. I need more of your medicine."

***

Wrestling back into cold, damp clothing after the warmth of the cocoon Obsidian Tears and I'd shared wasn't pleasant, but it was a relief. I knew what we'd done had been essential for her survival, and probably mine as well, and besides, nothing had happened between us that I should feel guilty about, but I did anyway. It didn't help that she wasn't awkward about the whole thing in the least and found perverse amusement in teasing me and seeing me blush.

The temperature had risen somewhat with the dawn, into the high fifties was my guess, but there was a light fog off the river and it was misting slightly. Not quite rain, but not pleasant either. I was grateful for our little cave.

After she'd bound her chest in the cloth wrap all the gals wore, I turned to Tears and gestured to her tattoos. "You have a lot more than Xochi. Hers are a record of the royal family. What are yours?"

"Some are a record of my mother and her mothers through time. Some celebrate battles I have fought and foes I have conquered. Others are protection from evil or to bring good fortune in war. Friar Bastía says that is idolatry and superstition and I should put my faith in God, not images on my skin, but it is our sacred tradition. Besides, I can have faith in both, no?"

"I suppose."

"Many of your brother warriors have skin pictures. Why don't you?"

"Just the way I was raised." I made air quotes. "'My body is a temple.'"

She laughed. "Friar Bastía says the same." She affected a deep, jolly voice. "*An nescitis quoniam membra vestra, templum sunt Spiritus Sancti, qui in vobis est, quem habetis a Deo, et non estis vestri?*"

"I'm going to take a wild guess and say 1 Corinthians 6:19."

"Correct!"

"I didn't realize so many of you knew Latin. I sure don't."

"Oh, I cannot speak in the tongue of the Word of God, but Friar Bastía teaches us out of his codex and explains the meanings of the words. He has us memorize the verses."

"It would be better to memorize them in your own tongue."

Tears looked scandalized. "But they are the words of God. They should be spoken in His tongue, as He wrote them."

"Latin isn't God's language. That verse was originally written by the Apostle Paul in Greek anyway."

"I will have to ask the friar about that. Do you speak this... Greek?"

"No, I learned the Bible in my own language. So I don't have to rely on a priest's interpretation. You should be able to read it for yourself."

"Who translated it from Greek to your tongue?"

"Uh... many people. King James commissioned the translation."

"But you don't know who?"

"Not exactly."

"Then you are trusting the interpretation of men you don't know."

"I suppose." I paused in lacing up my boots. "I mean, I have faith they were directed by the Holy Ghost."

"And I trust Friar Bastía to interpret correctly, whether this Greek tongue or Latin. He is a man of God and is filled with the Spirit."

"Fair enough."

"Princess Flower Eagle said you were a priest once, like the friar, for a time. How is it you do not know Latin?"

"Didn't need to learn it. I taught people the Word of God in Spanish."

"Spanish? That is Friar Bastía's native tongue."

"It is, but his dialect is very different from what I learned. We come from separate times in the history of our world. Almost five hundred years apart, I think."

"Why did you stop being a priest?"

"I wasn't actually a priest, not like your friar anyway. I was a missionary. I helped… spread the Word to those who didn't know it. It was just for two years."

"Ah, I see." She pulled on her plate carrier. "Do you miss being a man of God?"

"Sometimes. It was a good experience for the most part. I learned a lot about myself. I'd do it again for sure."

"It is good you are no longer a man of God and became Princess Flower Eagle's first consort. Do you think you will prove yourself as warrior in the trials or become a eunuch?"

"I'd prefer to not be a eunuch, thanks."

She nodded thoughtfully. "Then when I am ready to bear children, I will come to you for seed."

"Excuse me?"

"You are a good man. I would bear your children. One day. Not soon. I have many years left as a warrior."

"I don't think Xochi would agree to that. Or Friar Bastía. Or myself for that matter, no offense."

She frowned. "It is true the friar is not fond of the custom, but the princess would not object, I think. And it is not for *you* to decide."

She waved a hand dismissively. "You are just a man. Your seed belongs to the tribe. You should be honored that a warrior like myself would take your seed. I have many kills."

"But it's not *my* custom," I said.

"You are Kuauchanejkej now. Our customs are your customs. But there are many years yet before I will come to you. You will... how do you say? Come around? Sergeant Wilson has already agreed. I will take his seed too."

"Of course he did." I paused. "What did you mean, *first* consort?"

"The queen had five consorts, all eunuchs of course. If the princess becomes queen, she may choose to take others as well."

"Oh."

"Or she may not." Tears grinned. "I can see you do not like the idea. Friar Bastía does not either. Perhaps the custom will die in time. The friar is trying to institute a bond between one intact man and one woman. He calls it *El Sacramento del Matrimonio*. It is a strange custom."

"Right. The Sacrament of Marriage. If you recall, Friar Bastía married us. As *one* man and wife."

"Oh! I did not realize the princess agreed to be bound by this new custom. That is... interesting. And it binds your seed also?"

"Afraid so."

"That is unfortunate," she said as she wrapped her hair up into a topknot. "Many warriors will be disappointed."

"Mmhmm." I suppose I should've been flattered, but being treated like a stud horse didn't exactly thrill me. I'm sure Wilson was stoked though.

I'd turned off Tears's radio to save power overnight, and now I hooked on the earpiece as I switched it back on. "Any Crazy Horse element, this is Longshot. Radio check, over."

"Longshot, Xavier. Read you Lima Charlie. Was wondering if you two made it through the night. I see you survived the ordeal."

Very funny, Sergeant.

"Roger," I replied. "We're at a bend in the river. It looks fordable. We could attempt a crossing."

"Negative, Longshot. Hold your position. We're coming to you."

CHAPTER 27

It took a couple of hours for Wilson's team to find us, and by then the temperature was rising into the sixties. But the mist had turned into a soft drizzle, and the current looked stronger than it had earlier. Crossing would be tricky; Sanchez had been right to tell us to stay put.

"Bennett!" Wilson called across the river. "Was starting to wonder if we'd ever find you."

"Heya, Sarge," I called back. "Thanks for popping by."

He was standing on a shelf about ten feet above the river with Jade Talon and Falling Leaves, and he put his hands on his hips as he surveyed the churning water.

"Not too deep." He pointed to one part of the river. "Looks like you could follow that path of stones there to cross."

"Was thinking the same thing," I replied.

"You'll want to strip down," Wilson said. "You're gonna get soaked."

"No point. Clothes are already gross and wet."

"Roger that. Here, catch!" He threw out a coil of rope that unwound at it soared over the water, and I caught the other end. There wasn't anything suitable to anchor it to, so I just tied a bowline around my chest.

"Okay, you're first," I told Tears. "Wade across, facing the current, and use the rope to support you. Leaning back a little to put tension on the rope will help. Don't cross your legs and only move one foot at a time. Shuffle. Keep your hands on the rope at all times. Nice and slow. Got it?"

"Hooah, Corporal." She slung her rifle and slipped off the ledge and into the water as Wilson and I kept the line steady.

She had a couple of close calls, and at one point the water reached her chest and she lost her footing for a heart-stopping minute, but she made it across and scaled the short rise into the arms of her battle sisters.

"Your turn, bro," Wilson called to me.

I threw a mock salute and lowered myself from the shelf into the cold water, carefully feeling for purchase on the riverbed with my boots. The rocks were incredibly slippery, and with each step the undertow threatened to sweep my legs out from under me. As I moved diagonally against the current, Wilson took up the slack in the rope.

"Halfway there, bro," he called. "You got this!"

The churning torrent rose above my thighs, then my waist as I reached the midpoint, and it was getting harder to keep my footing as buoyancy took over. I shuffled my feet, unwilling to take a full step, and then something hit my thighs *hard* and my boots lost purchase. The river snatched at me, spinning my body around, and I was absolutely terrified something was trying to eat me. I kicked out with my legs, fighting to swim against the current as the rope snapped taut. Wilson was yelling something, but I couldn't hear him above the roar of the whitecaps buffeting my face.

I couldn't make out the shore; I couldn't make out anything. The undertow kept sucking me down before I could snatch a breath, and my lungs were on fire. Then my head hit a rock and I nearly passed out.

"Stop trying to swim, idiot!" Wilson screamed. "Stand up!"

Sputtering, I got my feet under me and tried to stand as the current ripped past my body, tugging at my clothes and gear. I was surprised to find I'd been nearly drowned in about three feet of water.

"Next time don't fight it," Wilson said. "Just let me reel you in."

"Let's hope there isn't a next time," I gasped, walking slowly against the current as he pulled, finally reaching the short cliff they were all watching from without further incident. "Something hit me and knocked my legs right out from under me. I panicked. Thought it was Toadzilla."

"Not today at least," Wilson said. "Probably a log or something. Lots of shit gets carried down rapids like these. Now get up here, 'tard."

"Moving, Sergeant." I reached for a handhold and hauled myself up as he pulled the rope. As soon as I reached the top, I flopped down and lay on my back, staring at the tops of the canyon walls far overhead and the stretch of permanently overcast sky. It was still raining, but I didn't care.

"I'm beat," I said. "Lost my boonie. Loved that boonie."

"I'm sure someone has a spare." Wilson keyed his radio without looking at me. "Xavier, Havok. The package is secure. En route. Havok out."

"'The package is secure,'" I muttered.

Wilson laughed. "Always wanted to say that. Get your soggy ass up, bro. We gotta di di mau. Oh shit, you're bleeding."

"'I ain't got time to bleed.' I always wanted to say *that*." I sat up and felt my face; my hand came away covered in blood.

"Damn," Wilson breathed. "Looks like you got scalped but they forgot to finish the job. It's just kinda… hanging there."

The gals had been ignoring us, watching the perimeter and chatting with each other, but at that moment Jade screamed.

I felt around my head, found the flap of skin, and pulled it back on, like a bloody skullcap. "Kind of you to mention it earlier, Sarge."

"Didn't notice. Musta flopped off when you laid down. Cold water stopped the bleeding for a bit, I guess."

"How's it look?" I asked. "On straight?"

"Uh…" Wilson reached up. "May I?"

"By all means. But get it on right. It's going to heal that way."

He grimaced and fussed for a minute, and Leaves made a gagging sound.

"There," Wilson said. "Perfect."

I turned to the gals. "Did he do it right or is he screwing with me?"

Tears scrunched up her nose, gave my loose scalp a little tug, cocked her head to the side, squinted, and then tugged a bit in the opposite direction. "Perfect."

I sighed. I had a headache, and my scalp itched horribly as the skin began fusing back together.

"That's hella freaky to watch," Wilson said. "Damn… there isn't even a scar."

"If it isn't straight, I'm going to scalp you and staple it back on crooked," I warned Wilson.

"Like you did to Wright's face?"

"Hey, that was my first time!"

***

We were down one canoe now, so Sanchez reorganized the crews to balance things out, putting me in charge of two of the lizardmen in addition to my original boat team. Thomas and Bartholomew, or so McKenzie told me. They all looked the same to me. They weren't much help with carrying our heavy dugout, either, and they apparently had a lot of opinions on how *we* should carry it. They chittered, squeaked, and clicked incessantly. None of which any of us could understand.

"Do they ever shut up?" Cohen asked as we sweated and grunted and maneuvered the canoe through yet another tangle of thorny scrub.

"Not really," I replied.

Thomas, or maybe Bartholomew, took a pinch of cocaine out of a pouch and snorted loudly before haranguing us with a litany of clicks and chirps as he pointed at us and the dugout. Bartholomew, or maybe it was Thomas, chittered in agreement.

"You want to carry it, small fry?" I snapped at the one I thought was Thomas.

He blinked his big eyes, licked a white-powdered nostril, and hissed something in reply.

"That's what I thought."

"Dakka," probably-Bartholomew said.

222

"Dakka!" most-likely-Thomas echoed.

"That's new," Cohen said. "Sounds like they're trying to say something in English."

"Dakka?" I asked Thomas. "What's that mean?"

Thomas pointed, saying "Dakka" to each of us in turn. Then he held his spear like a rifle. "Dakka dakka dakka."

Bartholomew jumped up and down. "Dakka dakka."

I shook my head. "Crazy pigmy lizard cokeheads."

Cohen laughed. "I think they're talking about our rifles, man."

Bartholomew jumped up and down again, then pantomimed carrying something heavy, pointed to us, and held his spear like a rifle. "Dakka dakka dakka." He pointed to himself and Thomas and chittered something ending in yet another "Dakka."

"They think they should have our rifles while we carry the boat, I bet," Cohen said. "You know, pull security."

I glared at them. "No dakka."

"Yaaasss dakka!" Thomas said. "Dakka dakka!"

There was no way I was arming the little freaks. It was bad enough that Peter was running around with a submachine gun. Besides, I doubted they could handle a full-scale battle rifle.

"Way too much dakka for you, kid," I told Thomas, shaking my head. "No dakka. Absolutely not."

"Yaaasss dakka!" he replied.

"No. Now shut up and go find something useful to do."

He flared his dewlap, gave me a gesture that I was pretty sure meant something highly offensive, clapped Bartholomew on the shoulder, and then the two of them strutted up the trail ahead of us chittering to each other and whipping their tails irritably.

***

It was noon when we finally got past the never-ending stretch of rapids—with no less than three waterfalls along the way. Ahead of us the canyon opened up considerably, its high walls stretching off to the horizon. Mist and vibrant vegetation hung from the cliffs, and tall trees choked the shore, some of them rising out of the wide river with stalk-like roots as if they were wading and holding their skirts up out of the water. Flying snakes flitted overhead, crisscrossing the canyon and diving into the water for fish.

"Oh look," I said to Pierce. "Flying snakes again. I'd missed them."

He made a sour face. "For once I'm happy to be dead."

It had been a while since I'd seen Pierce. Although I was relieved that he'd never shown up while I was… sheltering… with Obsidian Tears, I sometimes got worried when I hadn't seen him for a while. He was dead, after all, and I didn't know where he went when he wasn't with me. Sometimes he was doing other things—like hanging around Falling Leaves—but sometimes he just wasn't… anywhere. Or at least, he couldn't remember having been anywhere. Maybe at those times he really was dead.

He didn't like that idea, so I'd learned not to ask where he'd been. I was just happy when he came back.

Captain Brown consulted his map with Sanchez and mopped his brow with his boonie. It had gotten progressively warmer through the morning. With the sporadic rains, humidity, and backbreaking work of lugging those dugouts overland, most everyone's clothes were as saturated as Tears's and mine by now. Even Kiktú's fur was looking matted and droopy. The lads, on the other hand, seemed to love the rain and humidity.

"NCOs, gather 'round," Sanchez called out. "Don't start slapping yourselves on the back yet. We still got a long way to go."

Brown spread his map out on the ground, and we all took a knee. He stabbed his finger down. "If we'd been able to take the pass through to this chain of valleys, we'd be sitting pretty to link up with Clan Ónik. As it is, our evac via the river canyon has taken us southeast, to about here. This river meets up with the eastward sea in due course—making for the ocean would set us back considerably though. That's the bad news. Not so bad news is that a ways downriver we'll enter a delta, and if this map is accurate at all, we can cut up northward through it into this chain of canyons here. From there it's a straight shot to the battleground where the Compass is located. Unfortunately, that means bypassing Ónik territory, so no mounts."

"Is there good news, sir?" Takahashi asked.

"Nope," Brown replied. "Can't sugarcoat this one, I'm afraid. Wouldn't if I could."

"What is a 'delta'?" Flaming Feather asked.

"See here where the river flows into this marshland, before eventually draining out to the sea?" Brown said. "That's the delta. That river there, out of this chain of canyons up here, also drains into the swamp. We'll exit our river and go up that one."

"Navigating the channels is going to be some trick," Doc observed. "Waterways like that are always shifting. Islands appear and disappear overnight, rivers suddenly just… stop, and trying to portage these dugouts when we hit dead ends, which we *will*, is going to be…" He blew out his cheeks. "Well, not fun, I'll say that."

"Trust me, I know," Brown said. "My Black Hawk went down in —well, that doesn't matter—but it was a lot like how I imagine this territory will be."

"Been there, done that." Sanchez spat off to the side. "*A la mierda Laos.* It is what it is. The captain has the right idea. Our only other option is to go straight *through* the wetlands and make for the sea, then skirt up the coast." He traced his finger along the map. "I doubt this is to scale, but we'll never make it to the ocean. Not through all that. We'd just wander around lost forever until the mosquitos, and worse, have picked our bones clean."

Brown nodded. "Making for the northward chain of canyons is the lesser of several evils. I had hoped the alternate path we took through the pass would allow us to skirt around the opposition, but they're simply too strong. At that point we had no choice but to take the river. Landing here is suboptimal, but we'd have never made it through the pass."

"You picked the least bad of all the bad choices, and we live to fight another day," Wilson said. "No need to apologize, sir."

"He's not apologizing," Sanchez grunted.

Captain Brown looked at us each in turn. "I know this is the point in the novel where I make a big rousing speech and you all cheer and we go kick some ass, but this isn't a story and the good guys don't always win. This is as real as it gets. You've all been giving one hundred percent and then some, and I know you'll keep on giving it until the bitter end. And I'll be giving twice as much. That's all I can promise you." He paused and grinned. "But we *will* kick some ass before we're done, I can promise you *that* as well."

"Hooah, sir," Takahashi said. "That's good enough for me."

"In it to win it," Wilson said.

Flaming Feather crossed her arms over her chest, nodding grimly, and McKenzie flashed a savage smile through his bushy red beard.

"Aye," the big man said. "Death or glory, sir!"

CHAPTER 28

"But we know we win, sir," I told Captain Brown after the meeting had broken up. We were standing alone off to the side of the staging area, watching the river flow by. "At least this battle, I mean. We know we find the Compass. Xochi's vision shows her and me together again—with the Compass—the final battle, remember? Why didn't you just say that? We have hope—more than hope. We have fate on our side. You can promise them we'll get through this."

"Fate," Brown grunted.

"Yes, fate. I know *you* believe in fate. 'The future has already happened.'"

"Yes, it has. And Xochi's vision shows the two of you facing a great evil. But am *I* there? Is Diego? Hachirō or Dave? Jesus? Tim or Isaiah or Cory? Johnny? Our Kuauchanejkej sisters?"

"You tell me, sir. You know more about her vision than I do. All I know is it shows our future, her and I, *after* we face the evil. So, we win. You said back in Chlůmpu that the vision doesn't show us winning, but it *does*."

"You're jumping to a lot of conclusions there, Nephi. Yes, you two have a future, but that doesn't mean the two of you conquer the evil and win—it just means you both *survive*. And as I just pointed out, that's more than I can say for the rest of us. So no, I can't promise anyone anything. In the end, you may be the sole survivor of what was once Red Platoon. We've lost a lot of good men already. And women. We'll lose more."

"So her vision… it doesn't show you going home," I said softly.

Xochi had been unwilling to tell me much about her vision, but she'd talked to the captain about it—only for him to then be as tight-lipped with me as she was. The truth was, even though I was the one the vision was about, I knew almost none of it. And the captain was right: I had taken what little I did know, and had drawn conclusions that I now realized were unfounded.

Captain Brown stared silently at the river for several minutes. A large fish leaped from the water, sending ripples across the surface.

"Not explicitly," he said slowly. "It's unclear. It's *implicit*, but…" He paused. "Her vision is *your* fate, Nephi. The two of you. For the rest of us, it's only… hope."

I felt somehow… betrayed. I had thought—I had *concluded*—that the vision meant we'd win. That we'd go home. Yes, some of us would die along the way, but we all stood a chance. Now…

"With respect, sir, and speaking frankly, did everyone know this mission was based only on the *hope* that finding the Compass would get them home? That there was a chance it might not work? You didn't sugarcoat things a little, maybe?"

"They knew." He gazed down at me. "And no, I didn't."

I felt I'd crossed a line, but I pushed forward anyway. "And Cameron?"

"The situation changed. When we lost the ability to create portals, everything changed. Remember, Nephi, going into this we had easy, instant access to resupply and evac. We could've created a portal from Chlůmpu to the objective once we'd identified it. In and out. We had options. Easy options, even. And then we lost all of our options overnight. And then we lost Joe. You have to understand that Cory and Isaiah looked up to him. He served with Jesus for a long time back in the real world. Straight out of OSUT he was Jesus's battle buddy, and when Jesus made E5, Joe was assigned to his squad. And Ross and Joe had become good friends during our time here. You might not have liked him—hell, I didn't particularly care for him—but he was popular with the glower enlisted."

"You're saying Cameron and Stanley were friends?" Somehow out of everything, that tripped me up the most. I couldn't recall seeing either of them even giving the other the time of day.

Brown shrugged. "'Misery acquaints a man with strange bedfellows.'"

I took a breath. "I apologize for questioning you, sir."

He barked a laugh. "I'm not infallible, and I don't have an ego. I have zero issue with any of you speaking your mind to me in private. Even questioning me. So long as it doesn't undermine my authority in front of the rest of the platoon."

"You just seemed so confident when we launched this op."

"Little secret, son: bounded optimism is the key to being a good leader. I'm not going to blow sunshine up your ass, but I will always find the silver lining. Be realistic, yes, but always be hopeful in front of your men. Bullshit they can smell a mile away, but true confidence wins battles and saves lives."

"So… be a Pollyanna?"

"Damn, son." Brown shook his head. "I wouldn't go *that* far. Just remember, despair is contagious and so is hope. One will lead men to their grave and the other to victory."

***

<It is said the Salt Marsh Sea is home to a savage clan of the Kábi tribe,> Kiktú signed.

We were in the staging area by the river with the captain and the other NCOs for our indigenous asset briefing outlining the "Enemy Forces" section of our abbreviated OPORD. We'd already covered "Area of Operations" in the previous meeting. "Friendly Forces" would be skipped entirely, because there were none, and "Civilian Considerations" would also be skipped, because we didn't have any. Everything was a threat.

<They are primitive, barely even The People any longer, and have lost all knowledge of working stone and bronze. It is also said they practice the darkest forms of Unmaking, creating perversions of unlife through unholy rituals involving ritual cannibalism and the most horrific tortures. It is said even other clans of their tribe will not associate with them, because of their baseness.>

"And this is where we're going?" Takahashi asked once I'd interpreted.

"We're going to try to avoid it, by skirting the northwestern edge of the great marsh," Brown said. "But yes, we'll probably enter their territory. Hopefully only briefly."

"How solid is this intel?" Wilson asked. "Because I'm hearing a lot of 'It is said.'"

"No less than other intel I've had to act on," Brown said. "When we kicked off Grenada, all they gave us for operational planning were bad Xeroxes of tourist maps."

"Hopefully this will go better," Doc muttered. "That was a cluster."

"Okay, so we have psychotic cannibal jags," Wilson said, ticking off a finger. "What else?"

<It is a breeding ground for the imix.>

"Toadzilla breeding grounds," I interpreted.

"Even better." Wilson ticked off another finger.

<It is said blue fire demons lure travelers to their death.>

"Probably methane gas pockets," Brown said when I relayed that encouraging bit of info. "In other words, try not to get mesmerized by the will-o'-wisps. Low operational risk, unlike the imix and indigs which are a very high operational risk."

"Ignore the pretty lights." Wilson ticked off a third finger.

"Please continue, Kiktú," Brown said.

<Little more is known of the Salt Marsh Sea because so few return. But there are many dangers spoken of in travelers' tales. Land that swallows a man whole, leaving no trace...>

"Quicksand." Wilson ticked off another finger.

<Eels that will flay a man alive in moments...>

"Do the eels shriek?" Wilson asked.

<I do not know.>

"Just checking." He ticked off his thumb. "What about rodents of unusual size?"

"Sergeant," Sanchez growled.

"Real ugly critters," Wilson added. "Nasty, big, pointy teeth."

"That was a rabbit," I said. "*Not* a rodent. Different movie too."

Wilson shrugged.

<Yes, very large semiaquatic rodents infest the region, carrying disease and pestilence,> Kiktú signed.

"RUS's!" Wilson held up a finger on his other hand and grinned at Sanchez, who looked like he had a bad case of acid reflux. He was giving Wilson his platoon sergeant glare, which incidentally is very similar to the look my mom often gave me and my brothers. Wilson shut up.

"That's the condensed version of obvious threats," Brown said. He looked to Doc, who nodded.

"Not as obvious, but no less dangerous, are the threats of blood-borne diseases carried by biting insects, lack of potable water, and questionable food supplies," Doc said. "Insects should be mitigated by religious application of PFC Epasotl's ointment, and I do mean religious. I don't care how bad it smells. Water is a problem, because we'll be in a salt marsh. We can't purify it; it's simply not drinkable. We'll need to collect rainwater. Eels and these giant rodents could prove to be a food source, but we need to be able to cook or cure the meat somehow to avoid pathogens, and fuel sources will be limited."

"And fire attracts hostiles," Sanchez added.

"That too," Doc agreed.

"And navigation?" Takahashi asked the question we were all thinking. We'd gotten familiar with land nav sans compass or reliable maps—or any maps for that matter—mostly thanks to Epasotl's uncanny sense of direction, but how well she'd hold up in wetlands with constantly shifting landmarks and currents was a big open question.

"I was leaving that for last, because getting lost is the biggest threat," Brown said. "We'll effectively be traveling blind in a labyrinth, so we'll be relying on PFC Epasotl to chart our path, with a little help. PFC?"

Epasotl had been standing off to the side, speaking in a hush with the shrunken jaguar-man's head. Now her ears perked up and she joined the circle. "Yes, Big Kahuna?"

"Explain how we'll navigate the swamp between rivers."

"Is piece of pie," she said, holding up the head. "Have spirit of earth to help. Spirit of water better, but beggar can not be picky. Meet Tlalli."

"Heya," the head said, rising out of her hand to float above her shoulder. It had a deep, gravelly voice, and I pictured it chomping on a fat cigar like some sort of heavyset union foreman with bad tattoos.

Kiktú wasn't pleased, but she kept her protest to a low growl in the back of her throat.

"*Heya*? He speaks English?" I asked Epasotl.

"No duh. Is spirit. Live between worlds. Spirit know many things." She turned back to address the assembled NCOs. "Tlalli speak with land, find path."

"Sure," the head grunted. "Like I says to the captain earlier. No problemo. 'Cept I don't work no overtime or weekends. Fuhgettabout it. And I don't skimp on no breaks. Capiche? Rules are rules."

Maybe not a foreman. More like a mafioso from a really bad movie. Still union though. And definitely bad tattoos. And a cigar. Sounded like he smoked twelve a day.

"We have our mission, and we have a guide," Brown said. "Let's move with a purpose."

CHAPTER 29

Sanchez consolidated and reorganized the boat crews to optimize for the mission ahead. Takahashi, Wilson, Falling Leaves, and Jade Talon formed the crew for the lead boat, with Epasotl as navigator. Captain Brown's boat consisted of Flaming Feather and Heart-of-Darkness, with Dressed-in-Stars and Anderson's M240B. McKenzie and his lads all piled into one canoe, which was a tight squeeze, but the lizardmen weren't that big to begin with; they'd manage. Sanchez's crew consisted of Doc and Lawrence, with García and Kiktú's gun, and I kept Cohen, First-to-Dance, and Obsidian Tears in the trail boat. Pierce was there, too, which was unusual; he rarely showed up in big groups. He stayed quiet, though.

We cast off midafternoon and paddled with the current into the night and through to the next dawn. The river meandered through the canyon and out of the mountains, eventually entering a lowland jungle thick with the chatter of large-eyed monkeys who watched us drift past and the hissing shrieks of the ever-present brilliantly plumaged winged snakes flitting overhead between the tall trees. By early afternoon the river went from crystal clear to muddy with sediment, and the current slowed to a crawl; everyone had to pull to maintain a reasonable rate of progress. They were all getting pretty good at it too, and we kept up a steady three or four knots throughout the day.

As dusk began to fall, we tied off in a cluster of tall, stilt-like roots and set up on the shore for the night. By this point we'd been paddling for well over twenty-four hours, and everyone was tired and sore, even though we'd been taking shifts steering and paddling to let people rest. It was hard work, but as I reminded my team, it wasn't nearly as hard as it would be after we got past the salt marsh and had to start paddling *upstream*.

Not that the swamp was going to be any picnic either.

Dance and Cohen had first watch, so I gnawed on some dried meat cake and stretched out against my ruck. I was exhausted and very much looking forward to a few hours of sleep.

"How is it hanging?" Epasotl asked cheerfully just as I was about to drift off.

"Go away. I'm sleeping."

"No sleep. Must practice weaving."

I cracked an eye open. She was standing above me, arms akimbo, grinning in that unsettling way Chaneques do when they're trying to mimic a human smile.

"Seriously, Eps? I'm beat."

"Tell her to go away," Tears muttered irritably from off to the side.

"Tears says go away," I told Eps.

"Beat later. Weave now. Come."

I closed my eye. "Go to bed, Eps."

"Please?" Epasotl purred.

"No."

"With cherry on top?"

"No."

She kicked me.

"Stop it."

Another kick, this time harder.

"*Eps!*"

"Come. Weave with sister. Must remember how to weave like in faraway place. Is important."

I groaned. "I never *weaved*, Eps. I already told you that. That wasn't weaving. I don't even think anything really happened. I didn't *do* anything. People were sick, I prayed over them, and sometimes they got better. Not exactly an Earth-shattering miracle. Not like I brought anyone back from the dead or whatever."

"You bring First-to-Dance back from dead."

"That was you. And she wasn't dead."

"Super dead. As doornail."

"Really?"

"Yes. Come now."

"If you do not go with her, I am going to shoot you both," Tears grumbled.

"Fine." I got up and slung Sybil. "Where are we going?"

"Follow." She led me off a little ways. We were still inside the security perimeter but isolated enough that we wouldn't disturb anyone… too much.

"Now what?" I said.

"Sit."

I plopped down with my legs crossed. "Okay?"

She settled into a lotus position and placed her hands palms up on her knees. "Breathe. Feel juice flow inside."

"All I feel is sore from paddling for twenty-four hours."

"Close eyes. Breathe."

"If I close my eyes I'm gonna fall asleep."

"No sleep, meditate. Now close eyes, breathe. Feel juice flow around you. Inside you. Flow between here and there, me and you; between trees and rocks, land and river. Breathe in nose, out mouth."

I sighed and closed my eyes.

"You not breathe."

I inhaled through my nose, held it for a few heartbeats, and then exhaled through my mouth.

"Breathe in, breathe out," she said. "Juice flow in, juice flow out."

I must have drifted off, because the next thing I knew she'd jabbed me in the thigh with a sharp claw. "No sleep! Breathe. Focus."

"Okay, okay, I'm breathing."

We inhaled and exhaled in unison for several minutes. I'll admit it was relaxing; I'm certain I fell asleep a couple more times, but I must have managed to stay upright because I didn't get jabbed again.

"Feel juicy now, no?" Epasotl murmured.

"Not particularly. Can I go to bed now?"

"Hmm. We try something different. Maybe work. Do not know." She shifted so she was sitting directly in front of me and held out her hands.

"Oh, I know this game," I said. "I try to slap your hands before you pull them away."

"No slap. Hold hands."

I took her hands in mine. "Now what?"

"Close eyes. Breathe in, breathe out. In through nose, out mouth. Focus. Feel juice flow between us. My juice. You juice. Our juice."

"Oh my heck. Can we call it something other than *juice*?"

"What call it?"

"*I* don't know. God or sacred energy or divinity or qi or mana or just about anything but juice. Heck, even mojo works. Or why not call it what it's actually called? *Teōtl*."

"You think God is teōtl?"

"Well, no, because teōtl is a thing, not a being. I just want to stop saying juice."

"Big Kahuna say God is love. Love is thing."

"1 John 4:16," I said reflexively.

"What?"

"Sorry, old habit. But yes, if you want to say *what* God is, He is love, sure."

Epasotl looked thoughtful. "Like mojo better, but maybe that is trick. You need word you understand. Now close eyes. Breathe in, breathe out. In nose, out mouth. Focus. Feel love of you God flow between us. My love. You love. Our love."

I relaxed and focused on breathing in time with her. Slowly my hands, and then my arms, and then my core and even my face, tingled with warmth, as if an energy of some kind flowed from her into me and then back to her with each shared breath. I forgot my exhaustion; even the ever-present feeling of my body slowly dying around me seemed to fade away.

"You feel it, no? Feel *love*?"

"Yes." I did. I didn't know if *love* was the right word for it... but it was as close a word as I could think of.

"Is teōtl. Is *good* mojo. Is you God. Is same. Is what binds universe together. All things connected by many thread into whole cloth. Weave thread, change pattern, change what real. Is what I learn from healers in city. *Pure* weaving. No need sacrifice self or others. See threads in mind. See pattern. Weave new reality." She paused. "Oh!"

"What?" I asked, my eyes still closed. I was trying to see the threads, but they flitted from my mind's eye when I focused, always dancing out of view. I could almost catch the connections, feel the warp and weave connecting me to her, to the others, to the trees. Even the rocks. The land and the river.

"Open eyes."

I did.

"Oh," I said.

My veins glowed with a pure white radiance that pulsed in time with the beat of my heart.

"That is… cool," I said. "Also pretty disturbing. Can you turn it off? We're going to get in trouble with Sanchez for light discipline."

She let go of my hands. "Cannot turn off. Is coming from *you*."

"How do *I* turn it off then?"

"No know how."

"*What*? Eps, I'm lit up like that dude in *Tron*!"

I glanced around and saw that several people were staring at me, and the lads were chittering in alarm. The light coming from my veins wasn't *bright*, but it wasn't exactly tactical either. I rolled down my sleeves and tried to hide my hands, but my face was still glowing.

"What the hell is going on?" Sanchez hissed. "Put yourself out, Bennett."

"I… I don't know how, Sergeant."

He crossed over to us and threw a poncho over my head.

"Better figure it out," he grumbled.

***

I was still glowing the next morning, as if my blood had turned to white chem light fluid. It wasn't super obvious in the light of day, but it would make stealthy night operations difficult.

"How long am I going to look like the dude from *Tron*?" I asked Epasotl.

"Do not know. What is *Tron*?"

"A movie. Never mind. I look like a human glow stick."

"Clothes and gloves hide."

"Yeah, if I put a bag over my head."

"Paint face more?"

"That… actually that's not a bad idea. Camo paint might work. I still want it to stop, though—I'm *not* going to look like this forever. What exactly did we do last night?"

"Not sure. You touch weave. Summon much juice—mojo, love, whatever call it. You like grandfather ring now. Juiced up."

"I'm a teōtl battery?"

"Something like. Try not summon more for now, okay?"

"Trust me, I'm not planning to." I paused. "Why? What would happen if I did?"

"Not know. Maybe it consume you. Burn up. Crispy critter. But I think it not last too long maybe. Like ring. Go bad in time. Flat juice. Stale mojo. No good for weave."

Crispy critter. Despite her broken English, Epasotl had a way with words. I would be careful with… whatever this was.

Still, I had to ask.

"If I have teōtl… does that mean I can do the things that you can do? Shoot meteors? Make a wall of flame? Fly?"

She tsked. "I not fly. I make fall slow. Is different. Ueueokichtli teach me much about weaving, but still require sacrifice of self. Jag Makers teach more—pure weaving. Use you grandfather ring, help much. Still use potions some, but that different, that *naualotl*, is folk magic, like when heal you leg. That not weaving. Now I am *Teōicpauhqui*. Make god-weaving."

"And me?"

"Not know. Maybe you do weaving like me, maybe different. I teach you, and we see. Will be rad. But must draw juice every day or go flat. Go flat in ring, go flat in you."

And over the course of the day she proved to be right. I could feel the warm energy that filled me diffusing slowly, the light dimming. I was greatly relieved. And yet, at the same time, the energy was gradually replaced by the sensation of my body dying again. I could feel it once more, like a cancer, eating away at me. By dusk my veins had returned to the black spiderwebs I'd become accustomed to.

I was back to my familiar, death-touched, dying self.

Over the next few days Epasotl and I meditated together in the early dawn when the glowing veins in my face were less of a security risk. Now that we knew what we were doing, it was easier to fall into a mutual flow, and it had the same effect on me every time: my black veins turned a glowing white. This invited a lot of comments from the others in the platoon—Pierce said it was rad; Sanchez grumbled; the lads chittered and kept their distance—but pretty soon it became the new normal. Still, there seemed to be no point to it. I couldn't *use* the power inside me. I couldn't weave.

"Try make flame," Epasotl said one morning. "Like so." She cupped one hand, waved the other over it, and a small blue fire appeared, flickering above her palm. It floated and danced as she played her fingers over it like a puppeteer pulling at strings.

I screwed my eyes shut, rolled up my sleeves, and took a deep breath, focusing on seeing the energy in my mind's eye. The threads. The pattern of a flame.

"See pattern. Weave pattern," Epasotl coached. "Make what is not. Make *real*."

This was the magic Captain Brown called *evocation*. The creation of something from nothing. Weaving teōtl. Divine essence. Sacred energy. Manipulating the threads that bind and give shape to the tapestry of the universe. There is no word in English to describe the composition of the threads. They aren't material. They are neither good nor evil. They just… are. They exist. Have always existed. *Will* always exist.

"Cannot force weaving," Epasotl said. "Cannot force threads. Must guide gently. Show pattern to weave. Teach shape to form."

I held my hand out, palm up, slightly cupped, and placed my other hand over it like a lid. The air between my hands began to warm.

"Good," Epasotl said softly. "See fire. See pattern. Guide threads. Shape teōtl."

The air began to grow hot, and I pulled my hands slightly apart and cracked an eye open. Just above my palm, a small marigold cloud of light motes was beginning to form.

"I'm doing it!"

The little cloud burst with an explosion of heat that singed my fingers before winking out of existence.

"Ow! What the heck?"

"Lose focus, lose shape. Must focus."

I shook out my hands. "Why doesn't the flame burn *you*?"

"Must practice. Focus. Breathe. Try again."

"I'd rather not burn my hands off."

"Will heal. You heal fast. No worries."

"Still hurts."

"Stop whine like cub. Focus. Breathe. Try again."

I squared my shoulders. "Do or do not. There is no try."

"Good. Do, not try. I like. Very wise. Do again, but better. Breathe in nose, out mouth. Focus. Make weave. Not forget breathe. Very important."

"Wax on, wax off," I muttered with a smile.

"What?"

"Nothing, Mr. Miyagi."

"Shut mouth. Make talk too much. Focus. Breathe. Make weave. Make fire, no heat. No burn tender cub hands."

I breathed. I focused. I felt the warmth between my hands. Warm, but not hot. Fire without heat. A cool flame. I formed a picture... directed the threads...

And then in an instant, as if something had taken hold of my mind and *yanked*... my mental image shifted.

I saw Xochi—in pain. In *danger*. Suffocating darkness closing in around her from all sides. Darkness like a rupture in the fabric of the universe. An evil I could feel physically. An extra-dimensional entity existing outside of space and time.

Smoking Mirror.

Eternal, yet finite. A creature born of the void that thought itself a god. Unweaver. Unmaker. A being fueled by the torment of sentient life.

Xochi screamed, clutching at her belly, trying desperately to protect the light inside her. The *life* inside her. My life, her life. Our love made flesh in her womb. One and one made three.

But I couldn't reach her. Couldn't protect her or our unborn child.

My anger flashed, a white-hot flame erupting from my core as I emptied myself completely, igniting the darkness with burning radiance.

"What in the living hell was *that*?" Sanchez barked.

I opened my eyes. Epasotl was blinking, her eyelashes and hair singed, her skin glowing as if from a sunburn. Nearby a small tree had caught fire, and the ground was blasted clear in a two-meter radius around me. Even the rocks were smoking.

"Think enough practice for today," Epasotl said.

CHAPTER 30

"Ben-Ette make new trick," Epasotl said to Sanchez.

"Yeah, I saw that. So what, he's a human grenade now? Is he safe? Or could he go off at any time? We're damned lucked no one else was nearby."

I inspected my hands and clothes. No scorching. No burns. Veins were black, like normal. But it looked like a white phosphorus grenade had gone off in the area where I'd been sitting.

"You okay, Eps?" I asked.

"Am fine. Make shield last moment. No worries."

"I asked, is he *safe*?" Sanchez repeated.

"Should be, Little Kahuna."

"Should be? That's not good enough."

"What can say? No see that trick before." Epasotl spread her hands. "We more careful practice next time."

Sanchez grunted that we'd better, then stalked away.

"What happen?" Epasotl asked me.

"I had... a vision. Xochi is in danger. It was Smoking Mirror. I... was trying to protect her."

Epasotl looked at me curiously. "Could be vision now, could be vision future. Either way, you no can do anything about it."

"She was pregnant... so it must be the future."

"Maybe." Epasotl waggled her hand.

"What does that mean?"

"Not want tell you. Make worry."

"Tell me what?"

"Forget said anything. New trick is rad though, no? Do again?" She raised a hand. "But warn first. Sister almost crispy critter."

"What do you mean, you don't want me to worry?"

"You worry too much many things. No need more things to make worry."

"Oh my heck. Just spit it out."

"Well…"

"Well, what?"

"Congratulations?"

I glared at her.

"You mac daddy."

"Excuse me?"

"Strong seed." She flexed a skinny little arm.

"You mean she's pregnant? Now? How could you possibly know that?"

"Smell change before go on mission. She carry you cub."

"And you're just telling me now?"

"No make worry. See? You worry now. No point worry when no can do anything."

"She—*they*—could be in danger!"

She spread her hands. "What can do?"

My shoulders knotted and I gritted my teeth. "Absolutely nothing."

Epasotl placed a tiny hand on my arm and gazed up at me with her big, green, gold-flecked eyes. "Just need get back. Focus. Breathe. Charlie Mike, no?"

"Charlie Mike," I muttered.

Wilson strode by and slapped the back of my head playfully. "Heya, Willie Pete."

I grunted.

"What's up with him?" he asked Epasotl.

"No good time make joke, Broski."

Wilson's smile dropped. "Oh yeah?"

"It's nothing," I said.

"Ben-Ette worry about mate."

"Xochi?" He frowned. "You two know something I don't?"

"I said it's nothing. Nothing we can do anything about anyway."

"Ben-Ette have vision. Maybe now. Maybe future. No can tell."

"More visions, eh? Bad mojo?"

"Yeah, pretty bad," I grunted.

"Well, we're just gonna have to kick ass and take names and get back to her yesterday." He held out a fist. "In it to win it, bro!"

I gave him a desultory bump.

"Not going to kick much ass with that attitude, WP."

I sighed. It was a better nickname than "Lite-Brite" or "Glowstick," which had been the top contenders for the last few days.

"Oh, hey," Wilson said, snapping his fingers. "I got something for you. Almost forgot." He pulled a big square of lightweight olive drab patterned cloth out of a cargo pocket. "Meant to give this to you earlier."

"Uh, thanks. What is it?"

"Head wrap. Called a shemagh. Got it from this high-speed Green Bean back in Amoloyan who'd been to the Stan. Dude had some stories, bro."

"The Stan?"

"You know, Afghanistan. In the future. Anyway, it's to hide your face if you start glowing in the dark again."

"Huh. Smart thinking."

Wilson tapped his head. "Not just a hat rack, you know. Chin up, man. We'll beat this place and be back to your girl in no time flat. Gotta. Stars and I are overdue some serious fraternization. I've been Hand Solo too long for my health."

***

The river wound its course through the lowlands as the jungle transformed to mangrove swamp over the next few days. When it began to branch, Tlalli guided us through the ever-narrowing channels, keeping us on a northeast bearing, more or less, through the aquatic maze of thin waterways and tiny islands. We paddled day and night, taking shifts, as our food supply grew critically short. I still had my lone MRE, but I was committed to saving it for a special occasion, like sharing it with my team if starvation seemed imminent.

Literally starving to death actually takes a long time, so it stayed securely tucked in at the bottom of my ruck.

Three days after we'd entered the swamp, Captain Brown fell sick. Even Epasotl couldn't do anything to help him. On the fourth day, Heart-of-Darkness, García, Wilson, and Falling Leaves were delirious and burning up, and Sanchez called a halt at a large hillock rising out of the water.

"Some highly virulent fast-acting variant of malaria," Doc pronounced. "Nothing I can do other than keep them hydrated and just hope and pray they pull through."

"We stay here one day, then we have to press on," Sanchez said. "McKenzie's lads are going hunting. We'll cook some of it and smoke the rest. Then it's anchors up and Charlie Mike."

"There has to be something you can do," I said to Epasotl.

She gestured around the small island. "What herbs for potions? Not know plants here. Make worse maybe."

"I thought you didn't need potions anymore. Pure weaving, remember?"

"Still learn. Fix wound easy. This sick hard to see how pattern broken. Threads of sickness through whole body. Need potions. Seeds, herbs, plants."

Cohen fell ill that evening. By morning Lawrence was burning up as well.

The lads managed to catch some of the dreaded (but non-shrieking) piranha-eels and even an abnormally large, mangy rodent, which looked something like a giant beaver crossed with a rat. Even thoroughly cooked they tasted horrible, but we were hungry so no one complained.

The single-day stop turned into two, then three. Anderson and Doc fell ill too. Sanchez pulled Takahashi, Flaming Feather, McKenzie, and me into a huddle.

"We can't stay," he said. "We need to move. We've been here too long already. If there are hostiles in the area, they'll find us sooner rather than later."

"Sir McKenzie's craft has a full crew, but between the rest of us we have nine people fit to paddle and four boats," Takahashi said. "And that's assuming no one else gets sick."

"Could divvy up the lads," McKenzie offered. "Two per dugout. They seem immune to whatever this pathogen is."

"It may come to that," Sanchez agreed. He pursed his lips. "We'll keep the crews as they are for now. We've smoked a good amount of eel and that swamp rat. Should keep us going for a while. How's water?"

"Enough for a few days if we're careful, maybe four?" I replied.

"Same," Takahashi said.

"Yes," Flaming Feather agreed.

"I'm good. Lads are good," McKenzie said. "They can drink this soup."

I frowned. "Not sure that's a good idea."

"They've been doing it already," McKenzie answered with a shrug. "They don't understand why we cook the meat either. Says it ruins the flavor."

The very thought made me gag.

"Is there nothing Eps can do?" Takahashi asked.

"She's trying," I said. "She doesn't know the plants here, and most of them are probably toxic and would need special processing. She says she's 'experimenting,' but it doesn't sound promising."

Sanchez scowled. "What a shithole. Finally found somewhere worse than Laos." He gazed overhead. "Getting dark soon. I'd prefer to pull out now, but… too risky. It's the perfect setup for an ambush. But we leave at first light, no matter what." He paused for several long moments. "Yeah, I got a real bad feeling. No one sleeps tonight, hooah?"

If Sanchez's Spidey sense was tingling, that was more than enough to keep me wide awake all night.

After the huddle broke, I hurried back to my team's security position and low-crawled to where Dance and Tears were keeping watch over their sector in a foxhole. We hadn't been idle over the last three days and had dug in somewhat, creating concentric rings of defense we could fall back to if needed. Dance acknowledged me with a brief nod, but Tears was sleeping. I nudged her awake.

"We're on one hundred percent security tonight," I said. "Need everyone up and alert." I looked at Dance. "Anything?"

"No, Corporal. There was an RUS sniffing around, but Toadzilla got it."

"Have you checked the claymores?"

"Hooah, Corporal." Dance patted the clackers.

"Tears, I got one more in my ruck. Get it set up covering that angle over there."

"Moving," she said before crawling out of the hole and backwards out of sight.

"Has Epasotl found any way to help the sick?" Dance asked me.

I shook my head. We were all putting too much pressure on Epasotl. We'd grown reliant on her healing abilities.

"And you?" Dance asked. "What of your magic?"

I wanted to argue with her use of the word *magic*, but... I couldn't. Epasotl had been teaching me to do things that I couldn't explain in any other way. I was touching the threads of the universe, manipulating them. Magic was as good a word as any.

It had been hard enough to accept that magic existed in this world. Harder still to acknowledge that I was able to do it. Still, helping the sick was far beyond anything Eps had taught me.

"Disease is complicated," I said. "I might now be able to heal a cut or a scrape. They're localized, and relatively simple to repair, or so Epasotl says. But a disease is billions of tiny creatures spread throughout the body. How do you kill them without killing the whole body?"

"I thought disease was an evil spirit you must exorcise from the one who is sick."

"I wish it were that simple."

How *did* you kill them without killing the whole body? How did doctors back home do it? I had worked as a medic and administered medicine, but that didn't mean I had any idea how medicines actually worked inside the body. Were they able to identify what was the patient and what was the disease?

Every body had a pattern. A true weave. And disease would be… foreign, right? A tangle of threads that didn't belong. If you could see the pattern the foreign threads made, you could unravel it and…

"Oh my heck, I got it!" I exclaimed in a hush.

Dance glanced at me and raised an eyebrow.

"I think I know how to cure them."

***

"Could work," Epasotl said after I'd explained my theory. "But if you cut wrong thread, you maybe unravel wrong pattern, no? Kill person maybe."

We were standing near where all the sick had been laid out near the center of our perimeter. Epasotl had been nursing them while she and Maitl worked to try and find a cure.

"But good theory," Epasotl said. "Should work."

"So you'll try it?"

"No."

"Why not?"

"You theory. You try. Time put on big boy pants and make big weaving."

"Me? I can barely make a flame without burning myself."

"You sell self shorts. You fast learning."

"You just said I could kill someone doing this."

"Or they die if I do."

"You mean if it fails and someone dies, you don't want to be responsible."

She shot me with a finger gun. "This you weaving to make, broski. Big showtime. What be scared of? Probably they die either way. This way if not die, you hero. Is good."

"I don't want to be a hero."

"Time step up. Embrace destiny. Here, I make easy for you. Try on Touchdown first. If he die, no biggie."

"Eps!"

"Is true, no?"

"No. Even Anderson isn't expendable."

"Pffft. He private."

"So are you."

"I private *first class*. Not same. Much better."

"Maybe we should wait a bit longer. You could still find ingredients that work."

"Have tried everything. Nothing good. All plant here bad. This bad place. Everywhere death. Maitl, tell him nothing no good here."

The mummified virgin's hand stopped grinding whatever was in the mortar to give a thumbs-down.

"See? No option left. Try heal Touchdown. See if work."

"I'm not experimenting on Anderson, Eps. We'll have to find another way."

"Is no other way. If not work, Big Kahuna die, Doc die, everyone die. Worth try."

"They still might pull through."

"And monkey might fly out of butt."

"Try it on me," Captain Brown croaked.

I whipped my head around and then knelt beside him. "Say again, sir?"

"Whatever it is you're talking about. Try it on me first. I'm dead anyway."

"Don't say that, sir. You'll make it."

"Don't bullshit a bullshitter, son."

"Sir, with respect, you're delirious. Try to get some rest. Do you want some water?"

His eyelids fluttered and a fresh sweat broke out on his brow. "I have faith in you."

"Sorry, sir. Not happening."

His eyes shot open and he grabbed my chest plate, pulling me close. He tried to say something but turned over and dry-heaved instead. After retching bile and blood for a minute, he rolled onto his back and gasped. His hand still had an iron grip on my plate though, and he shook it forcefully. "You can do it, son. I have faith in you."

I looked at Epasotl, who just shrugged.

"Do what?" Sanchez asked softly from behind me.

Epasotl explained—skirting artfully around the part about why *she* couldn't do it—and I felt Sanchez's hand clasp my shoulder.

"If you think you might be able to do something that could help," he said, "it can't hurt to try. If you don't... we're dead anyway."

"But—"

His hand tightened on my shoulder.

"Yes, Sergeant."

Settling myself on my knees, I closed my eyes and let my hands drift over Captain Brown's body.

Focus.

Breathe.

In through the nose, out through the mouth.

Focus.

I sensed more than saw the threads that made up Captain Brown's body, and then the single strong thread that *was* him. Except the pattern was in disarray, and a shock of angry threads cut through the warp and weave. They weren't evil... just... *hungry*. And they were breaking the pattern apart. But *his* thread, the thread that was Captain Amos Brown, was stubborn, and held the pattern together by force of will alone.

It was clear, though, that it wouldn't be able to hold much longer. Sanchez was right. The captain was dead already. He just wasn't willing to let go.

I had to try.

Everything was so tangled, and I couldn't see which threads to cut and which to mend. Only then did I realize the danger was worse than I had feared: if I wove falsely, it wouldn't kill him; it would make him into something... different. Something possessing Brown's intellect, but in an altered form. Brown but not Brown.

Focus.

Breathe.

The fear and indecision were paralyzing.

And then Epasotl's consciousness touched mine.

"Eps?"

"I here."

"I thought you didn't want to be responsible if this doesn't work?"

"Not let you take all credit. What you see?"

"His pattern is so tangled. I can't see what it *should* be. The disease has consumed too much."

"Hmm. See problem."

"What should we do?"

"Could weave new form. What you think he like?"

"Be serious, Eps."

"Am serious."

"No. There has to be a way to restore him without turning him into a frog or a swamp rat."

"Hmm. Let teōtl decide."

"For real?"

"Is good idea."

"No, Eps, that's a terrible idea. Who knows what he could end up as? A tree? A rock?"

"Fine. Then let thread that is Big Kahuna decide. This weaving you not weave. This weaving Big Kahuna weave. He knows captain true form. He weave, you help."

"And what are you going to do?"

"Supervise."

"So you want the credit but not the responsibility."

"Am practicing."

"For what?"

"Promotion to E4."

I sighed and set to work. It was tedious and painstaking as I carefully pruned the threads of disease and fed new, pure threads into the pattern. I didn't try to shape it, I just fed and pruned, thread by thread. Over time the pattern began to take shape of its own accord—hopefully of Captain Brown's accord—and the process accelerated until the last of the disease had been cut away.

Exhausted, I leaned back and opened my eyes. Epasotl grinned at me and felt Brown's forehead. He appeared to be sleeping peacefully.

"No fever," Epasotl proclaimed.

No fever. And he hadn't been transformed into a swamp rat, either. My first real magic—complicated magic at that—had been a success. I wondered at the time if it was beginner's luck or if something, or *someone*, had been guiding my hands.

As my abilities continued to grow, I would find that it was very much the latter.

"That must've taken all night," I said.

"Only a few minutes," Sanchez commented. "It was... I don't know what you did, Bennett, but it was sure something to watch."

I took a deep breath and stood, stretching out my cramped legs. "Only eight more to go."

"You take half, I take half," Epasotl said. "Go faster."

"Solid plan," I agreed.

And then the first claymore went off.

CHAPTER 31

I fumbled to clip my earpiece on as the radio erupted in chatter. It sounded like people were calling in reports of enemy contact from all directions. Unslinging Sybil, I sprinted toward my team's position, where the claymore had gone off. I skidded down into the loamy soil and high-crawled over to Dance, who was snapping off rounds rapidly. Tears was already on the Mark 48, sending tightly controlled bursts downrange.

"What do we got, Dance?" I shouted.

"Multiple contacts," she yelled between shots. "Came out of nowhere. Claymore took out a squad-sized element about to overrun us. Tears! Shift left thirty degrees!"

Shadowy figures sprinted through tall marsh grass and leapt from islet to islet, advancing in waves. They appeared to be jags, but... *twisted* somehow. Thinner, darker, and faster.

"Belt out!" Tears called.

"They're coming too fast, Corporal!" Dance shouted at me.

"Get that new belt loaded, Tears." I lined up a snarling face with flashing fangs in my scope, fired, racked the bolt, found a new target, fired again. "We need to keep them from getting a foothold on the island." Several dark feline shapes leapt out of the water, launching a volley of javelins. "Tears! On your two."

Fire, work the bolt, fire, work the bolt. Fire again.

"Mag out!" I called.

I'd been trying to keep track of the radio chatter, but there was too much noise. From somewhere behind me a claymore went off, then another.

"Dance, get me AB on that group coming in from your eleven. Eighty meters. Better make it a double."

"Hooah!"

Thump.

Thump.

"All Crazy Horse elements, hostiles in the perimeter!" Sanchez called over the radio.

Getting up on a knee, I spun around to see a fan of flame erupt from Epasotl's hands, incinerating nearly a dozen mangy jags closing on her. Several went down instantly, and I took out the remaining five, firing as quickly as I could work the bolt.

"Mag out," I said automatically, scanning the interior of the island for threats as I swapped magazines. A javelin hissed past my head, and I spun back to face the perimeter and hit the deck.

"Red on ammo," Dance called to me.

"Tears!" I cried. "Stop that group before they reach—"

"Belt out!" Tears shouted back. "I'm black. Switching to rifle."

I scrambled for the clacker and detonated the claymore.

"Deadhead!" Dance yelled. "One o'clock, sixty meters and closing fast."

I swung Sybil and got the necromancer in my scope. He was leaping and bounding between islets, cloaked in a shroud of flame-shaped shadow. Somehow his image kept blurring in my scope. I fired, missed, fired again. Either I missed that time too or it didn't have any effect. I couldn't tell. He was eating up the distance alarmingly quickly. I took another shot, but he just kept coming. Forty meters. Thirty.

Tears was pouring fire into him ineffectually and raised herself out of her and Dance's foxhole to get a better shot.

I took another shot at twenty meters. No effect. There was no way I'd missed.

"Get down!" Dance shouted at Tears.

The shadow-shrouded spellcaster raised a bony hand, and a flash of dark energy erupted from it, striking Obsidian Tears center mass. She was thrown back into the foxhole, screaming as her flesh rotted away from her bones.

I took my last shot, and the Deadhead turned to me, flashing the whites of his eyes. Tossing Sybil to the side, I took a deep breath, summoning as much teōtl as I could in the moment.

Love.

Mojo.

Juice.

Call it what you will.

This time it wasn't just my veins that glowed. *Everything* glowed. I radiated light like a beacon.

And then I charged him.

Over a dozen skeletal jags fell in to form a protective phalanx around the necromancer as I barreled down the hill toward him. I was screaming. Don't ask me what. I can't remember.

I plowed into their formation, dodging bone-tipped spears, tackled the Deadhead, and let all the power I'd built up pour out of me in one burst of radiance that lit up the hillside like the noonday sun.

Somehow I was still standing.

And the Deadhead and all his minions were ash.

Roars echoed like rolling thunder across the marsh as the next wave advanced. I could see the massed spearmen coming, and I knew it was probably over for us, but I drew my sidearm anyway. I'd die in a pile of brass if it came to it.

Something shrieked overhead like heavy artillery. I looked up, following the comet's trail as it flew overhead toward the enemy. It detonated above them in a blinding burst of flame that turned bodies to ash and swamp water to steam.

Then the concussion wave hit me.

***

"Is he dead?" a woman's voice asked above me.

"Not dead," another woman replied. I recognized the voice as First-to-Dance. "See? He is breathing."

I cracked my eyes open. Jade Talon and Dance were squatting near my head. Above us the overcast sky was faintly beginning to

255

lighten in the east. I could hear the report of rifles and the occasional boom of a forty-millimeter grenade. I opened my mouth to speak, but it was too dry.

"I feel dead," I managed to croak after ungluing my tongue from the roof of my mouth.

"Not yet, Corporal," Dance said. She had deep scratches across her face.

"Tears?"

Dance frowned. "She fell. And then rose from the dead. She attacked us. She was like a Child of Mictlāntēcutli. I was forced to take her head."

"We need to move," Jade said. "It is not safe here."

"Can you move?" Dance asked.

I wiggled my fingers and toes and tested my limbs. I was pretty sure I'd broken some bones and suffered internal injuries when the blast wave hit me, but the damage seemed to have healed already. Rolling over, I got to my knees, and Dance and Jade helped me to my feet. I felt wobbly, but I nodded to Dance, and she led the way through the thick fog covering the ground and back up the hill to the top of the island that had become our little Alamo.

"Colossus three!" she shouted uphill, announcing our running password and number of friendlies.

The platoon was huddled in a tight perimeter at the top of the hill, picking off skirmishers. Only a few were still using their primaries; most were armed with the bows and spear-throwers we'd made. McKenzie's lads were the most effective in this sort of fight, flinging rocks from their slings with deadly accuracy. In hindsight, maybe I'd been too hard on these guys; I doubt any of us would have survived that assault without them.

"Welcome back," Sanchez said. "Thought you'd bought the farm, son."

"Not yet, Sarge. What's the situation?"

"Could be better. Red on ammo. They've made a few sustained pushes on our position." He paused to fire a rapid group with his pistol. The slide locked back, and he swapped magazines as he talked. "A couple times it's come down to hand weapons and really harsh language. But we're holding and they're starting to lose steam. Most of the opposition now is recycled troops."

"Recycled?"

"Undead. Reanimated. Whatever you call it. We got Deadheads out there raising cannon fodder."

"How long was I out?"

"Not long. Don't worry. You didn't miss much." He shouted at Flaming Feather and a couple others to adjust the sectors they were covering. "I need you on overwatch—where's your weapon?"

"I'm black on ammo for Sybil."

"McKenzie has the Barrett, get it from him and stand by. I'll call out HVTs." He threw a knife hand northward. "We're calling that our twelve."

"Hooah, Sarge."

The M107 was a beast of a rifle, about thirty pounds dry and over four feet long—twice what Sybil weighed and nearly a foot longer. Each magazine was a good five pounds alone. Not that I was complaining; I could handle the weight. Sybil was just so much more… elegant.

But looks can be deceiving. The Barrett is insanely accurate, and it can *really* reach out and touch someone. Sybil was effective out to about a klick and a half on the extreme end; the Barrett could beat that by several hundred meters. In sniper school back in Amoloyan, they'd told us kills out to three klicks and even farther weren't unheard of. Legendary shots, sure, but not impossible. A two-and-a-half-mile-plus kill was far beyond my skills, but it wasn't beyond the rifle's capabilities.

Sobering thought.

I got the rifle from McKenzie, along with the remaining magazines and a handful of Raufoss, then staged up near Sanchez where he could direct me. Epasotl was nearby, looking even more exhausted than I felt, with several tiny flaming meteors orbiting above her head.

"Epasotl!" Sanchez barked. "Give me two on that group of walking corpses at seven-thirty."

She shouted an acknowledgment hoarsely and threw out her hand. Two of the meteors streaked forth, arcing high above the swamp, before exploding into an advancing group of undead.

"Almost as good as a mortar team," Sanchez grumbled in satisfaction.

"Deadhead at ten, five hundred meters!" Takahashi called out.

"Take him down, Bennett," Sanchez directed.

I rushed to a small berm, set the Barrett up on its bipod, loaded a round of Raufoss—I wasn't about to mess around after five solid hits with .338 Lapua Magnum had failed to take one of these jerks down—and then got behind the scope to acquire the target. He was shrouded in shadow-flames, stalking across the marsh, raising corpses.

Breathe, relax, aim, squeeze.

The Barrett boomed. The round hit center mass.

And the spellcaster just… came apart.

After so long with Sybil, I'd anticipated more kick from the rifle, but the Barrett is surprisingly gentle considering the kinetic violence it can hurl downrange.

With the necromancer down, all of his reanimated forces stumbled and collapsed. But more were still coming.

"There's got to be another one out there," Sanchez called out. "Keep your eyes peeled for Deadheads, people."

I did a mental count of everyone in our little circle and came up one short. There should've been eight of us up and fighting, not counting the lads, but there were only seven. And Kiktú was nowhere to be seen, either.

I scanned the area for casualties. Nine of us were laid out sick from the malarial disease. And there was Kiktú, lying with them. She must have been badly wounded. Still, I was missing someone.

"Where's Stars?" I asked Jade.

She shook her head.

"Missing?"

"Dead."

That hit me hard. Of all the gals except my wife, I'd known Dressed-in-Stars the longest. It would hit Wilson harder. Much harder. And I had no idea how Flaming Feather was dealing with the loss of her younger sister.

I glanced over at her and got my answer.

With anger. And a whole lot of kinetic fury.

"Belt out!" Feather screamed, tossing the M240B aside. She brought up her SCAR-H and started taking out an advancing squad of reanimated jags with steady, controlled fire. Deadly calm and accurate. I'd expected her to go full auto and just dump a mag, but she had better fire discipline than that.

More people called black on ammo and switched bows and spear throwers. It was going to get close and furious real soon, real fast. And I saw now that a lot of people were badly hurt, not just Kiktú. They were fighting anyway. I prayed we'd all make it through.

Prayer.

Weaving.

Epasotl believed these two things were the same; I wasn't remotely convinced. It went against everything I'd been raised to believe.

And yet…

I don't know what came over me, but I took a knee and bowed my head, right there in the middle of it all with javelins incoming and undead jags storming the perimeter, getting close enough that people were making contact shots and hacking away with hand weapons.

"You can pray when we're dead!" Sanchez barked at me. He sounded so tired. Everyone did.

I ignored him, took a deep breath, and reached out.

I saw the threads of my friends. Brothers. Sisters. More than just a team. A family. Watched how their threads wove a pattern with mine to form Crazy Horse Platoon. Made it a living, breathing entity. And it was hurting—bad. It was bleeding out. We were moments from collapse.

If I could kill with threads of anger, maybe I could heal with threads of love.

I know, that sounds super corny now that I'm reading it back to myself. But it's what I was thinking at the time. I'm not macho. Never have been. Hallmark commercials make me cry.

I'm not the hero you're looking for.

I opened up and filled myself with teōtl until my skin burned and the swamp grass around me shriveled from the radiant heat.

I was *juiced up*.

Epasotl would say that.

Juiced up.

I prefer… *jacked*.

And then I sent it out to all the threads connected to my own in a wave of pure healing energy.

The entire platoon gave a collective sigh, and the opposition fell back a step.

It didn't turn the tide, but it gave my friends a second wind. Maybe even a fighting chance.

The battle raged on as the gray dawn crawled across the sky.

"Deadhead three o'clock, fifty meters!" McKenzie warned. "No, five o'clock, forty meters—bloody hell! Where'd the bugger go?"

"On our three, twenty-five meters!" Dance shouted.

"He's everywhere!" Jade cried.

I was swinging around, trying to get a fix, when the mist parted directly in front of Takahashi and an emaciated jag covered in writhing shadows stepped forward, reaching toward him with a gnarled staff decorated with scalps.

Then the mist swirled and he was gone again.

Takahashi stood and looked around dumbly.

"Get your ass down, Taks!" Sanchez barked.

"Deadhead at twelve, thirty meters!" Feather shouted.

I pivoted, bringing up the Barrett's heavy muzzle as the necromancer formed some kind of sphere of nothingness above his head.

"On me!" Epasotl cried. "Pull back. On me! Everyone on me!"

Someone, probably Sanchez, yanked my drag handle, and I lost my sight picture, but not before I saw the Deadhead cast the orb toward us.

Takahashi was still standing, looking confused, and I screamed at him, but it was too late.

The sphere of dark energy rippled through space, exploding in size as it approached, consuming *everything.*

Epasotl cast her hands up, and a shimmering blue dome fell over us and our sick. Outside her little shield everything within twenty meters of us just... died. Rotted away. Trees, grass, everything.

Takahashi.

I caught a moment of fear flash in his eyes as he too was consumed by the circle of death.

The protective dome flickered out of existence a moment later, and I snapped the Barrett to my shoulder and got the necromancer back in my scope. The mist was already swirling around him when I fired.

The fifty-caliber multi-purpose anti-materiel high-explosive incendiary armor-piercing round hit him dead center just as he was about to fade from view. Raufoss Mk 211 hits with the power of a twenty-millimeter auto-cannon, and it doesn't leave much of a man-sized, flesh-and-bone target behind.

A cloud of red mist floated away on the breeze while around our perimeter undead jaguar-warriors stumbled and fell.

Somewhere a bird began trilling to greet the dawn as the waterways churned with monsters gorging themselves on the dead.

CHAPTER 32

In addition to Takahashi, Obsidian Tears, and Dressed-in-Stars, we'd lost five of the lads: Andrew, James, Bartholomew, Thaddaeus, and Simon. Epasotl and I managed to bring all our sick back from the brink of death, although they all remained weak and would take time to recover. Kiktú was grievously wounded, but Epasotl did what she could. In fact nearly everyone was wounded to some degree or another, and my abilities as a healer were called into duty as well. I wasn't great at it, but I found I could weave a cut closed or mend a broken bone with some effort.

"I am sorry," Epasotl said as she handed me a twisted and melted lump of gold.

"My grandfather's ring?"

"Yes."

I turned the unrecognizable object around in my fingers. "It served its purpose, I suppose."

I looked back to where the others were staging the boats. It was still early in the morning, but we weren't planning on hanging around this graveyard any longer than necessary.

"Without it we not survive battle," Epasotl said.

"Then it was worth it." I sighed. "We'll have to find you a new 'battery.'"

"Many dead." She motioned around the island. "Already find something."

I grimaced. "Don't know if I'd trust anything *they* have. Could be cursed or something."

"Perhaps. Perhaps not. Take risk." She pulled an amulet out from behind her little plate carrier. It appeared to be obsidian, carved in the face of a tormented jaguar-man with ruby eyes and jade teeth.

"That definitely looks like something that would be cursed," I said.

"Found something for you too." She reached into her haversack and pulled out a tomahawk with a gleaming bronze head, a section of its darkly polished shaft wrapped in black leather. The blade was etched with strange glyphs, and the poll had been crafted to resemble a terrifying, snarling jaguar with emerald eyes. It was a masterpiece of craftsmanship, but I eyed it suspiciously.

"Looks… dunno. Evil," I said.

"Pffft. Is not evil. Is not good. Is weapon. Very good quality. Weapon for great warrior or king. You lucky to have it. Big Kahuna be jealous. Little Kahuna too. Everyone jealous."

I took it from her, handling it carefully. It had remarkable balance. I tested the edge with my thumb and drew blood.

"Ouch. Dang, that's sharp. Like a razor. I didn't know you could get bronze that sharp."

"See? Is good. Gift from sister. You welcome."

"Thanks, Eps. Who'd it, uh, come from?"

"How I know? All jaguar-people look same. He have big headdress and many scalps. Maybe great warrior. Dead warrior now. Not so great. Now is for you."

I dropped the tomahawk through a loop on my plate carrier. "Be careful with that amulet, Eps. It really doesn't look like something I'd want to play around with."

"You worry too much. Always worry."

"Maybe, but still…" Sanchez caught my eye and waved me over. "Come on, sis. Looks like we're about ready to cast off. I want to get as far away from this place as possible, as quickly as possible."

We hoofed it over to Sanchez. "Yes, Sarge?"

"I want your boat to lead the column. Take Epasotl with you to navigate." He made a sour face. "I hate leaving one of these tubs behind, but we don't have much choice. Not enough able-bodied people to crew them all. I'm putting Wilson on your boat. He's not combat-effective, so you're in charge until he recovers. Here." He handed me a handful of twenty-round 7.62 magazines. "That's for First-to-Dance. I split what's left between Flaming Feather and myself. That's it. That's all there is."

"Forty mike-mike?" I asked.

"Already divvied it up between me and First-to-Dance. Just have a few rounds of HE each. Claymores are all gone. Hand grenades all gone. Fair on nine-millimeter though. For now. I've distributed what we have left of arrows and made sure everyone got themselves a suitable battlefield pickup because the next fight is going to be up close and personal. There were plenty to choose from. See you found yourself something pretty."

"Yeah. Eps found it."

"I'm jealous. Know how to use it?"

"Sort of. Not really."

"If we ever get time, I'll show you, but it's a lot like knife work. Keep it close. Strike fast. You're not splitting wood. Try to hook a kidney or chop the femoral. Neck is good. Groin is almost better. That poll on the reverse will do some damage too, so don't forget about it. It's not just for looks."

"Thanks, Sarge."

He scratched his eye.

"Anything else, Sarge?"

"You've been pulling above your weight. Keep it up."

I tried to hide my surprise. That might have been the biggest compliment I'd heard him give anyone, ever. He paused, as if he wanted to say something more, but decided not to. Instead he asked me if I knew why he'd left Marine Recon in the Corps and signed on as a Cavalry Scout.

The randomness of the question caught me off-guard. I didn't know. But I had wondered. *Got tired of eating crayons, Sergeant?* Haha. Kidding. I didn't say that. I'm not suicidal.

"Because I was getting too old for shit like this." He gave a tired laugh. "Let's get the rest of the sick on board and put this shithole behind us."

***

It didn't rain for the next four days and nights. Not even a fine mist. The temperature soared even though the sky remained stubbornly overcast, and we ran out of water before we ran out of smoked eel and swamp rat. We wove through maze-like channels for hours on end until I lost all sense of direction. Epasotl tried to reassure me that her earth spirit was keeping us on course, but I was beginning to have my doubts. He was surly and uncooperative at the best of times.

"Are you sure Tlalli knows where he's going?" I asked her in a low voice on the morning of the fifth day. The fog was thick, and we could barely see a couple dozen meters ahead. "We're supposed to be going northeast, but I swear we've been going south for hours."

"Must follow rivers," she whispered.

"We were supposed to skirt the marsh, not go deeper into it."

"What can say? Tlalli speak to land. Find paths. Paths change day by day. Sometimes must find new path. Must trust."

"How much longer?"

"He say not many more dawns."

"Half the platoon is still recovering and we're out of water, Eps. If we don't find a source of drinkable water, we'll be dead in a few dawns." I glanced at Cohen, who was curled up at the bottom of the canoe looking pale. "Some of us sooner."

"What can do?" she hissed. "I do all can. We cure sick people but they not get better. Want I make water from thin air?"

"Could you?"

"If have rain spirit. But Atzi gone."

I looked at all the water flowing past and resisted the urge to dip my hand in and take a drink.

"Wait," I said. "Could we take this water and… I don't know… weave all the bad stuff out? Like we did with the disease?"

"Already try. No dice."

"Dang it."

"Anyway, what good weave out disease do? Everyone still sick."

"The fevers broke. They're not vomiting out of both ends. They just need rest and lots of water."

"Some need more. Some need good kick in balls." She glared back at Wilson who was wrapped in a poncho liner despite the heat and just… staring off into nothing. I figured she meant "pants," but then again maybe not.

"Take it easy on him. He just lost someone close."

"Broski gone. That not Broski. That someone else."

"He'll come back."

"He not make joke. He not eat. He not do anything but stare and ignore me."

"Give him time."

"Ahead," Dance called back to us softly.

I whipped my head around. Strange, tall, spindly shapes were emerging from the fog. I hefted the Barrett up and got behind the scope.

The shapes were scaffolds made from long poles. At least twenty of them were scattered in our path. Each held the body of a naked, horribly mutilated man suspended by ropes that stretched out his arms and legs. *Human* men, not jaguar-people.

I dialed in the magnification on my scope. They each had the unmistakable markings of men who'd been death-touched. And some of them were still alive, even as the ugly flying carrion lizards who infested this swamp pecked out their eyes and tore off strips of their flesh. It was revolting, and I couldn't help but feel for these crucified men—even though I knew they'd been sent by Smoking Mirror to kill us.

The feeling of disgust turned to nausea as my scope found the body of Sergeant Clark.

I wanted to vomit, but I was too dehydrated.

"Epasotl," I hissed. "We need to find another path. *Now*. These were put here as a warning."

She nodded and pulled out the shrunken jaguar-man head, shaking it like a Magic 8 Ball.

"He no answer," she said. "Probably on break."

"Well, get him *off* his break. This is urgent."

"No can do. Union rules."

"Spirits have an actual union?"

"Not know. What is union? Is thing he always say."

I shook my head. "Dance, stop paddling." I held up a fist to stop the canoes behind us, then keyed my radio, got nothing, checked that it was turned on, and tried again. Nothing.

"Dang it. Eps, your radio working?"

"Negatory."

"Mine is dead too," Dance confirmed.

"Hang tight here," I said.

We were next to a long, narrow sandbar, so I was able to get out of the dugout and run back to Sanchez's boat. He was gazing at the scaffolds through his binoculars and swearing softly to himself.

"We need to find another path, Sergeant," I said. "The course we're on takes us right through that horror show."

"What does our navigator say?"

"He's on break. Union rules or something."

"God, I hate unions." Sanchez spat over the side of his canoe. "Is that Sergeant Clark?"

"Yeah."

"Damn savages. Why didn't you just radio me?"

"Batteries are dead."

"Your whole boat?"

"Uh… maybe. Forgot to check Wilson's and Cohen's."

"We've been slack on doing radio checks the last few days. Get that solar charger out and juice 'em back up. We can't afford to lose comms."

"Yes, Sergeant." It would take most of the day to charge them with how overcast it was, but it was my fault they'd gone flat in the first place.

Sanchez bent down and fished around for something, then handed over a radio. "Here, use Touchdown's in the meantime. He sure as hell doesn't need it."

"How's he doing?"

Sanchez simply grunted in reply.

"What do you want to do, Sarge?"

He went back to peering through his binoculars for several minutes before keying his radio. "Mystique, Xavier. What's Bishop's status?"

"Sleeping," Flaming Feather replied. "Want me to wake him?"

"Negative. Xavier out." He lowered his binoculars and chewed on his lip. "Not much cover here. Vegetation is sparse. Except for that stand of trees about half a klick ahead. Should provide adequate concealment. Listen, if we have to go past the horror show, we go past it. Don't let it spook you. But I don't want to be exposed when the fog burns off, so we should hole up in those trees until nightfall. Go on ahead and clear it. We need to get all the boats in there."

CHAPTER 33

Dance and I paddled toward the stand of mangrove trees cautiously. It looked like a good covert to hide in, but that meant there could be others concealed there already.

We stopped paddling about a hundred meters away and let the canoe drift in the nearly stagnant current.

"What is our play?" Dance asked me in a low voice.

It never failed to amaze me how quickly our Kuauchanejkej allies had picked up not only English, but our slang and idioms as well. I'd been completely immersed in a Spanish-speaking culture for two years and I still had trouble with their idioms. And some of the slang just plain did not compute.

I scanned the thicket with my scope. There didn't seem to be any land approach, and I wasn't keen to try swimming in man-eating-eel-and-Toadzilla-infested waters. So we'd have to enter by boat.

There was probably a super high-speed way to do that, but our former Marine Recon platoon sergeant had failed to brief me on the particulars.

"I'll paddle us in," I told Dance. "You keep watch. Better load a round of HE in advance."

"Hooah."

"What I do?" Epasotl asked.

"Your staff got any charges left?"

"Cheah."

"Better get it out. And any other tricks you have up your sleeves." I glanced between the two of them. "Don't fire unless we're under direct threat. Hopefully we can just slip in, verify no one's home, and set up shop."

"And if someone home?" Epasotl asked.

"Ideally we slip back out without them knowing. Ready?"

They both flashed a thumbs-up.

I cut the paddle cleanly into the water and pulled us forward at a slow, steady pace. A pair of winged snakes burst out of the trees and danced in the sky, but otherwise all was still.

The mangrove thicket was larger than it had looked on the outside. It covered a few acres of still pools and gently flowing channels dotted with small islets overgrown with swamp grass. It was dark, too, but that wasn't a problem for Epasotl or me. Dance got out her NODs. After paddling in a ways, I stopped and let the canoe drift as I got out my thermal monocular. There were a lot of small heat signatures high in the trees, but given the soft chorus of discordant hissing we'd been hearing, that was to be expected.

Aside from the flying snakes, we appeared to be alone.

I started paddling again, taking us deeper in, pausing every few minutes to check on thermal.

Nothing.

I was about to call it good and radio Sanchez the all-clear when Epasotl tapped my shoulder and pointed.

I squinted in the direction she'd indicated. "What?" I subvocalized.

"House in trees," she hissed.

I looked harder and realized she was right. Off to our left, a large hut had been constructed in the trees, but it was so neglected and overgrown it looked like a big cluster of vegetation.

Or maybe it wasn't neglected. You couldn't ask for better camouflage.

"Want a closer look," I said, steering the dugout toward it. "Heads on a swivel."

Pierce was in the canoe with us, too. He'd been with me consistently of late. Didn't want to be running around on his own in a swamp, I guess.

"Mind checking it out?" I asked him.

"Can do, bro. Back in a jiffy."

Edging the dugout closer, I found a stalk of roots to rest the canoe against, and we waited.

And waited.

"Longshot, Xavier. Sitrep."

"Found a dwelling. Ghost is clearing it. Taking longer than it should. Stand by. Longshot out."

After another ten minutes I started to worry.

"Xavier, Longshot. Ghost is overdue. Going in with Gold One-Four."

"Roger. Fog's clearing. Try to speed things up. Xavier out."

"You rush a miracle man, you get rotten miracles," I muttered to myself. "Come on, Dance. We gotta see what's holding Pierce up. Stay frosty, Eps."

Epasotl shot me a shaka sign, and I tied the canoe off before climbing out along the latticework of stilt-like roots. I left the Barrett in the boat, but Dance kept her SCAR.

I signaled Dance to take point, and she flowed effortlessly past me. The Kuauchanejkej are literally born in trees and climb with a grace you have to see to believe. About halfway to the hut, I was regretting not sending Epasotl with Dance instead of me. Epasotl was a natural climber as well. Me, not so much. My tree-climbing career had been short-lived and had ended with a broken leg. My parents banned me from arboreal adventures after that incident. The ban didn't hold up all too well, but I never really got over my fear of heights afterward.

Scaling trunks meters above water swarming with deadly creatures… for the girls that was just another Tuesday. For me, not so much.

But we climbed, and I didn't break my leg. We found the door, eventually, and staged outside it.

I nodded to Dance, who swung inside gracefully. I followed right behind her, pistol drawn—not as gracefully—and cleared right as she cleared left. We bisected the room and staged up again on the opposite side next to a low doorway that led further into the structure.

The room we were in appeared to be some sort of common room, with rotting woven mats of the floor and mouldering herbs hanging from the ceiling. There were no windows, no furniture, and not much else to see. Toadstools grew on the floor of tightly woven branches, and vines edged through the thatched roof.

Dance nodded to me from behind her NODs, and I ducked and flowed through the doorway, again taking the right while she cleared the left.

The second room was bigger and had two exits. It looked like some sort of Stone Age laboratory. Shelves were lined with gourds and animal skulls, mangy pelts covered the floor, and a sort of low table squatted in the middle of the room covered with bones and stones all bearing strange markings. The table also held a mortar and pestle, some sort of pendant made from a rather large ruby, and a decidedly not Stone Age book swollen from water damage, its leather cover cracked and peeling.

I leaned in closer and squinted at the hand-painted gold leaf glyphs. It looked like it was a form of Mesoamerican writing, but I couldn't begin to identify it. I'm fascinated with Aztec and similar cultures—partly because of where I served on my mission, but also it's not an unusual subject of interest in my religion since we believe one of our scriptures came from an ancient American society—but I'm not a scholar by any stretch.

We cleared both of the exits—one led to a small sleeping chamber piled with stinking pelts and the other was obviously a toilet —and then stood once more by the low table.

"It does not look like anyone has been here for a very long time," Dance observed quietly. "We should go."

"Yeah, but where's Pierce?"

She shrugged. She looked nervous, which was very unlike her.

I moved to flip the cover of the book open with the barrel of my pistol, but Dance grabbed my arm and shook her head.

"This is obviously the home of a witch," she said. "I would not touch anything. We should go. We could be cursed already for stepping across the threshold."

Back in the real world I would've dismissed her as being superstitious, but magic was very real here. Curses, too. I should know.

"Epasotl will want to see this." I said. "Go back and send her up."

"And you?"

"I'm just going to wait. Maybe Pierce will show up. Don't worry, I won't touch anything."

She nodded and left the room.

I keyed my radio. "Xavier, Longshot. Dwelling is clear, but I want Kitty to check it out. Ghost is MIA."

"Roger. Clear to proceed?"

"Roger. All clear. Longshot out."

I scanned the room again and puffed out my cheeks. My eyes fell on the pendant again, and I leaned in closer. It wasn't Stone Age, either. The setting that held the ruby was exquisitely crafted, obviously by a master goldsmith, and the facets of the ruby were far too perfectly cut. It seemed to glow with an inner light, casting strange shadows around the table. Or maybe my eyes were playing tricks on me.

I wanted to pick it up, but resisted the temptation and just stood in the eerie silence trying unsuccessfully not to get too creeped out.

"Gnarly," Epasotl whispered, strolling into the room several minutes later.

"What do you make of all this?" I asked her.

She poked her head into the sleeping cubby and then the toilet. "No one here in long time. But smells of bad mojo. You touch anything?"

"Not a thing."

"Good."

"What do you think was going on here?" I asked, motioning to the table.

"Hmm." She scrunched up her nose. "Very strange. Not see markings like on bones and rocks before. Not Chaneque. Not jaguar-people as far as I know. What is that?" She pointed to the book.

"A book. Like a codex. Looks old. I think the writing on the cover is maybe Olmec or something like that. So is the design of the pendant, I think. The leather binding is strange."

"Is human skin," Epasotl said.

"Ah, and you'd know this because…? No—don't tell me." I thought of Brian McCoppin, one of the first of my platoon-mates to die here, flayed alive by Epasotl's people, in her own village. She might have even taken part in his torture. I'd never asked. I didn't want to know.

"Pendant look like could be good battery for juice," she said, reaching for it.

"Don't—" I began, but she'd already picked it up and was holding it to her eye, turning it around and squinting at it.

"Oh look!" she exclaimed. "Found Pierce."

"Say again?"

"At least think it Pierce. Look same. Like old alive Pierce, not dead rotting Pierce. But not big now. Tiny. See?" She thrust the pendant at me, and I took an involuntary step back.

"I'm not touching that."

"Do not whine like cub. Fine. I hold. You look. See if Pierce."

She held it out, and I moved cautiously toward it and peered into the ruby. There, trapped inside, was a miniature Pierce, waving and shouting at me. I couldn't hear him, but it was definitely Pierce. I waved back at him.

"How do we get him out?" I asked Epasotl.

"Not know. Never see this before."

"Sorry, bro," I said to the ruby, speaking loudly and slowly, enunciating each word. "We do not know how to get you out. Hang tight. Just… chill for a bit."

He shouted something, flipped me off, and then turned his back on me.

"Pierce pissed," Epasotl said.

"I'd be too if I was trapped in a ruby."

"Nice ruby though. Could be worse."

"I really don't think he cares that he's trapped in a one-hundred-carat rock, pretty as it is."

"Could store much juice," Epasotl said wistfully. She caught my expression and waved a hand. "Of course will not try! Might hurt Pierce. Pierce you friend. Not hurt you friend. Cross heart and hope you die." She held out the ruby again. "You take. Give to Falling Leaves. Make her happy have Pierce."

"I don't want to touch it."

"Take."

"No." I paused. I didn't quite trust her not to experiment with using it to store her spells. "Okay, fine."

She gave me the ruby pendant and then picked up the book and shoved it into her haversack before I could say anything. She then proceeded to circle the room, picking up random objects and inspecting them. Some went in her bag, some back on the shelves.

"I thought we weren't supposed to touch anything," I said.

"*You* not touch." She paused to unstopper a gourd and took a sniff, then resealed it and put it in her sack.

"But you said this was bad mojo."

"Hmm. Some bad mojo. Some just mojo mojo. What this?" She held up a creepy fanged skull etched with arcane symbols.

"No idea. Looks like a demon monkey. Can we go now?"

She shoved it in her bag too, then glanced around the room once more. "Okay, we go. Wonder where person went?"

I slipped the pendant under my plate carrier and into a blouse pocket. "Hopefully very, very far away from here, never ever to return. Or at least not until *we're* very, very far away from here."

Never to return.

Ever.

CHAPTER 34

Tlalli begrudgingly guided us out of the mangrove forest under the cover of fog and darkness and past the scaffolds of mutilated, crucified men. The night wind carried the tormented moans of those still clinging to life across the desolate marsh, and I shivered as I pulled my paddle through the water.

I tried not to think of Sergeant Clark hanging among them. He'd been a good guy, solid, a great leader—until he'd succumbed to the curse. I wanted to believe it wasn't his fault. That the curse had changed him, instead of bringing out a darkness that had always been inside him. We all had darkness inside us. It could've as easily have been me, if I hadn't had the love and support of Xochi and Captain Brown and even Friar Bastía. Even Sergeant Sanchez had prayed with me to give me strength to fight the curse and stay... *me*.

I didn't know. I still don't. I've always wanted to believe Sergeant Clark could've been saved... somehow. Christopher too, but after seeing him through my scope at the top of that cliff, after seeing the look of hatred in his eyes... I didn't really have much hope for that anymore. Christopher Bond, my friend, would have to be put down, like a rabid dog.

It didn't even matter whether his true nature was being brought forth or whether he was a good man who simply lacked the willpower to fight the curse. He was hunting me, hunting those I cared about, my brothers and sisters, and so... he would have to be dealt with.

"There are lights ahead," Dance said after a time. Her voice was low, tired, almost a rasp. I didn't know how long we'd been rowing. Just that I hadn't heard the moans from the scaffolds in a long while.

I could see the lights. Soft, like friendly campfires in the distance. They beckoned me. There we would find fellowship and rest. Refuge. I felt it.

I steered the canoe, aiming for a new channel in the dark labyrinth of small rivers and grassy knolls.

"What doing?" Epasotl hissed. "Stay on course."

I tried to work some spit into my mouth. I was so thirsty.

"The fires…" I croaked, my voice scratchy.

"Look pretty, don't they," Tlalli grunted as he floated above Epasotl's shoulder. "Hot food, water. Refuge. Ha! Fuhgettabout, *babbo*. They're a trap. Ghosts of the marsh. You'll never catch them. Drive you *pazzo*. Listen to Tlalli. I knows the way."

I stopped paddling and just stared at the lights.

"First-to-Dance!" Epasotl hissed. "Go left."

Dance had stopped paddling too and was staring at the ghostly lights that beckoned us. Our dugout drifted along the lazy current.

"Longshot, Xavier." I heard Sanchez's voice in my earpiece, but he sounded a world away. Epasotl was saying something, but I didn't care. The lights were calling. Refuge. Sanctuary.

Peace.

"Longshot, this is Xavier. Radio check, over."

"Xavier, this Kitty," Epasotl replied. "Longshot out of it. He all whacked in head. Lights charm him. Gold One-Four too. I take over. Steer boat right path. You follow."

"Say again?"

"Everyone charmed. Bad light call them. Not safe. No follow light. Repeat: no follow light. I steer. Follow Kitty. Hate call sign, by way. Not cat. Want new call sign."

Cohen had dragged himself up and was peering over the side of the canoe. He mumbled something and then stood unsteadily, shaking the boat.

"Get down, idiot," Epasotl hissed at him.

He ignored her and pointed at the lights.

Sanchez said something over the radio. I don't know what. I wasn't listening. The lights beckoned. Why weren't we going to them? We'd be safe if we followed them.

"Help!" Cohen screamed hoarsely, waving his arms. "Help! Over here!"

"Shut mouth!" Epasotl hissed.

I heard others from behind us calling for help too. There was a splash, and someone screamed.

Then my vision exploded in a burst of light as something cracked my skull. I swore and shook my head. Epasotl was standing in front of me with a broken paddle, her narrowed eyes glowing in the darkness.

"Wake. Up. Ben-Ette."

"Ow! What the heck, Eps?"

"Help get Cohen down. He going to jump overboard."

Cohen was waving his arms and shouting. He placed a foot on the gunwale. I glanced back at the other boats. People were standing up; some were shouting for help.

"Quick," I told Epasotl. "The sleep fog. Can you do it?"

"Can do," she said with a nod. "Good idea."

She drew her staff out of her haversack and waved it in the air. A silver-blue fog rose from the water and snaked out behind us, enveloping the other boats. Cohen wavered and fell back into the dugout, nearly dumping us all into the water.

One by one the cries for help went silent. I was feeling drowsy myself, but Epasotl waved something foul-smelling under my nose, and the lethargy fled.

"You not sleep too," she said. "You help. Must di di mau the hell out of Dodge. Bad guys come. Make big sacrifice. Everyone die slow. Bad mojo."

"So now you *don't* want to be tortured to death."

"Change mind. Stupid custom. Live better. Come. Must go. What do with everyone?"

"Um. Guess we'll have to tie the boats together and tow them."

"Solid plan. Hurry. Must shake ass."

***

Scrambling along a sandbar, I managed to get all four dugouts tied in a line, and Epasotl and I paddled for all we were worth as Tlalli grumbled and directed us through the maze of waterways. I considered waking up additional rowers several times, but the will-o'-the-wisps were still out there, and Epasotl and I didn't want to risk a repeat of people getting seduced by the comforting lights. I found I could resist the temptation if I squeezed my eyes shut and just focused on paddling. Which I pretty much had to do, pulling four dugouts with only Epasotl to help.

We didn't exactly set a blistering pace, but the fog obscured us. Distant growls and coughing barks carried over the night breeze, like a call and response between different parties; we were being hunted, and I prayed we could make enough distance from them before dawn broke and the fog burned off.

The spectral shapes of skeletal trees drifted past, and reeds scraped at the sides of the canoe.

"We need to go faster," I told Epasotl in a hushed voice.

"No can paddle harder," she said. "Arms tired. Back tired. Everything tired."

"Can Tlalli do anything?"

"Like what?"

"I don't know. Speed up the current or something?"

"Tlalli earth spirit. Not water spirit. Not in job description."

"Atzi was never this stubborn."

"Rules are rules, *mortadella*," Tlalli said to me, giving a bob in the air like a shrug as the canoe scraped against the bottom of the narrow river.

"It's getting too shallow," I hissed, looking around frantically. We were in the middle of a forest of dead trees overgrown with vines and tall marsh grass. The dugout bumped on the bottom again. Something cough-barked a short way off, and I held a finger to my lips. A thin gray line was beginning to lighten the sky to the east.

I dipped my paddle in carefully and felt it dredge through silt. The canoe scraped against the bottom again before coming to a dead stop.

Crap.

Epasotl gave me a *What do we do now?* gesture.

I glanced back at the canoes behind us, but I could see only Flaming Feather's dugout through the soupy fog. Everyone was still sleeping.

I leaned in close to one of Epasotl's ears. "We need to wake everyone up," I subvocalized.

She peered over the gunwale at the water and shook her head. She mouthed the word, "Toadzilla."

The water here was too shallow for those monstrosities, but the piranha-eels could still be a problem. Might already have *been* a problem. I'd heard someone go overboard in the night when we were all mesmerized by the swamp gas. Then again, I'd also done a count when I roped the boats together and didn't come up short.

Epasotl got my attention and hissed softly. "Use magic eyes."

"I can't see in this fog any better than you," I subvocalized.

"No. Not eyes. *Magic* eyes. Magic eye tube see through fog, no?"

Right. My thermal monocular. I dug it out and held it to my eye, scanning the fog. I tried to swallow the fear, but my throat was too dry. Lanky humanoid shapes stalked silently through the tall grass, weaving between the dead trees. They were circling us, drawing in the net.

The closest was no less than a hundred meters away.

"Multiple enemy," I told Epasotl. "Thirty or so. Getting closer. We need to wake everyone up. *Now.*"

"No time," she replied. She looked thoughtful for a moment and then held up a finger. "I have an idea. I will make it dark."

"It's already dark," I pointed out.

"No. So dark nothing can see. Not even magic eye tube."

Epasotl stood and pointed off into the fog. Tendrils of inky blackness flowed from her finger, snaking around our dugouts. The darkness was complete and total, a complete absence of light. It felt suffocating, like drowning in nothingness, and filled the space between the canoes, wrapping us like a shroud and pouring out across the water and over the islets around us. Within our cocoon of darkness, everything seemed to cease to exist, and I realized I was holding my breath. I exhaled softly. I could still hear us breathing and the occasional growl or coughing bark of our hunters, but the sensation of blindness was absolute.

I focused on my other senses to overcome the vertigo of being trapped within this void. It made me claustrophobic. My thermal monocular was useless; nothing visible on any wavelength penetrated Epasotl's magical darkness, and nothing escaped it.

Our hunters drew closer. They hissed and growled all around us. One let out a cough-bark not ten yards away that made me jump. They sounded confused.

Epasotl tapped my arm and pressed her lips to my ear.

"Can not keep dark much longer," she subvocalized. "What we do?"

I shook my head.

Minutes passed, and the darkness started to abate. I hefted the Barrett and brought it to my shoulder, training it on the sound of a deep predatory growl nearby.

"So sorry," Epasotl whispered in my ear. "I try. I fail."

And then the blackness swirled and dissolved like ink in water, and I saw the jag staring directly at me.

He stood so close I could've reached out and touched him.

CHAPTER 35

The jag was tall and emaciated, with mangy gray fur dotted with black rosettes. The kilt he wore was made of jaguar skin, and skulls hung from his knotted belt. We locked eyes for a moment and I saw into his twisted soul. His lips spread, exposing yellowed fangs, and he raised a club tipped with a sharp obsidian stone.

I jammed the Barrett's flash suppressor into his chest and pulled the trigger.

It wasn't loaded with Raufoss, but you can imagine what a contact shot with even conventional fifty-cal will do to a body.

I didn't bother to watch him come apart; I was already swinging the rifle around and firing at the next threat. I felt a wave of heat behind me and caught the flash of flame in my peripheral vision as Epasotl unleashed a fan of fire on the hostiles to my rear. I didn't think, I just reacted. Identify the threat. Neutralize it. It was like shooting fish in a barrel.

The thunderous roar of the Barrett must've woken people up, because I could hear the sharp cracks of rifles. First a couple, then several. And then the rolling thunder of small arms fire echoing across the marsh. The bark of 7.62. The pop of nine-millimeter. A symphony of kinetic fury.

It didn't last long.

I mounted the thermal monocular in front of my scope and scanned through the fog. Wherever this hunting party had come from, they appeared to be alone.

For the moment.

"What the hell is going on?" Sanchez barked.

"No time to explain," I called back. The canoe rocked, and I realized we were afloat again; the tide must have been coming back in. That was why we grounded. Tides.

"To oars!" I shouted, or something equally idiotic. To paddles? I don't know. The adrenaline dump made me a little stupid. "Don't look at the lights! Close your eyes and just paddle!"

We bent to pulling through the water, and as the sky lightened the current grew stronger, helping our progress. Everyone was lending a hand, even the sick. Tlalli griped and shouted directions as we... well, you don't exactly *speed* along in a forty-odd-foot dugout canoe, but after being at a dead stop and surrounded by cannibals, even three or four knots feels like racing with the wind.

We wound through the waterways past small islands and dead trees that gave way to verdant stands of mangrove. The fog slowly burned off and the gray sky grew brighter.

And the day grow hotter.

By early afternoon, it was obvious Dance was struggling, the effects of acute dehydration taking over. Cohen sort of slapped at the water, and Wilson's paddle just trailed in our wake. We were going against the current now, not a strong one, but it slowed us to a blistering one or two knots.

"How far?" I asked Tlalli.

The shrunken jaguar-man's head bobbed irritably above Epasotl's shoulder and fixed me with one burning eye. "*Mi fa arrabbiare.* How am I supposed to know?"

"You're our navigator!"

"Let me understand you something, Nancy boy. I asks the land which way, *per favore*, and the land it tells me which way. It don't say how far. *Capiche?*"

"Well, can you ask it how far?"

"*Mamma mia!* So demanding. You want I should make you a calzone too, kid?"

"Just ask."

"*Just ask*, he says," Tlalli grumbled. "I coulda had class, I coulda been a contender. I could've been somebody. Okay, you mook, I'll ask. But it's gonna cost you some dough. You gotta cough up the scratch."

"Can you believe this guy?" I asked Epasotl.

She shrugged.

"Okay, Tlalli. How much?"

"From now on, it's *Don* Tlalli. Capiche?"

"Don Tlalli?"

"You deaf or something, kid?"

"Fine." I pinched the bridge of my nose. "*Don* Tlalli, can you please ask the land how far?"

"*Please*, he says." Tlalli chuckled. "Might not be such an *imbarasso* after all. Heh. Well, the land says we're two gusts of the south wind and a swallow's flight away."

"Two gusts of the—seriously? What does that mean?"

"You asked, kid. No skin off my back if you don't like the answer."

"But that's not even remotely helpful."

"Well, *mi scusi*. Whadda you want from me?"

"Just keep us on course."

Tlalli grunted.

I paddled.

The current grew stronger.

***

By nightfall, we were paddling practically just to keep from being pushed backward by the current. The landscape hadn't changed much and a thick fog had settled, reducing visibility to mere meters. Dance was delirious, singing a song softly to herself in her native tongue. Tlalli was apparently off the clock, and Epasotl looked feverish. I thought I'd felt a gust of the south wind a few hours ago, and at dusk I *might* have seen a swallow fly overhead. I keyed my radio.

"Xavier, Longshot."

"Go for Xavier."

"If we go any slower, we're going to get carried downstream by the current. We might want to consider tying up for the night. I'm down to one and half paddlers."

"Tide's turning. Charlie Mike. Xavier out."

Dance dropped her paddle in the water and slumped over, muttering something I couldn't understand. It was hard to think. I had a horrible headache and felt dizzy. I didn't understand what Sanchez meant about the tide. What did that have to do with anything?

Charlie Mike.

I was paddling on autopilot. My hands itched from the constant healing as I sloughed off blisters and new skin regrew. My arms ached. My back ached. I just wanted to stop and sleep forever.

I let my paddle drag in the water.

Except we were still progressing upstream.

Upstream was now downstream.

Tides.

I scooped some water and tasted it before forcing myself to spit it out. Too salty. And probably swimming with pathogens. I keyed my radio.

"Xavier… Longshot."

"Go for Xavier." He sounded tired.

"Tide turned."

"Yes, Longshot?"

"I can't go on."

"Get some rest, but don't fall asleep. Just let the current carry us for a while."

"Need water."

"I know, son. Keep pushing."

"Excuse me," McKenzie broke in. I didn't know he even had a radio. He must've. Made sense. "But if we tie off, the lads could go hunting. Catch another swamp rat, eh? In Basra we drank blood from our camels when the water gave out."

"Great plan," Doc answered, sounding weak and delirious. "Then we die of dysentery instead of dehydration."

"Just a suggestion," McKenzie said. He sounded offended. "No need to be snippy, laddie."

"Charlie Mike," Sanchez grunted.

***

I must've dozed off, because it was the sound of the canoe's bottom scraping against rock that brought me back to my senses. The dugout bumped gently against something and came to a stop. Moments later Flaming Feather's boat knocked against mine, jolting me fully awake.

"Why are we stopping?" Feather hissed at me from her canoe.

"Ran aground," I called back. I had to raise my voice more than I liked to be heard above the thunderous pounding in my head. "I'll get out and push us back into the current."

I could barely see her through the mist and fog. The air was damp and chilly, and I shivered as a gust of wind hit me.

She nodded and climbed out of her dugout. "I will help. It is heavy."

"God, I'm so thirsty," I croaked.

"I fear we will not survive much longer. Many are close to death already."

We each bent down, got a shoulder behind the canoe, and heaved. It rocked a little, but didn't budge.

She said something I couldn't make out over the roar in my ears.

"What?" I practically yelled.

"I said there is too much weight. You will have to get everyone out."

"I can hardly hear you," I said. "What is that noise? It sounds like a—"

"Waterfall!" we said in unison.

At the thought of fresh water, we forgot the canoes, our teammates, security, everything, and ran to the source of the noise. The mist parted, and I laid eyes on the most beautiful sight I'd ever seen. The water fell silver-white like a bridal veil from high above, crashing into a large pool. I stripped off my plate carrier and ACU blouse, stumbled into churning water up to my thighs, and let the cascade pour over me. It was cold and tasted incredible. Fresh and pure and… probably full of pathogens. I didn't care at the moment. Flaming Feather danced beside me under the shower. She was giddy. Feather didn't *do* giddy. She was always the stoic one.

She embraced me fiercely, laughing.

"It tastes so good!" she cried.

"We should really purify—"

She interrupted me with a kiss and then shrieked a war cry.

"Come!" she said. "Let us get the others."

"We really shouldn't drink it without purifying it," I said, stumbling out of the pool behind her.

"It tastes clean."

"Doesn't mean it can't kill us."

She shrieked again, like a bird of prey, spun into my arms, kissed me a second time, deeper, and then laughed before sprinting away.

"I don't care!" she called over her shoulder.

"You will when you're vomiting blood out of both ends," I muttered, touching my lips and feeling guilty. I hadn't really kissed her back… much. But… she *was* a good kisser.

Xochi was probably going see to it that I became a eunuch—by her own hand.

"Come! Help me!" Feather called.

We went from boat to boat, rousing those we could raise and carrying others onto shore. I at least had the presence of mind to tie off the dugouts so they wouldn't drift away. I collected chlorine tablets and canteens and returned to the waterfall to fill them up. The water in the pool was slightly brackish, but the cascade was fresh. Feather came to help, and together we carried the canteens back to the rest of the platoon.

"Life tastes the freshest when you have stepped into the shadow of death," she said to me.

"We've been dancing in death's face for weeks. It *does* feel good to be alive, but it always makes me guilty too. For being the one who lived, that is. You know?"

A shadow flickered across her face, and I kicked myself mentally. She had just lost her younger sister.

"There is no sin in living when another has fallen, so long as you live well," she said. "To live a full life honors those who have traded their lives for yours. They have bought and paid for your future. To mourn is a waste of their gift. You should instead seek joy."

She squared her shoulders and smiled at me, but I saw the tears in her eyes. I turned my head to save her the indignity of drying them in front of me.

***

The fog cleared by midmorning, revealing the cliffs that surrounded us on all sides. We had entered some form of large open-ceiling cave through a low, narrow arch leading out to the marsh sea. The falls cascaded in two stages over a height of about thirty meters, and as I stood on the riverbank staring up at the top of the waterfall, I wondered how the heck we'd get the dugouts up there.

Probably we couldn't. Not without killing ourselves in the process.

I caught the scent of roasting meat on the wind, and my mouth watered. The lads had caught a small deer just before dawn, and McKenzie already had it cooking over a large fire.

I turned to survey our little camp. First-to-Dance was perched on a rock keeping watch, and waved to me with a smile. I caught sight of Jade Talon, also on watch, and Flaming Feather and Kiktú—now mostly recovered from her injury thanks to Epasotl's ministrations—seeing to nursing the platoon. Several people had fevers again, but I'd already examined them, and it wasn't magic healing they needed, just rest and hydration. Sanchez was still sleeping, and he could keep right on sleeping if you asked me. As far as I knew the man *never* slept.

But it did leave me as the senior NCO in the platoon at the moment. Me and my security detail of two. Captain Brown had been lucid for a while, but I'd convinced him to rest.

I have the watch, sir.

Epasotl came hobbling over to me using her staff as a crutch and gave me a Cheshire grin full of needle teeth.

"Swallowed a canary?" I asked her.

She looked puzzled, then stood a little straighter. "Learn new trick!"

"Oh yeah? What's that?"

"Watch and see." She fished the creepy obsidian jaguar-man skull amulet out of her shirt and held it in one hand. "Watching?"

"You have my undivided attention."

She turned and took a step away from me and then… *blinked* to a spot a hundred feet or so away. She waved, took a step toward me, and *blinked* again, this time appearing right in front of me. And naked except for the amulet around her neck.

"Uh, is that part of the trick?" I asked.

"No. That not happen before." She looked along the shore, and I followed her gaze. Her staff, her haversack, her clothes, everything, were scattered in all directions. A diminutive combat boot floated in the water lapping the shore.

"Amulet play trick," she sighed.

"I told you not to trust it. Here, I'll help you collect your things."

"Still, good trick, no?"

"Very good trick, aside from the naked part." I fished her boot out of the water. "How far can you teleport?"

"Not far. Just down beach and back." She picked up her ACU blouse and added it to the small bundle in her arms. "Good for fight, no? Jump around. Heal people. Play nasty tricks on bad guys."

"Yeah, again, aside from the part where all your stuff including your underwear might randomly get tossed out in all directions."

"Take off gear first. Jump naked." She tapped her head. "Not just coat rack."

I shrugged. "A naked Epasotl blinking around the battlefield would certainly have an adverse psychological effect on the enemy. *Very* demoralizing."

"What that mean?"

"Nothing."

"You be sarcastic. Make mean joke. Not nice to sister. Maybe *you* fight naked. Bad guy die laughing when see tiny disco stick."

"Disco stick? Never heard that one before."

"Boyfriend in Amoloyan teach."

"*Boyfriend?* No, wait. Forget I asked. I don't want to know."

She laughed. "You think *human*? Gag with spoons. Boyfriend Chaneque. Human look hella grody naked." She stuck her finger down her throat and made a vomiting sound.

"Either way, I don't want to hear about your love life."

"Why? I hear plenty *you* love life. Every night back with Xochi. 'Oh, Nephi, do not stop!'"

My face flushed. "We weren't *that* loud."

"Loud enough."

"Ugh."

She doubled over laughing. "You look like swallow fire chili."

"Uh-huh."

"Not be embarrassed. Make wife happy. Make cub. Is good. You daddy mac."

I picked up her haversack and handed it to her. "Were we really that loud?"

She flashed an evil grin. "Pretty loud."

CHAPTER 36

It turned out the person who fell overboard into piranha-eel-infested waters was Anderson, of course, but Sanchez somehow fished him out before he was flayed alive. Kid was the luckiest idiot I'd ever met.

After four days resting on the riverbank in our natural fortress enjoying fresh water and roast venison and the luxury of not having literally *everything* trying to kill us, we were in pretty good health and high spirits. Mostly. Except for Wilson, who remained subdued. The stubborn strength of his dark mood surprised me, because he'd always been that guy who just didn't seem to be affected by anything. I tried to talk to him, but he was only speaking in monosyllables. He'd take Jade and Leaves on patrols above the falls, and he did his best to fill Takahashi's combat boots as our squad leader, but otherwise he mostly kept to himself.

I didn't fault him. He'd lost a good friend and leader, one of his subordinates, *and* his lover all while he'd been laid out on his deathbed with malarial fever. I think he blamed himself for their deaths. He wasn't someone accustomed to being physically unable to step up, and it made him feel responsible. As if it was his fault for being sick. I suppose I would've felt the same, to some degree, but to watch a good friend beat himself up like that was both frustrating and heartbreaking.

I wandered the beach, chatting with squad-mates and friends, and came across Epasotl sitting cross-legged kneading a gross-looking lump of meat and fat on a broad leaf while the mummified virgin's hand busily ground away at a paste in the mortar.

"Hey guys," I said.

Maitl flipped me the bird.

"Been meaning to talk to you about that," I told Epasotl. "She flips off Captain or Sanchez, they're going to be bent."

"I not stupid, Ben-Ette. Maitl, show him how say hi to Big Kahuna."

The hand saluted.

"And Little Kahuna."

Maitl waved.

"See?"

"Oh," I said. "So I'm just special."

"Special Ed, maybe." Epasotl laughed, and the hand gave her a high-five.

"Hardy har har. What exactly are you making?"

"Food for platoon. New recipe. Found berries. Very good. Mix with secret ingredient. One bite, no need eat all day. No hungry. Big energy."

"Epasotl's new and improved pemmican. Sounds good." I didn't bother asking about the secret ingredient. We'd all learned long ago not to ask about her ingredients. "We'll have a good amount of smoked venison too. Should be in great shape when we set out."

"How Pierce?"

"Oh crap! I forgot all about him." I felt awful. I was of course aware that he hadn't been around, but that wasn't so unusual. Except now it was potentially permanent.

And we hadn't the first idea what to do about it.

"Pierce be pissed you forget."

I reached under my plate carrier and patted my pocket, just to be sure the ruby was still there.

"Will you give to Falling Leaves?"

"Haven't decided," I said. "What if it's dangerous?"

"Been in pocket for days. No bad happen. Is fine."

"Maybe, but I haven't *worn* it. What if wearing it activates something… like your amulet of naked teleportation?"

"Then we see what happen. Maybe useful."

"Or we all die."

"Could be. Doubt it. Think that just trap for soul. Trapped Pierce's soul when he go poking around where not belong."

"We were poking around too."

"One trap, one soul. If you go to house first, you soul trapped. No worries. I carry you. Give to Xochi. She keep you."

"Thanks for having my six."

"Sister always ride you ass."

"That you do."

"Go. Give to Falling Leaves. Make happy. Falling Leaves sad Obsidian Tears dead. Make happy. Go now. Sister busy making food for all platoon. Is much work. Anyone say thank you? No. Just say, 'PFC, do this' and 'PFC, do that.' Make joke about ugly kitty. No appreciate." She punched the lump of meat and fat. "I no kitty. Look nothing like cat. Kiktú cat. No see difference?"

Maitl gave me a shooing gesture.

"I could help," I offered.

Epasotl laid back her ears and hissed while she stared daggers at the lump in front of her.

"Everyone appreciates you, Epasotl. You've saved us more times than I can count."

"Sister on rag. No mind me. Go give pretty ruby to Falling Leaves. Make happy."

I decided to beat a strategic retreat before the claws came out. Literally. Walking away, I fished the ruby pendant out of my pocket. Pierce was still inside. He glared at me, tapped his wrist, and gave me the finger.

"Sorry, bro," I said. "Things have been… really busy. We're still trying to figure out how to get you out." I couldn't tell him the truth: that we didn't have the first clue how to get him out, didn't even know if it was possible. I scanned the beach and found Leaves sitting with Jade cleaning her rifle. "Hang tight, man. I got a surprise for you."

***

"What is up?" Leaves asked me after I'd asked Jade to give us a few minutes alone.

"There's something I've been meaning to tell you... about Stanford."

Her face fell.

"Nothing bad," I assured her quickly. "Well, not all bad. He kind of, well, came back, a while ago. As a ghost. Only I could see or hear him. For a long time I wondered if I was just imagining him."

"Oh, I know all about that. Everyone does."

"Everyone?"

"The platoon is not *that* big, Corporal. No one has any secrets. What did you want to tell me?"

"Do you want to see him?"

Her face broke out in a dazzling smile, and she nodded.

I held out my fist and uncurled my fingers, revealing the pendant.

She gasped. "That is the most beautiful stone I have ever seen. It is huge! Is it a ruby?" She gave me a confused look. "But what does it have to do with Stanford?"

"Look closer."

She squinted, then gave another gasp. "Is he *inside* the stone?"

"That's the bad news."

She smiled at the ruby and gave a little wave before glancing up at me. "Bad news?"

"He's trapped in there. It's some sort of prison, we think. Still not clear exactly how he got in there, or how to get him out."

"Is he safe?"

"I can't imagine any place safer at the moment."

"Can I talk to him?"

"Yes. He can hear you, but you won't be able to hear him."

She took the pendant from me carefully and cradled it in her palm. "Hello, baby. I have missed you so much. I think about you every day. I have so much to tell you."

"You can have it, for now, if you want," I said.

She clutched the pendant to her breast. "Thank you."

"Just be careful with it. It's obviously magic, and we don't know what… powers it may have. I'd recommend you don't—"

She slipped the golden chain over her head.

"—wear it." I finished with a scowl.

"Oh!" she cried. "I can hear him!"

"What?"

"Umhm? Yes!" she said to the ruby. "Oh my! Poor baby. You are very brave. I know! That was very thoughtless of him." She threw me an accusing glance and then kissed the pendant. "Oh yes, the battle was very fierce. You did? That is amazing. A maggoty corpse? No, you look as handsome as ever. No. Of course I would still love you." She giggled. "Me too. Oh! You are *evil*. Naughty boy."

"I'll just, ah, give you two some space," I said. She ignored me and continued to flirt with the pendant. "Just, do be careful with it, okay? It could be danger—never mind."

She wasn't listening anyway.

I sighed and strolled away, feeling somewhat lost. There was plenty to do, but I felt… Curly would probably say *somehow*. Not morose, just… not myself. I'd recovered from our ordeals in the swamp, physically at least, and the days of rest and good eating had already put a little weight back on that I'd lost. But my soul was weary. Heavy. My… condition… the curse, continued to gnaw away at me, and the sensation of a cancer consuming my body and soul was an ever-present companion. I was strong, fast, and could heal at an astonishing rate, but I was dying.

I found a secluded spot and sat down, crossing my legs and closing my eyes. I took a deep breath in through my nose, felt it coil in my core, and then exhaled slowly through my mouth.

Focus.

Breathe.

Visualize the threads connecting everything.

Feel the teōtl flowing through me.

Sacred energy. The divine essence that binds the universe together.

Mojo.

Juice.

Love.

God?

Threads of pure, raw intelligence weaving a grand pattern that forms the material world. The open-air cave we found sanctuary in. The brightly feathered winged serpents nesting high in the rocks. The waterfall. The trees and grass. The sandy beach. The brackish estuary feeding the marsh sea at low tide and in turn being fed when the tide rose, giving life to all the plants and animals that existed in that twilight ecosystem. Life in all its abundance. Goodness. Light and order.

And death. Corruption. Darkness and evil. Chaos. But those were not patterns woven by the threads. Those occurred where the pattern unraveled. Where the threads were cut and became tangled. Entropy was a force that strove unceasingly to unmake what had been made. To undo what had been done. The second law of thermodynamics wasn't the natural state of creation; it was a cancer. A disease.

But it was more than that. Entropy was *sentient*. Aware. It was a conscious embodiment of apathy for life, order, and goodness. An entity fueled by the threads of intellect that the Great Weaver had woven on His loom into the very fabric of reality. It was indifferent to the suffering it caused in its quest to consume all intelligence. Its ravenous appetite made it appear single-minded, but that was an illusion; the Unweaver was crafty. It plotted. It planned and schemed. It seduced sentient creatures into serving it with promises of power, when in the end they too would be devoured.

Everything would be consumed until the heat death of the universe extinguished all life. All intellect. Everything that was good. Love would be devoured by apathy in the end. And entropy, the Unmaker, would rest for eternity, bloated on creation. Unaware, unconscious, having consumed even itself.

Unless we fought back.

Unless we took part in the weaving.

All good men and women were weavers. Makers. Warriors against entropy. It wasn't magic. It wasn't supernatural. The carpenter building a house, the mother nurturing her child, the soldier sacrificing his life for the freedom of his people, the painter creating something beautiful; all were co-weavers fighting back the tide of apathy. Co-weavers with one another... and co-weavers with God.

I saw the unmaking in my body and soul. The curse that gave me strength and speed, the blight that healed me while paradoxically consuming me from the inside out. I saw the tears and tangles in the warp and weave, and I teased them apart, mending the threads, fixing what was broken inside me, cutting out the cancer.

Weaving myself anew.

***

When I came out of the trance, I was exhausted and starving. I opened my eyes slowly, surprised to see Captain Brown and Epasotl standing nearby, watching me. Others in the platoon were there, too. Several looked uneasy. Maybe even afraid.

"That was... something," Brown said. "Thought we'd lost you there for a while."

"Lost me, sir?"

"You go away," Epasotl said. "Only shape of soul stay. No body. Much light. Fill whole cave all night like noontime."

"All night?" I asked, looking at the gray sky. It was midmorning at the latest. "How long was I sitting here?"

"Twenty-four hours, give or take," Brown said.

I gazed at my hands, rolled up my sleeves, pulled up my shirt. The black veins were gone. I touched my face. The scars were gone too. It was as if I had a new body. Died and been resurrected. Something like that.

Born again.

"Yes, curse gone," Epasotl confirmed. "Dark skin from sun gone. All gone. Like newborn cub."

"Back to work," Brown called over his shoulder to the rest of the platoon. "Pack it up. We're moving out."

He strode over and helped me stand, then scratched his eye. "Seen a lot of strange things this last year, but that was the strangest. You feel okay?"

297

I turned my hands over. The skin was smooth and pink, no callouses. Even the ugly scar on my right hand I'd gotten when I was twelve was gone. I felt my face again.

"I think so, sir."

"Made some changes to the platoon. Check in with Sergeant Sanchez. We're pulling out. Been stationary too long already, but with your light show going on all night, it's bound to attract attention."

"Sorry about that, sir. I didn't know—"

He dismissed the apology with a wave. "That curse or whatever it was always made me uneasy. If you managed to beat it, that's what matters."

"Thank you, sir. How are you feeling?"

"Better," he grunted. "Much better. Now get. Don't want to keep the platoon sergeant waiting."

"Yessir."

Epasotl hurried beside me as I made my way over to where Sanchez was supervising the distribution of smoked venison and pemmican. He turned as I approached, arms akimbo, and scowled.

"Captain said you wanted to see me, Sarge?"

"Made some changes while you were... whatever you were doing. You're in charge of Blue Squad now. Flaming Feather is your ASL. You're keeping your original team from Gold, including Short Round. Keep him out of trouble; I'm tired of babysitting him. And I'm putting Kiktú under you. Hooah?"

"Hooah, Sarge. Will that be all?"

"Affirmative, Sergeant. Carry on."

I made to move and then paused. "Sergeant? Hooah! Thank you."

His lip twitched in what might have been a smile. "Don't thank me yet."

CHAPTER 37

"—along this chain of canyons into the highlands," Captain Brown said, running his finger northward along the map. We'd taken a knee with the captain on the beach, forming a little huddle. "As you can see, there's no pass indicated through this mountain range, but that doesn't mean there won't be one. And on the other side is our objective." He stabbed his finger down. "This plateau. More specifically, this location on the plateau." His finger rested on a stylized logogram that somewhat resembled a skeletal jaguar-man. "What we know about this location is that it's an extinct volcano surrounded by a dead sea, a great salt basin. The mountain was apparently excavated extensively with a network of tunnels and chambers. It's a cave city. At its center is a temple complex, carved into the heart of the volcano. That is where we will find the package."

"Inhabited?" Wilson asked.

"Abandoned, at least according to the high elder." Brown paused. "Which is not necessarily the same thing."

"Enemy forces?" McKenzie asked.

"Unknown," Brown replied. "This whole plateau is holy ground for both indigenous factions, so there are no settlements that we know of. But that doesn't mean we won't encounter opposition. We'll be ready for anything. Good news is there are no known settlements along our route. Bad news is this intel is considerably outdated and there are nomadic clans that we may encounter. So expect opposition. We're in no position to engage on any scale, so we'll move fast and avoid contact when possible."

"And if it's not possible?" I asked.

"Disengage at all costs. We cannot be drawn into a stand-up fight. Period."

"Guerrilla warfare," Sanchez commented. "And we're the guerrillas."

"There's also the threat from native flora and fauna," Brown said. "We've already encountered some of the dangers the environment can throw at us. Expect more of the same, if not worse."

"What's worse than murder vines and T-Rex?" Doc asked.

"Let's hope we don't find out," Sanchez said with a look of indigestion.

"And if we can't find a pass through these mountains, sir?" I asked.

"Then up and over," Brown replied.

I glanced back at the waterfall and the thirty-meter cliff rising to our egress from the open-ceiling sea cave. "Are we taking the dugouts?"

"Negative," Sanchez replied. "Wilson's scouted the area above extensively, and the canoes won't do us a lick of good, even if we could get them over the falls. It's all rapids and more falls, but it's traversable on foot, at least for the next twenty klicks. I didn't want his team going farther than that."

"Questions?" Brown asked.

I had a million, but none pertaining to anything facing us in the immediate future. Doc gave his usual spiel about water safety, and we broke to brief our people and move out. It was midday and we were burning daylight.

I gathered Blue Squad and downloaded everything Captain Brown had gone over until even Lawrence could recite it back verbatim.

"Ammo?" Flaming Feather asked.

"Sergeant Sanchez redistributed everything this morning," I said. "I have two mags for the Barrett, plus a few special rounds. Cohen has two mags of seven-six-two and Dance is down to one and a half. She also has four rounds of forty mike-mike, all HE."

"Yo, nothing for me?" Lawrence asked.

"I'm an ace with a bow," Cohen told me. "Short Round should have my rifle. Makes more sense."

I nodded. "Short Round, give Dance one of your mags."

"She gets two and a half and I only get one?" Lawrence complained. "I got jerked."

"She's a better shot than you," Cohen said pointedly.

"Everyone *should* have a full stack of nine-millimeter in their weapons," I said, giving Lawrence the eye. "I have extra and will redistribute as needed."

"Pistol mag's full, Corp—I mean Sarge," Lawrence said. He handed Dance one of his magazines of 7.62.

<Do you feel comfortable with your pistol?> I asked Kiktú. <I realize you haven't had much practice with live rounds.>

<The doctor has drilled me extensively on the weapon using what he called "dry fire" techniques.>

<Good,> I signed. "Everyone make sure your canteens and water bladder, if you have one, are topped off, and don't forget to add purification tablets, I don't care how clear the water looks or how good it tastes. Everyone should have an emergency med kit and food. Epasotl says you only need a bite or two of the pemmican a day, so go easy on it. Eat the smoked venison first. Hopefully we'll catch game along the way. We'll split into two teams on patrol: Dance and Kiktú, you're with me. Flaming Feather, you have Cohen and Short Round. Any questions?"

"How far to the objective?" Lawrence asked. "How long will it take?"

"No idea," I said. "The map isn't to scale and we have no other intel on the route. It'll take as long as it takes. Anything else? No? Good. Okay, let's police up the camp and get ready to move."

We'd already given the camp a good once-over, but it was worth a second look to make sure we hadn't left anything behind.

García caught me and pulled me aside.

"Congrats," he said. "I wanted you to have mine." He pulled his old rank insignia out of a pocket and affixed it to my uniform, then punched it hard. "Looks good on you, Bennett."

"Dang, man! Thanks." I'd never gotten insignia when I'd been made corporal—there wasn't exactly a PX handy in the area or anything. Wearing the three stripes somehow made it feel official.

"You earned it," he said. "Don't disgrace it… like I did."

"You didn't—"

He shook his head. "Just take care of your squad."

Wilson was standing nearby and strolled over to us with a grunt. He punched my rank too. Really hard. I reeled back a step and wheezed a thank you.

"More fun when they were pinned to the collar," he said. "I still have the scars."

Those were the most words I'd heard from him in days. He held out a hand, and I shook it.

"Welcome to the club, bro," he said.

A shadow flickered across García's face as he turned to leave, but Wilson threw an arm over his shoulder and then mine.

"Brothers," he said.

"Brothers," García agreed.

"Now we just gotta find Sanchez and Doc and get shitfaced," Wilson said with a laugh.

***

Six days. Six days of climbing waterfalls, crossing rapids, and trudging through a maze of canyons. Anderson broke his arm. Twice. I mended it each time. The last three days it'd been raining nonstop, heavy sheets that the wind whipped into our faces as we struggled ahead. We were saturated to the bone, huddled in our ponchos, as if they could do anything to protect us. At least it wasn't cold. Or too hot. It was just… miserable.

"God's weather!" Doc exclaimed at one point. "Ranger weather. Keeps the bad guys indoors."

"Glad you're enjoying it," I said.

"Embrace the suck, man. Could be worse."

He had a point. It *always* could be worse.

It got worse.

We climbed higher and the temperature began to drop. The canyons gave way to foothills, and by the morning of the seventh day we were staring through the downpours at a range of soaring white-capped mountains that looked like the backbone of the world.

Dance shivered beside me and pointed. "Why are the tops of the mountains white?"

"Snow."

"I have never seen white mountains. It is beautiful."

"It's cold."

"Colder than this?" she asked.

"Much colder."

Kiktú nudged me, and I interpreted for her.

<How could anything be colder than this?> she replied. She was completely bedraggled like a… well, a wet cat.

"Come on," I said. "We need to keep moving. Keep our body temperatures up."

The incessant wind and rain continued. We moved nonstop day and night, pausing only for short breaks to sleep for a couple of hours here and there, huddled together for warmth, before moving out again. Day and night. Even if fires weren't tactically unsound, I doubt we would've found anything to burn that wasn't too waterlogged.

"Still having fun?" I asked Doc.

He sneezed and glared at me in reply.

By the sixth… seventh?… day of the storm, Captain Brown ordered us to scout for shelter. The temperature had to be dropping into the forties by my guess, and people were showing signs of hypothermia. Even naked cuddling wasn't going to save us if we didn't find shelter soon.

Blue Squad was at the head of our little column, and we had Epasotl attached to us so Tlalli could navigate and "speak to the land" or whatever it was he did.

"Ahead, up that draw," Epasotl called out, pointing.

The wind was driving the rain near horizontally, and we had to walk half-bent into it as the trees groaned and creaked.

"Can you get hurricanes in the mountains?" Cohen shouted. "Because this feels like a hurricane."

"Isn't it too cold?" I asked.

He shrugged. "We're not far from the ocean. I can smell it."

We struggled up the steep draw, Feather's team on point. Soon we were climbing, using both our hands and feet, scrabbling through waterlogged rock and soil.

"Not far," Epasotl called back. "Tlalli say not far! Is cave ahead. Soon!"

"How soon?" I asked.

"Soon. Is close."

A large tree groaned and swayed dangerously ahead. I had barely shouted out a warning when it uprooted and came crashing down between our teams. Someone screamed—Lawrence, I think—and I double-timed it to close the gap between us. Cohen was shouting and Lawrence sounded panicked.

"Speak to me," I yelled as I clambered over the huge trunk.

"She's trapped!" Cohen shouted.

"Who's trapped?"

"Feather!"

"Ohmygodohmygodohmygod," Lawrence wailed.

"Shut him up," I told Cohen as I got over the tree and dropped down beside them. "Where's—? Oh shit."

Flaming Feather's face was a mask of pain; the tree had crushed her lower half, trapping her completely. There was blood on her mouth, her chin, and all down the front of her chest plate.

I carefully slid through the loose mud and scree to crouch down beside her. "Talk to me."

She rolled her eyes and coughed more blood.

"Where's Eps?" I called back to Cohen.

"Don't know."

"—ohmygodohmygod—"

"Shut him up!" I shouted. "Gag him if you have to."

Cohen grabbed Lawrence by the shoulders and turned him away from us.

I cradled Feather's head in my hands and leaned over her, trying to shield her from the pelting rain with my body. "Stay with me," I told her. "I got you. We're going to get you out. Okay? Just hang on."

Dance clambered over the tree beside me and held a hand to her mouth. Kiktú followed in a graceful bound.

Feather's eyes focused and unfocused on me and she tried to nod as she gagged on the blood filling her mouth. I turned her head carefully to the side, and she reached out weakly, grabbing my shoulders.

"Do not... leave... me."

"No one's leaving you. We got you." I keyed my radio. "Beast, Longshot. Friendly down. Tree fell. She's trapped. Crushed. Severe internal injuries."

"Right behind you, Longshot. Don't try to move her."

"Doc's on the way," I told Feather. "Hang in there."

She coughed more blood. She was drowning in it. I didn't know what to do to help her other than hold her head and stroke her hair. I felt useless. I could sense the weave of her life unraveling in my hands. I didn't know how to weave her back together, not with the tree crushing the life out of her. The most I could do was slow her death. Keep her alive. The tree trunk was massive, at least four feet across. It would take forever hacking away with my tomahawk to cut it.

"Where's Epasotl?" I shouted at Dance and Kiktú.

Dance shook her head.

"What do we got?" Doc asked, scrambling up beside me. "Oh. Okay." He hugged his med kit to his chest. "Okay. She's in shock... that's... a lot of blood." He put his kit aside and crawled under the trunk for a minute, then resurfaced. "Okay. Her lower torso and legs are trapped under the tree."

I'd closed my eyes and was focusing on keeping her airways clear. Doc clapped my shoulder. "You with me, Bennett? You're both... glowing. Are you doing something?"

I nodded.

"Okay, well whatever it is, keep doing it."

Her heart fluttered and I focused on keeping it beating, keeping the oxygen flowing to her brain. I couldn't sense her lower half. It was… cut off.

"We need to move the tree," I mumbled.

"Say again?" Doc asked.

"The tree. Move it."

"She's bleeding internally. If we remove the weight, we could make it worse."

"I can fix that… but I can't move… the tree." My eyes were still closed. I was focused intently on following the pattern of her body, sending life into her crushed organs and ruptured veins. "I need Epasotl."

"Anyone seen Eps?" Doc called out. "Anyone? Find her then!"

The tree shifted on its own, and Feather cried out. I screamed too. I felt her pain as if I shared her body. Her pain was my pain. I couldn't feel my legs. Someone was supporting me, holding me up.

"I got you," Doc said. "Just keep doing whatever it is you're doing. Don't let go of her. Sir! Sir, we need to move this tree."

"No good," I heard Captain Brown say. "It must weigh a couple dozen tons, and it's wedged between all the other trees it fell between. We don't have the tools or the manpower. Even if we did, it would take hours."

"Epasotl is MIA," Doc said. "We need to find her."

"Already on it," Brown replied.

"Dig," I said.

"What?" Doc asked. "Yeah, maybe. Worth a shot. Sir! I need a work detail. We're going to try and dig her out."

"Jesus!" Brown shouted above the rain and wind. "Get a pair of hands and a couple e-tools. Help Doc."

"Moving, sir!" I heard García reply.

"Sir, I need you to support Bennett and Feather while we dig."

"I got you, son," Brown said, moving in close and cradling both me and Feather in his arms.

"What do you need us to do, Doc?" García asked.

"Get on her left side. Heart, you have her right. We're going to try and dig around and under her through this muck enough that we can pull her out. Careful you don't get trapped yourself. The trunk's settling. It's unstable and probably weighs as much as a bus."

"Hooah!" García said.

Everything outside of me and Flaming Feather was far away. Distant. Another world. I followed those around me more by the light of their threads than through my physical senses. After several minutes something shifted and we cried out in unison. The crushing weight eased slightly, but with it, organs shifted, and ruptured veins pumped blood like a dam bursting and I couldn't control the flood. Feather was cold, and I poured warmth into her from my own body, feeding her feeble heartbeat with my life.

"Got them, sir?" I heard Doc ask from a world away. "Okay, real slow, real gentle… *pull.*"

CHAPTER 38

"I don't *know*," Doc echoed from somewhere in the darkness. "His vitals are returning to normal but he's unresponsive."

"Is okay." Epasotl's voice. "He sacrifice own life force. Need recover."

I worked enough spit into my dry mouth to talk, but it still came out like a hoarse croak. "Feather?"

"She's… alive," Doc said.

I cracked my eyes open. Firelight and shadow danced on the rough walls and ceiling of a small cave. I tried to get up, but Doc pushed me back down.

"Take it easy," he said.

"What happened to you?" I asked Epasotl.

"When tree fall I use amulet, make jump. Bad jump. Was trapped. Call for help, but no one come. Trapped many hours."

"How'd you get out?"

"Tlalli move earth. Make way to climb out."

"It took him *hours*? What kind of earth spirit is he?"

"Took him no time. Had to wait for him. Off the clock. Union rules." She scowled. "Union suck my ass."

"Amen," Doc said.

"You said Feather is alive, Doc. But…?"

"She can't walk."

"For how long?"

"Ever, likely. She has paraplegia. There's nothing I can do. With surgery and medication and extensive therapy, she could maybe recover partially. I don't know. I'm not a neurosurgeon. Not even close."

"Anything *we* can do?" I asked Epasotl.

"Not know. I try, but no bueno. Maybe you have better luck." She shrugged. "You better healer than me now."

"I don't know about that, Eps."

"Is true. You true healer. I just witch."

"I thought you were a Jedi," I said with a smile.

"If Jedi, move tree. I not Jedi. Just witch. Is fine. I good witch. You good healer. Only jealous a little."

"Well, I'm jealous of you both," Doc said. "I'd love to be able to do what you do. I just patch holes in people and cross my fingers."

"You do a lot more than that, Doc," I said.

"There you go, now I'm blushing. Get some rest, Bennett." He clapped my shoulder before leaving us.

I propped myself up a little and surveyed the cave. It wasn't as small as I'd thought; spacious enough for all of us, and someone had gotten a good fire going which warmed the cavern. People had staked out various spots around the fire and stripped down as they dried their clothes. Some ate and chatted softly while others slept. The lads played their game of knucklebones in a corner and chittered. I noticed Dance was sitting behind Feather, propping her up, while Leaves told her a story. Feather laughed.

"How long was I out?" I asked Epasotl.

"Not long. Do not know. No day or night in cave. Just warm and dry."

"If I can cure disease and repair extensive internal injuries, I should be able to heal a spinal injury, you'd think."

"Do not know. Not try now. You weak. Must heal self first. Sacrifice much to save her. Almost sacrifice everything."

"It was worth it."

"That why you good healer. Have much love for other. Maybe too much."

***

I woke from a disturbing dream I couldn't remember. Finding my clothes beside me, I dressed. Flaming Feather was sitting alone against a wall of the cave staring into the fire, and I joined her.

"Why are you sitting alone?" I asked.

"I wished for solitude."

"Should I go?"

"No."

She took my hand in hers and we watched the flames dance for several minutes before she spoke.

"You should have left me."

"Never."

She squeezed my hand and I saw a tear escape her eye. I brushed it away.

"I cannot walk," she said.

"For now," I said.

"I am a burden to the platoon. I cannot serve. I cannot fight. I am no longer a warrior. I will cut my hair and you will leave me here to die."

"That's a *bit* dramatic, Feather. No one's leaving anyone to die. I'll carry you myself if I have to. Don't give up so soon. I'll find a way. You'll walk again."

"Can you do this? Truly?"

I felt the connection between our hands and closed my eyes. The nervous system is so incredibly complex. Only a few weeks ago mending flesh and knitting bone had seemed impossible, but now it was simply a thing I could do. Still, the damage to her spine was exponentially more difficult to untangle than healing a cut or fracture. Even the disease that had infected Captain Brown and the others had had a shape to it that I could discern. This... this was completely different. Flaming Feather's weave had been severed in half. I could feel her numb legs atrophying already.

"I don't know," I said softly, meeting her eyes. "But I'll try. And I'll keep trying. I'm not giving up, and neither can you."

She squeezed my hand again.

Dance ran into the cave and bounced on the balls of her feet. "Snow!"

***

"It's so cold!" Dance exclaimed. "Is this the cold that turns rivers like stone?"

"Pretty close," I said.

"I can see my breath!"

We stood at the mouth of the cave, watching the blizzard. Heavy snowfall whipped through the branches of the trees and piled up in drifts against boulders. I held Feather in my arms, wrapped in a poncho liner, and she laughed. Falling Leaves and Heart-of-Darkness took turns sprinting out into the squall and dodging back into the cave. Jade Talon crossed her arms and frowned.

"People *live* in places with weather like this?" she asked me.

"It's not so bad," I said. "Well, *this* is—it's a serious snowstorm. You wouldn't want to be caught outside in this. But when the wind dies and the snow covers everything, there's a stillness, a silence, that's like a dream. It feels like magic. I can't believe it's actually snowing here though. I was surprised to see snow on the mountain peaks, but down here… I thought we're in a tropical zone. Or at least subtropical."

"Bomb cyclone," Captain Brown said from behind me. "Followed by a polar vortex. That's what's happening now."

"Then we're lucky we found shelter," I said.

"That's an understatement," he grunted.

An errant snowball flew past us and smacked the rock, showering us with snow.

"Sorry, sir!" Dance called out.

"Not yet, you aren't," he shouted, brushing past me.

"Uh-oh," I said to Feather. "Captain's bringing out the big guns. They're toast."

"Does weather like this make everyone behave like children?" Jade asked me as Brown scooped up a tremendous handful of snow and hurled it at Heart.

"Yeah, pretty much," I said.

Another snowball came flying toward us, and this time it hit Jade square in the face. She sputtered and gasped.

"Sorry!" Dance cried out with a laugh.

"You meant to do that!" Jade yelled, rushing out into the blizzard.

Feather tapped my shoulder. "I'm cold. Take me back in please."

"Of course."

We reentered the narrow crevasse that led into the larger chamber of the cavern, and I lowered her down gently by the fire and sat behind her to prop her up. I caught McKenzie watching us out of the corner of my eye. I couldn't read his expression. He looked… I don't know how to describe it, but it wasn't exactly friendly or sympathetic. It was *somehow,* as Curly would say.

"Off the record," I said to her quietly. "You and McKenzie… are you close?"

"What is 'off the record'?" she asked.

"Means whatever you say stays between us. Like… the vow of the confessional."

"Ah." She was silent for a minute. "Yes, we are. Or, we were. For a time." She sighed. "I know it is two-faced of me: I do not allow my sister warriors to enjoy physical companionship within the platoon. I know it is forbidden."

"I'm not going to judge. But he hasn't come within ten feet of you since the accident."

She shrugged.

"It just seems cold. I mean, if he loved you—"

"It is not like that. He is a man. I am a woman. Battle brings out passion, no? We sought release. But it was wrong of me to indulge when my sisters cannot. It was a moment of weakness, especially so for a leader. A few moments of weakness, to be truthful. I am shamed by my hypocrisy."

"Don't beat yourself up over it. We all make mistakes. But for him to ignore you after what happened to you is a dick move, if you ask me. Sorry if I'm being too blunt."

She laughed softly. "*La caballerosidad.* That is you to your core, Sergeant. *El caballero.* Friar Bastía often recited poetry to us of El Çid, a great and noble warrior, and of his loyal *caballeros.* That is what Princess Flower Eagle calls you among us in private. You are her El Çid—pure, faithful, and true."

"A chivalrous knight rescuing princesses and slaying dragons?" I chuckled. "I don't know how pure I am."

She glanced back at me and patted my cheek. "Like the snow."

She returned her gaze to the fire. "People like you and the princess live in a world of fantasy where love conquers all and righteousness always prevails. You are like children. Innocent."

I stiffened.

"Do not be offended." She shifted around to face me. "I mean no disrespect. I envy you. Both of you. What you have together. The world you live in. I would like to believe there is an El Çid waiting for me. But..." She sighed and laid her head against my chest. "But knights are rare men from another world. Love between a man and a woman is not common among my people. Few bond for life to raise children. A man is for pleasure or seed, not lifelong companionship. Our long-suffering friar is trying to change that with his *El Sacramento del Matrimonio*, but our roots are buried deep. For many years I thought he was foolish, but I have begun to think perhaps he is wise."

We sat in silence until I realized she had fallen asleep. I eased her down and lay with her head against my chest, supporting her with my arm. It wasn't exactly comfortable, but I didn't want to disturb her. I focused on her breathing, the crackle of the fire, the murmur of voices around us.

El Çid, I thought, and chuckled softly. Xochi had never told me about that. My heart ached for her. It felt like an eternity since I'd last seen her, and I wondered if I'd ever see her again. If her vision was true, we'd be reunited, eventually, but I was beginning to lose faith.

CHAPTER 39

A week passed before the storm fully lost its fury. But once the freak cold snap lifted and the air warmed, the snow began melting quickly. Even the whitecaps on the mountain peaks were shrinking.

"We'll make for that saddle there," Captain Brown said, pointing. "It's the closest thing we'll find to a pass. If the map is correct, we'll descend into the objective on the other side."

Sanchez lowered his binoculars and chewed on his lip. "Melt will swell the streams and rivers, but it can't be helped. We should head out today. Cabin fever's starting to set in anyway."

It was true. Everyone was getting antsy and irritable. Getting out and stretching our legs would be good for morale. I scanned the formidable mountain range, noting all the trees the storm had knocked down.

"Will be hard going," McKenzie commented. "Lots of deadfall and unstable ground."

As I looked at him, he turned, avoiding my gaze. I wasn't sure what was wrong. He wasn't being openly hostile, just frosty. I wondered if I should confront him about it, but thought better of it. At least for now. If it started affecting the functioning of the platoon, we'd have a word.

"Dave, I want Gold team in front, with you blazing the trail," Brown said.

"Hooah, sir," Wilson responded.

"And the lads forming a screen on our flanks," Brown added.

"Aye, sir," McKenzie replied crisply.

"Blue on rear security, sir?" I asked.

The captain nodded.

"What about the invalid, sir?" McKenzie asked.

I bristled, not so much at the word, but the way he said it. He might as well have said "garbage."

"I believe Nephi has a plan already for our comrade-in-arms," Brown said coolly. "Sergeant?"

"Yes, sir," I said. "We've engineered a harness system. Flaming Feather will be transported on Kiktú's back. Won't slow us down in the slightest, and if we make contact with hostile forces, she'll be combat-effective."

McKenzie grunted, but he still wouldn't meet my eye.

"You have a problem, *Sir* McKenzie?" I snapped. I regretted it instantly. I should've bit my tongue. It just slipped out.

"At ease, Sergeant," Sanchez growled.

Brown nodded to Wilson and Doc, and the three strode off, leaving McKenzie and me alone with the platoon sergeant.

"All right, gentlemen," Sanchez said. "Whatever's going on, I want it out in the open right here, right now. We kill it here and we leave it behind us to rot."

"No problem, Sergeant," McKenzie said. He actually clicked his heels. I wanted to punch him in the throat.

"I've been taking care of Flaming Feather, and he just stares at her like she's *garbage*," I said. "And then he just... glares at me."

"You have been awful close with your ASL," McKenzie said. "Seems a mite inappropriate, wouldn't you say? Sneaking off into the woods and all."

"Sneaking off into the—I was helping her to the latrine! In a snowstorm! I've been working with her every day trying to repair the damage. Nothing *inappropriate* is going on. Don't talk to me about 'inappropriate' when you were banging her behind the captain's back and then threw her away when she wasn't useful to you anymore, you sanctimonious son of a—"

I bit my tongue.

Too late.

Way, *way* too late.

Sanchez cleared his throat, and McKenzie shot me the evil eye.

"That will be all for now, Bennett," Sanchez said. "Walk with me, McKenzie."

I turned sharply and stalked away, swearing under my breath, both at McKenzie and myself, but mostly at myself. I was an idiot. And worse, unprofessional. An unprofessional idiot with a big mouth and loose lips.

I found Blue Squad outside the cave enjoying the relatively nice weather. Kiktú was leading them in knapping arrowheads out of flint. The gals were proficient in the technique, but Cohen and Lawrence had a long way to go. So did I.

"What is up, Sarge?" Dance said to me as I joined the circle.

"We'll be moving out today," I replied. "Start packing up." I held up a hand. "Not right this second. Finish what you're doing." I turned to Flaming Feather, who was sitting against a tree with a poncho liner wrapped around her legs. "We should attempt another session before we head out."

<I can carry her inside,> Kiktú signed.

Kiktú had been a huge help over the last several days, proving a willing and able nursemaid. The gals fawned over their disabled sister warrior of course, but Feather was large for a Kuauchanejkej woman, and they had difficulty moving her.

"Thanks," I said, "but I got her."

I moved over to Feather, picked her up in my arms, and returned to the cave. She might be large relative to her people, but that made her no more than five-four in combat boots—still small as far as I was concerned.

"You seem agitated," Feather said after I'd sat her down near the fire and gotten behind her to prop her up.

"It's nothing." I sighed. "I ran my mouth off when I should've bit my tongue."

"McKenzie?"

"Yeah."

"I told you to ignore him."

"I don't like the way he looks at you."

"Let him look however he wishes. I do not care. He is a selfish and unhappy man."

"But he used you and then just threw you away."

"He used me. I used him. You think in terms of love. It was not like that between us. Understand?"

"Maybe. What I *don't* understand is what you saw in him."

She laughed. "Do I need to be explicit?"

"No. Message received. Lima Charlie." I sighed again. "I also might've let slip to Sanchez about you and McKenzie."

"Might have? I am sure he already knew. Not much escapes him and the captain." She reached back and patted my cheek. "You are a sweet boy, and often foolish, and a little naïve—perhaps more than a little—but I love you for it. We all do. My sisters feel safe with you. They trust you. Obsidian Tears told me how you saved her from the cold sickness with the warmth of your body, but did not try to nest with her, even though your body was eager."

"*Eager?* She said that?"

"It is nothing to be embarrassed about. She was an attractive woman. You are a strong young man. You lay together flesh to flesh. What else would you expect? To not want her would be unnatural."

"I'm married, and I love my wife. I was trying to save Tears's life. I didn't want to do it."

"Are you defending yourself to me or to yourself? There is nothing to be ashamed of. You acted honorably. *La caballerosidad,* no?"

"Chivalry," I said. "I didn't feel particularly chivalrous that morning. Of course I'm ashamed."

She made a tsking sound. "Because you desired her?"

"Yes."

"Good. Then you are a virile man, and not a *chimouhqui,* which is lucky for the princess. That you did not try to nest with Obsidian Tears perhaps makes you an *exceptional* man. This concept of *La fidelidad* is strange to me and many of my people, but you and Princess Flower Eagle honor it, and that is to be commended. Try not to crucify yourself, little brother." She attempted to sit a little straighter. "Now, shall we begin?"

"Yes." I closed my eyes and focused on the feeling of her heart beating against my chest, visualizing all the threads that made her, and the bright single thread that *was* her. I followed her pattern until the weave that was her nervous system abruptly cut off. Again, as each time before, I was unsure how to proceed without causing more damage. I'd found I was at least able to reverse the atrophying of her limbs and keep the severed nerves alive, but I couldn't figure out how to repair them and make her whole.

She took hold of my hands and clasped them to her breast. "Relax, little brother. I can feel your racing thoughts."

"I don't want to hurt you."

She squeezed my hands. "I am not afraid."

I focused on my breathing once more, directing the teōtl to flow through me and into her. It was an intensely intimate feeling. Too intimate for my comfort. Too... sexual. When she gasped, I lost focus and felt a surge of guilt.

"Do not stop!" she breathed. "It is working. I can feel my legs!"

"I can't." I opened my eyes. We were both haloed in a white radiance that flickered and ebbed with the synchronized beating of our hearts. "I'm sorry."

The light pulsed and faded. She sighed in frustration.

"I'm sorry," I repeated.

"Look!" she said. "My toes!"

She wiggled them and clutched my hands tighter, then arched her neck and kissed my cheek. "Little brother, I can feel my legs!"

"Can you move them?"

"No... but my toes!" She settled herself against me and squared her shoulders. "Try again. Please."

"I don't think I can."

"Why not?" I could hear the frown in her voice.

"It's too much like..."

"What? Nesting?" She laughed. "Not like any nesting *I* have experienced. Not a nesting of the body. Not for pleasure. It was a pure union of souls."

"Yes. Exactly. It was too much like when Xochi and I... I'm sorry. I can't."

"You are not betraying her."

"It feels like it. I shouldn't share myself like that with another person. Only her."

Flaming Feather dropped my hands and pulled herself around. She studied my face for a long minute and then nodded.

"It is a gift, to feel that with another person," she said. "It is…"

"Sacred."

"Yes. I can see that." She bit her lip. "I will not lie. I am angry you would withhold yourself from me when you can heal me—purely out of loyalty to the princess. She would give me the gift of your soul in mine if we asked."

"But we can't ask. And it's not for her to give. I've promised myself to her. Mind, body, *and* soul. No other."

"This, you and me, it is not the same as you and her. Can you not see that? You love her in a way you can love no other. I see that in your soul. What you share with her is not the same as what you can share with me."

"It feels too much the same," I said. "It feels like a betrayal. I made a vow."

"And you would sacrifice my legs for a misplaced sense of loyalty? For a vow? *La fidelidad?* Sacrifice my future? My *life*? What I ask from you, it is not the same!"

Her voice was rising, and people were beginning to cast furtive glances at us.

Some not so furtive.

"I need to think," I said.

She glared into my eyes and then slapped me. Hard. She was crying.

"Get away from me!" She slapped me again and tried to crawl away. Leaves and Heart scurried over and held her as I scooted back and stood, shaking. I wasn't angry with her. I didn't blame her. I was just… confused.

Wilson approached, and I brushed past him.

"Bro…" he said.

"Not now!" I called back over my shoulder as I exited the cave. I needed air. I needed to think. I needed space.

I needed my wife, dammit.

CHAPTER 40

Dance found me sitting on a boulder in the forest some time later.

"You should not be so far from the cave," she said as she approached.

"I wanted to be alone."

"It is not safe."

I gestured around us. "There's no one here."

She rested her hands on her rifle as it dangled on the sling in front of her. "You do not even have your weapons or armor, Sergeant."

I patted the Glock 19 on my thigh.

"What happened?" she asked. "Flaming Feather will not speak to us. She cries and pushes us away. I have never seen her cry."

"She needs my help and... I can't."

Dance sat on the boulder beside me. "Why?"

"Honestly? It's probably stupid. A hang-up."

"But you *could* help her walk again?"

"Yes. I think so."

"But you won't. Because of a 'hang-up.' What is a hang-up?"

I took a deep breath. "When I heal people... I see inside them. What makes them. Body and spirit are interconnected. I see their soul. We're all made of patterns woven by threads of divinity. Where the pattern is broken or tangled, I weave it back together. Flaming Feather's pattern is worse than broken—it's severed. I can fix it, but... to touch another soul is intimate. And to fix her requires a level of intimacy so intense, it feels like..."

"Nesting with your wife? Nesting with someone you care for deeply and who cares deeply for you? I would not know," she added quickly. "I am a virgin. I am saving myself for"—she deepened her voice—"*El Sacramento del Matrimonio*." She laughed. "But I have talked with the friar much about nesting and love between a husband and wife."

"I doubt the friar would know much about that personally."

"Oh, no. He was bonded to a woman once. She died young, in childbirth. He became a friar after. He loved her deeply. He knows much of the world and of love and all things. He is very wise. We have spoken often of the nesting of souls that accompanies the nesting of the bodies when two truly become one through devotion and loyalty. *La fidelidad*. It is like the love between the Father and the Son or God and His creation." She gazed up into the branches of the trees. "Do you feel this with Princess Flower Eagle?"

"Yes."

"And you felt this with Flaming Feather when you tried to heal her today?"

"Yes. No. Not the same, but… close. Much too close. More than intimate. Almost erotic. No… it *was* erotic. It was *wrong*."

"And now you feel you have betrayed the princess, your wife and soulmate."

"Yes." I sighed. "Why do I feel like I'm in confession or something?"

"I have had lots of practice at confessions," Dance said with a laugh. "Especially after I met Sergeant Takahashi!" She blew out her cheeks. "His was not a good death. I miss him greatly, even if it was only, how do you say, a crush?"

I nodded.

"But"—she kicked her heels and her face brightened—"we are talking about you, *Sergeant* Bennett. I am still getting used to calling you 'Sergeant Bennett.' Sounds so grown up. Not that you are exactly young, but you do not look like an old man any longer."

"How old are you?" I asked.

"Eighteen rains."

"That's what you told Captain Brown when you volunteered for this mission, and that's what the other gals say, but how old are you really?"

"Old enough to be a warrior," she said proudly. "I have jumped from the tall tree."

I quirked an eyebrow.

"Sixteen."

"Figured."

"Princess Flower Eagle was *fifteen* rains when she jumped and still younger than me yet when she defeated a giant in single combat."

"Not questioning your ability as a warrior. Just curious."

"You are—what does Captain say? Deflecting?"

"You got me."

"So," she said seriously. "You feel you have committed adultery, no?"

"That's a harsh word. But… maybe. I don't know. I just know it felt wrong and so I stopped. But I don't think I can let it happen again."

"Even if Flaming Feather never walks again?"

"That also sounds harsh. Like I'm being selfish. I *want* to help her… but…"

"You want to be true to the princess."

"Yes."

"And the intimacy—the intensity of the bond you feel with Flaming Feather during the healing process is too *erotic*."

"For lack of a better word, yes," I said.

"What does that word mean? I am not sure I understand. Is it the same as *eros*? Friar Bastía speaks of eros. He says the Greek taught of several forms of love. It is one. The Greek are a people of your world, no?"

"Yes. I think the two words mean the same thing. More or less. I'm not sure exactly."

She held out one hand and then the other, as if weighing something. "Eros is love between a man and a woman. Sexual, yes, but also a creative love, a passionate love, a desire for oneness with another. Back when he was still in your world, Friar Bastía knew a nun, a mystic, whom he traveled to speak with often. Her name was Teresa, and she was blessed with exquisite visions of God's passionate love for us, his children. Angels visited her. Yes! They did. She spoke of the love she felt between herself and God as an intense desire. To use your word, an *erotic* love. She spoke often of the ecstasy of love she experienced and even used sexual language to describe it. Bastía believes she will be a saint someday." She caught my expression and shook her head. "No! Teresa was not talking about *nesting* with God. To say that would be a perversion of what she taught. But I think that is your problem. Have you read the Song of Songs?"

"I try not to. Frankly I think it's pornographic. I don't know why it's even in the Bible."

"What is 'pornographic'? I do not know the word."

"Dirty. Sexually dirty. Wrong. It's filth."

Dance laughed. "But the Song of Songs is not dirty or wrong. It is not filth. It is a love song between God and His creation. Can you not see? You mix things up and confuse them. This is why you feel that the intensity of love you experience when you enter Flaming Feather's soul to heal her is a betrayal of the vows you made to Princess Flower Eagle. What you are feeling is not sexual, but rather what we will all feel for each other and our God in Paradise. It is a divine passion."

I wasn't so sure. She made Heaven sound like an orgy. But maybe that was me confusing things. It would take time to parse the information overload I was feeling.

Dance shifted so she was facing me fully. "Let me put it another way. Do you believe what you felt with Flaming Feather when you tried to heal her to be a sin?"

"Yes. Maybe." I rubbed my face. "I don't know."

"Is it a sin to withhold help from someone in need?"

"Absolutely."

She held up a hand. "To help her is a sin." She held up her other hand. "And to not help her is a sin." She looked from one hand to the other and shrugged. "They cannot both be sins, *achtli*."

The word was specifically used by a younger sister for an older brother and was a term of affection among the Kuauchanejkej, much like *iuctli* was used by an older brother for a younger sister.

"You sure you're only sixteen?" I said.

She laughed. "I have an old soul, our friar says." She then brought her hands together. "You should pray about it, yes?"

"Not the worst idea."

"Come, we should return to the cave before Sergeant Sanchez sends out a search party."

"Also a good—"

I was cut off by a thick bag being pulled over my head. Dance started to scream, but was cut off quickly. Something hard slammed powerfully into my kidney, and the pain was so intense that I couldn't cry out.

Then everything went dark.

***

I woke with a raging headache and my kidney felt like it'd been ruptured. Not literally, but close enough. I couldn't see anything with the bag over my head, and my hands were bound to something in front of me. I swayed and felt dizzy. No, *I* didn't sway—the thing I was straddling swayed. The sensation was like I was riding something, but it was far wider than a horse. Then I heard a trumpeting call, and it became clear what I was mounted on. A thunder-stag. I was riding a dinosaur.

I breathed a sigh of relief. We'd been captured by Clan Ónik. They were the good guys. So this was all just a misunderstanding and I'd just have to explain—

"Ah, you're awake." The harsh tenor voice came from directly in front of me. It sounded familiar. It sounded like—

"Chris," I said.

Not a misunderstanding.

"You're a slippery bastard." He laughed. "Been tracking you a *long* time, Preacher."

"What do you want, Chris?"

"See you got a girlfriend," he said, ignoring me. "She's a whole lot prettier than that cat-gremlin abortion you used to roll with. Mmhmm. Even pretty for a native girl. Young, too. St. James likes 'em young. Younger the better. I like a mature woman, myself, but I'll take what I can get."

I was about to say what I'd do if they touched her, but I bit my tongue. This wasn't a movie and it'd only encourage him.

"Gone stoic, huh? That's fine. You never were much for conversation anyway. Matter of fact, it'd probably be better if you couldn't talk at all. Maybe Wright will cut out your tongue, add it to his necklace. You remember his necklace, right? It's damned heavy now with all the treasures he's collected."

"Wright's dead," I said.

"Wright, Preacher says you're dead," Bond called out.

"Take more than that to kill me, asshole," I heard Wright reply.

Crap.

I had seen Wright's body, mangled by a forty-millimeter air-burst grenade. He wasn't just dead, he was *very* dead.

Apparently not dead enough.

"Bet you're wishing you'd taken that shot at me when you had the chance." I heard Bond spit. "You always were a pussy, Preacher."

"I'm the pussy preacher around here!" Wright said with a laugh. He sounded closer. Too close. "And I got a *big* ol' sermon for your girl, Bennett."

I heard palms slapping, and Bond chuckled. "Just save some for me, Sarge."

"Always do!" Wright answered. More palm slapping. I ignored them and tested my restraints. Very secure. No point in trying. Not yet. The time would come.

I wasn't so much worried for myself, not that I wasn't, but thinking of what they might put Dance through terrified me. They wouldn't just abuse her; they'd degrade and humiliate her, completely and utterly.

And then they'd kill her.

Very, *very* slowly.

To keep myself from panicking I focused on listening. Judging by the thunder-stags' occasional trumpeting calls and responses, and the sounds of men speaking to each other in a guttural dialect of Nahuatl

I didn't recognize, I figured the group we traveled in was about a dozen strong. Perhaps more, but no less. And we were still moving through a forest; that much was clear from the monkeys, birds, and flying snakes I could hear high above.

Bond continued to needle me, but when I failed to get riled, he eventually grew bored and gave up.

I don't know how many miles we traveled that first day, or for how many hours. The bag on my head was claustrophobic and smelled rank, and my wrists were chafed and bleeding. Eventually we stopped, and Bond shoved me from the mount. I couldn't do anything to break my fall, and I hit the ground on my side hard enough to knock the wind out of me. He dropped softly beside me and then pulled me roughly into a kneeling position. It sounded like someone was pushed into the same position beside me. Dance. I could hear her breathing. Not panicked. Controlled. She was brave, I'll give her that.

Someone moved in front of me and the bag was pulled from my head. I lifted my eyes to see my old section leader staring down at me with a broad smile. He still wore his trademark *Magnum P. I.* mustache, and his hair was cropped as short as ever, in contrast to Wright, who stood nearby sporting dreads and a nasty-looking beard. In addition to the two of them, and Bond behind me, eight eagle warriors stood in a loose circle around us looking murderous.

"Bennett!" St. James said jovially, almost friendly-like. "I've been waiting for this reunion for a long, *long* time."

"What do you want, Sergeant?" I asked, forcing the tremor out of my voice.

"Well, for starters, you owe me some ass. I'll take payment now, with interest."

He punched me, hard, and I fell over, spitting blood. Bond hauled me up and St. James punched me again. And again. When he'd worked my face into a pulp, he started on my trunk until I vomited.

"Get him back up," St. James barked at Bond.

"Won't stay up, Sarge."

"Then hold him." St. James moved over to Dance. "What do we have here?" He pulled off her hood, and she spat at him. "Feisty one!

Shame. They always break the fastest. What's your name, sweetheart? I don't believe we've been introduced."

She told him to do something creative but anatomically impossible in her dialect of Nahuatl.

"Sergeant Wright," St. James said. "Teach her some manners—not the face! She's pretty and we're going to keep her that way—for a while anyway."

Wright nodded and laid a fist into her stomach. She curled up instantly and fell over, gasping.

"I asked your name, girl," St. James said, spitting on her.

Dance spat back, this time disparaging his parenthood.

Wright kicked her, and I heard something snap. Probably a rib. I wanted to call out her name to make it stop, but this was her fight. She was a warrior, and I'd only shame her.

She was wheezing now, barely able to make a sound.

"Your name," St. James repeated, leaning in close. Then he jumped back, holding his ear. "Bitch bit me!"

"I can take her teeth out," Wright said. "Don't need her teeth."

"We'll get there," St. James said, looking at the blood on his hand. "Bag her and get her up."

Wright shoved the bag over her head and hauled her up onto her knees as St. James stepped back in front of me once more. My vision was blurred, partly from one eye being swollen shut, partly from blood, and I could feel several gaps in my teeth. My ribs ached—nothing broken as far as I could tell—and I felt nauseous from all the blood I'd swallowed.

For the first time, I almost regretted weaving away my death-touch. No more magical healing—I was as mortal as anyone else. Then again, at least this put a limit on how much violence they could subject me to before they killed me. In my prior state, they could have tortured me… forever.

St. James must have been thinking along the same lines. "Our intel said you were like us, blessed by Mictlāntēcutli, but you obviously ain't."

"What do you want?" I repeated.

"You, Bennett! I want *you*," St. James said. "More specifically, I'm looking for something, and you're going to help me get it."

"Why would I help you?"

He tilted his head, considering.

"I can think of ten reasons off the top of my head. Sergeant Wright, show him one of them."

Wright pulled a nasty-looking knife out of his belt and stalked behind me. I felt my hands being grabbed, and a finger was pried away from my clenched fist. I told myself I wouldn't give them the satisfaction of screaming, but I did anyway. I howled. And sobbed.

I've already warned you: I'm not the hero you're looking for.

Wright came around and shoved my severed finger in front of my face.

"Which one did you take?" St. James asked.

"Preacher here thinks he's a sniper, so I took his trigger finger."

"Poetic. I approve."

"I'm still not going to help you," I muttered through the snot running down my face.

"Need another ten reasons?" St. James asked. "Sergeant, show him what I mean."

Bond laughed from behind me.

"You don't need to—" I began, but Wright had already started.

Dance didn't make a sound.

Wright tossed her finger into the dirt in front of me.

I had to restrain myself from doing my human incendiary hand grenade impression. I could take out all three of them at once. But I'd roast Dance, too, and there were still at least eight eagle warriors to contend with.

"Damn, your girl's got bigger balls than you do, Preacher," Bond said. "Guess I shouldn't be surprised."

"Captain Brown will find you," I told St. James. "He's on your trail now, and he'll catch up to you. He won't rest. He won't stop."

"Never shall I fail, never shall I leave a fallen comrade, blah, blah, blah," St. James drawled. "Only thing dumber than a Marine is a Ranger. Brown is a joke. How many men has he lost? How many of us are left? He led you all to your deaths. If you would've followed me, you'd be a king! We're the masters of this world, Bennett. Wright and Bond and I. We're kings. More than kings. Gods!"

He paced in front of me, eyes blazing. "How many slaves do you have, Sergeant?"

"More than I could ever kill," Wright said.

"How many women have you had, Bond?"

"More than I can count and never the same one twice, Sarge."

St. James leaned in close and whispered in my ear. "You could be a king too, Bennett. A god. Deliver the Compass to Tezcatlipoca. Kneel down before his throne and swear fealty, and everything you've ever wished for will be yours. He can make any dream a reality."

"Captain Brown will find you, and when he does, he'll kill you," I whispered back.

St. James straightened and laughed. "But we can't die! We're immortal!"

"Tell that to Sergeant Clark," I said.

"Oh, you saw that." He chuckled. "He's not dead. He's still hanging there. I crucified him along with his men. We had a... falling out, you could say."

They're not immortal, I reminded myself. *Just very hard to kill*. I closed my eyes and breathed deeply. I'd incinerate all of them. Dance, myself, everyone. I'd nuke the whole clearing and salt the earth with our ashes. I would *never* help them.

It ended here. It ended now.

CHAPTER 41

In through the nose. Out through the mouth.

Focus.

Breathe.

"What the hell is Preacher doing?" Wright asked. "Praying?"

St. James slapped me and I screwed my eyes tighter, opening myself to the teōtl…

But I felt… nothing.

He slapped me again. "Cut it out, Bennett. You look ridiculous."

I opened my eyes, and he grabbed something that hung around my neck and shoved it in my face. It looked like an amulet or pendant of some kind, but I couldn't focus on it.

"Can't do any magic tricks with this around your neck," St. James snarled. "We've been tracking you a long time, kid. Met some friends of yours. Nasty bunch of mangy indigs from out in the swamp where I left Clark to rot. They had some good stories. Gave us this in case we met up with you."

"Took some persuasion," Wright grunted.

"Some," St. James admitted.

My heart fell to my stomach. No, into a sinkhole. An abyss. We were screwed.

But Captain Brown…

He'd catch up. He'd save us.

He always did.

I had faith in my captain.

All we had to do was hang on for a little while.

"Think he needs another reason to help us, Sarge?" Wright asked, moving behind Dance.

I could hear her gritting her teeth.

"Not tonight," St. James replied. "We got plenty of days for him to change his mind. Plenty of fingers. And there are some other reasons to help us I want him to consider along the way. Bag him and get them back on the mounts. We're moving out."

***

I could tell by the change in temperature that we were climbing higher into the mountains. The trees grew sparser. The sounds of wildlife faded. We must have ridden through the night and into the next day, because when Bond shoved me off the mount and dragged my hood off, it was morning. St. James was standing in front of me, towering. Looming. He was a tall man. The black veins in his neck bulged. I stared at him through a haze of dried blood and pus. My right eye was swollen completely shut and my ribs still ached. The stump of my finger throbbed, and my stomach churned with acid.

"Hope you got a good night's rest, because today's a busy day, Specialist," St. James said cheerfully. "Did you have time to think about things?"

I'd had plenty of time. I hadn't slept at all. My answer hadn't changed.

"I'm not going to help you," I said as stoically as I could manage.

He motioned to Wright, and the big sergeant moved behind me and joined Bond in holding me down on my knees.

St. James glared down at me. "I've given you twenty reasons to help us, and over the next several days we're going to explore each one in detail. But—" He stepped aside, and my soul died. Ten yards in front of me First-to-Dance was staked out spread-eagle and naked on the ground. She wasn't struggling. She wasn't begging. She just stared up at the thick gray clouds. "Today I want to give you another reason."

My mouth was dry and my head spun. I didn't know what to do. It was too much.

"I'll help," I whispered.

"Can't hear you," St. James barked.

"I'll help, *Sergeant*!"

"Good. But I still think you need some motivation."

He spun on his heel and marched toward Dance as he undid his belt.

"I said I'd help!" I cried. "*Please!* Don't do this!"

"Shut him up," St. James called over his shoulder.

Weight shoved something foul-tasting into my mouth, and Bond held my head so I couldn't turn away.

"Close your eyes, Preacher, and I'll slice your eyelids off," Wright hissed into my ear.

St. James paused and turned back to me. "We're going to explore this reason every day, Bennett. *Every single day*. Until I'm convinced you're with us." He waved his hand, almost airily. "Along with all the other reasons you should help."

***

I have no words for what happened that morning.

When it was over… after St. James and Wright and Bond each… after the eagle warriors all stepped forward… after they had abused her with more than just their bodies… I was drowning in my own vomit. My eyes were dry only because I was so dehydrated I couldn't cry anymore.

Wright pulled the gag out of my mouth, and Bond let me fall to the ground. I coughed spasmodically, trying to clear the bile from my lungs. I was completely numb. Completely dead inside.

No. Not completely.

Somewhere deep inside an ember flickered.

Hate.

My time would come. And I would burn the world to its core.

***

Wright dragged Dance in front of me. She was wearing a baggy old T-shirt and her thighs were crusted with blood and filth. Her hooded head sagged, her limbs limp. She looked dead.

Every morning had been the same for the last three days.

They took more fingers. One from me. Two from Dance. They laughed and joked through it all.

I had begged, I had wept. Oh, how I'd wept. I'd pleaded and sobbed. It only made them laugh more. I told them everything I could possibly know about the Compass of the Gods—except for Xochi. I buried her so deep that even I lost her. When that wasn't enough, I made up things I didn't know.

I *wanted* to stay strong. Be stoic. For Dance. For her pride. But I couldn't. I was weak.

I'm not a hero.

"She's not gonna make it, Sarge," Wright said to St. James. "Can we have some fun this time? I want something for my necklace. Something new." He grabbed her breast roughly. "Nice, yeah? It'd look good strung up with my other treasures."

"Fine," St. James said. "She's all used up. I've lost interest. You boys have your fun."

"What do you want from me?" I spat. "I've told you everything I know. Agreed to everything you want. I don't need more damned reasons!"

St. James barked a laugh. "Oh, I know that. This is just entertainment for the troops."

Wright dropped Dance on the ground and pulled off her hood. Her face was unrecognizable. But her eyes… she was still there. Fighting. He grabbed her hair and started dragging her through the grass and scrub.

"If she dies, you'll never get the Compass!" I screamed.

St. James spun on me. "Say again, you ball-less sack of shit? You making demands now? There are things worse than death she can go through. You too. I haven't even started, boy."

"No." I tried to steady my voice. "No. I didn't mean that. It takes two to retrieve the Compass. Me. Me and… her. *We're* the key. Without her it won't work."

"That wasn't in the intel package," Bond said.

"I'm calling bullshit," St. James said. "You never said this before in all your blubbering."

"Me… and her. Us. Together. Me… and my… wife."

"Wife!" St. James exclaimed. "Screw me sideways. Or her, rather. All this time and she's your *wife*?"

Wright looked confused.

"Just makes it all so much sweeter, huh Sarge?" Bond said.

"Does indeed," St. James replied. "Well, no skin off my back to keep her alive a while longer. Even if he's lying, we'll have ourselves some fun with wifey. Bag 'em both and mount up. I want to reach the plateau before sundown."

***

That night they made camp for the first time. A proper camp. Tents were erected and the thunder-stags were put out to graze. I assume. I could only go off what I overheard. I was shoved in a tent and bound to the pole. They left the bag on my head. Some time later someone came in dragging something.

"Figured you'd want some alone time with your wife," Bond sneered. "Or what's left of her."

He propped her up beside me, and it sounded like she was being bound to the pole as well.

"Sweet dreams, Preacher."

We sat in silence for a long time. Outside I could hear men walking around, laughing, talking in slurred voices. They sounded drunk. Getting there at least.

"I'm so sorry," I said eventually. As if that meant anything by now.

I could hear her breathing, slowly, shallow, but she remained silent.

Footsteps approached our tent. Outside I heard Bond's voice.

"What are you doing?"

"I want my treasure," Wright slurred.

"Are you insane? St. James will have your balls if she dies."

Bond sounded drunk too.

"She'll live," Wright said. "I just want one of 'em."

"And if she doesn't?"

"She'll live. Don't be a pussy."

Bond dropped his voice to a whisper. "Sarge, listen, just wait a few more days, okay? Few more days and you can carve them both up. Maybe take her skin too, huh? Haven't done that in a while. Make Preacher watch. It'll be fun. I'll help."

Silence for a minute. Feet shuffling.

"Screw it." Wright belched. "What's a few more days."

The footsteps receded.

Dance exhaled slowly.

I realized I hadn't been breathing either.

"They are devils," she muttered after several long minutes.

I was surprised she still had the strength to speak. Anything I could think to say sounded trite, but I spoke anyway.

"I'm sorry I wasn't stronger. For you."

"It would have only made it worse."

"What could be worse?"

She was silent for a minute. "Many things."

"I'm sorry."

"Stop apologizing." She sounded so tired, so weak, and I could tell she was in unimaginable pain, yet there was a firmness to her voice. An edge. "You did nothing wrong."

"I let them break me."

"And what kind of man would you be if you hadn't broken?"

"A strong man."

"No. A heartless man, no better than they."

I didn't know what to say to that.

More silence.

"You were a priest once, no?" she asked.

"Of a sort. I still am, I think. Kind of."

"Friar Bastía says once a priest, always a priest. Will you hear my confession?"

I hesitated. We didn't really do confessions in my church… not the same anyway. And I'd certainly never been a Catholic priest.

"Will you?" she asked again.

Pleaded, almost.

"Yes."

"Forgive me, for I have sinned."

"Dance, what they did to you—that's not—"

"You misunderstand. In my despair I wished to die. It is a sin. A mortal sin."

"I'm absolutely certain God forgives you."

She sighed.

"Absolutely certain," I repeated.

"Do you truly think so?"

"Yes. I *know* so. With every fiber of my being."

"Then I can face whatever comes next."

"How do you do it?" I asked.

"Do what?"

"Stay so strong?"

"The Lord is my hiding place. He surrounds me with songs of deliverance."

She was so weak. I knew she was dying. I could hear it in her voice. Her faith, and her resolve to endure, humbled me to my core. I don't know much about the saints, but I knew I was sitting next to one.

"Will you hear *my* confession?" I asked her after the silence had stretched too thin.

"I am not a priest."

"Will you hear it anyway?"

"Yes."

"I wished to die because I couldn't bear to watch you suffer any longer. I would have abandoned you in death if I could have. And my cowardice fills me with shame."

"I cannot absolve you, because I am not a priest. But if I were, I would."

"But can *you* forgive me?"

She remained silent for a very, very long time. Eventually she spoke.

"I will try."

That was enough.

Feet shuffled covertly near the tent, and I heard the flap open. I felt Dance tense beside me. My hood was lifted, and I squinted at the shadow in front of me.

"Ross?" I asked in disbelief. It looked like him, but his face was bruised and swollen.

"They're all drunk," Cameron said quietly. "We've got to hurry. It'll be dawn soon. Can you walk?"

"Yes, I think so. What are you doing here?"

"No time. I'll explain later."

He removed Dance's hood, and I saw his face glisten with tears. Moving behind us, he quickly cut our restraints, then helped me to my feet and handed me a rifle. Dance's rifle. I slung it over my shoulder. Then he handed me my pistol and holster, and I fumbled to strap it on my leg. I was still in a great deal of pain, and I'd lost a couple fingers, including my favorite trigger finger, but that wouldn't be a problem; Captain Brown had seen to it we'd been trained to use our weapons in either hand.

"Do you have a weapon?" I asked him.

"Yes." He patted something slung behind his back. "Can she move?"

"No," Dance said.

"I got her," I said. "You lead."

I picked Dance up, shocked by how frail she felt, and Cameron handed her a bundle. "Your clothes, I think. Some mags. Forty mike-mike."

"Thank you," she said.

Cameron unslung his rifle, peeked out of the tent flap, then waved us forward. We scurried from shadow to shadow, working our way to the edge of the camp.

"Wait," I hissed, dropping to a knee and placing Dance gently on the ground.

"What?" Cameron asked. "We can't stop now!"

"Just a sec." I pulled the amulet from around my neck and held it in my hand. It was a carved totem of some kind. It was hideous. Perverse. Obscene. I closed my fist around it and felt a flash of heat, then tossed the ashes away.

Picking Dance back up, I nodded to Cameron, and we slipped away into the night.

CHAPTER 42

We moved like fugitives, never stopping, until the overcast sky warmed with the gray light of dawn. As we moved, I fed Cameron and myself energy to sustain us and did what I could to heal First-to-Dance and myself. She slept in my arms as we raced through the tall grass.

"I never thought we'd get so far so fast," Cameron said. "I feel like I could keep this pace forever."

"Not forever," I said. "Let's stop in that grove just ahead."

Once we were inside the safety of the trees, I laid Dance down and took a seat on a log.

"Where are we going?" I asked Cameron. "No. First, why—no—*how* are you here?"

He puffed out his cheeks. "*Really* long story, man. Chlůmpu was sacked. They took what captives they could manage, including me, and slaughtered the rest. Then they took us northward, to be sacrificed I suppose. We walked at a forced march for days. People, I mean jaguar-people, just stumbled out of the line and died where they fell. Then psycho St. James and company hooked up with them, and he saw me. He pulled me out and took me with his people. He wanted information about our platoon. About you, specifically. I tried to hold out, but"—he showed me his hands; all of his nails had been ripped out and his fingers were mangled—"eventually I broke. I'm sorry. I really tried to hold out. I tried so hard. But they worked me over for days and days. Eventually I told them everything, man. The route, the objective, the package. They made me draw the map from memory. They've been right on your ass for weeks. I was just waiting for them to kill me. I don't know why they didn't. Then they nabbed you and First-to-Dance and I managed to get away. It wasn't easy, but they were focused on you and Dance and they'd been getting lax on tying me up, and when an opportunity to slip away came up, I ran. To be honest I think I'd outworn my usefulness and St. James didn't care—or he would've sent his goons after me. That's the only explanation I can think of.

"Anyway, since then I've been trailing you, trying to find an opportunity to get you both out. I'm so sorry I couldn't do anything sooner."

"You got us out, Ross. That's what matters. We're alive. Thank you. It was only going to get worse." I sighed. "They'll have discovered we're gone by now. They'll be coming hot and heavy. Where are we going?"

Cameron waved a hand. "Away? I didn't really have a plan. I saw a chance to bust you out and took it."

"That's okay. The platoon can't be far. They'll connect with us. For now we press forward."

"Forward to where?" Cameron asked.

I walked to the edge of the thicket and pointed northward through the trees. "To the objective."

Through the hazy mist, a lone, sinister mountain rose above the horizon. It resembled a hunched eagle devouring its prey.

"We're going *there*?" Cameron protested. "But that's where *they're* going!"

"And we'll face them when the time comes."

"Face them? There's thirteen of them and only three of us. Two and a half, really. And they're like, *superhuman*, man. I've seen what they can do. Not just St. James and the others, but their eagle warriors too. They're not human anymore."

"Doesn't matter. That objective is our exfil. That's how we get out of this place. Charlie Mike." I smiled grimly. "Plus, I have a few surprises for them."

"Like a heavy infantry battalion hidden in your back pocket?"

"Not quite. Give me your hands."

"Say again?"

"Your hands. Let me see them."

He looked puzzled, but held out his tortured hands. I took them in mine and focused. White light skipped along my arms, down to his fingers. He inhaled sharply and pulled his hands away, gazing at them in wonder. "How… how did you do that?"

"Epasotl taught me some tricks, and I've learned a few of my own along the way. A lot has happened since Chlŭmpu. Come on, Ross. We need to get moving again. They can't be far behind us, and they're mounted. We need to move fast."

As if in response, we heard the trumpet of a thunder-stag in the distance.

I strode back to where Dance was sleeping and shook her shoulder gently. She woke with a start, cowering for a moment, and then relaxed.

"Where are we? I dreamed we were rescued. An angel carried me away through the night."

"We were," I said, motioning to Cameron. "Can you walk?"

She shook her head.

I nodded and closed my eyes, reaching out. I'd repaired some of the damage as we fled through the night, but not enough. I could see the savage rifts in her pattern clearly though, and I wove quickly. It was worse than I could have possibly imagined. There was none of the feeling of connection I'd experienced before. It was sterile, clinical work. As I healed her body, I also did what I could to heal her mind and soul.

I wondered who would heal mine.

She wasn't whole. That would take time, and there was still a lot of cosmetic damage, but it would be enough for now.

It would have to be.

"Get dressed," I told her, and Cameron and I turned to give her privacy. When she was ready, I handed her the rifle and ammo. She shoved the extra magazines into a cargo pocket and slung the bandoleer of forty mike-mike over her shoulder.

"Charlie Mike, Sergeant?" she asked. The joyful light she'd always had in her eyes was gone, replaced by an intense fire I'd never seen in her before.

I nodded.

"Sergeant, huh?" Cameron said.

"Like I said, a lot's happened."

***

We could see them in the distance behind us, pushing their mounts. The elephant-sized beasts were sprinting on their hind legs, kicking up dust and trumpeting a challenge.

"We need to find a ford," Cameron said. "The current is too strong. We'll be swept away."

We'd arrived at a river, wide and fast. A large tree swept past, spinning in the churning torrent. We had no choice but to cross, but it was clear we weren't going to find a place to ford.

"Better to be carried away than recaptured," Dance said. "I'll die before submitting to those devils again."

"No one's dying today," I said.

"If only it were cold," Dance lamented. "Cold enough to turn the river like stone. Then we could walk to the other side."

"Don't suppose making a river freeze over is one of those tricks you learned?" Cameron said to me. "Thick enough to support us, thin enough to turn away their mounts?"

"Not exactly, but... that does give me an idea. You both are going to have to stay close to me. Real close. And I need you to trust me."

I held out my hand, and Dance took it. Cameron took her other hand.

"What are we doing?" Cameron asked.

"Just trust me," I said. "Focus on the horizon. Don't look down."

I led them down the riverbank to the water's edge. The trumpeting grew nearer, and I could hear the eagle warriors shouting their war cry. The earth shook.

I took a deep breath and stepped out *onto* the water. Where my foot landed, ice crystals spread and thickened. Another hesitant step. And then another. The water knew the pattern I was trying to weave and complied energetically. Then we were walking. Then running.

Across the river, the water smooth as glass under our feet. Hard as ice, but only where our feet stepped. I didn't stop running when we reached the other bank. I sprinted until I heard Dance cry out behind me. She was standing with her hands on her knees, her face screwed up in pain.

"What's wrong?" I asked. "We have to hurry."

"I am bleeding."

"Where?" I started patting her down, looking for entrance or exit wounds. Had she been shot? I hadn't heard gunfire.

"From inside."

I stopped feeling for blood, realizing what she meant. "Oh."

Behind us, men and beasts bellowed in rage and frustration. I risked a glance back and saw eagle warriors urging their mounts into the water, but the river was too fast, too deep, and too wide, and the current swept them under and away.

"What's wrong?" Cameron asked, coming back to us.

"She can't run," I said. I looked her in the eye. "I'll carry you."

I picked her up, and Cameron and I ran.

***

We didn't stop until our legs gave out, then we collapsed by a stream. Ahead of us we could see the lone mountain looming above the horizon, storm clouds gathering around it. It was only midday, but the sky was growing dark, and I saw a flash of lightning.

"How the hell did you do that?" Cameron gasped. "How did we cross that river?"

"He turned the water to stone," Dance said weakly.

"Ice," I said, breathing hard. "We crossed on ice."

Cameron rubbed his face.

Dance gazed at the stream before us. "Do you think it is safe to drink?"

"No," I said. "Probably not." I moved over to the flow of clear water and dipped my hand in. I was so thirsty I wanted to drown in it. As I moved my hand, I saw the threads of pathogens within the pattern of the water. Teasing them apart from the flow was difficult, but I managed to bend and redirect them until I had a rivulet of pure water. I scooped some out and tasted it.

"Here," I told Dance and Cameron. "Drink from this spot. Nowhere else. It's safe here."

Dance thrust her head in and resurfaced with a gasp. She scooped up water and drank deeply.

"Not too much," I warned.

"No," she said. "But I am so thirsty."

"That's enough. Come here, kneel with me for a minute. I'll do what I can to help you. Running must have undone some of what I repaired. I'll do what I can. Then we need to get moving again."

I glanced back, searching for pursuers, finding none. But I knew they were back there. They would find a way to cross the river. They would never stop following us.

I placed my hands on Dance's shoulders and focused on mending the damage.

"I need to bathe," she said after a few minutes.

"No time. Do you think you can walk now?"

"Please?" she said. "I will be quick. I have not bathed since—"

Of course she wanted to wash. I mentally slapped myself for being so insensitive.

"Yes, of course. We'll keep watch."

Cameron and I took a knee in the tall grass, scanning the horizon for threats.

"How was Chlůmpu?" I asked him. "I mean, before it was sacked."

"Not bad. They were good people. Strange customs, but they were hospitable." He paused. "I don't know what kind of life I could've made for myself there, being the only human and all. I regretted my decision almost immediately."

"Figured you would." I saw movement in the distance and my heart started racing, but it was only a herd of wild thunder-stags. "Why did you decide to stay behind in the first place?"

He exhaled a long sigh. "Captain asked me the same question. I didn't know how to put it into words then, and I guess I don't now either, even though I've thought about it a lot. I just... gave up, I guess? And yeah I know how bad that sounds. I was so tired of… everything. I just wanted to sit back, crack open a cold beer, and watch a game."

"Not much opportunity for that in Chlůmpu," I said.

"You'd be surprised. They had this game they call *pitz*. Brutal ball game. Crazy rules. On a nice day in the stands drinking some… whatever it was… it was almost like being back home."

"Oh yeah, I actually know that game. I played a modern version of it called *ulama* on my mission. Not nearly as brutal as the original version, I imagine."

"They take it crazy seriously. I thought soccer fans were obsessed. No comparison to the jags." He paused, then gave me a sidelong glance. "I know everyone thinks I'm a coward and a deserter."

"You? No. Never thought that about you. I get it. I understand how someone could just… not be able to Charlie Mike and decide to go native. Even Wilson did."

"*Sergeant* Wilson? No way."

"Oh yeah. Stayed behind in Kuauchanko, remember?"

"That's because he was seriously injured."

I shook my head. "Not so much."

"Damn, you serious?"

I shrugged.

"He came back though," Cameron said.

"So did you. That's all that matters."

Cameron squinted off into the distance. "I suppose."

"Thank you," Dance called softly from behind us. "I am ready."

I was going to ask her if she felt better, and mentally slapped myself again. Of course she didn't.

"You both could use a bath too," she said, wrinkling her nose.

"It'll have to wait," I said, orienting myself to the mountain. Lightning flashed and thunder rolled. It started raining. "Let's move with a purpose."

CHAPTER 43

"Stay very still," I said, holding Dance's hands.

"Will it hurt?" she asked. She didn't sound frightened. Just curious.

"I don't know."

They'd taken the index and middle finger from her right hand, and half of the ring finger from her left. Rebuilding muscle, joining severed tendons, fusing skin, and knitting bone were one thing, but regrowing appendages was something else.

"I don't know if I can do this," I admitted.

"We walked on water," she said. "You can do this."

It was dusk, and the mountain towered over the wide savanna. We'd entered the foothills early in the day and were getting close… to whatever awaited us. Destiny. Fate. Whatever it was. Perhaps even our deaths. It didn't matter anymore, but I wasn't giving up. What would happen would happen.

"*Lo que será, será,*" Xochi often whispered to me when my mind was troubled with thoughts of the future. "It is in God's hands, my love."

But where was God when First-to-Dance was being brutalized?

Thou art my hiding place; thou shalt preserve me from trouble; thou shalt compass me about with songs of deliverance. Selah.

He was with her, I realized. Embracing her. Weeping with her. He was there all along. He never left her side. He didn't beg to flee from the sight of the horror.

Not like I had.

"I'm sorry," I said.

"You cannot do it?"

"I'm sorry I couldn't protect you. I'm sorry I abandoned you."

She sighed. "You must stop apologizing for what you could not control and for being human. You could not protect me. We were powerless. It would not matter what you said or did. They enjoyed tormenting us. They took pleasure in our suffering. What happened would have happened anyway." She gazed firmly into my eyes. "Did you break to their will in desperation to end my torture? What loving person would not? Did you wish to escape to death from the horrors you were forced to witness?" She took a deep breath and squeezed my hands. "I never felt abandoned by you, Nephi. You shared in my suffering. You were *with* me. You and our God. You wept for me. You begged for me. You even lied for me, which is a sin"—she cracked a wan smile—"but one that I think can be forgiven as it saved my life. Would I rather you had gazed silently and stoically in the face of another human being's degradation and pain? No. Your *humanity* gave me the strength to endure."

"I was weak and pathetic."

"You were *human*."

She straightened a little and gazed off into the distance for a minute, then looked back at me. "To endure, to not break, was my armor. Defiance shielded me. But now that it is over, I am defenseless. I am afraid. I need you more *now* than then. What I do not need are your apologies. Your self-pity does nothing for me. I need you to be strong for me now. I need you to carry me through the *after*. That is the part that terrifies me. The after. What has happened has happened. But what comes now? How do I take the next step? Who will walk with me? Even my sister warriors cannot tread my path because they have not been where I have gone. But you have." She paused and studied my eyes. "Are you strong enough to walk with me through the after, or will you abandon me to walk alone?"

"I won't abandon you."

"It will be a long road, achtli."

"I'll be there every step of the way, iuctli."

She smiled, and her face glowed with radiance. No, not her face —it was coming from our hands. Mine and hers. I'd healed us both. She wiggled ten perfect fingers and laughed softly.

"I knew you could do it."

***

As we drew closer to the mountain, I began to make out details on its surface. Great swaths of its face had been carved into colossal statues of jaguar-men warriors and façades resembling ancient Olmec buildings. The entire lower half of the volcano was a great stepped pyramid on a mind-bending scale. I stopped and stared in disbelief.

"Right?" Cameron said.

I realized my mouth was hanging open. "Who built this?"

"Aliens, I bet. Saw this show once about Mesoamerica and aliens. All those civilizations worshipped the jaguar, and the Olmecs in particular worshipped were-jaguars. Or they might have *been* were-jaguars themselves. In other words, jaguar-men. The jags used to travel the universe with their Compass thingy, right? My money says they set up shop on Earth too."

"But then where are they now?"

Cameron shrugged. "They left. Or not. Who knows."

"The Tlacaōcēlōtl are believed to be long gone from my world," Dance said. "But legends say some still live among us in human form. *Nagual,* they are sometimes called. They are powerful sorcerers."

I extended my hand toward the volcano-pyramid. "Even jags couldn't have built that."

"Dunno, man," Cameron said. "Someone built it. How are we going to find this Compass-whatever in there? It's huge."

"We'll find it," I said. "We're meant to find it."

"You mean *you're* meant to find it. The rest of us are just along for the ride. What makes you so special anyway?"

"Don't ask me," I replied. "I didn't sign up for this."

Dance patted my shoulder. "Sergeant Bennett rides the short bus."

"Hey!" I cried. "That's not nice."

Cameron busted out laughing.

"What?" Dance asked, looking puzzled. "Sergeant Wilson said the special children ride the short bus. What is a bus?"

"Means Bennett's a 'tard," Cameron wheezed, holding his sides.

"Tard? Is that like a Child of Prophesy? What is so funny about that, Specialist Cameron? You should be honored to serve with a Tard."

"I just… can't even…" He waved us away feebly, tears streaming down his face.

"I don't understand," Dance said irritably. "Are you making fun of me?"

"Tard—and short bus—is a rude way of saying someone isn't all there." I tapped my skull. "Like they got dropped on their head when they were a baby."

Realization dawned on her face, and she started laughing too. I had wondered if I'd ever hear her laugh again. It wasn't the same, not the joyous musical sound from before, but it was still good to hear.

"Like Touchdown," she said, wiping a tear from her eye.

"Little bit," I said. "Don't be too hard on the kid. He's a whiner sometimes, but he tries hard. He's just a little slow. And he has the worst luck imaginable."

Cameron took a deep breath and put his hands on his knees. "Come on, Sergeant Short Bus. Burning daylight."

"That nickname better not stick," I warned him.

"Oh, believe me. I'm telling *everyone* about this. It'll stick."

***

We heard the sound of battle from a long ways off and approached cautiously. The wind carried cough-bark roars of anger, yowls of pain, and the clash of weapons. And it didn't sound like a small battle, either. It sounded like the end of the world. It was midday, but the sky over the mountain was dark.

"Try to skirt around it?" Cameron said.

"Skirt where?" I asked. "It sounds like it's coming from everywhere ahead of us. Let's get eyes-on."

"Brilliant plan," Cameron said with a nod.

"Watch our six," I said. "Dance, on me."

We double-timed it up a draw and between hills to a small rise, the sounds of battle growing stronger. When we'd reached the military crest, we low-crawled until we could see over the ridge.

A huge white bowl stretched out between us and the mountain pyramid. The vast dead sea was filled for miles with an unbroken mass of jag warriors engaged in battle. The scale of the armies was beyond comprehension. It looked like two entire civilizations clashed in one titanic struggle to see who would be the last man standing. Literal hills of corpses littered the battlefield, and the sky was dark with carrion birds and volleys of arrows. Bright bursts of magical energy erupted here and there, tearing through ranks of warriors, and I watched in stunned horror as one entire battalion was reduced to slag. Sinkholes swallowed companies whole, and rotting plague swept through the masses like a maelstrom, accompanied by battalions of undead soldiers.

"How do we get through *that*?" Dance asked. She had to raise her voice to be heard over the frenzied slaughter.

"Can't go through it," I said. "Can't go around it. Wait for nightfall and slip past their camps?"

"Maybe." She sounded unconvinced.

"Then we wait and see."

"Could still go around maybe," she said without conviction.

"It would take days. The battle stretches to the horizons."

"Then we wait," she agreed.

I slipped back down behind the crest and called to Cameron. "No dice. No way through. No way around. We're going to have to wait it out."

"Fantastic," he replied.

"We need food and water."

"Preaching to the choir, man. But these hills are a wasteland. Nothing to eat or drink for miles."

I was starving. We all were. And thirsty. Food we could live without, but water? I'd already almost died from dehydration once. Can't recommend it. Two big thumbs down. I figured we had forty-eight hours before we shriveled up and died.

The battle couldn't possibly last that long.

Right?

It raged on through the night and into the next day. The numbers were dwindling, the fighting masses spreading out into ragged clumps among the sea of corpses. Cameron was watching with me as Dance covered our backs.

"This is so metal," Cameron said. "It's Bronze Age mayhem on an apocalyptic scale."

"There are women and children fighting too," I said. "I didn't notice before."

"How can you tell which ones are women?"

"No kilts, and they have tails."

"I thought female jags didn't fight?"

I shrugged.

"I'm so damn thirsty, man. We really need to get some water."

"Last stream we crossed was a day's hump from here. I don't want to backtrack. Not with Alpha on our trail."

"So what, we just sit here and die?"

"No. The armies are thinning out. See? There's a path through them. We could try after dark. There has to be water on that mountain."

Just then the earth trembled and a rift opened up in the basin below us, swallowing a mass of jags.

"Yeah, good plan," Cameron said.

"I never said it was a *good* plan."

By the next morning the armies had been whittled down to isolated groups of jaguar-men and women intent on annihilating one another. There were no more spectacular fireworks or flaming meteors. The tornadoes and earthquakes had stopped. Even the marching ranks of undead had fallen.

"I think the spellcasters are all dead," I said through cracked and bleeding lips. "Or they've finally run out of juice."

"Good," Dance replied hoarsely. "That stray fireball last night almost turned us to ashes."

"My mouth *tastes* like ashes," Cameron commented from behind us. "Oh shit."

"What?" I asked, turning back to him. Then I saw it too. Riders in the distance.

"Think they've spotted us?" Cameron asked.

"Let's not give them the chance," I said. "Up and over."

We scrambled over the crest in a crawl and skipped and slid down the reverse slope into the basin. We moved across the vast plain at a trot, skirting towering hills of rotting bodies and clouds of flies. The smell was overpowering.

"All this white... it looks like a winter wonderland," Cameron commented in a scratchy voice. "You know, apart from all the corpses and buzzards."

"Reminds me of the salt flats back in Utah," I rasped back. "Me and my brothers used to take our dirt bikes out there sometimes and race."

"Wish we had some bikes here. It's going to take all day to reach the base of the mountain. At *least* all day."

I looked back and saw that Dance had fallen. She wasn't trying to get back up. I hurried over and got her into a sitting position. Her head lolled back, and I had to support her neck.

"What's wrong?" Cameron asked.

"Think she just fainted. Oh, no—she's burning up."

"Need help?"

"No, I got her." I picked her up, and my knees almost buckled. She felt like she weighed twice as much as the last time I'd carried her. "Let's get her under cover." We weren't in direct sunlight—nothing was ever in direct sunlight in this permanently overcast land—but it was dry in the basin and the temperature was rising. "We need to get her into the shade."

"What cover?" Cameron asked, waving aimlessly. "What shade? I can't see the sun."

"You can still burn on an overcast day," I said. "I learned that the hard way one summer at Lake Powell."

"Please don't mention lakes," Cameron said. "Or rivers, or streams, or water of any kind."

We stumbled forward through the sea of dead, skirting small skirmishes of jags hacking each other apart. If they saw us, they didn't care.

"What about that?" Cameron asked, pointing to a huge jagged rock that had burst out of the ground.

"Yeah, that'll do."

The rock had erupted out of the hard-packed salt floor at an angle. I got Dance under the cover of its shadow and propped her up. Cameron scooted in beside me.

"At least there are fewer flies in this spot," he said. "You're right. Even this little bit of shade feels good."

"Hold her," I said. I scooted around the side of the rock and scanned the lip of the basin. If our pursuers were up there, they weren't silhouetting themselves.

I heard a yowl and jumped, spinning around. A jaguar-woman ran past, waving a broken war club in her hand. She charged another woman, and they clashed in a blur of fur and fangs. After she'd bashed the other woman's brains out, she turned toward us, panting. I lowered my hand to my pistol, but she seemed to be staring *through* us. She snarled and raced off in a different direction.

"Is it just me, or is it like she couldn't even see us?" Cameron asked.

"Not just you." I thought back to what the high elder had said about the final battle that exterminated his people. A battle that would happen far in the future.

"They can't see us because we're not witnessing the present," I said.

"Say again?"

"This battle happens in the future. We're seeing shades of the future. This isn't real."

"Flies are sure real. Sure smells real. You okay, Bennett?"

"We need to figure out how to get her temperature down."

"She needs *water*, man. We all do."

"Water…"

"Yeah, you know. Wet stuff?"

I gazed at the rock and ran my hand down its surface. "Water from a stone…" I mused.

"Please don't go crazy on me, man," Cameron pleaded. "I really don't want to die here."

Grasping at tenuous threads of teōtl, I began to weave. It was incredibly draining, this work of Making I was attempting. And I was exhausted. Out of juice.

A crack formed in the stone.

And from the crack trickled a stream of pure water.

CHAPTER 44

"You can regrow missing fingers, walk across rivers, and summon water from a stone," Cameron said. "I don't know if I should kiss you or start a new church."

I laughed.

We gathered handfuls of the coolest, freshest water I'd ever tasted, and drank deeply. The water wasn't just refreshing, it was energizing. It *healed*. I unwound the shemagh from around my neck, held it under the stream, and then wrapped it around Dance's head. I wet her lips and smiled as her eyes fluttered open a few minutes later.

"Heya, little sister. Have a drink of the sweetest water you've ever tasted." I held a cupped hand to her lips and poured it into her mouth.

She sighed. "That is amazing."

"Isn't it? Have some more."

"How did you find it?" she asked.

"He touched the rock and it just appeared!" Cameron said.

"Like Moisés." Dance smiled. "Better nickname than Short Bus."

"Oh, no. He's not getting out of that. It's Sergeant Short Bus for the rest of his days."

I flicked water at him.

"Can you sit?" I asked Dance.

"Yes, thank you."

I scooted around the rock, keeping low, and searched the rim of the basin again in the direction we'd come from. Bad news.

St. James and his crew had arrived.

Riders on thunder-stags were descending the slope. I counted only seven; perhaps the others had been lost crossing the river. I wished, not for the first time in the last few days, that I had my spotting scope. Or better yet the Barrett. A few rounds of Raufoss downrange from this position would solve quite a few problems.

I doubted even St. James could survive a hit from the Red Waterfall center mass.

"Dance, you still have four eggs left, right?" I asked without taking my eyes off the riders.

"Hooah."

I chewed on my lip. The grenade launcher didn't have great range, not compared to the rifles Alpha was toting. We had two long arms and a pistol. If it came to a shoot-out, they'd mow us down. Even the thumper wouldn't even those odds. Not much anyway. We'd cause some damage, but we'd be just as dead.

But they needed me alive. I couldn't trust that they wouldn't call my bluff about Dance, but I knew they wouldn't shoot *me*. That was my ace up the sleeve. Other than that, the hand I'd been dealt was pretty crappy.

"Okay guys, bad news is we got seven riders entering the basin," I said, still watching them.

"Dammit," Cameron said. "How long until they're here?"

"Ten minutes, maybe fifteen, if they make straight for us. They may not know where we are though."

"Fat chance," Cameron said. "With our luck they spotted us taking cover. I'm still waiting for the good news."

"I'm working on that," I said.

Question was if the smart play was to confront them or try and evade.

Or give myself up and hope Dance and Cameron could get away.

Surrender is not a Ranger word, I heard Captain Brown say.

I wasn't a Ranger.

But I embraced the Creed.

I am better trained and will fight with all my might.

What would Captain Brown do? If I ever got a tattoo, that would be it: *WWCBD*. Would he stand or run? Fight or flight?

He'd hit and fade.

I surveyed the terrain. Lots of cover. Plenty of piles of swollen fly-encrusted corpses.

And St. James wouldn't shoot me.

He could shoot you in the leg, I hear you say.

Bzzzt. Wrong answer.

Because femoral artery. Leg shot can be a kill shot just as good as center mass.

So I had that going for me. My ace up the sleeve.

I checked the riders once more. They'd entered the bowl and were walking their mounts directly toward us. Easy like a Sunday morning. Lazy, even. They were feeling confident.

Oh, for Carl G and a round or two of antipersonnel.

Don't wish for what you can't have.

I pulled back under the rock. "You're right, Ross—looks like they know exactly where we are. We have about ten minutes. If we run, they'll give chase. They'll ride us down."

"I'm *still* waiting for the good news," Cameron said.

"Dance, how far away do you think you could hit one of those thunder-stags with the thumper?" I asked.

"Three hundred meters," she said confidently.

"Then that's our line in the sand. This rock is good cover. They're coming in confident. Not even dispersing. *That's* your good news, Cameron. St. James is being cocky. He thinks he has us trapped. He's expecting us to maybe take a few potshots, and when we don't, he'll get even more confident. He thinks we're weak—"

"We *are* weak," Cameron said. He wasn't complaining, just stating facts. Couldn't fault him for that.

"He thinks we're weaker than we are. We still have teeth. When they get within three hundred meters, Dance, you hit those mounts with HE. Center mass. Nothing fancy. At the same time, I'll open up on them. Seven-six-two isn't going to hurt them much—they'll heal fast—but it will keep their heads down for a minute. It still hurts—I should know. And if I get lucky with a head shot, I might even take a couple of them out."

I pointed to other spots on the battlefield. "We're gonna go to that pile of corpses for cover, then that one, then that one. That'll keep them from flanking us. I'll cover you two the whole way. Give me your rifle, Cameron, and all your mags, Dance. You guys won't need them."

"And you get my rifle because…?" Cameron asked.

"Because I'm a better shot. And most importantly, because they won't shoot me. They need me alive. I'm your shield. That's why I'm covering you."

"Point," Cameron conceded. "Do I at least get the pistol?"

"Nine-millimeter is just going to piss them off, but you're welcome to it if it makes you feel better."

Cameron's eyes flicked to Dance meaningfully. I nodded and handed him my Glock in the holster without a word. He strapped it on.

"If I'm captured—" I began.

"Do not say 'leave me,' because we will not," Dance said. "You would not if it were one of us."

"Amen," Cameron said. "Remember the motto of our training regiment? *All for One and One for All*. We live or die here, now, together."

Dance nodded. "Together."

***

I placed one mag out in front of me, stuffed the other two in my cargo pocket, and then settled myself on the ground, wedged beside the rock, using a corpse as my shooting platform. It was a good position. Good cover. Good concealment. Good fields of fire. Dance hid on the other side, waiting for my call. She'd already loaded a round of HE in the tube and preset her sights. She was fast and she was accurate. I'd never seen someone work a grenade launcher like she could.

Cameron crouched near her. His job was to protect her while I was covering their fade. He and I had an unspoken agreement that under no circumstances would we allow First-to-Dance to be taken again. We'd shoot her first. And then ourselves. Surrender wasn't an option. Capture wasn't an option. I knew Dance wouldn't take her own life to avoid recapture; her religious convictions forbade it. But I'd go to Hell for eternity if that was the price I had to pay rather than let her fall into their hands again. I knew Cameron felt the same. I'd read it in his eyes in the way he looked at her when he asked for my pistol.

"Eight hundred meters and closing," I said quietly. "How you feeling, Thumper?"

She laughed softly. "You have never called me that before. The others do, but not you."

"Seemed appropriate."

"I am ready to lay the hate."

"Hooah," Cameron whispered.

"Five hundred," I warned. "Get ready. They're moving in a tight wedge. Not very tactical. Take the center riders. I have the flankers."

I waited, sighting in on the leftmost rider in the formation. Eagle warrior. I remembered him. I remembered all of them. St. James was in the rear of the wedge. Bond was on point. He'd take the first round of HE. Good. But I didn't see Wright, and I swore silently. St. James wasn't the only one who'd been too confident. I had too. There were more of them. They were flanking us.

"Cameron, keep your eyes peeled on our six. We're being flanked."

"Shit."

"Three hundred and fifty…"

I took a controlled breath.

"Thumper, now!"

Exhaling as I said the words, I squeezed the trigger and felt the SCAR-H slam into my shoulder.

The eagle warrior's head snapped back in a cloud of pink mist.

Thump!

I heard the smack of the egg hitting flesh, and a moment later the lead thunder-stag came apart along with Bond in a bloody haze.

Sayōnara, asshole.

My target swayed and ragdolled out of the saddle. I was already moving to the next. I wasn't going to be fancy with my shots. Not with a red dot at three hundred meters. Two shots, center mass. Move to the next target. Repeat.

Thump!

Another dinosaur became instant hamburger along with its rider. The explosion turned bone into shrapnel and knocked two more riders out of the saddle. They were down, but probably not out. The thunder-stags were panicking, trumpeting wildly and thrashing as their riders tried to control them.

Shift. Breathe. Aim. Fire. Recover. Fire.

St. James fell out of the saddle with two in the pipes and lungs.

Thump!

His mount exploded a moment later.

"Thumper! Save the last one. Wright's behind us."

"Where?" Dance cried.

"Don't know, but he's there."

I dropped an eagle warrior who was getting back up. He looked like someone had run him along a cheese grater for a few hours.

"Is this the part where we fade?" Cameron asked.

Riderless thunder-stages were running in all directions, shaking the ground and trumpeting in terror and confusion. Without knowing where Wright was, we couldn't fall back—we could run right into an ambush.

"Negative," I said. "New plan. We hold here."

Where are you, you son of a bitch?

A round impacted the swollen corpse I was shooting from, and it exploded. I blinked the filth from my eyes and snap-fired at St. James. The round hit him in the shoulder, and he half spun around, recovered, and raised his rifle.

He was *fast*.

But I was better trained.

A round snapped off the rock above me, showering me with needle shards. I returned fire, ignoring the burning pain across my back and scalp.

St. James staggered backwards and fell, clutching his throat.

Two of the eagle warriors had recovered and were advancing, holding their rifles out in front of them and spraying on full auto.

Whoever trained them needed to be flogged.

I ignored the rounds pelting the ground, raising plumes of salt and chunks of rotting jag.

Slow is smooth and smooth is fast.

I pink-misted the first one at one hundred fifty yards and dropped the second with two solid shots center mass. He'd be getting up again, but for now he was down.

Where are you?

"Three tangos. HE seven o'clock, seventy-five meters!" I yelled without looking. I didn't know *how* I knew Wright and two eagle warriors were there, behind us, but I knew.

Dance and I had been a team for so long by now, she didn't hesitate. She was already adjusting and firing almost before I'd finished giving the order.

Thump!

I heard the smack and then the explosion.

"One tango neutralized. Two wounded, including Wright. Black on ammo," Dance called.

"What the hell?" Cameron exclaimed. "She fired blind before they even rounded the corner. They rode right into it!"

"Cameron, get her a mag out of my cargo pocket. Thumper, keep their heads down."

"Hooah, Sarge!" Dance shouted.

A panicked thunder-stag raced by, shaking the ground.

I caught an eagle warrior creeping along a pile of corpses and sighted in calmly. Sixty yards. Easy shot.

His head snapped back and he dropped to the ground. Instant rag doll. A little pink cloud floated away on the breeze.

If my count was right, we had two in front, two behind. Wright and his buddy were a problem. We had absolutely no cover from them. We needed to move. I cast about and noticed a bizarre crystal formation about fifty yards to our right that had been hidden by a mound of corpses. It was spiny and spiked and very much unnatural, but it would provide good cover.

"Listen up. We're pulling back to that weird crystal formation on our three. Forget bounding. We move as one. I'll shield you." I swapped my partially spent magazine for a full one. "Ready? Go!"

They sprinted and I ran, half backwards, angling my body to try and get between them and any incoming. I could see St. James and an eagle warrior advancing, bounding from cover to cover from one direction, and Wright and his buddy coming from the other. I didn't bother with suppressive fire; no point wasting precious ammo.

"They're just going to flank us again," Cameron said as we crouched behind the large spindly crystal. I leaned around and took a shot at one of the eagle warriors who was feeling brave, nearly scalping him.

I muttered a word my mom doesn't approve of. I hate missing.

Incoming hit the crystal, and we all flinched as razor shards exploded in all directions.

"Anyone hit?" I asked.

"Not badly," Dance said.

"Same," Cameron said. "But this cover is going to kill us."

"Agreed." I cast about for better cover, but there was nothing other than the various piles of jag bodies. One of them would have to do. "See that closest pile of corpses? Go, I'll cover. Now!"

I hit the deck, rolling away from the deadly crystal and getting behind a body before snapping off a few rounds to keep Wright's head down. A quick shift, and I tagged St. James in the leg. It must have caused some serious damage, because he went down screaming bloody murder. Then one of the eagle warriors rushed me at a dead sprint, spraying everything with lead—he must've missed the memo about not killing me—and I hid behind my bloated cover until the frenzied fire stopped and all I could hear was his war cry.

I popped up and stitched him from navel to neck at twenty yards, then blew his head off for good measure.

After sending a few more rounds downrange to keep everyone occupied, I leapt up and sprinted back to Dance and Cameron. A round tagged my hip and I spun, landing in an ungainly sprawl. Cameron dashed forward and dragged me behind their cover.

"Let me look at you," he said.

"I'm fine."

"Let me look at you anyway."

"I said I'm fine."

"Shut up and stay still."

Dance crawled around and over the corpses to get a clear field of fire. I could hear the report of rifles and the smack of rounds hitting bodies.

"You're bleeding pretty bad," Cameron said. "But it looks like it grazed you."

"I said I'm fine."

"Mag out. I'm black," Dance called out.

I fished my partial magazine out of my pocket and handed it to Cameron, who tossed it to Dance.

"Help me up," I told Cameron. He gave me a hand and I winced as I stood. I could probably heal it, but that would take me out of the fight for precious seconds we didn't have.

"Arrrgh! They keep getting back up!" Dance screamed.

I clambered up the mound of bodies, doing my best to ignore the foulness, and got myself situated. Irritated flies buzzed in a black cloud around me. Did I mention the smell? Just… really no bueno. I was already covered in cuts and scrapes from rock and crystal shrapnel, and now I was coated in liquified rot. Definitely an infection risk. Doc would be furious.

St. James was stalking forward, and I snapped off a couple rounds to keep his head down. One of the eagle warriors—the last one left, I thought—popped up and sprayed our position, and Dance and I both got our heads down as rounds smacked into our fetid cover. Bloated corpses ruptured, splattering us with corruption. If we lived through this, we'd probably end up dying from some exotic disease.

I heard a break in the fire and got back up. For a minute, nothing moved.

Then Wright popped up, followed by St. James.

"I got the right!" I called out, shifting my aim and unloading on St. James. Three rounds center mass knocked him back a few steps. I lined up for the headshot and squeezed the trigger, but nothing happened.

I cursed. In all the excitement I didn't notice my bolt locking back.

"Black on ammo," I announced.

Dance ducked as a few rounds struck her position, then she returned fire.

"Black on ammo," she echoed.

"Well this sucks," Cameron said. "What now?"

CHAPTER 45

"It's over, Bennett," St. James called out. "You can't win."

I glanced at Cameron and Dance. Cameron shook his head slowly; Dance just closed her eyes.

"Come out," St. James called. "Let's talk. I just want to talk, Bennett. Man to man."

I took a deep breath and tried to steady my nerves. We'd had a brief reprieve, only a couple short minutes, but I'd had an idea and ran it by Cameron and Dance.

"I just want it on the record that I think this is a horrible plan," Cameron hissed.

"It will work," Dance replied calmly, looking over at me. Her steady gaze met my eye. "God is with you."

It wasn't even really a plan, as plans go. It wasn't even a desperate gamble. My connection to the flow of teōtl that bound the universe together was tenuous at best. There was so much death here, so much corruption, that the weave of the land itself seemed tangled and warped. This place… this was a place of eternal chaos, a nexus of entropy, where the final battle that exterminated The People was played out endlessly on repeat, through the past, present, and future. We stood on an ancient and future graveyard, the sediment of the dead sea filled with the crumbling bones of people who wouldn't fall in this battleground for another few millennia. It was a place outside of time.

And we'd run out of time.

I exhaled and stood, limping around the mound of corpses rotting in the heat, and looked up at the overcast sky. I couldn't see the sun above the gray clouds, but that was hardly notable in this land. What *was* notable was that I couldn't *feel* it. Ever since Epasotl had taught me how to channel teōtl, I'd always been able to feel the sun.

And calling the healing water from the stone had tapped me out. I didn't know if I could summon enough teōtl to cup a flame in my hand, let alone what I was planning to do.

And then I saw Bond. Alive. It was inconceivable. And yes, I know what that word means. I'd seen him come apart. There was no coming back from that kind of damage. I was sure of it.

Apparently I was wrong.

St. James stood twenty yards away from me, hands draped over the rifle slung around his front. Bond stood a little way to my right with an eagle warrior. Opposite, moving in from my left, were another two warriors. Obviously my count of tangos down had been wrong. They were far tougher than I'd thought.

I didn't see Wright, but I didn't need magical clairvoyance to know where he was. He'd flanked us again. My suspicion was confirmed when I heard Cameron shout a warning from behind me. It was cut off abruptly, followed by the sound of a body hitting the hard salt-crusted ground.

I moved slowly, angling myself so I could keep everyone in view. Wright appeared from behind the hill of corpses with Dance pinned in front of him, his savage knife to her throat. He was grinning, and I noticed his teeth had been filed down to sharp points. Somehow I'd missed that earlier. Behind him stalked two more eagle warriors. Could none of these guys just stay dead?

Eight-to-one was suicidal odds to begin with, but these guys… burn them, shoot them, blow them up, they'd put the pieces together and keep coming. Even hitting the kill switch only put them down for a while. Maybe they really were immortal. Had *I* been too? Again, I half-regretted curing myself. There were advantages to being cursed by the Lord of the Underworld.

I heard movement behind me and sighed. Correction: *nine*-to-one. There had been ten, hadn't there? Well, at least we'd somehow managed to put one down for good. So not immortal. Just insanely difficult to kill.

Or maybe that other guy was still busy regenerating.

"It's over," St. James repeated. "You see you can't win, don't you? We're gods."

"You're devils," Dance shouted.

"Well, you know what they say." St. James spread his hands. "Better to reign in Hell than serve in Heaven."

Thread by thread, I pulled twisted, tangled mats of divine energy into my core, carding it smooth, spinning it into fine threads. It would take time.

"You wanted to talk," I said. "So talk."

"I can give you everything you've always dreamed of," St. James said. "Anything you *can* dream of. And things you haven't even imagined."

"You mean Smoking Mirror can," I said. "You don't rule here, Sergeant. He does. This is Tezcatlipoca's world. His corruption. You don't reign. You *serve.* You're a slave. I already have everything I want. Everything I've ever dreamed of."

"What? Her?" St. James scoffed. "You're a simple man if all you can dream of is one woman."

"I have love and family," I said. "That's the greatest of all treasures."

It was true, too. What Xochi and I had was greater than anything I could possibly dream of. No amount of wealth or power could compete with what we had created together.

Bond started laughing, and even St. James couldn't help cracking a smile.

They could laugh. I didn't care if they mocked me. I just needed more time.

St. James flicked a hand, and two of the eagle warriors took Dance from Wright and held her between them. Wright stalked in front of her, his blade dangling lightly from his fingertips as she squared her shoulders.

And no, her being in their hands again wasn't part of my impossible eleventh-hour plan. I forced myself to stay calm. I had to focus.

I could hear the warrior behind me shuffling closer. Two warriors in front of me were spreading out, flanking, edging closer.

I swore silently.

I needed more time.

***

"This can go two ways, Bennett," St. James said calmly. "You work *with* us, or you work *for* us. I've tried to be reasonable. I've given you reasons—more than enough reasons, I thought—but you seem to have already forgotten them."

"I haven't forgotten anything," I replied. I tried to sound calm, but I couldn't keep the venom out of my voice.

"I think he has," St. James said to Bond.

"Yes, Sarge. Preacher's definitely forgotten, or he wouldn't be standing there acting like some kind of hardass." Bond started mimicking me crying and begging. He got down on his knees and clasped his hands and wailed. Then he began to laugh—a cruel, wicked laugh—and stood back up. He wiped a tear from his eye. "Do you have any idea how pathetic you are, Preacher? I've seen old women with bigger balls than you."

"Preacher don't even have balls," Wright commented. "Won't anyway, when I'm done. I'm gonna feed 'em to your little wife here, Preacher. Make you watch her chew 'em up. Remember when we did that before, Sarge? Fun times."

"It was sure as shit entertaining," St. James agreed.

"What do you say, Mrs. Bennett?" Wright asked Dance. "You gonna spit or swallow?"

"I think she's a spitter," Bond said.

First-to-Dance glared murder at Wright.

"She's forgot too, Sarge," Wright said to St. James. "Or maybe she liked it so much she wants more. That it, bitch? You want more?" He slapped her hard between the legs with the flat of his blade. "I won't be as gentle this time. But maybe that's your thing. Is that her thing, Preacher? Likes it rough?" He laughed. "Bond, guess we were too gentle the first time."

"Let's get this over with," St. James said. He sounded bored. "Last chance, Bennett. How do we find the Compass? What's the secret? What role do you play in all this?"

"I already told you *I don't know*," I said. "Somehow I find it. Somehow I'm led to it. I don't know *how*, only that I *do*."

"You said that; you also said a lot of other bullshit. We'll see." He motioned to the warriors flanking me. "Take him."

They advanced a few paces and then stopped, hesitating.

"Oh for Chrissakes, don't be pussies," St. James barked. "If he could do anything, he'd have already done it. Grab him and let's get this over with."

"We're not gonna cut them up?" Wright asked.

"If he doesn't cooperate, take something off her," St. James said. "Dealer's choice."

The eagle warriors closed in on me from all sides.

Now would be a choice time to do something, bro, I heard Wilson say.

I figured I *might* have enough juice built up to do my human incendiary grenade impression. Maybe. But that would only take out the three coming toward me. And that was assuming they couldn't come back from being turned to ash.

And yes, I'd given up on "the plan." Don't ask what it was. It made assumptions on bad intel. Like, for example, that I'd already killed most of them. And also, Dance not getting recaptured. And enough juice. Which was taking time. Time I didn't have.

"Run! Flee! Save yourself, big brother!" Dance cried to me in her native tongue.

"Shut your whore mouth," Wright growled, slapping her hard enough to break skin.

"God is with us, little sister," I replied calmly in her tongue, only half-believing it myself. I couldn't see a way to win this. Not anymore. St. James had me in check and was moving to mate. But I *could* see a way out. A final move. I'd help St. James, or make it look like it. I'd play along. Helping him wouldn't save us, I knew that; once he had the Compass, he'd take his time killing her first and then me. It would be so much worse than anything before, so much worse than anything we could imagine. But if I could get close enough to Dance, I knew I could at least kill *her*. Hopefully myself too. I had enough juice for at least that.

Stalemate.

When the moment came, I wouldn't hesitate.

***

After they'd bound my hands behind my back, the three warriors frog-marched me across the basin towards the base of the "pyramid." Air quotes intentional. The sheer scale of it screwed with your perception of size and distance. I was actually getting vertigo and had to keep reminding myself we were walking toward not a building, or even a temple, but a mountain. It towered over us ominously, like a crouching eldritch god, or something from the void between universes.

By now the ancient-and-future jags had stopped fighting, because there were none left alive to fight. They had slaughtered each other to the last man, woman, and child over the course of three days and three nights. The entire vast salt basin was a charnel house. A graveyard stretching for miles. I don't know how many Tlacaōcēlōtls died. Hundreds of thousands? A million? Maybe more. Probably more. It was complete and total scorched-earth racial suicide.

Or so I had thought.

But as we approached a courtyard at the base of a long steep stairway, I saw two jags remaining. And they were locked in mortal combat.

They were the two biggest jags I'd ever laid eyes on. Ten feet tall at least, and seriously pumped. Wrists as thick as my waist. Legs like tree trunks. Muscles like steel cables rippling under their matted and bloodstained fur. They fought like heavyweight boxers in the twelfth round, barely standing, exhausted, unable to make a sound other than the hoarse labored breathing that echoed off the stone walls. Broken weapons and shields lay all around them. And corpses. Lots of corpses. One had a great war club edged with obsidian blades, many of them shattered or missing. The other was armed with a bronze short sword. "Short" being a relative term. In my hands it would be a… well, very *long* sword. And impossibly heavy.

They weren't even swinging at each other. Just circling, lungs working like bellows. Each had been wounded so greatly it was impossible to tell where one injury ended and another began.

The giant jag with the war club raised his weapon wearily in one hand, attempted to roar, and then collapsed in a dead faint.

The other, the last of the Tlacaōcēlōtls, limped towards his fallen foe, bent down wearily, and then proceeded to saw his opponent's head off.

"Well I'll be damned," St. James said. "Would've paid good money to see that fight." He turned to me. "Okay, Bennett. How's this work? How do we find the Compass?"

The last Tlacaōcēlōtl stood, holding his enemy's head, and then threw it away with a snarl. He threw his sword away too, and surveyed the desolation spread out before him. His ears were limp, laid back on his head. He didn't look only weary and near death; he looked… sad. Profoundly sad.

And then his gaze fell on me—not through me, but *on* me—and we locked eyes. In that moment I felt—no, *shared*—a taste of his sorrow. The greatest sorrow imaginable. Here was a man who had spent a lifetime trying to stall the self-destruction of not only his people, but his entire species, and he had failed. He was the last of them, and soon he too would die.

He turned and began slowly climbing the steep steps.

"We follow him," I said.

CHAPTER 46

We followed the Last Tlacaōcēlōtl up the long, steep stairs and through an arched entrance, along vast abandoned halls and through cavernous chambers. Everything was ancient, but… untouched. Preserved. His entire people had vanished, ceased to exist overnight, millennia ago, or millennia from now, I wasn't sure there was a difference, but the structure remained, like a stage that had been set for a play and the actors never arrived.

The giant jaguar-man plodded forward slowly, but given the length of his stride, we still struggled at times to keep up. Yet whenever we lost sight of him around a corner or through a doorway, we always found him a short time later, as if he were waiting for us, guiding us. He *wanted* us to follow.

"This place gives me the creeps," Bond said at one point as we followed our guide through the abandoned never-ending structure. Some of the chambers were so vast they contained building and streets. Cities within a mountain. The scale was mind-bending.

"Don't be a pussy," Wright grumbled.

"Do you think it's haunted?" Bond asked him.

"I ain't afraid of no ghost."

"It's not haunted, Bond," St. James snapped. "Grow some balls."

The eagle warriors didn't look convinced.

As we proceeded, the chambers grew smaller, the hallways and passages narrower, and I sensed we were approaching the heart of the extinct volcano. The temple in the mountain. Their holy of holies. Reliefs of genocide and unimaginable tortures adorned the walls, joined by carvings of skeletal jaguar-men wearing necklaces of eyes and entrails dancing around bonfires stacked with corpses. It made Mictlan look like an amusement park for children.

"How much farther, Bennett?" St. James asked irritably. "We've been walking for hours."

"I don't know," I replied. "He's leading us somewhere."

"If the cat-man knows where it is, why don't we just catch him and make him tell us?" Bond sighed. "We don't need Bennett anymore."

"You won't be able to catch him, or interrogate him," I said. "He can't see you. You can't touch him. He's not here. He's a shade of the future."

"A ghost?" Wright snorted.

"'Shade of the future,'" Bond said mockingly, but there was a nervous edge to his voice. "That's the biggest load of bullshit I've ever heard."

"No, I think Bennett's right," St. James said. "We follow. And stay frosty, gentlemen. Intel says there are traps meant to keep people out."

"Like *Indiana Jones and the Temple of Doom*," Bond said.

"Don't be a retard," Wright snapped.

I was beginning to think maybe Bond wasn't so silly for worrying about this place being haunted though. *Things* flickered in dark corners and shadowy recesses. Creatures made of shadow. Monstrous shapes that flowed between the pools of wan yellow light cast by torches and braziers that somehow, impossibly, still burned after countless years.

Or maybe time simply didn't apply here. Maybe this temple existed in one single infinite moment. I'd have to ask Captain Brown what he thought. Maybe there was an *X-Men* story arc about something like this. He'd know.

I shook my head. I'd never get the chance to ask, because I was going to die here. Me and Dance, together. My wife's vision was wrong. There was no future where we stood side by side against a great evil. No future where we survived to raise a family together. Someone else would take my place in that timeline.

Someone not me.

***

St. James had us spread out in a column, with one of the eagle warriors taking point, followed by me and then St. James. Bond came next, and then two more warriors, followed by Dance with Wright behind her. The remaining three warriors held rear security. I'd considered making a rush back to her several times, but I'd have to get through everyone between us, and they were all armed with battle rifles and knives, obsidian-bladed war clubs, and tomahawks. Plus my hands were bound. My plans for forcing a stalemate weren't looking promising. Not now. But the time would come. There would be a moment, and I would seize it.

For now I just had to put one foot in front of the other and wait.

The warrior in front of me held up a fist and knelt.

"Whatcha got, Chimalli?" St. James asked.

"Tripwire, my lord," the warrior answered in a gravelly voice. "My lord would be wise to leave it be."

St. James nodded in agreement and called out the wire to those behind him. "Don't drag your dicks across the wire, men. Let's go."

Chimalli stepped carefully over the tripwire and was just starting to continue forward when suddenly the entire section of floor under and ahead of him swung like a teeter-totter, dumping him into darkness. It didn't sound like he fell far, but the sickening sound of flesh being punctured and torn adequately communicated his fate. As did his screams.

"Holy shit!" Bond cried.

St. James pushed past me and stepped carefully over the wire. The floor had already leveled out again, muffling Chimalli's screams. St. James got down on his knees and pushed hard on a section of the floor. It went down, and the opposite end fifteen feet away went up. He got out a flashlight and peered into the pit below.

"Shit," he said dispassionately. "Like a giant punji trap. Poor bastard's impaled on spikes. Well, he's not getting out of there unless he can get himself unstuck."

He let the floor level itself and stood.

The screaming was muffled again.

"Sucks to be him," Bond said with a shrug.

I would have been horrified at their indifference except I vividly remembered what this demon named Chimalli had done to Dance, and as far as I was concerned spending the rest of however long a death-touched might live impaled on spikes was too good for him.

"What now?" Wright called ahead. "How do we cross that seesaw?"

"We could run really fast?" Bond suggested.

"Don't be a retard," Wright snapped back.

St. James considered the problem for a minute and then laughed to himself and kicked the tripwire. There were two loud metallic clanks, and I sucked in my breath, waiting for something horrible to happen.

St. James tested the seesaw floor. It appeared to be rock-solid, locked in place. "Thought so. Someone has a perverse sense of humor. I approve. All clear, gentlemen. Citlalic, you're on point. Try to be more careful than Chimalli."

"As you command, my lord," Citlalic replied without emotion or any sign of hesitation. He moved past us and carefully crossed the treacherous section of floor, then waved us forward.

A few minutes later the passage opened into a circular room with four equally spaced exits. The Last Tlacaōcēlōtl, who appeared to have been waiting for us, disappeared through the left passage. Citlalic paused before entering the chamber and got down on one knee to examine the curious floor. Narrow paths of polished obsidian flagstones led to each exit, intersecting in the middle of the room in a wide jade-inlaid circle. The rest of the floor was composed of large, irregular basalt tiles, each with a different glyph carved on the surface.

"Pressure plates, my lord," Citlalic said, resting his hand lightly on a basalt tile. "We stick to the narrow path?"

"Seems too obvious," St. James said thoughtfully. "There must be a path through the tiles. Figure it out."

"As you command, my lord."

Citlalic studied the pattern of glyphs for a while and then took a hesitant step. When nothing happened, he took another. And another. As he proceeded, he grew more confident, step by step by—

Click.

He froze.

"Bet you fifty bucks if he takes his foot off that tile, something bad's gonna happen," Bond said.

I stepped back a bit, trying to maneuver myself behind St. James. Dance was only a few feet away. If I could just—

"Where you going?" St. James said to me, holding out his arm. "Don't be a pussy."

"My lord?" Citlalic asked.

"You don't be a pussy either. What's the worst that could happen? You'll heal. You're *immortal*, for Chrissakes. Grow a pair and get a move on."

"As you command, my lord."

Citlalic lifted his foot, and a searing jet of flame erupted out of the wall, immolating his head and shoulders. He reeled back, stepping into the jade-inlaid central circle—and vanished. One second he was there, flailing and burning, and the next he was just... gone. It was like he'd fallen into a black hole.

"Well, shit. At least we know not to step into the circle," St. James said. He glanced behind him. "Ahuatzi, you like puzzles. Front and center."

One of the warriors from the rear guard hurried past the others and bowed to St. James. "My lord?"

"Find the safe path." St. James pointed at the floor. "Citlalic almost had it. There, there, there, and there. *Not* there. See the pattern? Finish it. And don't step into that circle in the middle of the room." He pulled a chem light out of his cargo pocket and cracked it, then sliced off the top with his knife. "Dribble a little on each safe tile to mark the path."

"As you command, my lord."

The warrior stepped boldly across the maze of tiles, marking each one. At the point where Citlalic had erred, he paused, studying the glyphs. After a moment he took a different route and crossed confidently to the door on our left without further incident.

"You're next, Bennett," St. James said.

Keeping my balance with my hands tied behind my back was difficult, but the threat of being turned into a human barbecue motivated me, and I too crossed the tiles uncooked. One by one the others followed, and we continued on.

***

The floor sloped downward slowly, and the walls grew damp with humidity. Soon water began collecting on the floor, first in small puddles, but before long we found ourselves splashing through a couple inches of water. As we proceeded it continued to rise, inch by inch.

Ahuatzi held a fist up as the winding passage opened into a large, humid chamber dripping with condensation. Glowing fungus coated the walls, casting a dim light. I'm sure all the death-touched could see just fine, but I didn't have supernatural night vision anymore and couldn't make out much of anything.

But what I *could* see was hella creepy.

The walls bore carved reliefs of grotesque tentacled creatures like something out of a bad H. P. Lovecraft acid trip, and the ceiling was dripping with tendrils of fungi. The entire chamber smelled of stagnant water, mold, and despair.

Ahuatzi proceeded carefully, taking one slow step, then another. The room apparently had a sunken floor, for with each step he sank deeper into the water. When he reached the bottom, the water was above his waist. He and another warrior cleared the room, then waved us toward the room's only other exit.

The floor was slimy, and with my hands tied behind me, I lost my footing multiple times. Each time St. James had to haul me back up coughing and sputtering after I nearly drowned. Eventually he'd had enough and cut my bonds.

To be honest, the floor wasn't *that* slippery, and I'm not that clumsy. But I thought I'd done a good job of faking it.

I took another step forward, then almost lost my balance for real when a fungus tendril whipped down in front of me and snared an eagle warrior, hauling him up to the ceiling. He struggled and shouted as more tendrils wrapped around him. Coils snaked down across the room, snaring others. I saw Wright jerked up out of the water, and then Dance screamed as a slimy strand whipped around her neck. I dove toward her, caught her legs, and then wrenched her down far enough so I could leap up and take hold of the tendril, jerking it roughly until it snapped. She unwound it from her neck and threw it away, coughing roughly.

"You okay?" I asked.

She shook her head.

"Get as low as you can to the water. We're getting out of here."

In all the chaos, no one noticed us slipping toward the exit.

"My throat is burning," Dance said.

Mine was too. Spores had begun to fill the air.

"Try not to breathe," I whispered.

Her pace started to slow, and I practically had to haul her toward the short flight of stairs leading out of the room. For a moment I thought we were actually going to get away—but then I heard St. James shouting for someone to stop us, and I knew escape was impossible.

It was time to force the stalemate. There were no other moves left.

"I got you," I whispered, gathering her into my arms, holding her head against my own. "I got you, iuctli. Hang on. It will all be over soon."

"I do not want to die in this place of evil," she moaned.

"Nobody's dying," I lied.

"Achtli—"

"Shhh. I got you. It will be quick, I promise, and the pain will be gone. You'll never be in pain again."

I focused on the spools of teōtl wrapped around my core. It would have to all unwind at once. A surge of radiant power so intense it would consume us both. I focused, feeling the pressure building inside me, forcing it in on itself.

And then I released it all at once, like a white dwarf triggered into runaway nuclear fusion.

I willed myself to become a supernova.

CHAPTER 47

Nothing happened.

I didn't even glow. The tremendous surge of divine radiance just… evaporated.

I held First-to-Dance close, speechless and confused.

"What will be quick?" she asked. "Why will there be no pain?"

I would have cried, but I'd already expended a lifetime's worth of tears watching her suffer, and I had none left. My heart felt like a stone. I'd failed her. I'd failed us. I began to have desperate thoughts. I could still kill her. Could I make it quick? Painless? I could snap her neck. Could I? They make it look easy in the movies, but this wasn't Hollywood. This was real life. Was I even strong enough? I didn't want to botch it. I'd have to strangle her. It wouldn't be quick, but—

"Move your ass!" St. James hollered, jerking me by my collar. "On your feet!"

I dumbly got up, holding Dance in my arms. St. James led me with a firm hand on my shoulder farther down the passage. I was trying to figure out what had gone wrong. Dance and I should be dead. It wasn't supposed to happen like this. The terror of what would come *after* nearly paralyzed me, and St. James had to keep pushing me forward.

"Try and make a run for it again and I'll flay your bitch whore alive," he barked.

"Wasn't… trying to run. Just get… out of there."

"Hold here," he ordered.

Wright came splashing down the tunnel, ripping tendrils of fungus off his body. A couple of eagle warriors followed with Bond in tow.

I could hear another splashing along the passage behind them.

"Who we got?" St. James called back.

"Lost Huitzilin, Sarge," Bond replied.

"Motherf—" St. James punched the wall so hard that I heard bones break. He grimaced and shook out his hand. "Eztli, you're on point. Ahuatzi, Ilhicamina, take the girl. Let's get moving."

***

Our footsteps echoed off obsidian flagstones polished to a mirror sheen and walls of basalt reliefs continuing the now-familiar themes of horror, degradation, and despair in painstaking detail. Cressets containing perpetual heatless flame lit the way ahead. The passage we followed seemed to wrap itself around the heart of the dead volcano in an endless spiral leading ever downward. The passage grew tighter, narrower. Then it seemed almost to double back on itself and we found ourselves stepping into a large circular chamber. A vast dome overhead was pinpricked with lights that looked like the night sky, but it wasn't a sky I'd ever seen on Earth or in the Land of the Black Sun. These artificial stars provided the chamber's only light, a sickly marigold glow that seemed to writhe with a life of its own and cast deep shadows between the giant jade statues of otherworldly beasts that held up the ceiling with their paws, hands, claws, pincers, and other appendages I couldn't begin to describe.

The shadows writhed too.

The chamber held thirteen exits, and I saw the Last Tlacaōcēlōtl standing by one of them far across the open space between us. He looked back at me for a moment before vanishing into the darkness beyond the portal.

"Let's pick up the pace," St. James said, his irritation and exhaustion evident.

"Dragging this bitch's sorry ass is holding us up," Wright said. "Let's just slit her throat and get on with it."

"No," St. James said. "Bennett's only cooperating to keep her alive. We kill her and he'll start resisting. We don't have time to dick around with carving him up to force his assistance. She's his motivation to not screw around."

"We don't even need him, Sarge," Wright complained. "We can follow the cat bastard on our own. We should've slit both their throats hours ago."

"I'm not confident in that," St. James said. "For some reason Bennett's the key to finding what we're after. That creature is guiding *him,* not us. We need him, and because of that, we need her. Now let's get moving."

"I can carry her," I offered.

"Yeah, let Preacher haul his whore himself," Wright agreed.

St. James considered that for a moment, then shook his head. "Stop bitching, Wright. You're not even carrying her. It's your men doing the work. Are they getting tired already?"

"No, Sarge. I was just sayin'."

"Well, now you said. And I'm saying we need to start hauling—"

A shadow snaked out of a pool of darkness and coiled around the waist of one of the eagle warriors, slicing him neatly in half.

Shit went sideways, as they say.

More shadows erupted from everywhere and the stars above fell, hitting the ground like meteors. Men were shouting and screaming. Howling. The vast chamber erupted with the deafening echo of gunfire.

Seven-six-two doesn't do much against shadow creatures. They aren't substantial. Except for their razor claws. Those seemed to cut just fine.

A heavy splash of arterial blood hit me in the face as a shadow raked its talons across an eagle warrior's neck. His screams turned to a choking gargle as he fell and flopped on the ground beside me. Blinding muzzle flashes strobed in the darkness. Another warrior ran past me blindly, his face completely ripped away.

I cast about for Dance and saw her lying in a crumpled heap on the polished floor. I sprinted, heedless of the animated shadows, slipped on someone's entrails, and slid to a stop beside her.

Then I picked her up and ran as fast as I could toward the exit.

We barreled into the dark passage blindly. I could hear Wright gasping behind me, swearing to himself. I bounced off a wall and stumbled, catching both myself and Dance. St. James caught up to us and hauled me forward. There was light ahead. Dim, but growing brighter.

We came to a bend in the passage. Just ahead, the Last Tlacaōcēlōtl stood waiting. His sad eyes met mine, and he vanished through a doorway.

St. James called a halt. He was breathing hard. So was I. I glanced back and saw Wright holding his side, drenched in blood, grimacing, the livid scar on his face from my crappy stapling job pulsing like a long purple worm. Bond stood behind him, a hand on a brutal gash in his thigh. An eagle warrior came careening around the corner and stopped short.

"Who else got out?" St. James asked him. "You're it, Ahuatzi?"

The warrior nodded grimly, and St. James swore like only a cavalryman can.

"I'm so sick of this shit," he growled. "Let's get this over with. Move!"

He shoved me roughly and I stumbled forward, carrying Dance.

We reached the doorway, and I entered a chamber filled with shelves and shelves of books and scrolls. Ancient manuscripts from cultures I couldn't place and modern hardbound books from my own world, my own time. Clay tablets. Books with titles in languages I recognized and others with script so alien, it hurt to look at it for too long. Books bound with exotic skins and books made entirely of thin metal plates. The room seemed too small for the number of records it held. I felt like I was inside Epasotl's magic haversack.

And in the middle of the room, crowded by stacks of books and piles of scrolls, the Last Tlacaōcēlōtl sat on a cushion behind a low table staring at an orb of pure gold the size of a softball. It was etched in strange glyphs I couldn't begin to decipher and appeared to be made of multiple interlocking sections. It glowed buttery yellow in the orange light of the oil lamps scattered around the room, but its radiance seemed to come from within.

The Compass of the Gods.

"Is that it?" St. James asked me.

"Yes," I said.

"Doesn't look like much," Wright commented sourly. "I've got dinner plates worth more than that."

"I don't give a damn what it looks like," St. James said. "Only that we've found it." He pushed me roughly aside. "You know how many men I've lost chasing this Christmas decoration? Scores. Now we just have to mop up the rest of Red Platoon and we can leave this hellhole."

He reached for the Compass—but paused when the Last Tlacaōcēlōtl raised a hand.

"What?" St. James barked. He spun on me. "I thought he couldn't see the rest of us."

I gave a shrug.

"Screw it." He reached for the golden sphere again. There was a flash of light, and he whipped his hand away like he'd been bit, screaming.

Flames of sunlight licked along his fingers and consumed his entire hand, the blackened skin splitting and peeling until there was nothing left but a smoking stump. He cradled it to his chest as he sank to the floor, rocking and gritting his teeth.

I looked at the Last Tlacaōcēlōtl, and he met my gaze.

<It is not for him,> he signed.

By now I'd learned enough of their sign that I could understand this without needing Epasotl's nasty potion, and I nodded to him to show I understood.

"He says you can't have it," I told St. James in a flat voice.

"Wright, get the damn thing," St. James said through clenched teeth.

"I'm not touching it," Wright said. "Not for all the whores in Bangkok."

"Nope," Bond said.

Ahuatzi looked between the three of them and folded his arms.

"Then you get it, Bennett," St. James grunted.

"Can you stand?" I asked Dance. She nodded, and I set her on her feet.

"No," I told St. James.

"Excuse me?" he grated, pulling himself back to his feet. "What did you say?"

"I said no."

"You will collect it, and you will return with us to present it to Tezcatlipoca. Am I clear?"

"Go to hell, St. James."

"Wright!" he barked.

Weight grabbed Dance by the throat and whipped out his knife. I looked past him and nodded to Cameron, who had been standing in the doorway aiming my pistol steadily for some time now. He looked like shit, his face a mask of crusted blood, but I saw the steel in his eyes. The determination. He'd see this through. We'd made an unspoken promise, and he wouldn't fail First-to-Dance like I had.

The Glock barked in his hand, and her head snapped back in a spray of bone and brain matter.

Bond spun, inhumanly fast, and slammed his palm into Cameron's face with a sickening crunch.

"You didn't have to kill him, you retard!" Wright screamed. "We could've used the faggot as leverage."

"Stalemate," I said.

"Say again?" St. James growled.

"You've got no power over me, asshole."

Wright flicked his blade around in his hand. "You only need your hands to carry it for us, Preacher… if you catch my drift."

I caught it, but I didn't care. Not really. Dance was safe. Cameron was safe. I'd die eventually. No doubt in unimaginable pain. The thought made me nauseous, but that was my fate whether I helped them or not. I wasn't being flippant about it, just realistic. If I was going to suffer anyway, why let them win?

Wright made to close the distance between us, then stopped short, staring past me. I looked over my shoulder to see the Last Tlacaōcēlōtl standing, towering, seeming to fill the room, the Compass in his hand.

<This is not your fate, Consort of the Rainbow Lady,> he signed.
He held the Compass out to me, and I reached for it.
My fingers closed around the golden orb…

CHAPTER 48

"It's over, Bennett," St. James called out. "You can't win."

I glanced at Cameron and Dance. Cameron shook his head slowly; Dance just closed her eyes.

"Come out," St. James called. "Let's talk. I just want to talk, Bennett. Man to man."

I took a deep breath and exhaled a sigh of relief. This time would be different.

"I just want it on the record that I think this is a horrible plan," Cameron hissed.

"It will work," Dance replied calmly, looking over at me. Her steady gaze met my eye. "God is with you."

I felt the weight in my hand. It was heavy. Solid. Substantial.

"New plan," I said, holding up the Compass of the Gods.

"What the hell is that?" Cameron asked.

"It means we've already won," I replied. "Come with me."

I stood, limping around the mound of corpses rotting in the heat, and looked up at the overcast sky. I couldn't see the sun above the gray clouds, but I could feel its power.

Power I now held in my hand.

I glanced back, making sure Cameron and Dance were with me.

"Stay close," I said.

St. James stood twenty yards away from me, hands draped over the rifle slung around his front. Bond stood a little way to my right with an eagle warrior. Opposite, moving in from my left, were another two warriors. I knew Wright would be trying to flank us.

"Stop skulking, Wright," I called out. "I know you're back there."

Wright appeared from behind the hill of corpses. Behind him were two more eagle warriors. I could hear another approaching from my rear.

"How are they all still alive?" Cameron whispered. "It's not fair."

"Is that really the—?" Dance asked me.

"Yes."

"How?"

"Really, really long story. Just stay close to me."

"It's over," St. James repeated. "You see you can't win, don't you? We're gods."

"You're devils," Dance shouted.

"Well, you know what they say." St. James spread his hands. "Better to—"

"Reign in Hell than serve in Heaven?" I asked. "I know. You said that last time. I didn't buy your sales pitch then, and I'm not buying it now. You've lost, asshole."

He looked a little confused. Almost uncertain.

Good.

I raised my arm, a shining sphere floating above my palm. No, not just a shining sphere. A *sun*. A perfect, softball-sized, yellow-white, radiant sun in the palm of my hand.

I thought about throwing out a final pithy one-liner, maybe even something catchy, then shrugged. Why waste my breath?

The tiny sun in my hand blazed so brightly, St. James and the others had to shield their eyes.

"The Compass," he said in wonder. "How did you—"

I stretched out my hand toward him.

"Drop him!" St. James barked.

A ray of blinding radiance shot from my outstretched hand and hit St. James center mass. The ten-thousand-degree beam of focused sunlight didn't just cause him to spontaneously combust—it turned him instantly to ash.

I was already pivoting, sending beams of radiance downrange. Wright was immolated as he cried out in rage. Bond looked surprised as he was vaporized. Warrior after warrior flashed into cinders that rose spiraling into the air and drifted away on the wind.

The man-shaped column of ash that had been St. James collapsed in on itself, and the breeze carried him away too, scattering him far and wide across the salt basin.

I gazed at the Compass in my hand. It was an ordinary etched orb again, slightly warm and glowing softly like only pure gold does.

Cameron, slack-jawed, stared at the black scorch marks in the hardpacked salt, all that was left of Alpha and the eagle warriors.

Dance inspected the Compass. She reached out to it, but I drew it back.

"I wouldn't touch it," I warned.

"How?" she asked again.

I shook my head. I didn't really know, and I couldn't begin to explain. Maybe Captain Brown could parse what had happened.

"That was…" Cameron circled back and stared at the bauble in my hand. "So that's it? We can go home now? To the *real* world?"

"It's not that simple."

"So, what… I mean, we were sitting there, black on ammo and totally screwed… and it… did it just appear in your hand?"

"That's… not so simple either."

He blew out his cheeks. "Well at least we didn't die."

"Not this time around."

"What does that mean?" He held up his hands. "I know, not so simple. So, what now?"

I gazed out across the basin at the mounds of dead rotting under the oppressively gray sky. Black clouds were gathering around the top of the mountain, and lightning flashed. A peal of thunder echoed across the dead sea, and it began to rain.

"We find the others and leave this doomed world behind."

CHAPTER 49

"—so then Dance says, 'He rides the *short bus*!'" Cameron shouted.

Everyone burst out laughing, even Sanchez.

Wilson raised his drinking gourd. "Here's to Sergeant Short Bus!"

"Aye aye!" Doc yelled.

I raised my gourd to them and inclined my head.

"You will never live that down," Xochi said softly, grinning up at me. The side of her face was disfigured by a long scar, an old wound, but it only made her more beautiful to me, like kintsugi pottery.

"No, probably not," I agreed.

We stood under camo netting, with a cooling breeze wafting off the ocean smelling of salt and life. Hanging lanterns cast a warm glow on the faces of all my friends.

"I did not know what it meant!" Dance protested. She was smiling broadly, but there was a firmness around the corners of her mouth that made my heart heavy, and instead of sparkling cheerfully like they always used to, her amber eyes now held a glint of steel, like a bird of prey.

Xochi rubbed my back. "I missed you, my love."

I pulled my arm tighter around her slim waist. "You have no idea."

Flaming Feather walked up to us gracefully and bowed to my wife. "My blessings to you, Siuapilxochicuauhtli. And to the gift of new life you carry."

Xochi placed her hand on her stomach and bowed back. She wasn't starting to show yet, not much, just a hint of a bulge in her otherwise flat and toned abdomen. I'd expected her to be bigger, given how long we'd been away, but time worked oddly between the worlds, and what for us had been long months was only a few short weeks for the people who'd waited anxiously for our return.

The whole community of Kuauchanejkej refugees had turned out for the post-mission celebration, and people sang and danced throughout the night. But our small group, the few survivors who made up Crazy Horse Platoon, stayed apart and shared stories not meant for the ears of those who hadn't seen what we had seen and bled where we had bled.

"And my blessings to you, First Consort," Feather said, toasting my gourd with her own. "I look forward to watching you jump and thus earn your place among the sister warriors."

"Can't wait," I lied.

Doc wandered over and threw his arm across Feather's shoulder. He nodded to Xochi and then to me. "Princess. Short Bus."

I noticed Feather snake her arm around his waist. He inclined his head toward her.

"Care to dance?" he asked her.

She draped her other arm around his neck and kissed him. Rather deeply.

"I believe I would," she said.

Doc shot me a mock salute and a wink and pulled Feather away after him.

Wilson laughed loudly and whistled. I glanced over and noticed Jade Talon leading Anderson away into the darkness.

"Yeah, Touchdown!" Wilson shouted.

"I think the kid just got a new nickname," I said to Xochi. "Well, same name. *Totally* different meaning."

She reached down and grabbed my butt, gazing up at me with *that* look. "It is getting late, husband, no?"

I pulled back involuntarily at her playful touch. That part of me was… dead and gone. I just… I didn't think I could separate physical intimacy from the violence I'd witnessed done to First-to-Dance. It was too soon. My eyes darted over to Dance, and I frowned.

Xochi raised her hand to my waist and furrowed her brow. "What is it, my love? You smile at me with your mouth, but your eyes are dead. Please come home to me."

"I'm trying."

She'd seen me glance over at First-to-Dance and nodded slowly. "I think I understand. It will take time. Time and gentleness and love. For her too. She has no family, did you know that? No sisters or even brothers. Her mother died when Kuauchanko burned."

"Father?"

"Who can say? The tribe is her father, as is the way with many of our people." My wife paused as if considering something, and then nodded firmly. "We will take her in, as a sister-daughter. It is not uncommon. If you agree, of course."

"Of course."

"I will invite her to join our household." Xochi rubbed my back and stood on her toes to kiss me. "I love you."

"I love you too."

I gave her waist a squeeze, and she crossed over to where Dance was sitting surrounded by friends, yet alone, as if a vast sea separated her from the others.

My hand dropped to the pouch secured on my waist, a leather bag that held a heavy weight about the size of a softball. I still didn't understand how the Compass worked. The interlocking sections could be rotated to align different glyphs, forming a staggering number of combinations. It must have been preset to return us to the refugee camp, because once Dance and Cameron and I had reconnected with the rest of Crazy Horse Platoon, the Compass simply... *activated*... and we walked out of one world and back into another.

Just as if it had all been planned. And why not? It had all happened before. And would again.

Brown cleared his throat beside me, and I looked up. "Sir?"

"Walk with me?"

"Yes, sir."

We passed through the festive crowd and down to the beach, where breakers reflecting the bright starlight rolled onto the sand.

Brown stopped near the water's edge and looked out across the expansive bay.

We stood in silence for several minutes.

"The Kuauchanejkej call this body of water the Sea of Tears," he said.

I nodded. I had heard the legend of the goddess Chālchihuitl, who so despaired at the wickedness of her children that she drowned the world in her lament and turned all the people to fish. I waited for him to expand on the statement. He didn't usually spout trivia unless it led up to something. Epasotl came trudging through the sand and stood by us, gazing across the water, uncommonly silent.

"Twenty-one," Brown said eventually.

It took me a moment to realize he was speaking of those he'd lost here under his command. The men who had come with us from Panama and had died here.

"There are just ten of us left," he said after another long pause. "I promised them all I'd get them home. *All* of them. I swore an oath."

"Ten is better than none, sir," I offered. It sounded lame, and I regretted it immediately.

"It's unacceptable," he said. I didn't know if he was talking to me or himself. Maybe he hadn't been talking to me at all this whole time. Maybe he just needed to talk. It occurred to me that being an officer must get lonely at times. We gripe about them and crack jokes, sure, but it's not all rarified air and fancy balls and sharp uniforms and shiny medals for those who've been commissioned. Leadership is a heavy burden.

He picked up a stone, studied it for a minute, and then skipped it across the waves. "There *has* to be a way."

I waited, listening to the surf. When he didn't speak again, I asked, "A way for what, sir?"

He turned to me. "To get them all home. Every single one."

"You can't change the past," I said, quoting him. "And the future's already happened."

"We need to break out of this timeline."

"Time doesn't work like that. *You* told me that."

He pointed a thick finger at me. "You did it. We can too."

"Say again, sir?"

"You broke the timeline. You went back and changed the outcome. You went back and gave yourself the Compass, defeated St. James and his devils, and saved First-to-Dance and Cameron."

"I don't know *what* I did, sir. If I thought I could actually change the past, I'd go back a lot further. Certainly before Dance was... before anything happened. I don't think time is something we want to be playing around with, even if it's mutable, which you yourself said isn't possible. And besides, *I* didn't do anything. If anything happened, it was the Last Tlacaōcēlōtl who sent the Compass back, along with the knowledge of what would happen if I didn't stop St. James. I don't think *I* traveled through time at all. If I did, then that would mean I... replaced myself. So what happened to me? The other me?" I paused. "Or is that what you meant by 'someone else' taking my place in the timeline if I failed? *I* took my own place?"

I rubbed my face. It was all too confusing.

He looked thoughtful. "Could it be the same timeline, doubling back on itself?"

"Sorry, sir. I don't even remotely follow."

"He... spliced the timeline?"

"Like det wire, sir?"

"Maybe *that's* how we get everyone back home." He looked across the Sea of Tears and chewed on his lip. "We never leave Panama in the first place. We destroy the Compass. If Smoking Mirror never obtains it, then..."

My stone heart sank. Then we'd never leave Panama. I'd never meet Xochi. We'd never...

"No," I said.

That wasn't a word he heard very often. He looked at me and quirked an eyebrow.

"You'd be condemning my unborn child to death," I said. "Maybe Xochi too. All her people. Maybe this whole world. This universe. You have no idea what could happen." I shook my head. "No. Absolutely not. You could be condemning tens of millions of sentient beings to non-existence. It'd be genocide on a global scale. That's not worth the lives of twenty-one men. Not remotely."

He considered me for a long moment, then nodded slowly. "I hadn't considered the ramifications fully. I was thinking out loud." He sighed. "And it wouldn't work anyway. Any attempt to destroy the Compass would inevitably fail."

"Just like if we'd attempted to steal it in the first place," I said with a hint of a smile.

"Exactly."

"The future's already happened," I repeated.

"And the past can't be changed."

"Except for when it can."

"Yeah, that's a head-scratcher." He blew out his cheeks. "This sucks, Nephi."

"Really does, sir."

"Maybe suck even more," Epasotl said.

I'd forgotten she was there. She was never that quiet for that long.

"What might suck even more?" I asked her.

She pulled the book out of her haversack. The one bound in human skin with the title written in a strange Mesoamerican language.

"Been looking at book. Cannot read all yet, not much, some, but has many pictures. Maps of stars. Some I know, some never see before. Strange charts. Many much formulas. Difficult math. Book has drawings of Compass also. Think it will show way to get brothers home. But cannot do on own. Need Quetzalcoatl to help. Will be hard."

"That's going to be difficult, for sure. But why does it suck?" I asked.

"Found something else. Something think you not like, Ben-Ette."

"And that is...?"

"Man who write book, he lost in time and space. Trying hard to get home. Return to woman he love." She gazed up at me, her large, green-and-gold-flecked eyes glowing in the starlight. "Think *you* write book."

ABOUT THE AUTHORS

JASON ANSPACH (1979-) is the award-winning, Associated Press Best-selling author of Galaxy's Edge, Wayward Galaxy, and Forgotten Ruin. He is an American author raised in a military family (Go Army!) known for pulse-pounding military science fiction and adventurous space operas that deftly blend action, suspense, and comedy.

Together with his wife, their seven (not a typo) children, and a border collie named Charlotte, Jason resides in Puyallup, Washington. He remains undefeated at arm wrestling against his entire family.

Galaxy's Edge: www.InTheLegion.com

Author website: www.JasonAnspach.com

twitter.com/TheJasonAnspach

Ryan Williamson draws inspiration for his writing from his love of history and mythology as well as his past experience as a Cavalry Scout in the U.S. Army. His debut novel, "The Widow's Son" has been praised by readers and critics alike for its thrilling action, complex characters, and immersive worldbuilding. He is also the co-author of "Doomsday Recon," an epic new military fantasy series from WarGate Books. Ryan lives in the Pacific Northwest with his wife and children. When he is not writing, he enjoys exploring the back roads on his motorcycles. You can find him on Twitter as @rywilwrite or visit his website at **ryanwilliamson.com**.

WARGATE BOOKS

Discover more titles like DEATH OR GLORY, including several free options, at **www.WarGateBooks.com**.